WARNING!
APPROACH THESE PAGES
WITH STAKE IN HAND!

For from the moment you enter these realms of horror, you will be pitted against perils created in the fertile imaginations of true masters of terror. And now that you have been warned, venture further if you dare into the fright-filled worlds of:

Fritz Leiber's "The Girl with the Hungry Eyes"—She was a model with a unique allure and a life of mystery, and she could make his fortune as a photographer as long as he resisted the temptation to follow her into the night. . . .

August Derleth's "The Drifting Snow"—She came with the storm and unless you hardened your heart against her, she could freeze your blood. . . .

Tanith Lee's "Red As Blood"—Bianca was Snow White with one very important difference, a difference which could turn the Witch Queen to an angel and earn Bianca herself a sleep to end all evil. . . .

VAMPS

VAMPS

AN ANTHOLOGY OF FEMALE VAMPIRE STORIES

EDITED BY
Martin H. Greenberg
&
Charles G. Waugh

DAW BOOKS, INC.
DONALD A. WOLLHEIM, PUBLISHER

1633 Broadway, New York, NY 10019

ACKNOWLEDGMENTS

King—"One for the Road" by Stephen King appeared in MAINE Magazine, March/April 1977. Copyright by MAINE Magazine, Company, Inc., from the book NIGHT SHIFT. Reprinted by permission of Doubleday & Company, Inc.

Tenn—Copyright © 1956 by King-Size Publications; reprinted by permission of the author and his agent, Virginia Kidd.

Keller—Copyright © 1947 by David H. Keller. Copyright renewed. Reprinted by arrangement with the Estate of David H. Keller and John P. Trevaskis, Jr.

Bloch—Copyright © 1939 by Street & Smith Publications, Inc.; renewed © 1967 by Robert Bloch. Reprinted by permission of Kirby McCauley, Ltd.

Wellman—Copyright © 1951 by *Weird Tales* for *Weird Tales*, May 1951. Reprinted by permission of Karl Edward Wagner, Literary Executor for Manly Wade Wellman.

Leiber—Copyright © 1949; renewed © 1977 by Fritz Leiber. Reprinted by permission of Richard Curtis Associates, Inc.

Quinn—Reprinted by permission of the agents for the author's Estate, the Scott Meredith Literary Agency, Inc., 845 Third Avenue, New York, NY 10022.

Derleth—Copyright © 1939 by *Weird Tales*. Copyright renewed. Reprinted by permission of the Scott Meredith Literary Agency, Inc., 845 Third Avenue, New York, NY 10022.

Wellman ("When It Was Moonlight")—Copyright © 1940 by Street & Smith Publications, Inc. for UNKNOWN, February 1940. Copyright renewed © 1968 by The Conde Nast Publications, Inc. Reprinted by permission of Karl Edward Wagner, Literary Executor for Manly Wade Wellman.

Matheson—Copyright © 1951; renewed © 1979 by Richard Matheson. Reprinted by permission of Don Congdon Associates, Inc.

Lee—Copyright © 1979 by Mercury Press, Inc.; © 1983 by Tanith Lee. From THE MAGAZINE OF FANTASY AND SCIENCE FICTION. Reprinted by permission of the author and DAW Books, Inc.

TABLE OF CONTENTS

INTRODUCTION

Why There Are So Many "Ladies of the Night"

Women vampires are among the most common and popular subjects for monster stories. This book contains sixteen examples, spanning one hundred and forty-six years, from "Clarimonde" (1836) to "Red as Blood" (1979).

The first short story featuring a woman vampire appears to have been "Wake Not the Dead," which has been attributed to J. L. Tieck. After its anthologization in 1823, at least sixteen additional examples were produced by other nineteenth century writers such as Alexandre Dumas ("The Pale Lady," 1848) and Sir Arthur Conan Doyle ("The Parasite," 1892). We have included three of the best: Théophile Gautier's previously mentioned "Clarimonde," Sheridan Lefanu's oft filmed "Carmilla" (1872), and Julian Hawthorne's Halloween tale, "Ken's Mystery" (1888?).

The twentieth century has seen the publication of many more feminine vampire stories. Our earliest selection is "Luella Miller (1902), Mary Wilkins Freeman's portrait of a psychic vampire. Seven tales are from the influential years of *Weird Tales (1923–1954)* and *Unknown* (1939–1943): Seabury Quinn's "Restless Souls" (1928), Robert Bloch's "The Cloak" (1939), August Derleth's "The Drifting Snow" (1939), Manly Wade Wellman's "When It Was Moonlight" (1940), David

H. Keller's "Heredity" (1947), and Manly Wade Wellman's "The Last Grave of Lill Warran" (1951). The most recent story is Tanith Lee's "Red as Blood," a biting revision of "Snow White."

Assuming vampires aren't real (and it's something I wouldn't stake my life on), there are at least seven possible reasons for their acceptance and popularity.

Vampiric animals and insects exist in the real world. Examples include female mosquitoes and certain types of bats and moths. Such creatures have obviously provided springboards for fertile imaginations.

Bruce Wallace (*Omni*, June, 1979) suggests vampiric fears may derive from prehistoric cave-dwellers. During earlier stages of the disease, those bitten by rabid bats would retreat further into the darkness to avoid light. During later stages, they emerged as aggressive madmen, attempting to bite others. New bite victims recapitulated the cycle. Since sensitivity to, and avoidance of, such creatures had survival value, it is possible that, as a result of selection over many centuries, such characteristics even became part of humanity's genetic heritage.

Basil Cooper (*The Vampire in Legend and Fact*, 1973) notes that throughout history, some profoundly disturbed individuals have derived "a morbid physical satisfaction . . . by drinking the blood of the living or—even more horrible—of the newly dead."

Douglas Hill (*The History of Ghosts, Vampires and Werewolves*, 1970) suggests premature burial may have occurred frequently before the medical revolution of the last one hundred years. When people died inexplicably from various plagues—among other things—superstitious villagers may have searched for vampires by disinterring bodies. Those who had "been buried prematurely, awakened in the grave, and died trying hopelessly to claw (their) way out" would have been found in a different position and with "a fearful expression on (their) face(s) and blood on (their) hands and finger-nails."

For adults, scary tales of vampires, ghosts, and werewolves provide excitement and a change from mundane matters. For parents, such threats (such as the danger of staying out after dark) can be used to control their children's behavior. For outgroups and the powerless, hinting at supernatural revenge may offer a desperate form of protection.

Reasons for the popularity of feminine vampires would also seem to be numerous.

Fans of fantastic literature include a large percentage of adolescent males, terrified of young women. (See Fritz Leiber's autobiography in *The Ghost Light*, 1984). From this point of view, writing about women as vampires makes good market sense. It introduces sexual overtones and permits women to be caricaturized as uncertain mixtures of danger and allure.

Since vampires tend to accomplish their ends through seduction and hypnosis, feminine vampires fit into the Judeo-Christian tradition of Eve the temptress. Writers also can also use them without having to wrestle over problems of size and strength.

Other contributing factors could be women's closer association with blood; a tendency toward greater paleness as a result of fashion, largely indoor activities, and a higher chance for iron deficiency anemia; and a kind of ying/yang masters of the night vs. masters of the day symbolism.

Though much of what has just been said seems negative, feminine vampire stories may have positive characteristics also. That is why we compiled this anthology. Many of these stories are entertaining works: well written and plotted, with memorable characters and original ideas. Some highlight inequities women face in life, some permit direct or comparative presentation of strong and assertive women, and some provide feminists familiar themes to startle the uneducated through revision and transcendence.

Charles G. Waugh

STEPHEN KING

One for the Road

It was quarter past ten and Herb Tooklander was thinking of closing for the night when the man in the fancy overcoat and the white, staring face burst into Tookey's Bar, which lies in the northern part of Falmouth. It was the tenth of January, just about the time most folks are learning to live comfortably with all the New Year's resolutions they broke, and there was one hell of a northeaster blowing outside. Six inches had come down before dark and it had been going hard and heavy since then. Twice we had seen Billy Larribee go by high in the cab of the town plow, and the second time Tookey ran him out a beer—an act of pure charity my mother would have called it, and my God knows she put down enough of Tookey's beer in her time. Billy told him they were keeping ahead of it on the main road, but the side ones were closed and apt to stay that way until next morning. The radio in Portland was forecasting another foot and a forty-mile-an-hour wind to pile up the drifts.

There was just Tookey and me in the bar, listening to the wind howl around the eaves and watching it dance the fire around on the hearth. "Have one for the road, Booth," Tookey says, "I'm gonna shut her down."

He poured me one and himself one and that's when the door

cracked open and this stranger staggered in, snow up to his shoulders and in his hair, like he had rolled around in confectioner's sugar. The wind billowed a sand-fine sheet of snow in after him.

"Close the door!" Tookey roars at him. "Was you born in a barn?"

I've never seen a man who looked that scared. He was like a horse that's spent an afternoon eating fire nettles. His eyes rolled toward Tookey and he said, "My wife—my daughter—" and he collapsed on the floor in a dead faint.

"Holy Joe," Tookey says. "Close the door, Booth, would you?"

I went and shut it, and pushing it against the wind was something of a chore. Tookey was down on one knee holding the fellow's head up and patting his cheeks. I got over to him and saw right off that it was nasty. His face was fiery red, but there were gray blotches here and there, and when you've lived through winters in Maine since the time Woodrow Wilson was President, as I have, you know those gray blotches mean frostbite.

"Fainted," Tookey said. "Get the brandy off the backbar, will you?"

I got it and came back. Tookey had opened the fellow's coat. He had come around a little; his eyes were half open and he was muttering something too low to catch.

"Pour a capful," Tookey says.

"Just a cap?" I asks him.

"That stuff's dynamite," Tookey says. "No sense overloading his carb."

I poured out a capful and looked at Tookey. He nodded. "Straight down the hatch."

I poured it down. It was a remarkable thing to watch. The man trembled all over and began to cough. His face got redder. His eyelids, which had been at half-mast, flew up like window shades. I was a bit alarmed, but Tookey only sat him up like a big baby and clapped him on the back.

The man started to retch, and Tookey clapped him again.

"Hold onto it," he says, "that brandy comes dear."

The man coughed some more, but it was diminishing now. I got my first good look at him. City fellow, all right, and from somewhere south of Boston, at a guess. He was wearing kid gloves, expensive but thin. There were probably some more of those grayish-white patches on his hands, and he would be lucky not to lose a finger or two. His coat was fancy, all right; a three-hundred-dollar job if ever I'd seen one. He was wearing tiny little boots that hardly came up over his ankles, and I began to wonder about his toes.

"Better," he said.

"All right," Tookey said. "Can you come over to the fire?"

"My wife and my daughter," he said. "They're out there . . . in the storm."

"From the way you came in, I didn't figure they were at home watching the TV," Tookey said. "You can tell us by the fire as easy as here on the floor. Hook on, Booth."

He got to his feet, but a little groan came out of him and his mouth twisted down in pain. I wondered about his toes again, and I wondered why God felt he had to make fools from New York City who would try driving around in southern Maine at the height of a northeast blizzard. And I wondered if his wife and his little girl were dressed any warmer than him.

We hiked him across to the fireplace and got him sat down in a rocker that used to be Missus Tookey's favorite until she passed on in '74. It was Missus Tookey that was responsible for most of the place, which had been written up in *Down East* and the *Sunday Telegram* and even once in the Sunday supplement of the Boston *Globe*. It's really more of a public house than a bar, with its big wooden floor, pegged together rather than nailed, the maple bar, the old barn-raftered ceiling, and the monstrous big fieldstone hearth. Missue Tookey started to get some ideas in her head after the *Down East* article came out, wanted to start calling the place Tookey's Inn or Tookey's Rest, and I admit it has sort of a Colonial ring to it, but I prefer plain old Tookey's Bar. It's one thing to get uppish in the summer, when the state's full of tourists, another thing altogether in the winter, when you and your neighbors have to trade together. And there had been plenty of winter nights, like this one, that Tookey and I had spent all alone together, drinking scotch and water or just a few beers. My own Victoria passed on in '73, and Tookey's was a place to go where there were enough voices to mute the steady ticking of the deathwatch beetle—even if there was just Tookey and me, it was enough. I wouldn't have felt the same about it if the place had been Tookey's Rest. It's crazy but it's true.

We got this fellow in front of the fire and he got the shakes harder than ever. He hugged onto his knees and his teeth clattered together and a few drops of clear mucus spilled off the end of his nose. I think he was starting to realize that another fifteen minutes out there might have been enough to kill him. It's not the snow, it's the wind-chill factor. It steals your heat.

"Where did you go off the road?" Tookey asked him.

"S-six miles s-s-south of h-here," he said.

Tookey and I stared at each other, and all of a sudden I felt cold. Cold all over.

"You sure?" Tookey demanded. "You came six miles through the snow?"

He nodded. "I checked the odometer when we came through t-town. I was following directions . . . going to see my wife's s-sister . . . in Cumberland . . . never been there before . . . we're from New Jersey. . . ."

New Jersey. If there's anyone more purely foolish than a New Yorker it's a fellow from New Jersey.

"Six miles, you're sure?" Tookey demanded.

"Pretty sure, yeah. I found the turnoff but it was drifted in . . . it was. . . ."

Tookey grabbed him. In the shifting glow of the fire his face looked pale and strained, older than his sixty-six years by ten. "You made a right turn?"

"Right turn, yeah. My wife—"

, "Did you see a sign?"

"Sign?" He looked up at Tookey blankly and wiped the end of his nose. "Of course I did. It was on my instructions. Take Jointner Avenue through Jerusalem's Lot to the 295 entrance ramp." He looked from Tookey to me and back to Tookey again. Outside, the wind whistled and howled and moaned through the eaves. "Wasn't that right, mister?"

"The Lot," Tookey said, almost too soft to hear. "Oh my God."

"What's wrong?" the man said. His voice was rising. "Wasn't that right? I mean, the road looked drifted in, but I thought . . . if there's a town there, the plows will be out and . . . and then I. . . ."

He just sort of tailed off.

"Booth," Tookey said to me, low. "Get on the phone. Call the sheriff."

"Sure," this fool from New Jersey says, "that's right. What's wrong with you guys, anyway? You look like you saw a ghost."

Tookey said, "No ghosts in the Lot, mister. Did you tell them to stay in the car?"

"Sure I did," he said, sounding injured. "I'm not crazy."

Well, you couldn't have proved it by me.

"What's your name?" I asked him. "For the sheriff."

"Lumley," he says, "Gerard Lumley."

He started in with Tookey again, and I went across to the telephone. I picked it up and heard nothing but dead silence. I hit the cutoff buttons a couple of times. Still nothing.

I came back. Tookey had poured Gerard Lumley another tot of brandy, and this one was going down him a lot smoother.

"Was he out?" Tookey asked.

"Phone's dead."

"Hot damn," Tookey says, and we look at each other. Outside the wind gusted up, throwing snow against the windows.

Lumley looked from Tookey to me and back again.

"Well, haven't either of you got a car?" he asked. The

anxiety was back in his voice. "They've got to run the engine to run the heater. I only had about a quarter of a tank of gas, and it took me an hour and a half to . . . Look, will you *answer* me?" He stood up and grabbed Tookey's shirt.

"Mister," Tookey says, "I think your hand just ran away from your brains, there."

Lumley looked at his hand, at Tookey, then dropped it. "Maine," he hissed. He made it sound like a dirty word about somebody's mother. "All right," he said. "Where's the nearest gas station? They must have a tow truck—"

"Nearest gas station is in Falmouth Center," I said. "That's three miles down the road from here."

"Thanks," he said, a bit sarcastic, and headed for the door, buttoning his coat.

"Won't be open, though," I added.

He turned back slowly and looked at us.

"What are you talking about, old man?"

"He's trying to tell you that the station in the Center belongs to Billy Larribee and Billy's out driving the plow, you damn fool," Tookey says patiently. "Now why don't you come back here and sit down, before you bust a gut?"

He came back, looking dazed and frightened. "Are you telling me you can't . . . that there isn't . . . ?"

"I ain't telling you nothing," Tookey says. "You're doing all the telling, and if you stopped for a minute, we could think this over."

"What's this town, Jerusalem's Lot?" he asked. "Why was the road drifted in? And no lights on anywhere?"

I said, "Jerusalem's Lot burned out two years back."

"And they never rebuilt?" He looked like he didn't believe it.

"It appears that way," I said, and looked at Tookey. "What are we going to do about this?"

"Can't leave them out there," he said.

I got closer to him. Lumley had wandered away to look out the window into the snowy night.

"What if they've been got at?" I asked.

"That may be," he said. "But we don't know it for sure.
I've got my Bible on the shelf. You still wear your Pope's
medal?"

I pulled the crucifix out of my shirt and showed him. I was
born and raised Congregational, but most folks who live
around the Lot wear something—crucifix, St. Christopher's
medal, rosary, something. Because two years ago, in the span
of one dark October month, the Lot went bad. Sometimes,
late at night, when there were just a few regulars drawn up
around Tookey's fire, people would talk it over. Talk around
it is more like the truth. You see, people in the Lot started to
disappear. First a few, then a few more, than a whole slew.
The schools closed. The town stood empty for most of a year.
Oh, a few people moved in—mostly damn fools from out of
state like this fine specimen here—drawn by the low property
values, I suppose. But they didn't last. A lot of them moved
out a month or two after they'd moved in. The others . . .
well, they disappeared. Then the town burned flat. It was at
the end of a long dry fall. They figure it started up by the
Marsten House on the hill that overlooked Jointner Avenue,
but no one knows how it started, not to this day. It burned out
of control for three days. After that, for a time, things were
better. And then they started again.

I only heard the word "vampires" mentioned once. A
crazy pulp truck driver named Richie Messina from over
Freeport way was in Tookey's that night, pretty well liquored
up. "Jesus Christ," this stampeder roars, standing up about
nine feet tall in his wool pants and his plaid shirt and his
leather-topped boots. "Are you all so damn afraid to say it
out? Vampires! That's what you're all thinking, ain't it?
Jesus-jumped-up-Christ in a chariot-driven sidecar! Just like a
bunch of kids scared of the movies! You know what there is
down there in 'Salem's Lot? Want me to tell you? Want me
to tell you?"

"Do tell, Richie," Tookey said. It had got real quiet in the
bar. You could hear the fire popping, and outside the soft

drift of November rain coming down in the dark. "You got the floor."

"What you got over there is your basic wild dog pack," Richie Messina tells us. "That's what you got. That and a lot of old women who love a good spook story. Why, for eighty bucks I'd go up there and spend the night in what's left of that haunted house you're all so worried about. Well, what about it? Anyone want to put it up?"

But nobody would. Richie was a loudmouth and a mean drunk and no one was going to shed any tears at his wake, but none of us were willing to see him go into 'Salem's Lot after dark.

"Be screwed to the bunch of you," Richie says. "I got my four-ten in the trunk of my Chevy, and that'll stop anything in Falmouth, Cumberland, *or* Jerusalem's Lot. And that's where I'm goin'."

He slammed out of the bar and no one said a word for a while. Then Lamont Henry says, real quiet, "That's the last time anyone's gonna see Richie Messina. Holy God." And Lamont, raised to be a Methodist from his mother's knee, crossed himself.

"He'll sober off and change his mind," Tookey said, but he sounded uneasy. "He'll be back by closin' time, makin' out it was all a joke."

But Lamont had the right of that one, because no one ever saw Richie again. His wife told the state cops she thought he'd gone to Florida to beat a collection agency, but you could see the truth of the thing in her eyes—sick, scared eyes. Not long after, she moved away to Rhode Island. Maybe she thought Richie was going to come after her some dark night. And I'm not the man to say he might not have done.

Now Tookey was looking at me and I was looking at Tookey as I stuffed my crucifix back into my shirt. I never felt so old or so scared in my life.

Tookey said again, "We can't just leave them out there, Booth."

"Yeah, I know."

We looked at each other for a moment longer, and then he reached out and gripped my shoulder. "You're a good man, Booth." That was enough to buck me up some. It seems like when you pass seventy, people start forgetting that you are a man, or that you ever were.

Tookey walked over to Lumley and said, "I've got a four-wheel-drive Scout. I'll get it out."

"For God's sake, man, why didn't you say so before?" He had whirled around from the window and was staring angrily at Tookey. "Why'd you have to spend ten minutes beating around the bush?"

Tookey said, very softly, "Mister, you shut your jaw. And if you get the urge to open it, you remember who made that turn onto an unplowed road in the middle of a goddamned blizzard."

He started to say something, and then shut his mouth. Thick color had risen up in his cheeks. Tookey went out to get his Scout out of the garage. I felt around under the bar for his chrome flask and filled it full of brandy. Figured we might need it before this night was over.

Maine blizzard—ever been out in one?

The snow comes flying so thick and fine that it looks like sand and sounds like that, beating on the sides of your car or pickup. You don't want to use your high beams because they reflect off the snow and you can't see ten feet in front of you. With the low beams on, you can see maybe fifteen feet. But I can live with the snow. It's the wind I don't like, when it picks up and begins to howl, driving the snow into a hundred weird flying shapes and sounding like all the hate and pain and fear in the world. There's death in the throat of a snowstorm wind, white death—and maybe something beyond death. That's no sound to hear when you're tucked up all cozy in your own bed with the shutters bolted and the doors locked. It's that much worse if you're driving. And we were driving smack into 'Salem's Lot.

"Hurry up a little, can't you?" Lumley asked.

I said, "For a man who came in half frozen, you're in one hell of a hurry to end up walking again."

He gave me a resentful, baffled look and didn't say anything else. We were moving up the highway at a steady twenty-five miles an hour. It was hard to believe that Billy Larribee had just plowed this stretch an hour ago; another two inches had covered it and it was drifting in. The strongest gusts of wind rocked the Scout on her springs. The headlights showed a swirling white nothing up ahead of us. We hadn't met a single car.

About ten minutes later Lumley gasps: "Hey! What's that?"

He was pointing out my side of the car; I'd been looking dead ahead. I turned, but was a shade too late. I thought I could see some sort of slumped form fading back from the car, back into the snow, but that could have been imagination.

"What was it? A deer?" I asked.

"I guess so," he says, sounding shaky. "But its eyes— they looked red." He looked at me. "Is that how a deer's eyes look at night?" He sounded almost as if he were pleading.

"They can look like anything," I says, thinking that might be true, but I've seen a lot of deer at night from a lot of cars, and never saw any set of eyes reflect back red.

Tookey didn't say anything.

About fifteen minutes later, we came to a place where the snowbank on the right of the road wasn't so high because the plows are supposed to raise their blades a little when they go through an intersection.

"This looks like where we turned," Lumley said, not sounding too sure about it. "I don't see the sign—"

"This is it," Tookey answered. He didn't sound like himself at all. "You can just see the top of the signpost."

"Oh. Sure." Lumley sounded relieved. "Listen, Mr. Tooklander, I'm sorry about being so short back there. I was cold and worried and calling myself two hundred kinds of fool. And I want to thank you both—"

"Don't thank Booth and me until we've got them in this car," Tookey said. He put the Scout in four-wheel drive and slammed his way through the snowbank and onto Jointner

Avenue, which goes through the Lot and out to 295. Snow
flew up from the mudguards. The rear end tried to break a
little bit, but Tookey's been driving through snow since
Hector was a pup. He jockeyed it a bit, talked to it, and on
we went. The headlights picked out the bare indication of
other tire tracks from time to time, the ones made by Lumley's
car, and then they would disappear again. Lumley was leaning forward, looking for his car. And all at once Tookey said,
"Mr. Lumley."

"What?" He looked around at Tookey.

"People around these parts are kind of superstitious about
'Salem's Lot," Tookey says, sounding easy enough—but I
could see the deep lines of strain around his mouth, and the
way his eyes kept moving from side to side. "If your people
are in the car, why, that's fine. We'll pack them up, go back
to my place, and tomorrow, when the storm's over, Billy will
be glad to yank your car out of the snowbank. But if they're
not in the car—"

"Not in the car?" Lumley broke in sharply. "Why wouldn't
they be in the car?"

"If they're not in the car," Tookey goes on, not answering, "we're going to turn around and drive back to Falmouth
Center and whistle for the sheriff. Makes no sense to go
wallowing around at night in a snowstorm anyway, does it?"

"They'll be in the car. Where else would they be?"

I said, "One other thing, Mr. Lumley. If we should see
anybody, we're not going to talk to them. Not even if they
talk to us. You understand that?"

Very slow, Lumley says, "Just what are these superstitions?"

Before I could say anything—God alone knows what I
would have said—Tookey broke in. "We're there."

We were coming up on the back end of a big Mercedes.
The whole hood of the thing was buried in a snowdrift, and
another drift had socked in the whole left side of the car. But
the taillights were on and we could see exhaust drifting out of
the tailpipe.

"They didn't run out of gas, anyway," Lumley said.

Tookey pulled up and pulled on the Scout's emergency brake. "You remember what Booth told you, Lumley."

"Sure, sure." But he wasn't thinking of anything but his wife and daughter. I don't see how anybody could blame him, either.

"Ready, Booth?" Tookey asked me. His eyes held on mine, grim and gray in the dashboard lights.

"I guess I am," I said.

We all got out and the wind grabbed us, throwing snow in our faces. Lumley was first, bending into the wind, his fancy topcoat billowing out behind him like a sail. He cast two shadows, one from Tookey's headlights, the other from his own taillights. I was behind him, and Tookey was a step behind me. When I got to the trunk of the Mercedes, Tookey grabbed me.

"Let him go," he said.

"Janey! Francie!" Lumley yelled. "Everything okay?" He pulled open the driver's-side door and leaned in "Everything—"

He froze to a dead stop. The wind ripped the heavy door right out of his hand and pushed it all the way open.

"Holy God, Booth." Tookey said, just below the scream of the wind. "I think it's happened again."

Lumley turned back toward us. His face was scared and bewildered, his eyes wide. All of a sudden he lunged toward us through the snow, slipping and almost falling. He brushed me away like I was nothing and grabbed Tookey.

"How did you know?" he roared. "Where are they? What the hell is going on here?"

Tookey broke his grip and shoved past him. He and I looked into the Mercedes together. Warm as toast it was, but it wasn't going to be for much longer. The little amber low-fuel light was glowing. The big car was empty. There was a child's Barbie doll on the passenger's floormat. And a child's ski parka was crumpled over the seatback.

Tookey put his hands over his face . . . and then he was gone. Lumley had grabbed him and shoved him right back into the snowbank. His face was pale and wild. His mouth was working as if he had chewed down on some bitter stuff he couldn't yet unpucker enough to spit out. He reached in and grabbed the parka.

"Francie's coat?" he kind of whispered. And then loud, bellowing: *"Francie's coat!"* He turned around, holding it in front of him by the little fur-trimmed hood. He looked at me, blank and unbelieving. "She can't be out without her coat on, Mr. Booth. Why . . . why . . . she'll freeze to death."

"Mr. Lumley—"

He blundered past me, still holding the parka, shouting: *"Francie! Janey! Where are you? Where are youuu?"*

I gave Tookey my hand and pulled him onto his feet. "Are you all—"

"Never mind me," he says. "We've got to get hold of him, Booth."

We went after him as fast as we could, which wasn't very fast with the snow hip-deep in some places. But then he stopped and we caught up to him.

"Mr. Lumley—" Tookey started, laying a hand on his shoulder.

"This way," Lumley said. "This is the way they went. Look!"

We looked down. We were in a kind of dip here, and most of the wind went right over our heads. And you could see two sets of tracks, one large and one small, just filling up with snow. If we had been five minutes later, they would have been gone.

He started to walk away, his head down, and Tookey grabbed him back. "No! No, Lumley!"

Lumley turned his wild face up to Tookey's and made a fist. He drew it back . . . but something in Tookey's face made him falter. He looked from Tookey to me and then back again.

"She'll freeze," he said, as if we were a couple of stupid kids. "Don't you get it? She doesn't have her jacket on and she's only seven years old—"

"They could be anywhere," Tookey said. "You can't follow those tracks. They'll be gone in the next drift."

"What do you suggest?" Lumley yells, his voice high and hysterical. "If we go back to get the police, she'll freeze to death! Francie *and* my wife!"

"They may be frozen already," Tookey said. His eyes caught Lumley's. "Frozen, or something worse."

"What do you mean?" Lumley whispered. "Get it straight, goddamn it! Tell me!"

"Mr. Lumley," Tookey said, "there's something in the Lot— "

But I was the one who came out with it finally, said the word I never expected to say. "Vampires, Mr. Lumley. Jerusalem's Lot is full of vampires. I expect that's hard for you to swallow—"

He was staring at me as if I'd gone green. "Loonies," he whispered. "You're a couple of loonies." Then he turned away, cupped his hands around his mouth, and bellowed, *"FRANCIE! JANEY!"* He started floundering off again. The snow was up to the hem of his fancy coat.

I looked at Tookey. "What do we do now?"

"Follow him," Tookey says. His hair was plastered with snow, and he did look a little bit loony. "I can't just leave him out here. Booth. Can you?"

"No," I says. "Guess not."

So we started to wade through the snow after Lumley as best we could. But he kept getting further and further ahead. He had his youth to spend, you see. He was breaking the trail, going through that snow like a bull. My arthritis began to bother me something terrible, and I started to look down at my legs, telling myself: A little further, just a little further, keep goin', damn it, keep goin'. . . .

I piled right into Tookey, who was standing spread-legged in a drift. His head was hanging and both of his hands were pressed to his chest.

"Tookey," I says, "you okay?"

"I'm all right," he said, taking his hands away. "We'll

stick with him, Booth, and when he fags out he'll see reason.''

We topped a rise and there was Lumley at the bottom, looking desperately for more tracks. Poor man, there wasn't a chance he was going to find them. The wind blew straight across down there where he was, and any tracks would have been rubbed out three minutes after they was made, let alone a couple of hours.

He raised his head and screamed into the night: *"FRANCIE! JANEY! FOR GOD'S SAKE!"* And you could hear the desperation in his voice, the terror, and pity him for it. The only answer he got was the freight-train wail of the wind. It almost seemed to be laughin' at him, saying: *I took them Mister New Jersey with your fancy car and camel's-hair topcoat. I took them and I rubbed out their tracks and by morning I'll have them just as neat and frozen as two strawberries in a deepfreeze. . . .*

"Lumley!" Tookey bawled over the wind. "Listen, you never mind vampires or boogies or nothing like that, but you mind this! You're just making it worse for them! We got to get the—"

And then there *was* an answer, a voice coming out of the dark like little tinkling silver bells, and my heart turned cold as ice in a cistern.

"Jerry . . . Jerry, is that you?"

Lumley wheeled at the sound. And then she came, drifting out of the dark shadows of a little copse of trees like a ghost. She was a city woman, all right, and right then she seemed like the most beautiful woman I had ever seen. I felt like I wanted to go to her and tell her how glad I was she was safe after all. She was wearing a heavy green pullover sort of thing, a poncho, I believe they're called. It floated all around her, and her dark hair streamed out in the wild wind like water in a December creek, just before the winter freeze stills it and locks it in.

Maybe I did take a step toward her, because I felt Tookey's hand on my shoulder, rough and warm. And still—how can I say it?—I *yearned* after her, so dark and beautiful with that green poncho floating around her neck and shoulders, as exotic and strange as to make you think of some beautiful woman from a Walter de la Mare poem.

"Janey!" Lumley cried. *"Janey!"* He began to struggle through the snow toward her, his arms outstretched.

"No!" Tookey cried. *"No, Lumley!"*

He never even looked . . . but she did. She looked up at us and grinned. And when she did, I felt my longing, my yearning turn to horror as cold as the grave, as white and silent as bones in a shroud. Even from the rise we could see the sullen red glare in those eyes. They were less human than a wolf's eyes. And when she grinned you could see how long her teeth had become. She wasn't human anymore. She was a dead thing somehow come back to life in this black howling storm.

Tookey made the sign of the cross at her. She flinched back . . . and then grinned at us again. We were too far away, and maybe too scared.

"Stop it!" I whispered. "Can't we stop it?"

"Too late, Booth!" Tookey says grimly.

Lumley had reached her. He looked like a ghost himself, coated in snow like he was. He reached for her . . . and then he began to scream. I'll hear that sound in my dreams, that man screaming like a child in a nightmare. He tried to back away from her, but her arms, long and bare and white as the snow, snaked out and pulled him to her. I could see her cock her head and then thrust it forward—

"Booth!" Tookey said hoarsely. "We've got to get out of here!"

And so we ran. Ran like rats, I suppose some would say, but those who would weren't there that night. We fled back down along our own backtrail, falling down, getting up again, slipping and sliding. I kept looking back over my shoulder to see if that woman was coming after us, grinning that grin and watching us with those red eyes.

We got back to the Scout and Tookey doubled over, holding his chest. "Tookey!" I said, badly scared. "What—"

"Ticker," he said. "Been bad for five years or more. Get me around in the shotgun seat, Booth, and then get us the hell out of here."

I hooked an arm under his coat and dragged him around and somehow boosted him up and in. He leaned his head back and shut his eyes. His skin was waxy-looking and yellow.

I went back around the hood of the truck at a trot, and I damned near ran into the little girl. She was just standing there beside the driver's-side door, her hair in pigtails, wearing nothing but a little bit of a yellow dress.

"Mister," she said in a high, clear voice, as sweet as morning mist, "won't you help me find my mother? She's gone and I'm so cold—"

"Honey," I said, "honey, you better get in the truck. Your mother's—"

I broke off, and if there was ever a time in my life I was close to swooning, that was the moment. She was standing there, you see, but she was standing *on top* of the snow and there were no tracks, not in any direction.

She looked up at me then, Lumley's daughter Francie. She was no more than seven years old, and she was going to be seven for an eternity of nights. Her little face was a ghastly corpse white, her eyes a red and silver that you could fall into. And below her jaw I could see two small punctures like pinpricks, their edges horribly mangled.

She held out her arms at me and smiled. "Pick me up, mister," she said softly. "I want to give you a kiss. Then you can take me to my mommy."

I didn't want to, but there was nothing I could do. I was leaning forward, my arms outstretched. I could see her mouth opening, I could see the little fangs inside the pink ring of her lips. Something slipped down her chin, bright and silvery, and with a dim, distant, faraway horror, I realized she was drooling.

Her small hands clasped themselves around my neck and I was thinking: Well, maybe it won't be so bad, not so bad, maybe it won't be so awful after a while—when something black flew out of the Scout and struck her on the chest. There was a puff of strange-smelling smoke, a flashing glow that was gone an instant later, and then she was backing away, hissing. Her face was twisted into a vulpine mask of rage, hate, and pain. She turned sideways and then . . . and then she was gone. One moment she was there, and the next there was a twisting knot of snow that looked a little bit like a human shape. Then the wind tattered it away across the fields.

"Booth!" Tookey whispered. "Be quick, now!"

And I was. But not so quick that I didn't have time to pick up what he had thrown at that little girl from hell. His mother's Douay Bible.

That was some time ago. I'm a sight older now, and I was no chicken then. Herb Tooklander passed on two years ago. He went peaceful, in the night. The bar is still there, some man and his wife from Waterville bought it, nice people, and they've kept it pretty much the same. But I don't go by much. It's different somehow with Tookey gone.

Things in the Lot go on pretty much as they always have. The sheriff found that fellow Lumley's car the next day, out of gas, the battery dead. Neither Tookey nor I said anything about it. What would have been the point? And every now and then a hitchhiker or a camper will disappear around there someplace, up on Schoolyard Hill or out near the Harmony Hill cemetery. They'll turn up the fellow's packsack or a paperback book all swollen and bleached out by the rain or snow, or some such. But never the people.

I still have bad dreams about that stormy night we went out there. Not about the woman so much as the little girl, and the way she smiled when she held her arms up so I could pick her up. So she could give me a kiss. But I'm an old man and the time comes soon when dreams are done.

You may have an occasion to be traveling in southern Maine yourself one of these days. Pretty part of the countryside. You may even stop by Tookey's Bar for a drink. Nice place. They kept the name just the same. So have your drink, and then my advice to you is to keep right on moving north. Whatever you do, don't go up that road to Jerusalem's Lot.

Especially not after dark.

There's a little girl somewhere out there. And I think she's still waiting for her good-night kiss.

WILLIAM TENN

She Only Goes Out At Night . . .

In this part of the country, folks think that Doc Judd carries magic in his black leather satchel. He's *that* good.

Ever since I lost my leg in the sawmill, I've been all-around handyman at the Judd place. Lots of times when Doc gets a night call after a real hard day, he's too tired to drive, so he hunts me up and I become a chauffeur too. With the shiny plastic leg that Doc got me at a discount, I can stamp the gas pedal with the best of them.

We roar up to the farmhouse and, while Doc goes inside to deliver a baby or swab grandma's throat, I sit in the car and listen to them talk about what a ball of fire the old Doc is. In Groppa County, they'll tell you Doc Judd can handle *anything*. And I nod and listen, nod and listen.

But all the time I'm wondering what they'd think of the way he handled his only son falling in love with a vampire. . . .

It was a terrifically hot summer when Steve came home on vacation—real blister weather. He wanted to drive his father around and kind of help with the chores, but Doc said that after the first tough year of medical school anyone deserved a vacation.

"Summer's a pretty quiet time in our line," he told the boy. "Nothing but poison ivy and such until we hit the polio

31

season in August. Besides, you wouldn't want to shove old Tom out of his job, would you? No, Stevie, you just bounce around the countryside in your jalopy and enjoy yourself.''

Steve nodded and took off. And I mean took off. About a week later, he started coming home five or six o'clock in the morning. He'd sleep till about three in the afternoon, lazy around for a couple of hours and, come eight-thirty, off he'd rattle in his little hot-rod. Road-houses, we figured, or maybe some girl. . . .

Doc didn't like it, but he'd brought up the boy with a nice easy hand and he didn't feel like saying anything just yet. Old buttinsky Tom, though—I was different. I'd helped raise the kid since his mother died, and I'd walloped him when I caught him raiding the ice-box.

So I dropped a hint now and then, kind of asking him, like, not to go too far off the deep end. I could have been talking to a stone face for all the good it did. Not that Steve was rude. He was just too far gone in whatever it was to pay attention to me.

And then the other stuff started and Doc and I forgot about Steve.

Some kind of weird epidemic hit the kids of Groppa County and knocked twenty, thirty, of them flat on their backs.

''It's almost got me beat, Tom,'' Doc would confide in me as we bump-bump-bumped over dirty back-country roads. ''It acts like a bad fever, yet the rise in temperature is hardly noticeable. But the kids get very weak and their blood count goes way down. And it stays that way, no matter what I do. Only good thing, it doesn't seem to be fatal—so far.''

Every time he talked about it, I felt a funny twinge in my stump where it was attached to the plastic leg. I got so uncomfortable that I tried to change the subject, but that didn't go with Doc. He'd gotten used to thinking out his problems by talking to me, and this epidemic thing was pretty heavy on his mind.

He'd written to a couple of universities for advice, but they didn't seem to be of much help. And all the time, the parents of the kids stood around waiting for him to pull a cellophane-wrapped miracle out of his little black bag, because, as they said in Groppa County, there was nothing could go wrong with a human body that Doc Judd couldn't take care of some way or other. And all the time, the kids got weaker and weaker.

Doc got big, bleary bags under his eyes from sitting up nights going over the latest books and medical magazines he'd ordered from the city. Near as I could tell he'd find nothing, even though lots of times he'd get to bed almost as late as Steve.

And then he brought home the handkerchief. Soon as I saw it, my stump gave a good, hard, extra twinge and I wanted to walk out of the kitchen. Tiny, fancy handkerchief, it was, all embroidered linen and lace edges.

"What do you think, Tom? Found this on the floor of the bedroom of the Stopes' kids. Neither Betty nor Willy have any idea where it came from. For a bit, I thought I might have a way of tracing the source of infection, but those kids wouldn't lie. If they say they never saw it before, then that's the way it is." He dropped the handkerchief on the kitchen table that I was clearing up, stood there sighing. "Betty's anemia is beginning to look serious. I wish I knew . . . I wish . . . Oh, well." He walked out to the study, his shoulders bent like they were under a sack of cement.

I was still staring at the handkerchief, chewing on a fingernail, when Steve bounced in. He poured himself a cup of coffee, plumped it down on the table and saw the handkerchief.

"Hey," he said. "That's Tatiana's. How did it get here?"

I swallowed what was left of the fingernail and sat down very carefully opposite him. "Steve," I asked, and then stopped because I had to massage my aching stump. "Stevie, you know a girl who owns that handkerchief? A girl named Tatiana?"

"Sure. Tatiana Latianu. See, there are her initials embroidered in the corner—T. L. She's descended from the Rumanian nobility; family goes back five hundred years. I'm going to marry her.''

''She the girl you've been seeing every night for the past month?''

He nodded. ''She only goes out at night. Hates the glare of the sun You know, poetic kind of girl. And Tom, she's so *beautiful.* . . .''

For the next hour, I just sat there and listened to him. And I felt sicker and sicker. Because I'm Rumanian myself, on my mother's side. And I knew why I'd been getting those twinges in my stump.

She lived in Brasket Township, about twelve miles away. Tom had run into her late one night on the road when her convertible had broken down. He'd given her a lift to her house—she'd just rented the old Mead Mansion—and he'd fallen for her, hook, line and whole darn fishing rod.

Lots of times, when he arrived for a date, she'd be out, driving around the countryside in the cool night air, and he'd have to play cribbage with her maid, an old beak-faced Rumanian biddy, until she got back. Once or twice, he'd tried to go after her in his hot-rod, but that had led to trouble. When she wanted to be alone, she had told him, she wanted to be *alone.* So that was that. He waited for her night after night. But when she got back, according to Steve, she really made up for everything. They listened to music and talked and danced and ate strange Rumanian dishes that the maid whipped up. Until dawn. Then he came home.

Steve put his hand on my arm. ''Tom, you know that poem—*The Owl and the Pussy-Cat?* I've always thought the last line was beautiful. 'They danced by the light of the moon, the moon, they danced by the light of the moon.' That's what my life will be like with Tatiana. If only she'll have me. I'm still having trouble talking her into it.''

I let out a long breath. ''The first good thing I've heard,'' I said without thinking. ''Marriage to *that* girl—''

When I saw Steve's eyes, I broke off. But it was too late.

"What the hell do you mean, Tom: *that* girl? You've never even met her."

I tried to twist out of it, but Steve wouldn't let me. He was real sore. So I figured the best thing was to tell him the truth.

"Stevie. Listen. Don't laugh. Your girl friend is a vampire."

He opened his mouth slowly. "Tom, you're off your—"

"No, I'm not." And I told him about vampires. What I'd heard from my mother who'd come over from the old country, from Transylvania, when she was twenty. How they can live and have all sorts of strange powers—just so long as they have a feast of human blood once in a while. How the vampire taint is inherited, usually just one child in the family getting it. And how they go out only at night, because sunlight is one of the things that can destroy them.

Steve turned pale at this point. But I went on. I told him about the mysterious epidemic that had hit the kids of Groppa County—and made them anemic. I told him about his father finding the handkerchief in the Stopes' house, near two of the sickest kids. And I told him—but all of a sudden I was talking to myself. Steve tore out of the kitchen. A second or two later, he was off in the hot-rod.

He came back about eleven-thirty, looking as old as his father. I was right, all right. When he'd wakened Tatiana and asked her straight, she'd broken down and wept a couple of buckets-full. Yes, she was a vampire, but she'd only got the urge a couple of months ago. She'd fought it until her mind began to break when the craving hit her. She'd only touched kids, because she was afraid of grownups—they might wake up and be able to catch her. But she'd kind of worked on a lot of kids at one time, so that no one kid would lose too much blood. Only the craving had been getting stronger. . . .

And still Steve had asked her to marry him! "There must be a way of curing it," he said. "It's a sickness like any other sickness." But she, and—believe me—I thanked God, had said no. She'd pushed him out and made him leave. "Where's Dad?" he asked. "He might know."

I told him that his father must have left at the same time he did, and hadn't come back yet. So the two of us sat and thought. *And thought*.

When the telephone rang, we both almost fell out of our seats. Steve answered it, and I heard him yelling into the mouthpiece.

He ran into the kitchen, grabbed me by the arm and hauled me out into his hot-rod. "That was Tatiana's maid, Magda," he told me as we went blasting down the highway. "She says Tatiana got hysterical after I left, and a few minutes ago she drove away in her convertible. She wouldn't say where she was going. Magda says she thinks Tatiana is going to do away with herself."

"*Suicide?* But if she's a vampire, how—" And all of a sudden I knew just how. I looked at my watch. "Stevie," I said, "drive up to Crispin Junction. And drive like holy hell!"

He opened that hot-rod all the way. It looked as if the motor was going to tear itself right off the car. I remember we went around curves just barely touching the road with the rim of one tire.

We saw the convertible as soon as we entered Crispin Junction. It was parked by the side of one of the three roads that cross the town. There was a tiny figure in a flimsy nightdress standing in the middle of the deserted street. My leg stump felt like it was being hit with a hammer.

The church clock started to toll midnight just as we reached her. Steve leaped out and knocked the pointed piece of wood out of her hands. He pulled her into his arms and let her cry.

I was feeling pretty bad at this point. Because all I'd been thinking of was how Steve was in love with a vampire. I hadn't looked at it from her side. She'd been enough in love with him to try to kill herself the *only* way a vampire could be killed—by driving a stake through her heart on a crossroads at midnight.

And she was a pretty little creature. I'd pictured one of these siren dames: you know, tall, slinky, with a tight dress. A witch. But this was a very frightened, very upset young lady who got in the car and cuddled up in Steve's free arm like she'd taken a lease on it. And I could tell she was even younger than Steve.

So, all the time we were driving back, I was thinking to myself *these kids have got plenty trouble*. Bad enough to be in love with a vampire, but to be a vampire in love with a normal human being. . . .

"But how *can* I marry you?" Tatiana wailed. "What kind of home life would we have? And Steve, one night I might even get hungry enough to attack *you!*"

The only thing none of us counted on was Doc. Not enough, that is."

Once he'd been introduced to Tatiana and heard her story, his shoulders straightened and the lights came back on in his eyes. The sick children would be all right now. That was most important. And as for Tatiana—

"Nonsense," he told her. "Vampirism might have been an incurable disease in the fifteenth century, but I'm sure it can be handled in the twentieth. First, this nocturnal living points to a possible allergy involving sunlight and perhaps a touch of photophobia. You'll wear tinted glasses for a bit, my girl, and we'll see what we can do with hormone injections. The need for consuming blood, however, presents a somewhat greater problem."

But he solved it.

They make blood in a dehydrated, crystalline form these days. So every night before Mrs. Steven Judd goes to sleep, she shakes some powder into a tall glass of water, drops in an ice cube or two and has her daily blood toddy. Far as I know, she and her husband are living happily ever after.

DAVID H. KELLER

Heredity

Dr. Theodore Overfield was impressed.

The size of the estate, the virgin timber, the large stone house, and, above all, the high iron fence, which surrounded the place, indicated wealth and careful planning. The house was old, the trees were very old, but the fence was new. Its sharp, glistening pickets ranged upward, looking like bayonets on parade.

When he had accepted the invitation to make a professional visit to that home, he had counted on nothing more than a case of neurasthenia, perhaps an alcoholic psychosis or feminine hysteria. As he drove through the gateway and heard the iron shutters clank behind him, he was not so sure of its being a commonplace situation or an ordinary patient. A few deer ran, frightened, from the roadside. They were pretty things. At least, they were one reason for the fence.

At the house, a surly, silent, servant opened the door and ushered him into a room that seemed to be the library. It not only held books in abundance, but it seemed that the books were used. Not many sets, but many odd volumes were there—evidently first editions. At one end of the room was a winged Mercury; at the other end, a snow white Venus.

Between them, on one side, was the fireplace with several inviting chairs.

"A week here with pay will not be half bad," mused the Doctor. But his pleasant thought was interrupted by the entrance of a small, middle-aged man, with young eyes, but with hair that would soon be white. He introduced himself.

"I am Peterson, the man who wrote you. I presume that you are Dr. Overfield?"

The two men shook hands and sat down by the fireplace.

It was early September, and the days were chill in the mountains.

"I understand that you are a psychiatrist, Dr. Overfield," the white-haired man began. "At least, I was told that you might be helpful to me in the solving of my problem."

"I do not know what your trouble is," answered the Doctor, "but I have not made any appointments for the next week; so that time and my ability are at your disposal. You did not mention in your letters just what the trouble was. Do you care to tell me now?"

"Not now. Perhaps after dinner. You may be able to see for yourself. I am going to take you to your bedroom, and you may come down at six and meet the rest of the family."

The room that Overfield was taken to seemed comfortable in every way. Peterson left the room, hesitated, and came back.

"Just a word of advice, Doctor. When you are alone in here, be sure to keep the door locked."

"Shall I lock it when I leave?"

"No. That will not be necessary. No one will steal anything."

The Doctor shut the door, locked it according to advice, and went to the windows. They overlooked the woods. In the distance he could see a few deer. Nearer, white rabbits were playing on the lawn. It was a pretty view, but the windows were barred!

"A prison?" he asked himself. "Bars on the windows! Advice to keep the door locked! What can he be afraid of?

Evidently, not of thieves. Perhaps he has a phobia. I wonder whether all the rooms are barred? This seems interesting. And then that fence? It would be a brave man who would try to go over that, even with a ladder. He did not impress me as being a neurasthenic, but, at the same time, he wanted to delay the interrogation. Evidently, he feels that it would be easier if I found out some things for myself.''

The Doctor was tired from the long drive, so he took off his shoes and collar, and started to go to sleep. The silence was complete. The slightest sound was magnified into a startling intensity. Minutes passed. He thought that he heard a doorknob turn and was sure that it was his door, but no one knocked and there was no sound of footsteps. Later, thinking about everything, he went to sleep. It was growing dark when he awoke and looked at his watch. It was ten minutes to six. Just time enough to dash into his dinner clothes. He did not know whether people dressed for dinner at that place, but there was no harm in doing so.

Downstairs, Peterson was waiting for him. Mrs. Peterson was also there. She must have known that the Doctor would dress for dinner; and, not wanting to embarrass him, also had dressed formally for the occasion. But her husband wore the same suit that he had on all day. He had even neglected to comb his hair.

At the table, the white-haired man kept silent. The wife was a sparkling conversationalist, and the Doctor enjoyed her talk as much as he did the meal. Mrs. Peterson had been to places and had seen many things, and she had a way of telling about them that was even more vivid than the average travelogue. She appeared to be interested in everything.

"Here is a woman of culture," thought Overfield. "This woman knows a little bit about everything and is able to tell it at the right time."

He might have added that she was beautiful. Subconsciously, he felt that; and even more deeply wondered why such a woman should have married a fossil like Peterson.

Nice enough man, all right, but certainly not fit mate for such a woman.

The woman was small, delicately formed, yet radiant with health and vitality. Someone was sick in the family, but it evidently was not she. Dr. Overfield studied the husband. Perhaps there was his patient? Silent, moody, suspicious, locked doors and barred windows! It might be a case of paranoia, and the wife was forcing the conversation and trying to be gay simply as a defense reaction.

Was she really happy? At times, a cloud seemed to come over her face, to be chased away at once by a smile or even a merry laugh. At least, she was not altogether happy. How could one be with a husband like that!

The surly, silent, servant waited on the table. He seemed to anticipate every need of his mistress. His service was beyond the shadow of reproach; but in some way, for some reason, the Doctor disliked him from the beginning. He tried to analyze that dislike, but failed. Later on he found the reason. His mind was working fast, trying to solve the problem of his being there, the invitation to spend a week. Suddenly, he awoke to the fact that there was a vacant chair. The table had been set for four, and just then the door opened and in walked a young lad followed by a burly man in black.

"This is my son, Alexander, Dr. Overfield. Shake hands with the gentleman, Alexander."

Closely followed by the man in black, the youth walked around the table, took the Doctor's hand, and then sat down at the empty place. An ice was served. The man in black stood in back of the chair and carefully supervised every movement the boy made. Conversation was now blocked. The dessert was eaten in silence. Finished, Peterson spoke.

"You can take Alexander to his room, Yorry."

"Very well, Mr. Peterson."

Again there were but three at the table, but the conversation was not resumed. Cigarettes were smoked in silence. Then Mrs. Peterson excused herself.

"I am designing a new dress, and I have gotten to a very

interesting place. I cannot decide on snaps or buttons; and if there are to be buttons, there must be an originality about them that will make their use logical. So, I shall have to ask you gentlemen to excuse me. I hope that you will spend a comfortable week with us, Dr. Overfield.''

"I am sure of that, Mrs. Peterson," replied the Doctor, rising as she left the table. The white-haired man did not rise. He simply kept looking into the wall ahead of him, looking into it without seeing the picture on it—without seeing anything that there was to see! At last, he crushed the fire out of his cigarette and rose.

"Let us go into the library. I want to talk."

Once there, he tried to make the Doctor comfortable.

"Take off your coat and collar if you wish, and put your feet up on the stool. We shall be alone tonight, and there is no need of formality."

"I judge you are not very happy, Mr. Peterson?" the Doctor began. It was just an opening wedge to the mental catharsis that he hoped would follow. In fact, it was a favorite introduction of his to the examination of a patient. It gave the sick person confidence in the Doctor, a feeling that he understood something about him, personally. And many people came to his office because they were not happy.

"Not very," was the reply. "I am going to tell you something about it, but part I want you to see for yourself. It starts back at the time when I began in business. I had been called Philip by my parents, Philip Peterson. When in school, I studied about Philip of Macedonia, and there were parts of his life that I rather admired. He was a road breaker, if you know what I mean. He took a lot of countries and consolidated them. He reorganized the army. Speaking in modern slang, he was a 'go-getter.' Of course, he had his weaknesses— such as wine and women—but in the main, he was rather fine.

"There was a difference between being King of Macedonia and becoming president of a leather company, but I thought that the same principles might be used and would probably lead to success. At any rate, I studied the life of Philip and tried to profit by it. At last, I became a rich man.

"Then I married. As you saw, my wife is a gifted, cultured woman. We had a son. At his birth, I named him Alexander. I wanted to follow in the course of the Macedonian. I ruled the leather business in America, and I hoped that he would rule it in the entire world. You saw the boy tonight at supper."

"Yes, I saw him."

"And your diagnosis?"

"Not exactly true to form, but resembles the type of mental deficiency known as *mongolian idiocy* more than anything else."

"That is what I have been told. We kept him at home for two years, and then I placed him in one of the best private schools in America. When he reached the age of ten, they refused to keep him any longer, no matter what I paid them. So I fixed this place up, sold out my interests, and came here to live. He is my son, and I feel that I should care for him."

"It is rather peculiar that they do not want him in a private school. With your wealth. . . ."

"Something happened. They felt that they could not take the responsibility for his care."

"How does he act? What does his mother think about it?"

"Do you know much about mothers in general?"

"A little."

"Then you can understand. His mother thinks that he is perfect. At times, she refuses to believe that he is feeble-minded. She uses the word 'retarded' and thinks that he will outgrow the condition and some day become normal."

"She is mistaken."

"I am afraid so. But I cannot convince her. When the matter is argued, she becomes angry; and she is very unpleasant when she is that way. We moved here. You saw our servants. The butler serves in several capacities. He has been in the family for many years and is to be trusted. He is deaf-mute."

"I understand," the Doctor exclaimed. "That accounts for his surly, silent, personality. All mutes are queer."

"I presume that is true. He keeps house for us. You see, others servants are hard to keep. They come, but they won't stay after they learn about Alexander."

"Do they object to his mentality?"

"No, it is the way he acts that worries them. I have given you the facts. They will not stay here. The man, Yorry, is an ex-pugilist. He is without nerves and without fear. He is very good to the boy; but, at the same time, he makes him obey. Since he has been here, it is possible to bring the lad to the table, and that makes Mother very happy. But, of course, he cannot be on duty all the time. When he has his hours off, he lets Alexander run in the park."

"The boy must like it out there. I saw the deer and the rabbits."

"Yes, it gives him exercise. He likes to chase them."

"Don't you think he ought to have some playmates?"

"I used to think so. I even went so far as to adopt another boy. He died. After that, I could not repeat the experiment."

"But any child might die," the Doctor replied. "Why not bring another boy in, even for a few hours a day, for him to talk to and play with?"

"No, never again! But you stay here and watch the boy. Examine him and see if you can give me advice."

"I am afraid that there is not much to be done for him beyond training him, and correcting any bad habits that he may have."

The white-haired man looked puzzled as he replied:

"That is the trouble. Some years ago, I consulted a specialist. I told him all about it, and he said that he thought the child had better be allowed a certain freedom of action. He said something about desires and libido and thought that the only chance for improvement was in letting him have his own way. That is one reason why we are here with the deer and the rabbits."

"You mean that the boy likes to play with them?"

"Not exactly. But you study him. I have told Yorry that he is to answer all your questions. He knows the boy better than I do; and God forgive me for saying it, but I know him too well. Of course, it is hard for me to talk about it. I would rather have you get the details from Yorry. It is growing late and perhaps you had better go to bed. Be sure to lock the door."

"I'll do that," the Doctor said, "but you told me that nothing would be stolen."

The Doctor went to his room, thoroughly puzzled. He knew the variety of mental deficiency known as *mongolian idiocy*. He had helped examine and care for several hundred of such cases. Young Alexander was one, yet, he was different. There was something about him that did not quite harmonize with that diagnosis. His habits? Perhaps that was it. Was his father afraid of him? Was that why he had a strong man to train him? Was that why the bars were on the windows? But why the rabbits and the little deer?

Almost before he was asleep he was roused by a knock at the door. Going to it, he called without opening the door.

"What is it?"

"This is Yorry," was the response. "Are you all right?"

"Yes."

"Let me in."

The Doctor opened the door, allowed the man to enter, and locked it behind him.

"What is the trouble?"

"Alexander is out of his room. We do not mind it in the daytime, but at night it is bad. Look over at the window!"

There was a white thing at one of the windows, holding on to the bars and shaking them in an effort to break them. Yorry shook his head.

"That lad, that lad! This is no place for him, but what are the poor people to do? Well, if you are safe, I will go out and try to get him. You lock the door behind me."

"Are you afraid of him?"

"Not for myself, but for others. I do not know fear. Mr.

Peterson said you wanted to examine the boy. What time tomorrow?''

"At ten. Right here will do."

"I'll have him here. Good night, and be sure to lock the door."

The Doctor was tired, so he went to sleep with all the questions unsolved. The next morning breakfast was served to him in his room by the deaf-mute. At ten, Yorry came in with Alexander. The boy seemed frightened, but obeyed the commands of his attendant.

In most respects, the examination showed the physical defects of the mongolian idiot. There were a few minor differences. Though the boy was small for his age, the musculature was good, and the teeth were perfect. Not a cavity was present. The upper canines were unusual.

"He has very fine teeth, Yorry," the Doctor commented.

"He has, Sir, and he uses them," replied the man.

"You mean in eating his food?"

"Yes. Just that."

"They are the teeth of a meat-eater."

"That is what he is."

"I wish that you would tell me about it, honestly. Why did they turn him out of that private school?"

"It was his habits."

"What kind of habits?"

"Suppose you see for yourself. The three of us will go in the woods. It is safe as long as you are with me, but you must not go by yourself."

The Doctor laughed.

"I am accustomed to abnormals."

"Perhaps, but I do not want anything to happen to you. Come with me, Alexander."

The boy went with them, and seemed to be perfectly docile.

Once in the woods, Yorry helped the boy undress. Naked, the lad started to run through the forest.

"He cannot get out?" the Doctor asked.

"No, nor for that matter, neither can the deer and the little rabbits. We will not try to follow him. When he finishes, he will come back."

An hour passed, and then two hours. At last, Alexander came creeping through the grass on all fours. Yorry took a wet towel from his pockets, wiped the blood from the boy's face and hands, and then started to dress him.

"So that is what he does?" asked the Doctor.

"Yes, and sometimes more than that."

"And that is why they did not want him in the school?"

"I suppose so. His father told me that when he was young, he started in with flies and bugs and toads."

The Doctor thought fast.

"There was a little child brought here to be his playmate. The boy died. Do you know anything about that?"

"No. I do not know anything about that. I do not want to know anything about it. It probably happened before I came here."

Overfield knew that the man was not telling the truth. But even in his lie, he was handing out useful information. The Doctor decided to have another talk with the boy's father. There was no use trying to help unless all the facts were given to him.

At the noonday meal, the conversation was not as sparkling as it had been the evening before. Peterson seemed moody. Mrs. Peterson was polite, but decidedly restrained. It seemed that most of the conversation was forced. After the meal was over, there was one part of the conversation that seemed to stand out in the mind of the specialist. Peterson remarked that one of his teeth was troubling him, and that he would have to see a dentist. His wife replied, "I have perfect teeth. I have never been to a dentist."

In the library, while he was waiting for Peterson to come, Dr. Overfield recalled that statement.

"I have examined your son, Mr. Peterson," began the specialist, "and I have seen him in the woods. Yorry told me about some things and lied to me about others. Up to the present time, no one seems willing to tell me the entire truth. I have one question that I must have answered. How did the boy die? The one you had for a playmate?''

"I am not sure. And when I say that, I am perfectly honest. We found him dead in his room one morning. A glass had been broken in the bedroom window. A lot of broken glass was around him. There was a deep cut in one side of his throat. The Coroner thought that he had walked in his sleep, struck the window pane, and that a piece of glass had severed the jugular vein. He certified that as the cause of death.''

"What do you think, Mr. Peterson?''

"I have stopped thinking.''

"Was it before that, or afterward, that you had the bars placed in the windows?''

"After that. Can you help the boy?''

"I am afraid not. The advice that the other man gave you years ago was bad. It has kept the boy in fine physical condition, but there are other things to be considered besides physical health. If he were my son, I would remove the deer and the rabbits, those that are still alive. And I would try and train him in different habits.''

"I will think that over. I paid you for your opinion, and I value it. Now, one more question: Is this habit of the boy's a hereditary one? Do you think, that in the past, some ancestor of his did something like that?''

It was a puzzling question. Perhaps Dr. Overfield was right in answering it with another question.

"Any insanity in the family?''

"None that I ever heard of.''

"Good! How about your wife's family?''

"Her heredity is as good as mine, perhaps better.''

"Then all that we can say is that *mongolianism* can come in any family; and, as far as the boy's habit is concerned, suppose we call it an atavism? At one time, all our ancestors ate raw meat. The Mongolian type of mental deficiency comes to us from the cradle of the human race. The boy may have brought it with him as he leaped forward two million years, brought raw meat-eating with his slanting eyebrows.''

"I wish I were sure," commented the father. "I would give anything to be sure that I was not to blame for the boy's condition.''

"Or your wife?" the Doctor asked.

"Oh! There is no question about her," was the half smiling reply. "She is one of the nicest women God ever made.''

"Perhaps there is something in her subconscious, something that does not show on the surface?"

The husband shook his head.

"No. She is just good through and through.''

This ended the conversation. The Doctor promised to spend the rest of the week, though he felt that there was little use in his doing so. He joined the retired leather man and his wife at dinner. Mrs. Peterson was more beautiful than ever, in a white evening dress, trimmed with gold sequins. Peterson looked tired; but his wife was brilliant in every way, in addition to her costume. She talked as though she would never tire, and everything that she said was worth listening to. She had just aided in the organization of a milk fund for undernourished children. Charity, it seemed, was one of her hobbies. Peterson talked about heredity, but little attention was paid to him or his thoughts. He soon stopped talking.

Through it all there was something that Dr. Overfield could not understand. When he said good night to the white-haired man, he told him as much.

"I do not understand it either," commented Peterson, "but perhaps, before I die, I shall understand. I cannot help feeling that there is something in heredity, but I cannot prove it.''

Dr. Overfield locked the door of his bedroom, and retired at once. He was sleepy, and, at the same time, nervous. He thought that a long night's rest would help. But he did not sleep long. A pounding on the door brought him to consciousness.

"Who is there?" he asked.

"It's me, Yorry. Open the door!''

"What is the trouble?"

"It is the boy, Alexander. He has slipped away from me again, and I cannot find him."

"Perhaps he has gone to the woods?"

"No. All the outside doors are locked. He must be in the house."

"Have you hunted?"

"Everywhere. The butler is safe in his room. I have been all over the house except in the Master's room."

"Why not go there? Wait till I get some clothes on. Just a minute. He keeps the doors locked, doesn't he? He told me to keep my door locked. You are sure he has his door locked?"

"It was locked earlier in the evening. I tested it. I do that every night with all the bedrooms."

"Anyone with duplicate keys?"

"No one except Mrs. Peterson. I think she must have a set; but she sleeps in her room, and her door was locked. At least it was, earlier in the evening."

"I think we ought to go to their rooms. The boy has to be somewhere. Perhaps he is with one of his parents."

"If he is with his mother, it is all right. They understand each other. She can do anything with him."

They rushed upstairs. The door to Mrs. Peterson's room was open, the room empty, and the bed untouched. That was something not to be expected. The door to the next room, Peterson's room, was closed—but not locked. Opening it, Yorry turned on the electric lights.

Before he did so, from the dark room came an odd, low, snarling, noise. Then the lights were on, and there was the Peterson family on the floor. Peterson was in the middle. He had his shirt torn off, and he was very quiet. On the right side, tearing at the muscles of the arm, was Alexander, his face and hands smeared with blood. On the other side, at the neck, the Peterson woman was fastened, drinking blood from the jugular vein. Her face and dress were stained with blood, and as she looked up, her face was that of an irritated, but otherwise contented demon. She seemed disturbed over the interruption, but too preoccupied to understand it. She kept on drinking, but the boy snarled his anger. Overfield pulled Yorry through the doorway, turned out the lights, and slammed the door in back of them. Then he dragged the dazed man down the steps to the first floor.

"Where is the telephone?" he yelled.

Yorry finally showed him. The Doctor jerked off the receiver.

"Hullo! Hullo! Central. Give me the Coroner. No, I don't know the number. Why should I know the number? Get him for me. Hullo! Is this the Coroner? Can you hear me? This is a doctor talking, Dr. Overfield. Come to Philip Peterson's house at once. There has been a murder committed here. Yes. The man is dead. What killed him? Heredity. You can't understand? Why should you? Now, listen to me. He had his throat cut, perhaps with a piece of broken glass, perhaps not. Can you understand that? Do you remember the little boy? Come up, and I will wait for you here."

The Doctor hung up the receiver. Yorry was looking at him.

"The master was always worried about the boy," Yorry said.

"He can stop worrying now," answered the Doctor.

THÉOPHILE GAUTIER

Clarimonda

You ask me, brother, if I have ever loved. I have. It is a strange story, and though I am sixty, I scarce venture to stir the ashes of that remembrance. I mean to refuse you nothing, but to no soul less tried than yours would I tell the story. The events are so strange that I can hardly believe they did happen. I was for more than three years the plaything of a singular and diabolical illusion. I, a poor priest, I led in my dreams every night—God grant they were dreams only!—the life of the damned, the life of the worldly, the life of Sardanapalus. A single glance, too full of approval, cast upon a woman, nearly cost me the loss of my soul. But at last, by the help of God and of my holy patron, I was able to drive away the evil spirit which had possessed me. My life was complicated by an entirely different nocturnal life. During the day I was a priest of God, chaste, busied with prayers and holy things; at night, as soon as I had closed my eyes, I became a young nobleman, a connoisseur of women, of horses and dogs, gambling, drinking, and cursing, and when at dawn I awoke, it seemed to me rather that I was going to sleep and dreaming of being a priest. Of that somnambulistic life there have remained in my remembrance things and words I cannot put away, and although I have never left the walls of my presbytery, you will be apt to think, on hearing me, that I am a man who, having worn out everything and having given up the world and entered religion, means to end in the bosom of God days too greatly agitated, rather than a humble student in a seminary, who has grown old in a forgotten parish in the depths of a forest, and who has never had anything to do with the things of the day.

Yes, I have loved, as no one on earth ever loved, with an insensate and furious love, so violent that I wonder it did not break my heart. Ah! what nights! what nights I have had!

From my youngest childhood I felt the vocation to the priesthood and all my studies were therefore bent in that direction. My life until the age of twenty-four was nothing but one long novitiate. Having finished my theological studies, I passed successfully through the minor orders, and my superiors considered me worthy, in spite of my youth, of crossing the last dread limit. The day of my ordination was fixed for Easter week.

I had never gone into the world. The world, to me, lay within the walls of the college and of the seminary. I knew vaguely that there was something called a woman, but my thoughts never dwelt upon it; I was utterly innocent. I saw my old, infirm mother but twice a year; she was the only connection I had with the outer world. I regretted nothing; I felt not the least hesitation in the presence of the irrevocable engagement I was about to enter into; nay, I was joyous and full of impatience. Never did a young bridegroom count the hours with more feverish ardor. I could not sleep; I dreamed that I was saying Mass; I saw nothing more glorious in the world than to be a priest. I would have refused, had I been offered a kingdom, to be a king or a poet instead, for my ambition conceived nothing finer.

What I am telling you is to show you that what happened to me ought not to have happened, and that I was the victim of the most inexplicable fascination.

The great day having come, I walked to the church with so light a step that it seemed to me that I was borne in the air, or that I had wings on my shoulders; I thought myself an angel, and I was amazed at the somber and preoccupied expression of my companions—for there were several of us. I had spent the night in prayer, and was in a state bordering on ecstasy. The bishop, a venerable old man, seemed to me like God the Father bending from eternity, and I beheld the heavens through the vault of the dome.

You are acquainted with the details of the ceremony: the benediction, the Communion in both kinds, the anointing of the palms of the hands with the oil of the catechumens, and finally the sacred sacrifice offered in conjunction with the bishop. I will not dwell on these things. Oh! how right was Job. "Imprudent is he who has not made a covenant with his eyes!" I happened to raise my head, which until then I had kept bent down, and I saw before me, so close that I might have touched her, although in reality she was a long way off, on the other side of the railing, a young woman of wondrous beauty dressed with regal magnificence. It was as though scales had fallen from my eyes. I felt like a blind man suddenly recovering his sight. The bishop, so radiant but now, was suddenly dimmed, the flame of the tapers on their golden candlesticks turned pale like stars in the morning light, and the whole church was shrouded in deep obscurity. The lovely creature stood out against this shadow like an angelic revelation. She seemed illumined from within, and to give forth light rather than to receive it. I cast down my eyes, determined not to look up again, so as to avoid the influence of external objects, for I was becoming more and more inattentive and I scarcely knew what I was about. Yet a moment later I opened my eyes again, for through my eyelids I saw her dazzling with the prismatic colors in a radiant penumbra, just as when one has gazed upon the sun.

Oh, how beautiful she was! The greatest painters had never approached this fabulous reality, even when, pursuing ideal beauty in the heavens, they brought back to earth the divine portrait of the Madonna. Neither the verse of the poet nor the palette of the painter can give you an idea of her. She was rather tall with the figure and the port of a goddess. Her hair, of a pale gold, was parted on her brow and flowed down her temples like two golden streams; she looked like a crowned queen. Her forehead, of a bluish whiteness, spread out broad and serene over the almost brown eyebrows, a singularity which added to the effect of the sea-green eyes, the brilliancy and fire of which were unbearable. Oh, what eyes! With one flash they settled a man's fate. They were filled with a life, a limpidity, an ardor, a moist glow, which I have never seen in any other human eyes. From them flashed glances like arrows, which I distinctly saw striking my heart. I know not whether the flame that illumined them came from heaven or hell, but undoubtedly it came from one or the other place. That woman was an angel or a demon, perhaps both. She certainly did not come from the womb of Eve, our common mother. Teeth of the loveliest pearl sparkled through her rosy smile, and little dimples marked each inflection of her mouth in the rosy satin of her adorable cheeks. As to her nose, it was of regal delicacy and pride, and betrayed the noblest origin. An agate polish played upon the smooth, lustrous skin of her half-uncovered shoulders, and strings of great fair pearls, almost similar in tone to her neck, fell upon her bosom. From time to time she drew up her head with the undulating movement of an adder or of a peacock, and made the tall embroidered ruff that surrounded her like a silver trellis tremble slightly. She wore a dress of orange-red velvet, and out of the broad, ermine-lined sleeves issued wondrously delicate patrician hands, with long, plump fingers, so ideally transparent that the light passed through them as through the fingers of Dawn.

All these details are still as vivid to me as if I had seen her but yesterday, and although I was a prey to the great agitation, nothing escaped me; the faintest tint, the smallest dark spot on the corner of the chin, the scarcely perceptible down at the corners of the lips, the velvety brow, the trembling shadow of the eyelashes on her cheeks—I noted all with astonishing lucidity.

As I gazed at her, I felt open within me doors hitherto fast-closed; passages obstructed until now were cleared away in every direction and revealed unsuspected prospects; life appeared in a new guise; I had just been born into a new order of ideas. Frightful anguish clutched my heart, and every minute that passed seemed to me a second and an age. Yet the ceremony was proceeding, and I was being carried farther from the world, the entrance to which was fiercely besieged by my nascent desires. I said "yes," however, when I meant to say "no," when everything in me was revolting and protesting against the silence my vow was doing to my will. An occult force dragged the words from my mouth in spite of myself. It is perhaps just what so many young girls do when they go to the altar with a firm resolve to boldly refuse the husband forced upon them. Not one carries out her intention. It is no doubt the same thing which makes so many poor novices take the veil, although they are quite determined to tear it to pieces at the moment of speaking their vows. No one dares to cause such a scandal before everybody, nor to deceive the expectations of so many present. The numerous wills, the numerous glances, seem to weigh down on one like a leaden cloak. And then, every precaution is so carefully taken, everything is so well settled beforehand in a fashion so evidently irrevocable that thought yields to the weight of fact and completely gives way.

The expression of the fair unknown changed as the ceremony progressed. Her glance, tender and caressing at first, became disdainful and dissatisfied as if to reproach me with dullness of perception. I made an effort, mighty enough to have overthrown a mountain, to cry out that I would not be a priest, but I could not manage it; my tongue clove to the roof of my mouth and it was impossible for me to express my will by the smallest negative sign. I was, although wide-awake, in a state similar to that of nightmare, when one seeks to call out a word on which one's life depends, and yet is unable to do so.

She seemed to understand the martyrdom I was suffering,

and as if to encourage me, she cast upon me a look full of divine promise. Her eyes were a poem, her every glance was a canto; she was saying to me:

"If you will come with me, I will make you more happy than God Himself in Paradise. The angels will be jealous of you. Tear away the funeral shroud in which you are about to wrap yourself. I am beauty and youth and love; come to me, and together we shall be Love. What can Jehovah offer you in compensation? Our life shall pass like a dream, and will be but one eternal kiss. Pour out the wine in that cup and you are free. We will go away to unknown isles and you shall sleep on my bosom on a bed of massive gold under a pavilion of silver. For I love you and mean to take you from your God, before whom so many youthful hearts pour out floods of love that never reach Him."

It seemed to me that I heard these words on a rhythm of infinite sweetness, for her glance was almost sonorous, and the phrases her eyes sent me sounded within my heart as if invisible lips had breathed them. I felt myself ready to renounce God, but my hand was mechanically accomplishing the formalities of the ceremony. The beauty cast upon me a second glance so beseeching, so despairing that sharp blades pierced my heart, and I felt more swords enter my breast than did the Mother of Sorrows.

Never did any human face exhibit more poignant anguish. The maiden who sees her betrothed fall suddenly dead by her side, the mother by the empty cradle of her child, Eve seated on the threshold of the gate of Paradise, the miser who finds a stone in place of his treasure, the poet who has accidentally dropped into the fire the only manuscript of his favorite work—not one of them could look more inconsolable, more stricken to the heart. The blood left her lovely face and she turned pale as marble. Her beautiful arms hung limp by her body as if the muscles had been unknotted, and she leaned against a pillar, for her limbs were giving way under her. As for me, livid, my brow covered with a sweat more bloody than that of Calvary, I staggered toward the church door. I was stifling; the vaulting seemed to press down on me and my hand to upbear alone the weight of the cupola.

As I was about to cross the threshold, a woman's hand suddenly touched mine. I had never touched one before. It was cold like the skin of a serpent, yet it burned me like the print of a red-hot iron. It was she. "Oh, unfortunate man! unfortunate man! What have you done? she whispered; then disappeared in the crowd.

The old bishop passed by. He looked severely at me. My appearance was startlingly strange. I turned pale, blushed red, and flames passed before my eyes. One of my comrades took pity on me and led me away; I was incapable of finding alone the road to the seminary. At the corner of a street, while the young priest happened to look in another direction, a quaintly dressed Negro page approached me and without staying his steps handed me a small pocket-book with chased gold corners, signing to me to conceal it. I slipped it into my sleeve and kept it there until I was alone in my cell. I opened it. It contained but two leaves with these words: "Clarimonda, at the Palazzo Concini." I was then so ignorant of life that I did not know of Clarimonda, in spite of her fame, and I was absolutely ignorant where the Palazzo Concini was situated. I made innumerable conjectures of the most extravagant kind, but the truth is that, provided I could see her again, I cared little what she might be, whether a great lady or a courtesan.

This new-born love of mine was hopelessly rooted within me. I did not even attempt to expel it from my heart, for I felt that that was an impossibility. The woman had wholly seized upon me; a single glance of hers had been sufficient to change me; she had breathed her soul into me, and I no longer lived but in her and through her. I indulged in countless extravagant fancies; I kissed on my hand the spot she had touched, and I repeated her name for hours at a time. All I needed to do to see her as plainly as if she had been actually present was to close my eyes; I repeated the words which she had spoken to me, "Unfortunate man! unfortunate man! what have you done?'' I grasped the full horror of my situation, and the dread, somber aspects of the state which I had embraced were plainly revealed to me. To be a priest; that is, to remain chaste, never to love, never to notice sex or age; to turn aside from beauty, to voluntarily blind myself, to crawl in the icy shadows of a cloister or a church, to see none but the dying, to watch by strangers' beds, to wear mourning for myself in the form of the black cassock, a robe that may readily be used to line your coffin.

Meanwhile I felt life rising within me like an internal lake, swelling and overflowing; my blood surged in my veins; my youth, so long suppressed, burst out suddenly like the aloe that blooms but once in a hundred years, and then like a thunder-clap. How could I manage to see Clarimonda again? I could find no pretext to leave the seminary, for I knew no one in town. Indeed, my stay in it was to be very short, for I was merely waiting to be appointed to a parish. I tried to loosen the bars of the window, but it was at a terrific height from the ground, and having no ladder, I had to give up that plan. Besides, I could go out at night only, and how should I ever find my way through the labyrinth of streets? All these difficulties, which would have been slight to other men, were tremendous for me, a poor seminarist, in love since yesterday, without experience, without money, and without clothes.

"Ah, if only I had not been a priest, I might have seen her every day; I might have been her lover, her husband," I said to myself in my blindness. Instead of being wrapped in my gloomy shroud, I should have worn silk and velvet, chains of gold, a sword and a plume, like handsome young cavaliers. My hair, instead of being dishonored by a broad tonsure, would have fallen in ringlets around my neck; I should have worn a handsome waxed mustache; I should have been a valiant man. A single hour spent before an altar, a few words scarcely breathed, had cut me off forever from the living; I had myself sealed the stone of my tomb; I had pushed with my own hand the bolts of my prison door.

I looked out the window. The heavens were wondrously

blue, the trees had assumed their spring-time livery, nature exhibited ironical joy. The square was full of people coming and going. Young dandies and young beauties in couples were going toward the gardens and the arbors; workmen passed by, singing drinking songs; there was an animation, a life, a rush, a gaiety, which contrasted all the more painfully with my mourning and my solitude. A young mother was playing with her child on the threshold of a door. She kissed its little rosy lips still pearly with drops of milk, and indulged, as she teased it, in those many divine puerilities which mothers alone can invent. The father, who stood a little way off, was smiling gently at the charming group, and his crossed arms pressed his joy to his heart. I could not bear the sight. I closed the windows and threw myself on my bed, my heart filled with frightful hatred and jealousy, and I bit my fingers and my coverlet as if I had been a tiger starving for three days.

I know not how long I remained in this condition, but in turning over in a furious spasm, I perceived Father Serapion standing in the middle of the room gazing attentively at me. I was ashamed of myself, and letting fall my head upon my breast, I covered my face with my hands.

"Romualdo, my friend, something extraordinary is taking place in you," said Serapion after a few moments' silence. "Your conduct is absolutely inexplicable. You, so pious, so calm, and so gentle, you have been raging in your cell like a wild beast. Beware, my brother, and do not listen to the suggestions of the devil. The evil spirit, angered at your having devoted yourself to the Lord, prowls around you like a ravening wolf, and is making a last effort to draw you to himself. Instead of allowing yourself to be cast down, dear Romualdo, put on the breastplate of prayer, take up the shield of mortification, and valiantly fight the enemy. You will overcome him. Trial is indispensable to virtue, and gold emerges finer from the crucible. Be not dismayed nor discouraged; the best guarded and the strongest souls have passed through just such moments. Pray, fast, meditate, and the evil one will flee from you.''

The father's discourse brought me back to myself, and I became somewhat calmer. ''I was coming,'' he said, ''to inform you that you are appointed to the parish of C——. The priest who occupied it has just died, and his lordship the Bishop has charged me to install you there. Be ready tomorrow.''

I signed that I would be ready, and the father withdrew.

I opened my breviary and began to read my prayers, but the lines soon became confused; I'd lost the thread of my thoughts, and the book slipped from my hands without my noticing it.

To leave tomorrow without having seen her again! To add one more impossibility to all those that already existed between us! To lose forever the hope of meeting her unless a miracle occurred! Even if I were to write to her, how could I send my letter? Considering the sacred functions which I had assumed, to whom could I confide, in whom could I trust? I felt terrible anxiety. Then what Father Serapion had just said to me of the wiles of the devil recurred to my memory. The strangeness of the adventure, the supernatural beauty of Clarimonda, the phosphorescent gleam of her glance, the burning touch of her hand, the trouble into which she had thrown me, the sudden change which had occurred in me, my piety vanished in an instant—everything went to prove plainly the presence of the devil, and that satin-like hand could only be the glove that covered his claws. These thoughts caused me much terror. I picked up the breviary that had fallen to the ground from my knees, and I again began to pray.

The next day Serapion came for me. Two mules were waiting for us at the door, carrying our small valises. He got on one and I on the other as well as I could. While traversing the streets of the town, I looked at every window and every balcony in the hope of seeing Clarimonda, but it was too early, and the town was not yet awake. My glance tried to pierce through the blinds and curtains of all the palaces in front of which we were passing. No doubt Serapion thought my curiosity was due to the admiration caused in me by the beauty of the architecture, for he slackened his mule's speed to give me time to look. Finally we reached the city gate and began to ascend the hill. When we reached the top, I turned around once again to gaze at the spot where lived Clarimonda. The shadow of a cloud covered the whole town; the blue and red roofs were harmonized in one uniform half-tint, over which showed, like flecks of foam, the morning smoke. By a singular optical effect there stood out bright under a single beam of light a building that rose far above the neighboring houses, wholly lost in the mist. Although it was certainly three miles away, it seemed quite close; the smallest detail could be made out—the turrets, the platforms, the windows, even the swallow-tailed vanes.

"What is that palace yonder lighted by a sunbeam?" I asked Serapion.

He shaded his eyes with his hand, and after having looked, answered: "That is the old palazzo which Prince Concini gave to Clarimonda the courtesan. Fearful things take place there."

At that moment—I have never known whether it was a reality or an illusion—I thought I saw on the terrace a slender white form that gleamed for a second and vanished. It was Clarimonda. Oh! did she know that at that very moment, from the top of her rough road which was taking me away from her, ardent, and restless, I was watching the palace she dwelt in, and which a derisive effect of light seemed to draw near to me as if to invite me to enter it as its master? No doubt she knew it, for her soul was too much in sympathy with mine not to have felt its every emotion, and it was that feeling which had urged her, still wearing her night-dress, to ascend to the terrace in the icy-cold dew of morning.

The shadow reached the palace, and all turned into a motionless ocean of roofs and attics in which nothing was to be distinguished save swelling undulations. Serapion urged on his mule; mine immediately started too, and a turn in the road concealed forever from me the town of S——, for I was never to return there. After three days' traveling through a monotonous country, we saw rising above the trees the weather-cock of the steeple of the church to which I had been appointed; and after having traversed some tortuous streets bordered by huts and small gardens, we arrived before the facade, which was not very magnificent. A porch adorned with a few moldings and two or three sandstone pillars roughly cut, a tiled roof, and buttresses of the same sandstone as the pillars— that was all. On the left, the cemetery overgrown with grass, with a tall iron cross in the center; to the right, in the shadow of the church, the presbytery, a very plain, poor, but clean house. We entered. A few hens were picking up scattered grain. Accustomed, apparently, to the black dress of ecclesiastics, they were not frightened by our presence, and scarcely moved out of the way. A hoarse bark was heard, and an old dog ran up to us; it was my predecessor's dog. Its eye was dim, its coat was gray, and it exhibited every symptom of the greatest age a dog can reach. I patted it gently with my hand, and it immediately walked beside me with an air of inexpressible satisfaction. An old woman, who had been housekeeper to the former priest, also came to meet us, and after having shown us into the lower room, asked me if I intended to keep her. I told her that I should do so, and the dog and the hens also, and whatever furniture her master had left her at his death, which caused her a transport of joy, Father Serapion having at once paid her the price she had set upon it.

Having thus installed me, Father Serapion returned to the seminary. I therefore remained alone and without any other help than my own. The thought of Clarimonda again began to haunt me, and in spite of the efforts I made to drive it away, I was not always successful. One evening as I was walking through the box-edged walks of my little garden, I thought I saw through the shrubbery a female form watching my movements, and two sea-green eyes flashing amid the foliage, but it was merely an illusion. Having passed on the other side of the walk, I found only the imprint of a foot on the sand, so small that it looked like a child's foot. The garden was shut in by very high walls. I visited every nook and corner of it, but found no one. I have never been able to explain the fact, which, for the matter of that, was nothing by comparison with the strange things that were to happen to me.

I had been living in this way for a year, carefully fulfilling all the duties of my profession, praying, fasting, exhorting, and succoring the sick, giving alms even to the extent of depriving myself of the most indispensable necessaries; but I felt within me extreme aridity, and the sources of grace were closed to me. I did not enjoy the happiness which comes of fulfilling a holy mission; my thoughts were elsewhere, and Clarimonda's words often recurred to me. O my brother, ponder this carefully. Because I had a single time looked at a woman, because I had committed a fault apparently so slight, I suffered for several years the most dreadful agitation and my life was troubled forever.

I shall not dwell longer upon these inward defeats and victories which were always followed by greater falls, but I shall pass at once to a decisive circumstance. One night there was a violent ringing at my door. The housekeeper went to open it, and a dark-complexioned man, richly dressed in a foreign fashion, wearing a long dagger, showed under the rays of Barbara's lantern. Her first movement was one of terror, but the man reassured her, and told her that he must see me at once on a matter concerning my ministry. Barbara brought him upstairs. I was just about to go to bed. The man told me that his mistress, a very great lady, was dying and asking for a priest. I replied that I was ready to follow him, took what was needed for extreme unction, and descended quickly. At the door were impatiently pawing and stamping two horses black as night, breathing out long jets of smoke. He held the stirrup for me and helped me to mount one, then sprang on the other, merely resting his hand upon the pommel of the saddle. He pressed in his knees and gave his horse its head, when it went off like an arrow. My own, of which he held the bridle, also started at a gallop and kept up easily with the other. We rushed over the ground, which flashed by us gray and streaked, and the black silhouettes of the trees fled like the rout of an army. We traversed a forest, the darkness of which was so dense and icy that I felt a shudder of superstitious terror. The sparks which our horses' hoofs struck from the stones formed a trail of fire, and if any one had seen us at that time of night, he would have taken us for two specters bestriding nightmares. From time to time will-o'-the-wisps flashed across the road, and the jackdaws croaked sadly in the thickness of the wood, in which shone here and there the phosphorescent eyes of wildcats. Our horses' manes streamed out wildly, sweat poured down their sides, and their breath came short and quick through their nostrils; but when the equerry saw them slackening speed, he excited them by a guttural cry which had nothing of human in it, and the race began again madder than ever. At last our whirlwind stopped. A black mass dotted with brilliant points suddenly rose before us. The steps of our steeds rounded louder upon the iron-bound flooring, and we entered under an archway the somber mouth of which yawned between two huge towers. Great excitement reigned in the château. Servants with torches in their hands were traversing the courts in every direction, and lights were ascending and descending from story to story. I caught a confused glimpse of vast architecture—columns, arcades, steps, stairs, a perfectly regal and fairy-like splendor of construction. A Negro page, the same who had handed me Clarimonda's tablets, and whom I at once recognized, helped me to descend, and a majordomo, dressed in black velvet, with a gold chain around his neck and an ivory cane, advanced toward me. Great tears fell from his eyes and flowed down his cheeks upon his white beard. "Too late, my lord priest. But if you have not been able to save the soul, come and pray for the poor body." He took me by the arm and led me to the room of death. I wept as bitterly as he did, for I had understood that the dead woman was none else than Clarimonda, whom I had loved so deeply and madly. A prie-dieu was placed by the bedside; a bluish flame rising from a

bronze cup cast through the room a faint, vague light, and
here and there brought out of the shadow the corner of a piece
of furniture or of a cornice. On a table, in a chased urn, was a
faded white rose, the petals of which, with a single excep-
tion, had all fallen at the foot of the vase like perfumed tears.
A broken black mask, a fan, and disguises of all kinds lay
about on the armchairs, showing that death had entered this
sumptuous dwelling unexpectedly and without warning. I
knelt, not daring to cast my eyes on the bed, and began to
recite the psalms with great fervor, thanking God for having
put the tomb between the thought of that woman and myself,
so that I might add to my prayers her name, henceforth
sanctified. Little by little, however, my fervor diminished,
and I fell into a reverie. The room had in no wise the aspect
of a chamber of death. Instead of the fetid and cadaverous air
which I was accustomed to breathe during my funeral watches,
a languorous vapor of Oriental incense, a strange, amorous
odor of woman, floated softly in the warm air. The pale light
resembled less the yellow flame of the night-light that flickers
by the side of the dead than the soft illumination of volup-
tuousness. I thought of the strange chance which made me
meet Clarimonda at the very moment when I had lost her
forever, and a sigh of regret escaped from my breast. I
thought I heard some one sigh behind me, and I turned
involuntarily. It was the echo. As I turned, my eyes fell upon
the state-bed which until then I had avoided looking at. The
red damask curtains with great flowered pattern, held back by
golden cords, allowed the dead woman to be seen, lying full
length, her hands crossed on her breast. She was covered
with a linen veil of dazzling whiteness, made still more
brilliant by the dark purple of the hangings; it was so tenuous
that it concealed nothing of the charming form of her body,
and allowed me to note the lovely lines, undulating like the
neck of a swan, which even death itself had been unable to
stiffen. She looked like an alabaster statue, the work of some
clever sculptor, intended to be placed on a queen's tomb, or a
young sleeping girl on whom snow had fallen.

I was losing my self-mastery. The sensuous air intoxicated me, the feverish scent of the half-faded rose went to my brain, and I strode up and down the room, stopping every time before the dais to gaze at the lovely dead woman through her transparent shroud. Strange thoughts came into my mind; I imagined that she was not really dead, that this was but a feint she had employed to draw me to her château and to tell me of her love. Once indeed I thought I saw her foot move under the white veil, disarranging the straight folds of the shroud.

Then I said to myself, "But is it Clarimonda? How do I know? The black page may have passed into some other woman's service. I am mad to grieve and worry as I am doing." But my heart replied, as it beat loud, "It is she—it is none but she." I drew nearer the bed and gazed with increased attention at the object of my uncertainty. Shall I confess it? The perfection of her form, though refined and sanctified by the shadow of death, troubled me more voluptuously than was right, and her repose was so like sleep that any one might have been deceived by it. I forgot that I had come here to perform the funeral offices, and I imagined that I was a young husband entering the room of his bride who hides her face through modesty and will not allow herself to be seen. Sunk in grief, mad with joy, shivering with fear and pleasure, I bent toward her and took up the corner of the shroud; I raised it slowly, holding in my breath for fear of waking her. My arteries palpitated with such force that I felt the blood surging in my temples and my brow was covered with sweat as if I had been lifting a marble slab. It was indeed Clarimonda, such as I had seen her in the church on the day of my ordination. She was as lovely as then, and death seemed to be but a new coquetry of hers. The pallor of her cheeks, the paler rose of her lips, the long closed eyelashes showing their brown fringes against the whiteness, gave her an inexpressibly seductive expression of melancholy chastity and of pensive suffering. Her long hair, undone, in which were still a few little blue flowers, formed a pillow for her head and protected with its curls the nudity of her shoulders. Her lovely hands, purer and more diaphanous than the Host, were crossed in an attitude of pious repose and of silent prayer that softened the too great seduction, even in death, of the exquisite roundness and the ivory polish of her bare arms from which the pearl bracelets had not been removed. I remained long absorbed in mute contemplation. The longer I looked at her, the less I could believe that life had forever forsaken that lovely frame. I know not whether it was an illusion or a reflection of the lamp, but it seemed to me that the blood was beginning to course again under the mat pallor; yet she still remained perfectly motionless. I gently touched her arm; it was cold, yet no colder than her hand on the day it touched me under the porch of the church. I resumed my position, bending my face over hers, and let fall upon her cheeks the warm dew of my tears. Oh, what a bitter despair and powerlessness I felt! Oh, what agony I underwent during that watch! I wished I could take my whole life in order to give it to her, and breathe upon her icy remains the flame that devoured me. Night was passing, and feeling the moment of eternal separation approaching, I was unable to refuse myself the sad and supreme sweetness of putting one kiss upon the dead lips of her who had had all my love. But, oh, wonder! a faint breath mingled with mine, and Clarimonda's lips answered to the pressure of mine. Her eyes opened, became somewhat brighter, she sighed, and moving her arms, placed them around my neck with an air of ineffable delight. "Oh, it is you, Romualdo!" she said in a voice as languishing and soft as the last faint vibrations of a harp. "I waited for you so long that I am dead. But now we are betrothed; I shall be able to see you and to come to you. Farewell, Romualdo, farewell! I love you; that is all I wish to say to you, and I give you back the life which you have recalled to me for one moment with your kiss. Good-bye, but not for long."

Her head fell back, but her arms were still around me as if to hold me. A wild gust of wind burst in the window and rushed into the room; the last leaf of the white rose fluttered for a moment like a wing at the top of the stem, then broke away and flew out of the casement, bearing Clarimonda's soul. The lamp went out and I swooned away on the bosom of the lovely dead.

When I recovered my senses, I was lying on my bed in my little room in my house, and the old dog of the former priest was licking my hand that was hanging out from under the blanket. Barbara, shaky with old age, was busy opening and closing drawers and mixing powders in glasses. On seeing me open my eyes, the old woman uttered a cry of joy, while the dog yelped and wagged his tail; but I was so weak that I could neither move nor speak. I learned later that I had remained for three days in that condition, giving no other sign of life than faint breathing. These three days are cut out of my life. I do not know where my mind was during that time, having absolutely no remembrance of it. Barbara told me that the same copper-complexioned man who had come to fetch me during the night, had brought me back the next morning in a closed litter and had immediately departed. As soon as I could collect my thoughts, I went over in my own mind all the circumstances of that fatal night. At first I thought I had been the dupe of some magical illusion, but real and palpable circumstances soon shattered that supposition. I could not believe I had been dreaming, since Barbara had seen, just as I had the man with two black horses, and described his dress and appearance accurately. Yet no one knew of any château in the neighborhood answering to the description of that in which I had again met Clarimonda.

One morning I saw Father Serapion enter. Barbara had sent him word that I was ill, and he had hastened to come to me. Although his eagerness proved affection for and interest in me, his visit did not give me the pleasure I should have felt. The penetration and the inquisitiveness of his glance troubled me; I felt embarrassed and guilty in his presence. He had been the first to notice my inward trouble, and I was annoyed by his clear-sightedness. While asking news of my health in a hypocritically honeyed tone he fixed upon me his two yellow, lion-like eyes, and plunged his glance into my soul like a sounding-rod. Then he asked me a few questions as to the way in which I was working my parish, if I enjoyed my position, how I spent the time which my duties left me, if I had made any acquaintances among the inhabitants of the place, what was my favorite reading, and many other details of the same kind. I answered as briefly as possible, and he himself, without waiting for me to finish, passed on to something else. The conversation evidently had nothing to do with what he meant to say to me. Then, without any preparation, as if it were a piece of news which he had just recollected and which he was afraid to again forget, he said, in a clear, vibrant voice that sounded in my ear like the trump of the Last Judgment:—

"The great courtesan Clarimonda died recently, after an orgy that lasted eight days and nights. It was infernally splendid. They renewed the abominations of the feasts of Belshazzar and Cleopatra. What an age we are living in! The guests were served by dark slaves speaking an unknown language, who, I think, must have been fiends; the livery of the meanest of them might have served for the gala dress of an emperor. There have always been very strange stories about this Clarimonda; all her lovers have died a wretched and violent death. It is said that she was a ghoul, a female vampire, but I am of opinion that she was Beelzebub in person."

He was silent and watched me more attentively than ever to see the effect his words produced upon me. I had been unable to repress a start on hearing the name of Clarimonda, and the news of her death, besides the grief it caused me, through the strange coincidence with the nocturnal scene of which I had been a witness, filled me with a trouble and terror that showed in my face in spite of the efforts I made to master myself. Serapion looked at me anxiously and severely; then he said: "My son, I am bound to warn you that you have one foot over the abyss. Beware lest you fall in. Satan has a long arm, and tombs are not always faithful. The stone over

Clarimonda should be sealed with a triple seal, for it is not, I am told, the first time that she has died. May God watch over you, Romualdo!''

With these words he walked slowly toward the door, and I did not see him again, for he left for S——almost immediately.

I had at last entirely recovered, and had resumed my usual duties. The remembrance of Clarimonda and the words of the old priest were ever present to my mind; yet no extraordinary event had confirmed Serapion's gloomy predictions. I therefore began to believe that his fears and my terrors were exaggerated; but one night I dreamed a dream. I had scarcely fallen asleep when I heard the curtains of my bed open and the rings sliding over the bars with a rattling sound. I sat up abruptly, learning on my elbow, and saw the shadow of a woman standing before me. I at once recognized Clarimonda. In her hand she bore a small lamp, of the shape of those put into tombs, the light of which gave to her slender fingers a rosy transparency that melted by insensible gradations into the opaque milky whiteness of her bare arm. Her sole vestment was the linen shroud that had covered her upon her state bed, and the folds of which she drew over her bosom as if she were ashamed of being so little clothed, but her small hand could not manage it. It was so white that the color of the drapery was confounded with that of the flesh under the pale light of the lamp. Enveloped in the delicate tissue which revealed all the contours of her body, she resembled an antique marble statue of a bather rather than a woman filled with life. Dead or living, statue or woman, shadow or body, her beauty was still the same; only the green gleam of her eyes was somewhat dulled, and her mouth, so purple of yore, had now only a pale, tender rose-tint almost like that of her cheeks. The little blue flowers which I had noticed in her hair were dried up and had lost most of their leaves. And yet she was charming, so charming that in spite of the strangeness of the adventure and the inexplicable manner in which she had entered the room, I did not experience a single thrill of terror.

She placed the lamp on the table and sat down on the foot

of my bed. Then bending toward me, she said in the silvery, velvety voice which I had heard from no one but her:—

"I have made you wait a long time, dear Romualdo, and you must have thought I had forgotten you. But I have come from a very long distance, from a bourne whence no traveler has yet returned. There is neither moon nor sun in the country whence I have come; neither road nor path; naught but space and shadow; no ground for the foot, no air for the wing; and yet I am here, for love is stronger than death and overcomes it. Ah, what worn faces, what terrible things I have seen on my way! What difficulty my soul, which returned to this world by the power of will, experienced before it could find its own body and reenter it! What efforts I had to make before I could push up the tombstone with which they had covered me! See! the palms of my poor hands are all bruised. Kiss them and cure them, my dear love." And one after the other, she put the cold palms of her hands upon my lips. I did kiss them many a time, and she watched me with a smile of ineffable satisfaction.

I confess it to my shame—I had wholly forgotten the counsels of Father Serapion and my own profession; I had fallen without resisting and at the first blow; I had not even endeavored to drive away the tempter. The freshness of Clarimonda's skin penetrated mine, and I felt voluptuous thrills running through my body. Poor child! In spite of all that I have seen of her, I find it difficult to believe that she was a demon; she certainly did not look like one, and never did Satan better conceal his claws and horns. She had pulled her feet up under her, and was curled up on the edge of my bed in an attitude full of nonchalant coquetry. From time to time she passed her little hand through my hair and rolled it into ringlets as if to try how different ways of dressing it would suit my face. I allowed her to go on with the most guilty complaisance, and while she toyed with me she chatted brightly. The remarkable thing is that I experienced no astonishment at so extraordinary an adventure, and with the facility we enjoy in dreams of admitting as quite simple the most amazing events, it seemed to me that everything that was happening was quite natural.

"I loved you long before I had seen you, dear Romualdo, and I had looked for you everywhere. You were my dream, and when I saw you in church at that fatal moment, I at once said, 'It is he!' I cast on you a glance in which I put all the love which I had had, which I had, and which I was to have for you; a glance that would have damned a cardinal and made a king kneel before my feet in the presence of his whole court. But you remained impassible; you preferred your God to me. Oh, I am jealous of God, whom you loved, and whom you still love more than me! Unfortunate that I am—oh, most unfortunate! Your heart will never be wholly mine, though you brought me back to life with a kiss, though I am Clarimonda, who was dead and who for your sake burst the cerements of the tomb, and has come to devote to you a life which she has resumed only to make you happy!"

With these words she mingled intoxicating caresses which penetrated my senses and my reason to such a degree that I did not hesitate, in order to console her, to utter frightful blasphemies and to tell her that I loved her as much as I did God.

Her eyes brightened and shone like chrysoprase. "True? Quite true? as much as God?" she said, clasping me in her lovely arms. "Since that is so, you will go with me, you will follow me where I will. You shall cast off your ugly black clothes, you shall be the proudest and most envied of men, you shall be my lover. Oh, the lovely, happy life we shall lead! When shall we start?"

"Tomorrow! tomorrow!" I cried in my delirium.

"Tomorrow be it," she replied. "I shall have time to change my dress, for this one is rather scanty and not of much use for traveling. Then I must also warn my people, who think me really dead, and who are mourning as hard as they can. Money, clothes, and carriage—everything shall be ready, and I shall call for you at this same hour. Good-bye, dear heart," and she touched my brow with her lips.

The lamp went out, the windows were closed, and I saw no more. A leaden, dreamless sleep overcame me and held me fast until the next morning. I awoke later than usual, and the remembrance of the strange vision agitated me the livelong day. At last I managed to persuade myself that it was a mere fever of my heated brain. Yet the sensation had been so intense that it was difficult to believe it was not real, and it was not without some apprehension of what might happen that I went to bed, after having prayed God to drive away from me evil thoughts and to protect the chastity of my sleep.

I soon fell fast asleep and my dream continued. The curtains were opened, and I saw Clarimonda, not as the first time, wan in her pale shroud, and the violets of death upon her cheeks, but gay, bright, and dainty, in a splendid traveling-dress of green velvet with gold braid, caught up on the side and showing a satin under-skirt. Her fair hair escaped in great curls from below her broad black felt hat with capriciously twisted white feathers. She held in her hand a small riding-whip ending in a golden whistle. She touched me lightly with it and said: "Well, handsome sleeper, is that the way you get ready? I expected to find you up. Rise quickly, we have no time to lose."

I sprang from my bed.

"Come, put on your clothes and let us go," she said, pointing to a small parcel which she had brought. "The horses are impatiently champing their bits at the door. We ought to be thirty miles away by now."

I dressed hastily, and she herself passed me the clothes, laughing at my awkwardness and telling me what they were when I made a mistake. She arranged my hair for me, and when it was done, she held out a small pocket-mirror of Venice crystal framed with silver filigree and said to me, "What do you think of yourself? Will you take me as your valet?"

I was no longer the same man and did not recognize myself. I was no more like myself than a finished statue is like a block of stone. My former face seemed to me but a coarse sketch of the one reflected in the mirror. I was handsome, and my vanity was sensibly tickled by the metamorphosis. The elegant clothes, the rich embroidered jacket, made me quite a different person, and I admired the power of transformation possessed by a few yards of stuff cut in a certain way. The spirit of my costume entered into me, and in ten minutes I was passably conceited. I walked up and down the room a few times to feel more at my ease in my new garments. Clarimonda looked at me with an air of maternal complaisance and appeared well satisfied with her work.

"Now, that is childishness enough. Let us be off, dear Romualdo; we are going a long way and we shall never get there." As she touched the doors they opened, and we passed by the dog without waking it.

At the door we found Margheritone, the equerry who had already conducted me. He held three horses, black like the first, one for me, one for himself, and one for Clarimonda. The horses must have been Spanish jennets, sired by the gale, for they went as fast as the wind, and the moon, which had risen to light us at our departure, rolled in the heavens like a wheel detached from its car. We saw it on our right spring from tree to tree, breathlessly trying to keep up with us. We soon reached a plain where by a clump of trees waited a carriage drawn by four horses. We got into it and the horses started off at a mad gallop. I had one arm around Clarimonda's waist and one of her hands in mine; she leaned her head on my shoulder, and I felt her half-bare bosom against my arm. I had never enjoyed such lively happiness. I forgot everything at that moment. I no more remembered having been a priest, so great was the fascination which the evil spirit exercised over me. From that night my nature became in some sort double. There were in me two men unknown to each other. Sometimes I fancied myself a priest who dreamed every night he was a nobleman: sometimes I fancied I was a nobleman who dreamed he was a priest. I was unable to distinguish between the vision and the waking, and I knew not where reality began and illusion ended. The conceited libertine rallied the priest; the priest hated the excesses of the young nobleman. Two spirals, twisted one within the other and confounded without ever touching, very aptly represent this bicephalous life of mine. Yet, in spite of the strangeness of this position, I do not think that for one instant I was mad. I always preserved very clearly the perception of my double life. Only there was an absurd fact which I could not explain; it was that the feeling of the same self should exist in two men so utterly different. That was an anomaly which I did not understand, whether I believed myself to be the parish priest of the little village of —— or il Signor Romualdo, the declared lover of Clarimonda.

What is certain is that I was, or at least believed that I was, in Venice. I have never yet been able to make out what was true and what was imaginary in that strange adventure. We dwelt in a great marble palace on the Canaleio, full of frescoes and statues, with two paintings in Titian's best manner in Clarimonda's bedroom. It was a palace worthy of a king. Each of us had his own gondola and gondoliers, his own livery, music-room, and pet. Clarimonda liked to live in great style, and she had something of Cleopatra in her nature. As for me, I lived like a prince's son, and acted as if I belonged to the family of the twelve Apostles or the four Evangelists of the Most Serene Republic; I would not have got out of my way to let the Doge pass, and I do not think that since Satan fell from heaven there was any one so proud and so insolent as I. I used to go to the Ridotto and gamble fearfully. I met the best society in the world, ruined eldest sons, swindlers, parasites, and swashbucklers; yet in spite of this dissipated life, I remained faithful to Clarimonda. I loved her madly. She would have awakened satiety itself and fixed inconstancy. I should have been perfectly happy but for the accursed nightmare which returned every night, and in which I thought myself a parish priest living an ascetic life and doing penance for his excesses of the daytime. Reassured by the habit of being with her, I scarcely ever thought of the strange manner in which I had made her acquaintance. How-

ever, what Father Serapion had told me about her occasionally occurred to my mind and caused me some uneasiness.

For some time past Clarimonda's health had been failing.
Her complexion was becoming paler and paler every day.
The doctors, when called in, failed to understand her disease
and knew not how to treat it. They prescribed insignificant
remedies, and did not return. Meanwhile she became plainly
paler, and colder and colder. She was almost as white and as
dead as on that famous night in the unknown château. I was
bitterly grieved to see her thus slowly pining away. She,
touched by my sorrow, smiled gently and sadly at me with
the smile of one who knows she is dying.

One morning I was seated by her bed breakfasting at a
small table, in order not to leave her a minute. As I pared a
fruit I happened to cut my finger rather deeply. The blood
immediately flowed in a purple stream, and a few drops fell
upon Clarimonda. Her eyes lighted up, her face assumed an
expression of fierce and savage joy which I had never before
beheld. She sprang from her bed with the agility of an
animal, of a monkey or of a cat, and sprang at my wound,
which she began to suck with an air of inexpressible delight.
She sipped the blood slowly and carefully like a gourmand
who enjoys a glass of sherry or Syracuse wine; she winked
her eyes, the green pupils of which had become oblong
instead of round. From time to time she broke off to kiss my
hand, then she again pressed the wound with her lips so as to
draw out a few more red drops. When she saw that the blood
had ceased to flow, she rose up, rosier than a May morn, her
face full, her eyes moist and shining, her hand soft and warm;
in a word, more beautiful than ever and in a perfect state of
health.

"I shall not die! I shall not die!" she said, half mad with
joy, as she hung around my neck. "I shall be able to love you
a long time yet. My life is in yours, and all that I am comes
from you. A few drops of your rich, noble blood, more
precious and more efficacious than all the elixirs in the world,
have restored my life."

The scene preoccupied me a long time and filled me with strange doubts concerning Clarimonda. That very evening, when sleep took me back to the presbytery, I saw Father Serapion, graver and more care-worn than ever. He looked at me attentively, and said to me: "Not satisfied with losing your soul, you want to lose your body also. Unfortunate youth, what a trap you have fallen into!" The tone in which he said these few words struck me greatly, but in spite of its vivacity, the impression was soon dispelled and numerous other thoughts effaced it from my mind. However, one evening I saw in my mirror, the perfidious position of which she had not taken into account, Clarimonda pouring a powder into the cup of spiced wine she was accustomed to prepare for me after the meal. I took the cup, feigned to carry it to my lips, and put it away as if to finish it later at leisure, but I profited by a moment when my beauty had turned her back, to throw the contents under the table, after which I withdrew to my room and went to bed, thoroughly determined not to sleep, and to see what she would do. I had not long to wait. Clarimonda entered in her night-dress, and having thrown it off, stretched herself in the bed by me. When she was quite certain that I was asleep, she bared my arm, drew a golden pin from her hair, and whispered, "One drop, nothing but a little red drop, a ruby at the end of my needle! Since you still love me, I must not die. Oh, my dear love! I shall drink your beautiful, brilliant, purple blood. Sleep, my sold treasure, my god and my child. I shall not hurt you, I shall only take as much of your life as I need not to lose my own. If I did not love you so much, I might make up my mind to have other lovers whose veins I would drain; but since I have known you, I have a horror of every one else. Oh, what a lovely arm! how round and white it is! I shall never dare to prick that pretty blue vein." And as she spoke, she wept, and I felt her tears upon my arm which she held in her hands. At last she made up her mind, pricked me with the needle, and began to suck the blood that flowed. Though she had scarcely imbibed a few drops, she feared to exhaust me. She tied my arm with a narrow band, after having rubbed my wound with an unguent which healed it immediately.

I could no longer doubt; Father Serapion was right. However, in spite of the certainty, I could not help loving Clarimonda, and I would willingly have given her all the blood she needed in order to support her factitious existence. Besides, I was not much afraid, for the woman guarded me against the vampire; what I had heard and seen completely reassured me. At that time I had full-blooded veins which would not be very speedily exhausted, and I did not care whether my life went drop by drop. I would have opened my arm myself and said to her, "Drink, and let my life enter your body with my blood." I avoided alluding in the least to the narcotic which she had poured out for me and the scene of the pin, and we lived in the most perfect harmony.

Yet my priestly scruples tormented me more than ever, and I knew not what new penance to invent to tame and mortify my flesh. Although all these visions were involuntary and I in no wise took part in them, I dared not touch the crucifix with hands so impure and a mind so soiled by such debauch, whether real or imaginary. After falling into these fatiguing hallucinations, I tried to keep from sleeping. I kept my eyes open with my fingers, and remained standing by the wall struggling against slumber with all my strength; but soon it would force itself into my eyes, and seeing that the struggle was useless, I let fall my arms with discouragement and weariness, while the current carried me again to the perfidious shores. Serapion exhorted me most vehemently, and harshly reproached me with weakness and lack of fervor. One day, when he had been more agitated than usual, he said to me:—

"There is but one way of ridding you of this obsession, and although it is extreme, we must make use of it. Great evils require great remedies. I know where Clarimonda is buried. We must dig her up, and you shall see in what a pitiful condition is the object of your love. You will no longer be tempted to lose your soul for a loathsome body devoured

by worms and about to fall into dust. It will assuredly bring
you back to your senses."

For myself, I was so wearied of my double life that I
accepted, wishing to know once for all whether it was the
priest or the nobleman who was the dupe of an illusion. I was
determined to kill, for the benefit of the one or the other, one
of the two men who were in me, or to kill them both, for
such a life as I had been leading was unendurable. Father
Serapion provided a pick, a crowbar, and a lantern, and at
midnight we repaired to the cemetery of ——, the place of
which he knew accurately, as well as the disposition of the
graves. Having cast the light of our lantern upon the inscriptions on several tombs, we at last reached a stone half hidden
by tall grass and covered with moss and parasitical plants,
on which we made out this partial inscription: "Here lies
Clarimonda, who in her lifetime was the most beautiful woman
in the world. . . ."

"This is the spot," said Serapion, and putting down the
lantern, he introduced the crowbar in the joints of the stone
and began to raise it. The stone yielded, and he set to work
with the pick. I watched him, darker and more silent than the
night itself. As for him, bending over this funereal work, he
perspired heavily and his quick breath sounded like the rattle
in a dying man's throat. It was a strange spectacle, and any
one who might have seen us would have taken us rather for
men profaning the tomb and robbing the shrouds than for
priests of God. Serapion's zeal had something harsh and
savage which made him resemble a demon rather than an
apostle or an angel, and his face, with its austere features
sharply brought out by the light of the lantern, was in no wise
reassuring. I felt an icy sweat break out on my limbs, my hair
rose upon my head. Within myself I considered the action of
the severe Serapion an abominable sacrilege, and I wished
that from the somber clouds that passed heavily over our
heads might flash a bolt that would reduce him to powder.
The owls, perched on the cypresses, troubled by the light of
the lantern, struck the glass with their dusty wings and uttered

plaintive cries. The foxes yelped in the distance, and innumerable sinister noises rose in the silence.

At last Serapion's pick struck the coffin, which gave out the dull, sonorous sound which nothingness gives out when it is touched. He pulled off the cover, and I saw Clarimonda, pale as marble, her hands clasped, her white shroud forming but one line from her head to her feet. A little red drop shone like a rose at the corner of her discolored lips. Serapion at the sight of it became furious.

"Ah! there you are, you demon, you shameless courtesan! You who drink blood and gold!" and he cast on the body and the coffin quantities of holy water, tracing with the sprinkler a cross upon the coffin. The holy dew no sooner touched poor Clarimonda than her lovely body fell into dust and became only a hideous mass of ashes and half-calcined bones. "There is your mistress, my lord Romualdo," said the inexorable priest, as he pointed to the remains. "Are you now still tempted to go to the Lido and Fusino with your beauty?"

I bowed my head. Something had been shattered within me. I returned to my presbytery, and lord Romualdo, the lover of Clarimonda, left the poor priest with whom he had so long kept such strange company. Only the next night I saw Clarimonda. She said to me, as the first time under the porch of the church, "Unfortunate man! unfortunate man! What have you done? Why did you listen to that foolish priest? Were you not happy? What have I done to you, that you should go and violate my poor tomb and lay bare the wretchedness of my nothingness? All communion between our souls and bodies is henceforth broken. Farewell; you will regret me."

She vanished in air like a vapor, and I never saw her again. Alas! she spoke the truth. I have regretted her more than once, and I still regret her. I purchased the peace of my soul very dearly. The love of God was not too much to replace her love.

Such, brother, is the story of my youth. Never look upon a woman, and walk always with your eyes cast on the ground, for chaste and calm though you may be, a single minute may make you lose eternity.

ROBERT BLOCH

The Cloak

The sun was dying, and its blood spattered the sky as it crept into its sepulcher behind the hills. The keening wind sent the dry, fallen leaves scurrying toward the west, as though hastening them to the funeral of the sun.

"Nuts!" said Henderson to himself, and stopped thinking.

The sun was setting in a dingy red sky, and a dirty raw wind was kicking up the half-rotten leaves in a filthy gutter. Why should he waste time with cheap imagery?"

"Nuts!" said Henderson, again.

It was probably a mood evoked by the day, he mused. After all, this was the sunset of Halloween. Tonight was the dreaded Allhallows Eve, when spirits walked and skulls cried out from their graves beneath the earth.

Either that, or tonight was just another rotten cold fall day. Henderson sighed. There was a time, he reflected, when the coming of this night meant something. A dark Europe, groaning in superstitious terror, dedicated this Eve to the grinning Unknown. A million doors had once been barred against the evil visitants, a million prayers mumbled, a million candles lit. There was something majestic about the idea, Henderson reflected. Life had been an adventure in those times, and men walked in terror of what the next turn of a midnight road might bring. They had lived in a world of demons and ghouls and elementals who sought their souls—and by Heaven, in those days a man's soul meant something. This new skepticism had taken a profound meaning away from life. Men no longer revered their souls.

"Nuts!" said Henderson again, quite automatically. There was something crude and twentieth-century about the coarse expression which always checked his introspective flights of fancy.

The voice in his brain that said "nuts" took the place of humanity to Henderson—common humanity which would voice the same sentiment if they heard his secret thoughts. So now Henderson uttered the word and endeavored to forget problems and purple patches alike.

He was walking down this street at sunset to buy a costume for the masquerade party tonight, and he had much better concentrate on finding the costumer's before it closed than waste his time daydreaming about Halloween.

His eyes searched the darkening shadows of the dingy buildings lining the narrow thoroughfare. Once again he peered at the address he had scribbled down after finding it in the phone book.

Why the devil didn't they light up the shops when it got dark? He couldn't make out numbers. This was a poor, run-down neighborhood, but after all—

Abruptly, Henderson spied the place across the street and started over. He passed the window and glanced in. The last rays of the sun slanted over the top of the building across the way and fell directly on the window and its display. Henderson drew a sharp intake of breath.

He was staring at a costumer's window—not looking through a fissure into hell. Then why was it all red fire, lighting the grinning visages of fiends?

"Sunset," Henderson muttered aloud. Of course it was, and the faces were merely clever masks such as would be displayed in this sort of place. Still, it gave the imaginative man a start. He opened the door and entered.

The place was dark and still. There was a smell of loneli-
ness in the air—the smell that haunts all places long undisturbed; tombs, and graves in deep woods, and caverns in the
earth, and—

"Nuts."

What the devil was wrong with him, anyway? Henderson
smiled apologetically at the empty darkness. This was the
smell of the customer's shop, and it carried him back to
college days of amateur theatricals. Henderson had known
this smell of moth balls, decayed furs, grease paint and oils.
He had played amateur Hamlet and in his hands he had held a
smirking skull that hid all knowledge in its empty eyes—a
skull, from the costumer's.

Well, here he was again, and the skull gave him the idea.
After all, Halloween night it was. Certainly in this mood of
his he didn't want to go as a rajah, or a Turk, or a pirate—
they all did that. Why not go as a fiend, or a warlock, or a
werewolf? He could see Lindstrom's face when he walked
into the elegant penthouse wearing rags of some sort. The
fellow would have a fit, with society crowds wearing their
expensive Elsa Maxwell take-offs. Henderson didn't greatly
care for Lindstrom's sophisticated friends anyway; a gang of
amateur Noel Cowards and horsy women wearing harnesses
of jewels. Why not carry out the spirit of Halloween and go
as a monster?

Henderson stood there in the dusk, waiting for someone to
turn on the light, come out from the back room and serve
him. After a minute or so he grew impatient and rapped
sharply on the counter.

"Say in there! Service!"

Silence. And a shuffling noise from the rear, then—an
unpleasant noise to hear in the gloom. There was a banging
from downstairs and then the heavy clump of footsteps.
Suddenly Henderson gasped. A black bulk was rising from
the floor!

It was, of course, only the opening of the trapdoor from the basement. A man shuffled behind the counter, carrying a lamp. In that light his eyes blinked drowsily.

The man's yellowish face crinkled into a smile.

"I was sleeping, I'm afraid," said the man, softly. "Can I serve you, sir?"

"I was looking for a Halloween costume."

"Oh yes. And what was it you had in mind?"

The voice was weary, infinitely weary. The eyes continued to blink in the flabby yellow face.

"Nothing usual, I'm afraid. You see, I rather fancied some sort of monster getup for a par— Don't suppose you carry anything in that line?"

"I could show you masks."

"No. I mean, werewolf outfits, something of that sort. More of the authentic."

"So. The *authentic*."

"Yes." Why did this old dunce stress the word?

"I might—yes, I might have just the thing for you, sir." The eyes blinked, but the thin mouth pursed in a smile. "Just the thing for Halloween."

"What's that?"

"Have you ever considered the possibility of being a vampire?"

"Like Dracula?"

"Ah—yes, I suppose—Dracula."

"Not a bad idea. Do you think I'm the type for that, though?"

The man appraised him with that tight smile. "Vampires are of all types, I understand. You would do nicely."

"Hardly a compliment," Henderson chuckled. "But why not? What's the outfit?"

"Outfit? Merely evening clothes, or what you wear. I will furnish you with the authentic cloak."

"Just a cloak—is that all?"

"Just a cloak. But it is worn like a shroud. It is shroud-cloth, you know. Wait, I'll get it for you."

The shuffling feet carried the man into the rear of the shop again. Down the trapdoor entrance he went, and Henderson waited. There was more banging, and presently the old man reappeared carrying the cloak. He was shaking dust from it in the darkness.

"Here it is—the genuine cloak."

"Genuine?"

"Allow me to adjust it for you—it will work wonders, I'm sure."

The cold, heavy cloth hung draped about Henderson's shoulders. The faint odor rose mustily in his nostrils as he stepped back and surveyed himself in the mirror. The light was poor, but Henderson saw that the cloak effected a striking transformation in his appearance. His long face seemed thinner, his eyes were accentuated in the facial pallor heightened by the somber cloak he wore. It was a big, black shroud.

"Genuine," murmured the old man. He must have come up suddenly, for Henderson hadn't noticed him in the glass.

"I'll take it," Henderson said. "How much?"

"You'll find it quite entertaining, I'm sure."

"How much?"

"Oh. Shall we say five dollars?"

"Here."

The old man took the money, blinking, and drew the cloak from Henderson's shoulders. When it slid away he felt suddenly warm again. It must be cold in the basement—the cloth was icy.

The old man wrapped the garment, smiling, and handed it over.

"I'll have it back tomorrow, Henderson promised.

"No need. You purchased it. It is yours."

"But—"

"I am leaving business shortly. Keep it. You will find more use for it than I, surely."

"But—"

"A pleasant evening to you."

Henderson made his way to the door in confusion, then turned to salute the blinking old man in the dimness.

Two eyes were burning at him from across the counter—two eyes that did not blink.

"Good night," said Henderson, and closed the door quickly. He wondered if he were going just a trifle mad.

At eight, Henderson nearly called up Lindstrom to tell him he couldn't make it. The cold chills came the minute he put on the cloak, and when he looked at himself in the mirror his blurred eyes could scarcely make out the reflection.

But after a few drinks he felt better about it. He hadn't eaten, and the liquor warmed his blood. He paced the floor, attitudinizing with the cloak—sweeping it about him and scowling in what he thought was a ferocious manner. He was going to be a vampire all right! He called a cab, went down to the lobby. The driver came in, and Henderson was waiting, black cloak furled.

"I wish you to drive me," he said, in a low voice.

The cabman took one look at him in the cloak and turned pale.

"Whazzat?"

"I ordered you to come," said Henderson gutturally, while he quaked with inner mirth. He leered ferociously and swept the cloak back.

"Yeah, yeah. O.K."

The driver almost ran outside. Henderson stalked after him.

"Where to boss—I mean, sir?"

The frightened face didn't turn as Henderson intoned the address and sat back.

The cab started with a lurch that set Henderson to chuckling deeply, in character. At the sound of the laughter the driver got panicky and raced his engine up to the limit set by the governor. Henderson laughed loudly, and the impressionable driver fairly quivered in his seat. It was quite a ride, but Henderson was entirely unprepared to open the door and find it slammed after him as the cabman drove hastily away without collecting a fare.

"I must look the part," he thought complacently, as he took the elevator up to the penthouse apartment.

There were three or four others in the elevator; Henderson had seen them before at other affairs Lindstrom had invited him to attend, but nobody seemed to recognize him. It rather pleased him to think how his wearing of an unfamiliar cloak and an unfamiliar scowl seemed to change his entire personality and appearance. Here the other guests had donned elaborate disguises—one woman wore the costume of a Watteau shepherdess, another was attired as a Spanish ballerina, a tall man dressed as Pagliacci, and his companion had donned a toreador outfit. Yet Henderson recognized them all; knew that their expensive habiliments were not truly disguises at all, but merely elaborations calculated to enhance their appearance. Most people at costume parties gave vent to suppressed desires. The women showed off their figures, the men either accentuated their masculinity as the toreador did, or clowned it. Such things were pitiful; these conventional fools eagerly doffing their dismal business suits and rushing off to a lodge, or amateur theatrical, or mask ball in order to satisfy their starving imaginations. Why didn't they dress in garish colors on the street? Henderson often pondered the question.

Surely, these society folk in the elevator were fine-looking men and the women in their outfits—so healthy, so red-faced, and full of vitality. They had such robust throats and necks. Henderson looked at the plump arms of the woman next to him. He stared, without realizing it, for a long moment. And then, he saw that the occupants of the car had drawn away from him. They were standing in the corner, as though they feared his cloak and scowl, and his eyes fixed on the woman. Their chatter had ceased abruptly. The woman looked at him, as though she were about to speak, when the elevator doors opened and afforded Henderson a welcome respite.

What the devil was wrong? First the cab driver, then the woman. Had he drunk too much?

Well, no chance to consider that. Here was Marcus
Lindstrom, and he was thrusting a glass into Henderson's
hand.

"What have we here? Ah, a bogeyman!" It needed no
second glance, to perceive that Lindstrom, as usual at such
affairs, was already quite bottle-dizzy. The fat host was
positively swimming in alcohol.

"Have a drink, Henderson, my lad! I'll take mine from the
bottle. That outfit of yours gave me a shock. Where'd you get
the make-up?"

"Make-up? I'm not wearing any make-up."

"Oh. Sure you're not. How . . . silly of me."

Henderson wondered if he were crazy. Had Lindstrom
really drawn back? Were his eyes actually filled with a
certain dismay?

"I'll . . . I'll see you later," babbled Lindstrom, edging
away and quickly turning to the other arrivals. Henderson
watched the back of Lindstrom's neck. It was fat and white.
It bulged over the collar of his costume and there was a vein
in it. A vein in Lindstrom's fat neck. Frightened Lindstrom.

Henderson stood alone in the anteroom. From the parlor
beyond came the sound of music and laughter; party noises.
Henderson hesitated before entering. He drank from the glass
in his hand—Bacardi rum, and powerful. On top of his other
drinks it almost made the man reel. But he drank, wondering.
What was wrong with him and his costume? Why did he
frighten people? Was he unconsciously acting his vampire
role? That crack of Lindstrom's about make-up, now—

Acting on impulse, Henderson stepped over to the long
panel mirror in the hall. He lurched a little, then stood in the
harsh light before it. He faced the glass, stared into the
mirror, and saw nothing.

*He looked at himself in the mirror, and there was no one
there!*

Henderson began to laugh softly, evilly, deep in his throat.
And as he gazed into the empty, unreflecting glass, his
laughter rose in black glee.

"I'm drunk," he whispered. "I must be drunk. Mirror in my apartment made me blurred. Now I'm so far gone I can't see straight. Sure I'm drunk. Been acting ridiculously, scaring people. Now I'm seeing hallucinations—or not seeing them, rather. Visions. Angels."

His voice lowered. "Sure, angels. Standing right in back of me, now. Hello, angel."

"Hello."

Henderson whirled. There she stood, in the dark cloak, her hair a shimmering halo above her white, proud face; her eyes celestial blue, and her lips infernal red.

"Are you real?" asked Henderson, gently. "Or am I a fool to believe in miracles?"

"This miracle's name is Sheila Darrly, and it would like to powder its nose if you please."

"Kindly use this mirror through the courtesy of Stephen Henderson," replied the cloaked man, with a grin. He stepped back a ways, eyes intent.

The girl turned her head and favored him with a slow, impish smile. "Haven't you ever seen powder used before?" she asked.

"Didn't know angels indulged in cosmetics," Henderson replied. "But then there's a lot I don't know about angels. From now on I shall make them a special study of mine. There's so much I want to find out. So you'll probably find me following you around with a notebook all evening."

"Notebooks for a vampire?"

"Oh, but I'm a very intelligent vampire—not one of those backwoods Transylvanian types. You'll find me charming, I'm sure."

"Yes, you look like the sure type," the girl mocked. "But an angel and a vampire—that's a queer combination."

"We can reform one another," Henderson pointed out. "Besides, I have a suspicion that there's a bit of the devil in you. That dark cloak over your angel costume; dark angel, you know. Instead of heaven you might hail from my home town."

Henderson was flippant, but, underneath his banter, cyclonic thoughts whirled. He recalled discussions in the past; cynical observations he had made and believed.

Once, Henderson had declared that there was no such thing as love at first sight, save in books or plays where such a dramatic device served to speed up action. He asserted that people learned about romance from books and plays and accordingly adopted a belief in love at first sight when all one could possibly feel was desire.

And now this Sheila—this blonde angel—had to come along and drive out all thoughts of morbidity, all thoughts of drunkenness and foolish gazings into mirrors, from his mind; had to send him badly plunging into dreams of red lips, ethereal blue eyes and slim white arms.

Something of his feelings had swept into his eyes, and as the girl gazed up at him she felt the truth.

"Well," she breathed. "I hope the inspection pleases."

"A miracle of understatement, that. But there was something I wanted to find out particularly about divinity. Do angels dance?"

"Tactful vampire! The next room?"

Arm in arm they entered the parlor. The merrymakers were in full swing. Liquor had already pitched gaiety at its height, but there was no dancing any longer. Boisterous little grouped couples laughed arm in arm about the room. The usual party gagsters were performing their antics in corners. The superficial atmosphere, which Henderson detested, was fully in evidence.

It was reaction which made Henderson draw himself up to full height and sweep the cloak about his shoulders. Reaction brought the scowl to his pale face, caused him to stalk along in brooding silence. Sheila seemed to regard this as a great joke.

"Pull a vampire act on them," she giggled, clutching his arm. Henderson accordingly scowled at the couples, sneered horrendously at the women. And his progress was marked by the turning of heads, the abrupt cessation of chatter. He walked through the long room like Red Death incarnate. Whispers trailed in his wake.

"Who is that man?"

"We came up with him in the elevator, and he—"

"His eyes—"

"Vampire!"

"Hello, Dracula!" It was Marcus Lindstrom and a sullen-looking brunette in Cleopatra costume who lurched toward Henderson. Host Lindstrom could scarcely stand, and his companion in cups was equally at a loss. Henderson liked the man when sober at the club, but his behavior at parties had always irritated him. Lindstrom was particularly objectionable in his present condition—it made him boorish.

"M' dear, I want you t' meet a very dear friend of mine. Yessir, it being Halloween and all, I invited Count Dracula here, t'gether with his daughter. Asked his grandmother, but she's busy tonight at a Black Sabbath—along with Aunt Jemima. Ha! Count, meet my little playmate."

The woman leered up at Henderson.

"Oooh Dracula, what big eyes you have! Oooh, what big teeth you have! Ooooh—"

"Really, Marcus," Henderson protested. But the host had turned and shouted to the room.

"Folks, meet the real goods—only genuine living vampire in captivity! Dracula Henderson, only existing vampire with false teeth."

In any other circumstances Henderson would have given Lindstrom a quick, efficient punch on the jaw. But Sheila was at his side, it was a public gathering; better to humor the man's clumsy jest. Why not be a vampire?

Smiling quickly at the girl, Henderson drew himself erect, faced the crowd, and frowned. His hands brushed the cloak. Funny, it still felt cold. Looking down he noticed for the first time that it was a little dirty at the edges; muddy or dusty. But the cold silk slid through his fingers as he drew it across his breast with one long hand. The feeling seemed to inspire him. He opened his eyes wide and let them blaze. His mouth opened. A sense of dramatic power filled him. And he looked at Marcus Lindstrom's soft, fat neck with the vein standing in the whiteness. He looked at the neck, saw the crowd watching him, and then the impulse seized him. He turned, eyes on that creasy neck—that wabbling, creasy neck of the fat man.

Hands darted out. Lindstrom squeaked like a frightened rat. He was a plump, sleek white rat, bursting with blood. Vampires liked blood. Blood from the rat, from the neck of the rat, from the vein in the neck of the squeaking rat.

"Warm blood."

The deep voice was Henderson's own.

The hands were Henderson's own.

The hands that went around Lindstrom's neck as he spoke, the hands that felt the warmth, that searched out the vein. Henderson's face was bending for the neck, and, as Lindstrom struggled, his grip tightened. Lindstrom's face was turning purple. Blood was rushing to his head. That was good. Blood!

Henderson's mouth opened. He felt the air on his teeth. He bent down toward that rat neck, and then—

"Stop! That's plenty!"

The voice, the cooling voice of Sheila. Her fingers on his arm. Henderson looked up, startled. He released Lindstrom, who sagged with open mouth.

The crowd was staring, and their mouths were all shaped in the instinctive O of amazement.

Sheila whispered, "Bravo! Served him right—but you frightened him!"

Henderson struggled a moment to collect himself. Then he smiled and turned.

"Ladies and gentlemen," he said, "I have just given a slight demonstration to prove to you what our host said of me was entirely correct. I *am* a vampire. Now that you have been given fair warning, I am sure you will be in no further danger. If there is a doctor in the house, I can, perhaps, arrange for a blood transfusion.''

The O's relaxed and laughter came from startled throats. Hysterical laughter, in part, then genuine. Henderson had carried it off. Marcus Lindstrom alone still stared with eyes that held utter fear. *He* knew.

And then the moment broke, for one of the gagsters ran into the room from the elevator. He had gone downstairs and borrowed the apron and cap of a newsboy. Now he raced through the crowd with a bundle of papers under his arm.

''Extra! Extra! Read all about it. Big Halloween Horror! Extra!''

Laughing guests purchased papers. A woman approached Sheila, and Henderson watched the girl walk away in a daze.

''See you later,'' she called, and her glance sent fire through his veins. Still, he could not forget the terrible feeling that came over him when he had seized Lindstrom. Why?

Automatically, he accepted a paper from the shouting pseudo-newsboy. ''Big Halloween Horror,'' he had shouted. What was that?

Blurred eyes searched the paper.

Then Henderson reeled back. That headline! It was an *Extra* after all. Henderson scanned the columns with mounting dread.

''Fire in costumer's . . . shortly after 8 p.m. firemen were summoned to the shop of . . . flames beyond control . . . completely demolished . . . damage estimated at . . . peculiarly enough, name of proprietor unknown . . . skeleton found in—''

''No!'' gasped Henderson aloud.

He read, reread *that* closely. The skeleton had been found in a box of earth in the cellar beneath the shop. The box was a coffin. There had been two other boxes, empty. The skeleton had been wrapped in a cloak, undamaged by the flames—

And in the hastily penned box at the bottom of the column were eyewitness comments, written up under scareheads of heavy black type. Neighbors had feared the place. Hungarian neighborhood, hints of vampirism, of strangers who entered the shop. One man spoke of a cult believed to have held meetings in the place. Superstition about things sold there— love philters, outlandish charms and weird disguises.

Weird disguises—vampires—cloaks—his eyes!

"This is an authentic cloak."

"I will not be using this much longer. Keep it."

Memories of these words screamed through Henderson's brain. He plunged out of the room and rushed to the panel mirror.

A moment, then he flung one arm before his face to shield his eyes from the image that was not there—the missing reflection. *Vampires have no reflections.*

No wonder he looked strange. No wonder arms and necks invited him. He had wanted Lindstrom. Good God!

The cloak had done that, the dark cloak with the stains. The stains of earth, grave-earth. The wearing of the cloak, the cold cloak, had given him the feelings of a true vampire. It was a garment accursed, a thing that had lain on the body of one undead. The rusty stain along one sleeve was blood.

Blood. It would be nice to see blood. To taste its warmth, its red life, flowing.

No. That was insane. He was drunk, crazy.

"Ah! My pale friend the vampire."

It was Sheila again. And above all horror rose the beating of Henderson's heart. As he looked at her shining eyes, her warm mouth shaped in red invitation, Henderson felt a wave of warmth. He looked at her white throat rising above her dark, shimmering cloak, and another kind of warmth arose. Love, desire, and a—hunger.

She must have seen it in his eyes, but she did not flinch. Instead her own gaze burned in return.

Sheila loved him, too!

With an impulsive gesture, Henderson ripped the cloak from about his throat. The icy weight lifted. He was free. Somehow, he hadn't wanted to take the cloak off, but he had to. It was a cursed thing, and in another minute he might have taken the girl in his arms, taken her for a kiss and remained to—

But he dared not think of that.

"Tired of masquerading?" she asked. With a similar gesture she, too, removed her cloak and stood revealed in the glory of her angel robe. Her blonde, statuesque perfection forced a gasp to Henderson's throat.

"Angel," he whispered.

"Devil," she mocked.

And suddenly they were embracing. Henderson had taken her cloak in his arm with his own. They stood with lips seeking rapture until Lindstrom and a group moved noisily into the anteroom.

At the sight of Henderson the fat host recoiled.

"You—" he whispered. "You are—"

"Just leaving." Henderson smiled. Grasping the girl's arm, he drew her toward the empty elevator. The door shut on Lindstrom's pale, fear-filled face.

"Were we leaving?" Sheila whispered, snuggling against his shoulder.

"We were. But not for earth. We do not go down into my realm, but up—into yours."

"The roof garden?"

"Exactly, my angelic one. I want to talk to you against the background of your own heavens, kiss you amidst the clouds, and—"

Her lips found his as the car rose.

"Angel and devil. What a match!"

"I thought so, too," the girl confessed. "Will our children have halos or horns?"

"Both, I'm sure."

They stepped out onto the deserted rooftop. And once again it was Halloween.

Henderson felt it. Downstairs it was Lindstrom and his society friends, in a drunken costume party. Here it was night, silence, gloom. No light, no music, no drinking, no chatter which made one party identical with another; one night like all the rest. This night was individual here.

The sky was not blue, but black. Clouds hung like the gray beards of hovering giants peering at the round orange globe of the moon. A cold wind blew from the sea, and filled the air with tiny murmurings from afar.

It was also quite cold.

"Give me my cloak," Sheila whispered. Automatically, Henderson extended the garment, and the girl's body swirled under the dark splendor of the cloth. Her eyes burned up at Henderson with a call he could not resist. He kissed her, trembling.

"You're cold," the girl said. "Put on your cloak."

Yes, Henderson, he thought to himself. Put on your cloak while you stare at her throat. Then, the next time you kiss her you will want her throat and she will give it in love and you will take it in—hunger.

"Put it on, darling—I insist," the girl whispered. Her eyes were impatient, burning with an eagerness to match his own.

Henderson trembled.

Put on the cloak of darkness? The cloak of the grave, the cloak of death, the cloak of the vampire? The evil cloak, filled with a cold life of its own that transformed his face, transformed his mind?

"Here."

The girl's slim arms were about him, pushing the cloak onto his shoulders. Her fingers brushed his neck, caressingly, as she linked the cloak about his throat.

Then he felt it—through him—that icy coldness turning to a more dreadful heat. He felt himself expanded, felt the sneer across his face. This was Power!

And the girl before him, her eyes taunting, inviting. He saw her ivory neck, her warm slim neck waiting. It was waiting for him, for his lips.

For his teeth.

No—it couldn't be. He loved her. His love must conquer this madness. Yes, wear the cloak, defy its power, and take her in his arms as a man, not as a fiend. He must. It was the test.

"Sheila, I must tell you this."

Her eyes—so alluring. It would be easy!

"Sheila, please. You read the paper tonight."

"Yes."

"I . . . I got my cloak there. I can't explain it. You saw how I took Lindstrom. I wanted to go through with it. Do you understand me? I meant to . . . to bite him. Wearing this thing makes me feel like one of those creatures. But I love you, Sheila."

"I know." Her eyes gleamed in the moonlight.

"I want to test it. I want to kiss you, wearing this cloak. I want to feel that my love is stronger than this—thing. If I weaken, promise me you'll break away and run, quickly. But don't misunderstand. I must face this feeling and fight it; I want my love for you to be that pure, that secure. Are you afraid?"

"No." Still she stared at him, just as he stared at her throat. If she knew what was in his mind!

"You don't think I'm crazy? I went to this costumer's—he was a horrible little old man—and he gave me the cloak. Actually told me it was a real vampire's. I thought he was joking, but tonight I didn't see myself in the mirror, and I wanted Lindstrom's neck, and I want you. But I must test it."

The girl's face mocked. Henderson summoned his strength. He bent forward, his impulses battling. For a moment he stood there under the ghastly orange moon, and his face was twisted in struggle.

And the girl lured.

Her odd, incredibly red lips parted in a silvery, chuckly laugh as her white arms rose from the black cloak she wore to circle his neck gently. "I know—I knew when I looked in the mirror. I knew you had a cloak like mine—got yours where I got mine—"

Queerly, her lips seemed to elude his as he stood frozen for an instant of shock. Then he felt the icy hardness of her sharp little teeth on his throat, a strangely soothing sting, and an engulfing blackness rising over him.

F. MARION CRAWFORD

For the Blood
is the Life

We had dined at sunset on the broad roof of the old tower, because it was cooler there during the great heat of summer. Besides, the little kitchen was built at one corner of the great square platform, which made it more convenient than if the dishes had to be carried down the steep stone steps, broken in places and everywhere worn with age. The tower was one of those built all down the west coast of Calabria by the Emperor Charles V early in the sixteenth century, to keep off the Barbary pirates, when the unbelievers were allied with Francis I against the Emperor and the Church. They have gone to ruin, a few still stand intact, and mine is one of the largest. How it came into my possession ten years ago, and why I spend a part of each year in it, are matters which do not concern this tale. The tower stands in one of the loneliest spots in Southern Italy, at the extremity of a curving rocky promontory, which forms a small but safe natural harbor at the southern extremity of the Gulf of Policastro, and just north of Cape Scalea, the birthplace of Judas Iscariot, according to the old local legend. The tower stands alone on this hooked spur of the rock, and there is not a house to be seen within three miles of it. When I go there I take a couple of sailors, one of whom is a fair cook, and when I am away it is in charge of a gnome-like little being who was once a miner and who attached himself to me long ago.

My friend, who sometimes visits me in my summer solitude, is an artist by profession, a Scandinavian by birth, and a cosmopolitan by force of circumstances. We had dined at sunset; the sunset glow had reddened and faded again, and the evening purple steeped the vast chain of the mountains that embrace the deep gulf to eastward and rear themselves higher and higher toward the south. It was hot, and we sat at the landward corner of the platform, waiting for the night breeze to come down from the lower hills. The color sank out of the air, there was a little interval of deep-gray twilight, and a lamp sent a yellow streak from the open door of the kitchen, where the men were getting their supper.

Then the moon rose suddenly above the crest of the promontory, flooding the platform and lighting up every little spur of rock and knoll of grass below us, down to the edge of the motionless water. My friend lighted his pipe and sat looking at a spot on the hillside. I knew that he was looking at it, and for a long time past I had wondered whether he would ever see anything there that would fix his attention. I knew that spot well. It was clear that he was interested at last, though it was a long time before he spoke. Like most painters, he trusts to his own eyesight, as a lion trusts his strength and a stag his speed, and he is always disturbed when he cannot reconcile what he sees with what he believes that he ought to see.

"It's strange," he said. "Do you see that little mound just on this side of the boulder?"

"Yes," I said, and I guessed what was coming.

"It looks like a grave," observed Holger.

"Very true. It does look like a grave."

"Yes," continued my friend, his eyes still fixed on the spot. "But the strange thing is that I see the body lying on the top of it. Of course," continued Holger, turning his head on one side as artists do, "it must be an effect of light. In the first place, it is not a grave at all. Secondly, if it were, the body would be inside and not outside. Therefore, it's an effect of the moonlight. Don't you see it?''

"Perfectly; I always see it on moonlight nights."

"It doesn't seem to interest you much," said Holger.

"On the contrary, it does interest me, though I am used to it. You're not so far wrong, either. The mound is really a grave."

"Nonsense!" cried Holger, incredulously. "I suppose you'll tell me what I see lying on it is really a corpse!"

"No," I answered, "it's not. I know, because I have taken the trouble to go down and see."

"Then what is it?" asked Holger.

"It's nothing."

"You mean that it's an effect of light, I suppose?"

"Perhaps it is. But the inexplicable part of the matter is that it makes no difference whether the moon is rising or setting, or waxing or waning. If there's any moonlight at all, from east or west or overhead, so long as it shines on the grave you can see the outline of the body on top."

Holger stirred up his pipe with the point of his knife, and then used his finger for a stopper. When the tobacco burned well he rose from his chair.

"If you don't mind," he said, "I'll go down and take a look at it."

He left me, crossed the roof, and disappeared down the dark steps. I did not move, but sat looking down until he came out of the tower below. I heard him humming an old Danish song as he crossed the open space in the bright moonlight, going straight to the mysterious mound. When he was ten paces from it, Holger stopped short, made two steps forward, and then three or four backward, and then stopped again. I knew what that meant. He had reached the spot where the Thing ceased to be visible—where, as he would have said, the effect of light changed.

Then he went on till he reached the mound and stood upon it. I could see the Thing still, but it was no longer lying down; it was on its knees now, winding its white arms round

Holger's body and looking up into his face. A cool breeze stirred my hair at that moment, as the night wind began to come down from the hills, but it felt like a breath from another world.

The Thing seemed to be trying to climb to its feet, helping itself up by Holger's body while he stood upright, quite unconscious of it and apparently looking toward the tower, which is very picturesque when the moonlight falls upon it on that side.

"Come along!" I shouted. "Don't stay there all night!"

It seemed to me that he moved reluctantly as he stepped from the mound, or else with difficulty. That was it. The Thing's arms were still round his waist, but its feet could not leave the grave. As he came slowly forward it was drawn and lengthened like a wreath of mist, thin and white, till I saw distinctly that Holger shook himself, as a man does who feels a chill. At the same instant a little wail of pain came to me on the breeze—it might have been the cry of the small owl that lives among the rocks—and the misty presence floated swiftly back from Holger's advancing figure and lay once more at its length upon the mound.

Again I felt the cool breeze in my hair, and this time an icy thrill of dread ran down my spine. I remembered very well that I had once gone down there alone in the moonlight; that presently, being near, I had seen nothing; that, like Holger, I had gone and had stood upon the mound; and I remembered how, when I came back, sure that there was nothing there, I had felt the sudden conviction that there was something after all if I would only look behind me. I remembered the strong temptation to look back, a temptation I had resisted as unworthy of a man of sense, until, to get rid of it, I had shaken myself just as Holger did.

And now I knew that those white, misty arms had been round me too; I knew it in a flash, and I shuddered as I remembered that I had heard the night owl then too. But it had not been the night owl. It was the cry of the Thing.

I refilled my pipe and poured out a cup of strong southern

wine; in less than a minute Holger was seated beside me again.

"Of course there's nothing there," he said, "but it's creepy, all the same. Do you know, when I was coming back I was so sure that there was something behind me that I wanted to turn round and look? It was an effort not to."

He laughed a little, knocked the ashes out of his pipe, and poured himself out some wine. For a while neither of us spoke, and the moon rose higher, and we both looked at the Thing that lay on the mound.

"You might make a story about that," said Holger after a long time.

"There is one," I answered. "If you're not sleepy, I'll tell it to you."

"Go ahead," said Holger, who likes stories.

Old Alario was dying up there in the village behind the hill. You remember him, I have no doubt. They say that he made his money by selling sham jewelry in South Africa, and escaped with his gains when he was found out. Like all those fellows, if they bring anything back with them, he at once set to work to enlarge his house, and as there are no masons here, he sent all the way to Paola for two workmen. They were a rough-looking pair of scoundrels—a Neapolitan who had lost one eye and a Sicilian with an old scar half an inch deep across his left cheek. I often saw them, for on Sundays they used to come down here and fish off the rocks. When Alario caught the fever that killed him the masons were still at work. As he had agreed that part of their pay should be their board and lodging, he made them sleep in the house. His wife was dead, and he had an only son called Angelo, who was a much better sort than himself. Angelo was to marry the daughter of the richest man in the village, and, strange to say, though their marriage was arranged by their parents, the young people were said to be in love with each other.

For that matter, the whole village was in love with Angelo,

and among the rest a wild, good-looking creature called
Cristina, who was more like a gipsy than any girl I ever saw
about here. She had very red lips and very black eyes, she
was built like a greyhound, and had the tongue of the devil.
But Angelo did not care a straw for her. He was rather a
simple-minded fellow, quite different from his old scoundrel
of a father, and under what I should call normal circumstances I really believe that he would never have looked at
any girl except the nice plump creature, with a fat dowry,
whom his father meant him to marry. But things turned up
which were neither normal nor natural.

On the other hand, a very handsome young shepherd from
the hills above Maratea was in love with Cristina, who seems
to have been quite indifferent to him. Cristina had no regular
means of subsistence, but she was a good girl and willing to
do any work or go on errands to any distance for the sake of a
loaf of bread or a mess of beans, and permission to sleep
under cover. She was especially glad when she could get
something to do about the house of Angelo's father. There is
no doctor in the village, and when the neighbors saw that old
Alario was dying they sent Cristina to Scalea to fetch one.
That was late in the afternoon, and if they had waited so
long, it was because the dying miser refused to allow any
such extravagance while he was able to speak. But while
Cristina was gone matters grew rapidly worse, the priest was
brought to the bedside, and when he had done what he could
he gave it as his opinion to the bystanders that the old man
was dead, and left the house.

You know these people. They have a physical horror of
death. Until the priest spoke, the room had been full of
people. The words were hardly out of his mouth before it was
empty. It was night now. They hurried down the dark steps
and out into the street.

Angelo, as I have said, was away, Cristina had not come
back—the simple woman-servant who had nursed the sick
man fled with the rest, and the body was left alone in the
flickering light of the earthen oil lamp.

Five minutes later two men looked in cautiously and crept forward toward the bed. They were the one-eyed Neapolitan mason and his Sicilian companion. They knew what they wanted. In a moment they had dragged from under the bed a small but heavy iron-bound box, and long before anyone thought of coming back to the dead man they had left the house and the village under cover of the darkness. It was easy enough, for Alario's house is the last toward the gorge which leads down here, and the thieves merely went out by the back door, got over the stone wall, and had nothing to risk after that except the possibility of meeting some belated country-man, which was very small indeed, since few of the people used that path. They had a mattock and shovel, and they made their way here without accident.

I am telling you this story as it must have happened, for, of course, there were no witnesses to this part of it. The men brought the box down by the gorge, intending to bury it until they should be able to come back and take it away in a boat. They must have been clever enough to guess that some of the money would be in paper notes, for they would otherwise have buried it on the beach in the wet sand, where it would have been much safer. But the paper would have rotted if they had been obliged to leave it there long, so they dug their hole down there, close to that boulder. Yes, just where the mound is now.

Cristina did not find the doctor in Scalea, for he had been sent for from a place up in the valley, halfway to San Domenico. If she had found him, he would have come on his mule by the upper road, which is smoother but much longer. But Cristina took the short cut by the rocks, which passes about fifty feet above the mound, and goes round that corner. The men were digging when she passed, and she heard them at work. It would not have been like her to go by without finding out what the noise was, for she was never afraid of anything in her life, and, besides, the fishermen sometimes come ashore here at night to get a stone for an anchor or to gather sticks to make a little fire. The night was dark, and

Cristina probably came close to the two men before she could see what they were doing. She knew them, of course, and they knew her, and understood instantly that they were in her power. There was only one thing to be done for their safety, and they did it. They knocked her on the head, they dug the hole deep, and they buried her quickly with the iron-bound chest. They must have understood that their only chance of escaping suspicion lay in getting back to the village before their absence was noticed, for they returned immediately, and were found half an hour later gossiping quietly with the man who was making Alario's coffin. He was a crony of theirs, and had been working at the repairs in the old man's house. So far as I have been able to make out, the only persons who were supposed to know where Alario kept his treasure were Angelo and the one woman-servant I have mentioned. Angelo was away; it was the woman who discovered the theft.

It is easy enough to understand why no one else knew where the money was. The old man kept his door locked and the key in his pocket when he was out, and did not let the woman enter to clean the place unless he was there himself. The whole village knew that he had money somewhere, however, and the masons had probably discovered the where-abouts of the chest by climbing in at the window in his absence. If the old man had not been delirious until he lost consciousness, he would have been in frightful agony of mind for his riches. The faithful woman-servant forgot their exis-tence only for a few moments when she fled with the rest, overcome by the horror of death. Twenty minutes had not passed before she returned with the two hideous old hags who are always called in to prepare the dead for burial. Even then she had not at first the courage to go near the bed with them, but she made a pretense of dropping something, went down on her knees as if to find it, and looked under the bedstead. The walls of the room were newly whitewashed down to the floor, and she saw at a glance that the chest was gone. It had been there in the afternoon, it had therefore been stolen in the short interval since she had left the room.

There are no carabineers stationed in the village; there is not so much as a municipal watchman, for there is no municipality. There never was such a place, I believe. Scalea is supposed to look after it in some mysterious way, and it takes a couple of hours to get anybody from there. As the old woman had lived in the village all her life, it did not even occur to her to apply to any civil authority for help. She simply set up a howl and ran through the village in the dark, screaming out that her dead master's house had been robbed. Many of the people looked out, but at first no one seemed inclined to help her. Most of them, judging her by themselves, whispered to each other that she had probably stolen the money herself. The first man to move was the father of the girl whom Angelo was to marry; having collected his household, all of whom felt a personal interest in the wealth which was to have come into the family, he declared it to be his opinion that the chest had been stolen by the two journeyman masons who lodged in the house. He headed a search for them, which naturally began in Alario's house and ended in the carpenter's workshop, where the thieves were found discussing a measure of wine with the carpenter over the half-finished coffin, by the light of one earthen lamp filled with oil and tallow. The search party at once accused the delinquents of the crime, and threatened to lock them up in the cellar till the carabineers could be fetched from Scalea. The two men looked at each other for one moment, and then without the slightest hesitation they put out the single light, seized the unfinished coffin between them, and using it as a sort of battering ram, dashed upon their assailants in the dark. In a few moments they were beyond pursuit.

That is the end of the first part of the story. The treasure had disappeared, and as no trace of it could be found the people naturally supposed that the thieves had succeeded in carrying it off. The old man was buried, and when Angelo came back at last he had to borrow money to pay for the miserable funeral, and had some difficulty in doing so. He hardly needed to be told that in losing his inheritance he had lost his bride. In this part of the world marriages are made on strictly business principles, and if the promised cash is not forthcoming on the appointed day the bride or the bridegroom whose parents have failed to produce it may as well take themselves off, for there will be no wedding. Poor Angelo knew that well enough. His father had been possessed of hardly any land, and now that the hard cash which he had brought from South Africa was gone, there was nothing left but debts for the building materials that were to have been used for enlarging and improving the old house. Angelo was beggared, and the nice plump little creature who was to have been his turned up her nose at him in the most approved fashion. As for Cristina, it was several days before she was missed, for no one remembered that she had been sent to Scalea for the doctor, who had never come. She often disappeared in the same way for days together, when she could find a little work here and there at the distant farms among the hills. But when she did not come back at all, people began to wonder, and at last made up their minds that she had connived with the masons and had escaped with them.

I paused and emptied my glass.

"That sort of thing could not happen anywhere else," observed Holger, filling his everlasting pipe again. "It is wonderful what a natural charm there is about murder and sudden death in a romantic country like this. Deeds that would be simply brutal and disgusting anywhere else become dramatic and mysterious because this is Italy and we are living in a genuine tower of Charles V built against genuine Barbary pirates."

"There's something in that," I admitted. Holger is the most romantic man in the world inside of himself, but he always thinks it necessary to explain why he feels anything.

"I suppose they found the poor girl's body with the box," he said presently.

"As it seems to interest you," I answered, "I'll tell you the rest of the story."

The moon had risen high by this time; the outline of the Thing on the mound was clearer to our eyes than before.

The village very soon settled down to its small, dull life. No one missed old Alario, who had been away so much on his voyages to South Africa, that he had never been a familiar figure in his native place. Angelo lived in the half-finished house, and because he had no money to pay the old woman-servant she would not stay with him, but once in a long time she would come and wash a shirt for him for old acquaintance's sake. Besides the house, he had inherited a small patch of ground at some distance from the village; he tried to cultivate it, but he had no heart in the work, for he knew he could never pay the taxes on it and on the house, which would certainly be confiscated by the Government, or seized for the debt of the building material, which the man who had supplied it refused to take back.

Angelo was very unhappy. So long as his father had been alive and rich, every girl in the village had been in love with him; but that was all changed now. It had been pleasant to be admired and courted, and invited to drink wine by fathers who had girls to marry. It was hard to be stared at coldly, and sometimes laughed at because he had been robbed of his inheritance. He cooked his miserable meals for himself, and from being sad became melancholy and morose.

At twilight, when the day's work was done, instead of hanging about in the open space before the church with young fellows of his own age, he took to wandering in lonely places on the outskirts of the village till it was quite dark. Then he slunk home and went to bed to save the expense of a light. But in those lonely twilight hours he began to have strange waking dreams. He was not always alone, for often when he sat on the stump of a tree, where the narrow path turns down the gorge, he was sure that a woman came up noiselessly over the rough stones, as if her feet were bare; and she stood under a clump of chestnut trees only half a dozen yards down the path, and beckoned to him without speaking. Though she was in the shadow he knew that her lips were red, and that when they parted a little and smiled at him she showed two small sharp teeth. He knew this at first rather than saw it, and he knew that it was Cristina, and that she was dead. Yet he was not afraid; he only wondered whether it was a dream, for he thought that if he had been awake he should have been frightened.

Besides, the dead woman had red lips, and that could only happen in a dream. Whenever he went near the gorge after sunset she was already there waiting for him, or else she very soon appeared, and he began to be sure that she came a little nearer to him every day. At first he had only been sure of her blood-red mouth, but now each feature grew distinct, and the pale face looked at him with deep and hungry eyes.

It was the eyes that drew him. Little by little he came to know that some day the dream would not end when he turned away to go home, but would lead him down the gorge out of which the vision rose. She was nearer now when she beckoned to him. Her cheeks were not livid like those of the dead, but pale with starvation, with the furious and unappeased physical hunger of her eyes that devoured him. They feasted on his soul and cast a spell over him, and at last they were close to his own and held him. He could not tell whether her breath was as hot as fire or as cold as ice; he could not tell whether her red lips burned his or froze them, or whether her five fingers on his wrist seared scorching scars or bit his flesh like frost; he could not tell whether he was awake or asleep, whether she was alive or dead, but he knew that she loved him, she alone of all creatures, earthly or unearthly, and her spell had power over him.

When the moon rose high that night the shadow of that Thing was not alone down there upon the mound.

Angelo awoke in the cool dawn, drenched with drew and chilled through flesh, and blood, and bone. He opened his eyes to the faint gray light, and saw the stars still shining overhead. He was very weak, and his heart was beating so slowly that he was almost like a man fainting. Slowly he turned his head on the mound, as on a pillow, but the other face was not there. Fear seized him suddenly, a fear unspeakable and unknown; he sprang to his feet and fled up the gorge, and he never looked behind him until he reached the door of the house on the outskirts of the village. Drearily he went to his work that day, and wearily the hours dragged themselves after the sun, till at last it touched the sea and sank, and the great sharp hills above Maratea turned purple against the dove-colored eastern sky.

Angelo shouldered his heavy hoe and left the field. He felt less tired now than in the morning when he had begun to work, but he promised himself that he would go home without lingering by the gorge, and eat the best supper he could get himself, and sleep all night in his bed like a Christian man. Not again would he be tempted down the narrow way by a shadow with red lips and icy breath; not again would he dream that dream of terror and delight. He was near the village now; it was half an hour since the sun had set, and the cracked church bell sent little discordant echoes across the rocks and ravines to tell all good people that the day was done. Angelo stood still a moment where the path forked, where it led toward the village on the left, and down to the gorge on the right, where a clump of chestnut trees overhung the narrow way. He stood still a minute, lifting his battered hat from his head and gazing at the fast-fading sea westward, and his lips moved as he silently repeated the familiar evening prayer. His lips moved, but the words that followed them in his brain lost their meaning and turned into others, and ended in a name that he spoke aloud—Cristina! With the name, the tension of his will relaxed suddenly, reality went out and the dream took him again, and bore him on swiftly and surely like a man walking in his sleep, down, down, by the steep path in the gathering darkness. And as she glided beside him, Cristina whispered strange, sweet things in his ear, which somehow, if he had been awake, he knew that he could not quite have understood; but now they were the most wonderful words he had ever heard in his life. And she kissed him also, but not upon his mouth. He felt her sharp kisses upon his white throat, and he knew that her lips were red. So the wild dream sped on through twilight and darkness and moonrise, and all the glory of the summer's night. But in the chilly dawn he lay as one half dead upon the mound down there, recalling and not recalling, drained of his blood, yet strangely longing to give those red lips more. Then came the fear, the awful nameless panic, the mortal horror that guards the confines of the world we see not, neither know of as we know of other things, but which we feel when its icy chill freezes our bones and stirs our hair with the touch of a ghostly hand. Once more Angelo sprang from the mound and fled up the gorge in the breaking day, but his step was less sure this time, and he panted for breath as he ran; and when he came to the bright spring of water that rises halfway up the hillside, he dropped upon his knees and hands and plunged his whole face in and drank as he never drunk before—for it was the thirst of the wounded man who has lain bleeding all night long upon the battle-field.

She had him fast now, and he could not escape her, but would come to her every evening at dusk until she had drained him of his last drop of blood. It was in vain that when the day was done he tried to take another turning and to go home by a path that did not lead near the gorge. It was in vain that he made promises to himself each morning at dawn when he climbed the lonely way up from the shore to the village. It was all in vain, for when the sun sank burning into the sea, and the coolness of the evening stole out as from a hiding-place to delight the weary world, his feet turned toward the old way, and she was waiting for him in the shadow under the chestnut trees; and then all happened as before, and she fell to kissing his white throat even as she flitted lightly down the way, winding one arm about him. And as his blood failed, she grew more hungry and more thirsty every day, and every day when he awoke in the early dawn it was harder to rouse himself to the effort of climbing the steep path to the village; and when he went to his work his feet dragged painfully, and there was hardly strength in his arms to wield the heavy hoe. He scarcely spoke to any one now, but the people said he was "consuming himself" for love of the girl he was to have married when he lost his inheritance; and they laughed heartily at the thought, for this is not a very romantic country. At this time, Antonio, the man who stays here to look after the tower, returned from a visit to his people, who live near Salerno. He had been away all the time since before Alario's death and knew nothing of what had happened. He has told me that he came back late in the afternoon and shut himself up in the tower to eat and sleep, for he was very tired. It was past midnight when he awoke, and when he looked out the waning moon was rising over the shoulder of the hill. He looked out toward the mound, and he saw something, and he did not sleep again that night. When he went out again in the morning it was broad daylight, and there was nothing to be seen on the mound but loose stones and driven sand. Yet he did not go very near it; he went straight up the path to the village and directly to the house of the old priest.

"I have seen an evil thing this night," he said; "I have seen how the dead drink the blood of the living. And the blood is the life."

"Tell me what you have seen," said the priest in reply.

Antonio told him everything he had seen.

"You must bring your book and your holy water tonight," he added. "I will be here before sunset to go down with you, and if it pleases your reverence to sup with me while we wait, I will make ready."

"I will come," the priest answered, "for I have read in old books of these strange beings which are neither quick nor dead, and which lie ever fresh in their graves, stealing out in the dusk to taste life and blood."

Antonio cannot read, but he was glad to see that the priest understood the business; for, of course, the books must have instructed him as to the best means of quieting the half-living Thing for ever.

So Antonio went away to his work, which consists largely in sitting on the shady side of the tower, when he is not perched upon a rock with a fishing-line catching nothing. But on that day he went twice to look at the mound in the bright sunlight, and he searched round and round it for some hole through which the being might get in and out; but he found none. When the sun began to sink and the air was cooler in the shadows, he went up to fetch the old priest, carrying a little wicker basket with him; and in this they placed a bottle of holy water, and the basin, and sprinkler, and the stole which the priest would need; and they came down and waited in the door of the tower till it should be dark. But while the light still lingered very gray and faint, they saw something moving, just there, two figures, a man's that walked, and a woman's that flitted beside him, and while her head lay on his shoulder, she kissed his throat. The priest has told me that, too, and that his teeth chattered and he grasped Antonio's arm. The vision passed and disappeared into the shadow. Then Antonio got the leathern flask of strong liquor, which he kept for great occasions, and poured such a draught as made the old man feel almost young again; and he got the lantern, and his pick and shovel, and gave the priest his stole to put on and the holy water to carry, and they went out together toward the spot where the work was to be done. Antonio says that in spite of the rum his own knees shook together, and the priest stumbled over his Latin. For when they were yet a few yards from the mound the flickering light of the lantern fell upon Angelo's white face, unconscious as if in sleep, and on his upturned throat, over which a very thin red line of blood trickled down into his collar; and the flickering light of the lantern played upon another face that looked up from the feast—upon two deep, dead eyes that saw in spite of death—upon parted lips redder than life itself— upon two gleaming teeth on which glistened a rosy drop. Then the priest, good old man, shut his eyes tight and show- ered holy water before him, and his cracked voice rose almost to a scream; and then Antonio, who is no coward after all, raised his pick in one hand and the lantern in the other, as he sprang forward, not knowing what the end should be; and then he swears that he heard a woman's cry, and the Thing was gone, and Angelo lay alone on the mound unconscious, with the red line on his throat and the beads of deathly sweat on his cold forehead. They lifted him, half-dead as he was, and laid him on the ground close by; then Antonio went to work, and the priest helped him, though he was old and could not do much; and they dug deep, and at last Antonio, standing in the grave, stooped down with his lantern to see what he might see.

His hair used to be dark brown, with grizzled streaks about the temples; in less than a month from that day he was as gray as a badger. He was a miner when he was young, and most of these fellows have seen ugly sights now and then, when accidents have happened, but he had never seen what he saw that night—that Thing which is neither alive nor dead, that Thing that will abide neither above ground nor in the grave. Antonio had brought something with him which the priest had not noticed. He had made it that afternoon—a sharp stake shaped from a piece of tough old driftwood. He had it with him now, and he had his heavy pick, and he had taken the lantern down into the grave. I don't think any power on earth could make him speak of what happened then, and the old priest was too frightened to look in. He says he heard Antonio breathing like a wild beast, and moving as if he were fighting with something almost as strong as himself; and he heard an evil sound also, with blows, as of something violently driven through flesh and bone; and then the most awful sound of all—a woman's shriek, the unearthly scream of a woman neither dead nor alive, but buried deep for many days. And he, the poor old priest, could only rock himself as he knelt there in the sand, crying aloud his prayers and exorcisms to drown these dreadful sounds. Then suddenly a small iron-bound chest was thrown up and rolled over against the old man's knee, and in a moment more Antonio was beside him, his face as white as tallow in the flickering light of the lantern, shoveling the sand and pebbles into the grave with furious haste, and looking over the edge till the pit was half full; and the priest said that there was much fresh blood on Antonio's hands and on his clothes.

I had come to the end of my story. Holger finished his wine and leaned back in his chair.

"So Angelo got his own again," he said. "Did he marry the prim and plump young person to whom he had been betrothed?"

"No; he had been badly frightened. He went to South America, and has not been heard of since."

"And that poor thing's body is there still, I suppose," said Holger. "Is it quite dead yet, I wonder?"

I wonder, too. But whether it be dead or alive, I should hardly care to see it, even in broad daylight. Antonio is as gray as a badger, and he has never been quite the same man since that night.

MANLY WADE WELLMAN

The Last Grave
of Lill Warran

The side road became a rutted track through the pines, and the track became a trail. John Thunstone reflected that he might have known his car would not be able to travel the full distance, and in any case a car seemed out of place in these ancient and uncombed woods. A lumber wagon would be more in keeping; or riding a mule, if John Thunstone were smaller and lighter, a fair load for a mule. He got out of the car, rolled up the windows, and locked the door. Ahead of him a path snaked through the thickets, narrow but well marked by the feet of nobody knew how many years of tramping.

He set his own big feet upon it. His giant body moved with silent grace. John Thunstone was at home in woods, or in wilder places.

He had dressed roughly for this expedition. He had no intention of appearing before the Sandhill woods people as a tailored and foreign invader. So he wore corduroys, a leather jacket that had been cut for him from deer hides of his own shooting and a shabby felt hat. His strong-boned, trim-mustached face was sober and watchful. It did not betray excitement, or any advance on the wonder he expected to feel when he finished his quest. In his big right hand he carried a walking stick of old dark wood.

"Yep, yep," the courthouse loafers at the town back on the paved road had answered his questions. "Lill Warran—that's her name, Lill, not Lily. Not much lily about her, nothin' so sweet and pure. She was a witch, all right, mister. Sure she was dug out of her grave. Nope, we wasn't there, we just heard about the thing. She was buried, appears like, in Beaver Dam churchyard. And somebody or several somebodies, done dug her up outa there and flung her body clear of the place. Old-time folks believe it's poison bad luck to bury a witch in church ground. You do that and leave her, you might's well forget the church 'cause it won't be blessed no more. Ain't saying we believe that personal; it's country belief."

But the courthouse loafers had not denied the belief in the necessity of digging up a witch. One or two of them contributed tales of Lill Warran. How she was no dry, stooped, gnarled old crone, but a "well-growed" woman, tall and fully and finely made, with a heavy massive wealth of black hair. She wore it knotted into a great loaf at her nape, they said, and that hair shone like fresh-melted tar. Her eyes, they said, were green as green glass, in a brown face, and her mouth—

"Huh!" they'd agreed to Thunstone. "You've come a far piece, and it's like you seen a many fine-looking women. But, mister, ain't no possible argument, you seen Lill Warran and that red mouth she had on her, you'd slap a mortgage on your immortal soul to get a kiss of it."

And the inference was, more than one man had mortgaged his immortal soul for a kiss of Lill Warran's mouth. She was dead now. How? Bullet, some said. Accident, said others. But she was dead, and she'd been buried twice over, and dug up the both times.

Gathering this and other information, John Thunstone was on the trail of the end of the story. For it has been John Thunstone's study and career to follow such stories to their end. His story-searches have brought him into adventures of which only the tenth part has been told, and that tenth part the simplest and most believable. His experiences in most cases he has kept to himself. Those experiences have helped, perhaps, to sprinkle gray in his smooth black hair, to make somber his calm, strong face.

The trail wound, and climbed. Here the wooded land sloped upward. And brush of a spiny species grew under the pines, encroaching so that John Thunstone had to force his way through, like a bull in a swamp. The spines plucked at his leather-clad arms and flanks, like little detaining fingers.

At the top of the slope was the clearing he sought.

It was a clearing in the strictest sense of the word. The tall pines had been axed away, undoubtedly their strong, straight trunks had gone to the building of the log house at the center. And cypress, from some swamp near by, had been split for the heavy shingles on the roof. All around the house was bare sand. Not a spear of grass, not a tuft of weed, grew there. It was as naked as a beach by the sea. Nobody moved in that naked yard, but from behind the house came a noise. *Plink, plink*, rhythmically. *Plink, plink*. Blows of metal on something solid, like stone or masonry.

Moving silently as an Indian, John Thunstone rounded the corner of the log house, paused to make sure of what was beyond, then moved toward it.

A man knelt there, of a height to match John Thunstone's own, but lean and spare, after the fashion of Sandhills brush dwellers. He wore a shabby checked shirt and blue dungaree pants, worn and frayed and washed out to the blue of a robin's egg. His sleeves were rolled to the biceps, showing gaunt, pallid arms with sharp elbows and knotty hands. His back was toward Thunstone. The crown of his tow head was beginning to be bald. Before him on the ground lay a flat rectangle of liver-colored stone. He held a short-handled, heavy-headed hammer in his right hand, and in his left a narrow-pointed wedge, such as is used to split sections of log into fire wood. The point of the wedge he held set against the face of the stone, and with the hammer he tapped the wedge butt. *Plink, plink*. He moved the point. *Plink*.

Still silent as a drifting cloud, Thunstone edged up behind him. He could see what the gaunt man was chiseling upon the stone. The last letter of a series of words, the letters irregular but deep and square:

HERE LIES

LILL   WARREN

TWICE BURIED AND TWICE DUG UP

BY FOOLS AND COWARDS

NOW SHE MAY

REST IN PEACE .

SHE WAS A ROSE OF SHARON

A LILY OF THE VALLEY

John Thunstone bent to read the final word, and the bright afternoon sun threw his shadow upon the stone. Immediately the lean man was up and his whole body whipped erect and away on the other side of his work, swift and furtive as a weasel. He stood and stared at John Thunstone, the hammer lowered, the lean-pointed wedge lifted a trifle.

"Who you?" the gaunt man wheezed breathily. He had a sharp face, a nose that projected like a pointed beak, with forehead and chin sloping back from it above and below. His eyes were dark, beady and close-set. His face was yellow and leathery, and even the whites of his eyes looked clouded, as with biliousness.

"My name is John Thunstone," Thunstone made reply, as casually as possible. "I'm looking for Mr. Parrell."

"That's me. Pos Parrell."

Pos . . . It was plain to see where the name suited the man. That lean, pointed snout, the meager chin and brow, the sharp eyes, looked like those of an opossum. A suspicious, angry, dangerous opossum.

"What can I do for you?" demanded Pos Parrell. He sounded as if he would like to do something violent.

"I want to ask about Miss Lill Warran," said Thunstone, still quietly, soothingly, as he might speak to a restive dog or horse. "I see you're making a gravestone for her." He pointed with his stick.

"And why not?" snapped Pos Parrell. His thin lips drew back from lean, strong teeth, like stained fangs. "Ain't she to be allowed to rest peacefully in her grave sometime?"

"I hope she will," said Thunstone. "I heard at the county seat about how she'd been dragged out of her grave at the churchyard."

Pos Parrell snorted. His hands tightened on hammer and wedge. "Now, mister, what almighty pick is it of yours? Listen, are you the law? If you are, you just trot your law back to the county seat. I'm not studying to hear any law. They won't let her stay buried at Beaver Dam, I've buried her here, and here she'll stay."

"No," Thunstone assured him. "I'm not the law."

"Then what are you? One of them reporters from the newspapers? Whatever you are, get off my place."

"Not until we've talked a bit, Mr. Parrell."

"I'll put you off. I got a right to put you off my place."

Thunstone smiled his most charming. "You do have the right. But could you put me off?"

Pos Parrell raked him with the beady eyes. "You about twice as big as me, but—"

He dropped the hammer. It struck the sand with a grim thud. He whipped the lean wedge over to his right hand, holding it daggerwise.

"Don't try that," warned Thunstone, and his walking stick lifted in his own hand.

Pos Parrell took a stamping stride forward. His left hand clutched at the tip of Thunstone's stick, the wedge lifted in his right.

But Thunstone drew back on the stick's handle. There was a metallic whisper. The lower part of the stick, clamped in

Parrell's grasp, stripped away like the sheath of a sword, revealing a long, straight skewer of gleaming blade that set in the handle as in a heft. As Parrell drove forward with his wedge, Thunstone delicately flicked the point of his sword cane across the back of Parrell's fist. Parrell squeaked with pain, and the wedge fell beside the hammer. Next instant Parrell was backing away hurriedly. Thunstone moved lightly, calmly after him, the sword point quivering inches from Parrell's throat.

"Hey!" protested Parrell. "Hey!"

"I'm sorry, but you'll have to listen to me."

"Put that thing down. I quit!"

Thunstone lowered the point, and smiled.

"Let's both quit. Let's talk."

Parrell subsided. He still held the hollow lower length of the stick. Thunstone took it from him and sheathed his blade.

"You know what?" said Parrell, rather wearily. "That's about the curiousest place I ever seen a man carry a stab weapon."

"It's a sword cane," explained Thunstone, friendly again. "It was made hundreds of years ago. The man who gave it to me said it was made by Saint Dunstan."

"Who was that?"

"He was an Englishman."

"Foreigner, huh?"

"Saint Dunstan was a silversmith," Thunstone told Parrell. "This blade in my stick is made out of silver. Among other things, Saint Dunstan is said to have twisted the devil's nose."

"Lemme see that thing again," Parrell said, and again Thunstone cleared the blade. "Huh!" grunted Parrell. "It got words on it. I can't make 'em out."

Thunstone's big finger tapped the engraved lettering. *"Sic pereant omnes inimici tui, Domine,"* he read aloud. "That means, "So perish all thine enemies, O God.' "

"Bible words or charm words?"

"Perhaps both," said Thunstone. "Now, Parrell, I want to be your friend. The people in town are pretty rough in their talk about you."

"And about Lill," said Parrell, so faintly that Thunstone could hardly hear. "But I loved her. Lots of men has loved her, but I reckon I was the only one loving her when she died."

"Tell me," urged Thunstone.

Parrell tramped back toward the cabin, and Thunstone followed. Parrell sat on the door sill and scuffed the dirt with his coarse shoes. He studied the back of his right hand, where Thunstone's skillful flick of the silver blade had raised a thin wale and shed a drop of blood.

"You know, you could have hurt me worse if you'd had a mind," he said.

"I didn't have a mind," Thunstone told him.

Again the shoes scuffed the sand. "I prized up my door stoop stone to make that marker for Lill's grave."

"It's a good one."

Parrell gestured to the edge of the clearing. There, in the shade of the pines, showed a mound of sand, dark with fresh digging, the size and shape of a body.

"I buried her there," he said, "and there she'll stay. At the last end, I reckon, she knowed I loved her and nothing could change it."

A rose of Sharon, a lily of the valley. Lill Warran had been no sweet lily, the courthouse loafers had insisted. Thunstone squatted on his heels.

"You know," he said, "you'll feel better if you talk about it to somebody who will listen."

"Reckon I will."

And Pos Parrell talked.

Later Thunstone wrote down Parrell's story from memory, as a most interesting record of belief in the supernatural, and also belief in a most beautiful and willful woman.

* * *

Lill Warran was called a witch because her mother had been one, and her grandmother had been one. Folks said she could curse pigs thin, and curse hens out of laying, and make trees fall on men cutting them. They wouldn't hear of things like that happening by chance. The preacher at Beaver Dam had sworn she said the Lord's Prayer wrong—"Our Father, who *wert* in heaven." Which meant Satan, who'd fallen from the Pearly Gates, the way it says in the book of Isaiah. No, the preacher hadn't read Lill Warran out of church, but she stopped coming, and laughed at the people who mumbled. The old folks hated her, the children were afraid and the women suspicious. But the men!

"She could get any man," said Parrell. "She got practically all of them. A hunter would leave his gun, a drinker would leave his bottle of stump-hole whiskey, a farmer would leave his plough standing in the field. There was a many wives crying tears because their husbands were out at night, following after Lill Warran. And Nobe Filder hanged himself, everybody knows, because he was to meet Lill and she didn't come, but went that night to a square dance with Newton Henley. And Newton grew to hate her, but he took sick and when he was dying he called on her name."

Pos Parrell had just loved her. She never promised to meet him, she tossed him smiles and chance words, like so many table scraps to a dog. Maybe it was as well. Those who were lovers of Lill Warran worshipped her, then feared and hated her.

That, at least, was witch history as Thunstone had read it and researched it. The old books of the old scholars were full of evidence about such seductive enchantresses, all the way back to the goddesses of dark love—Ishtar, Astoreth, Astarte, various names for the same force, terrible in love as the God of War is terrible in battle. To Thunstone's mind came a fragment of the Epic of Gilgamesh, lettered on a Chaldean tablet of clay five millennia ago. Gilgamesh had taunted Ishtar's overtures:

> Thou fellest in love with the herdsman
> Who ever scattered grain for thee,
> And daily slaughtered a kid for thee;
> Thou smotest him,
> Turned him into a wolf . . .

"It didn't prove nothing," Parrell was protesting. "Only that she was easy to fall in love with and hard to keep."

"What did she live on?" asked Thunstone. "Did her family have anything?"

"Shucks, no. She was orphaned. She lived by herself—they've burned the cabin now. People said she knew spells, so she could witch meat out of smokehouses into her pot, witch meal out of pantries onto her table."

"I've heard of people suspecting that of witches," nodded Thunstone, careful to keep his manner sympathetic. "It's an easy story to make yourself believe."

"I never believed it, not even when—"

Parrell told the climax of the sorry, eerie tale. It had happened a week ago. It had to do with a silver bullet.

For silver bullets are sure death to demons, and this was known to a young man by the name of Taylor Howatt, the latest to flutter around the fascinating flame that was Lill Warran. His friends warned him about her, and he wouldn't listen. Not Taylor! Not until there was prowling around his cabin by something that whined and yelped like a beast-varmint—a wolf, the old folks would say, except that wolves hadn't been seen in those parts since the old frontier days. And Taylor Howatt had glimpsed the thing once or twice by moonlight. It was shaggy, it had pointy ears and a pointy muzzle, but it stood up on its two legs, part of the time at least.

"The werewolf story," commented Thunstone, but Parrell continued.

Taylor Howatt knew what to do. He had an old, old deer rifle, the kind made by country gunsmiths as long back as the

War with the North. He had the bullet mold, too, and he'd melted down half a silver dollar and cast him a bullet. He'd loaded the deer rifle ready, and listened for several nights to the howls. When the thing came peeking close to an open window, he caught its shape square against the rising moon and fired.

Next day, Lill Warran was found dead on the footpath leading to her own home, and her heart was shot through.

Of course, there'd been a sheriff deputy down. Taylor Howatt was able to claim it was accidental. The people had gathered at Lill's cabin, and there they'd found stuff, they said. One claimed a side of bacon he said had hung in his smokehouse. And another found a book.

"Book?" said John Thunstone quickly. For books are generally interesting properties in stories like the story of Lill Warran.

"I've been told about it by three folks who swore they seen it," replied Parrell. "Me myself, I didn't see it, so I hold I ain't called on to judge it."

"What did those people tell you about it?"

"Well—it was hairy like. The cover all hairy and dark, like the skin of a black bear. And inside it had three parts."

"The first part," said Thunstone, "was written with red ink on white paper. The second part, with black ink on red paper. And the third, black paper, written on with—"

"You been talking to them other folks!" accused Parrell, half starting up.

"No. Though I heard the book mentioned at the court-house. It's just that I've heard of such books before. The third part of the book, black paper, is written on with white ink that will shine in the dark, so that it can be read without light."

"Then them folks mocking me heard what you heard about the like of the book. They made it up to vex my soul."

"Maybe," agreed Thunstone, though he doubted that the people of the Sandhills brush would have so much knowledge of classical and rare grimoires. "Go on."

The way Parrell had heard the book explained, the first part—red ink on white paper—was made up of rather simple charms, to cure rheumatism or sore eyes, with one or two more interesting spells that concerned the winning of love or the causing of a wearisome lover to depart. The second, the black ink on red, had the charm to bring food from the stores of neighbors, as well as something that purported to make the practitioner invisible, and something else that aided in the construction of a mirror in which one could see far away scenes and actions.

"And the black part of the book?" asked Thunstone, more calmly than he felt.

"Nobody got that far."

"Good," said Thunstone thankfully. He himself would have thought twice, and more than twice, before reading the shiny letters in the black third section of such a book.

"The preacher took it. Said he locked it in his desk. Next day it was gone. Folks think it went back to Satan himself."

Folks might not be far wrong, thought Thunstone, but did not say as much aloud.

Parrell's voice was wretched as he finished his narrative. Lill Warran had had no kinsmen, none who would claim her body at least. So he, Parrell, had claimed it—bought a coffin and paid for a plot in Beaver Dam churchyard. He and an undertaker's helper had been alone at the burying of Lill Warran.

"Since nobody wanted to be Christian, nothing was said from the Bible at the burying," Parrell told Thunstone. "I did say a little verse of a song I remembered, I always remembered, when I thought of her. This it what it was."

He half-crooned the rhyme:

> "The raven crow is a coal, coal black.
> The jay is a purple blue,
> If ever I forget my own fair love,
> Let my heart melt away like dew."

Thunstone wondered how old the song was. "Then?" he prompted.

"You know the rest. The morning after, they tore her up out of the grave and flung her in my yard. I found her lying near to my doorstep, the one I just now cut for her grave-stone." Parrell nodded toward where it lay. "I took her and buried her again. And this morning it was the same. There she lay. So let them all go curse. I buried her yonder, and yonder she'll stay, or if anybody says different I'll argue with something more than a law book. Did I do wrong, mister?"

"Not you," said Thunstone. "You did what your heart told you."

"Thanks. Thank you kindly. Like you said, I do feel better for talking it over." Parrell rose. "I'm going to set up that stone."

Thunstone helped him. The weight of the slab taxed their strength. Parrell drove it into the sand at the head of the grave. Then he looked to where the sun was sinking behind the pines.

"You won't be getting back away from here before it's dark and hard to pick the way. I'll be honored if you stopped here tonight. Not much of a bed or supper doings, but if you'll be so kind—"

"Thank you," said Thunstone, who had been wondering how to manage an overnight stay.

They entered the front room of the little cabin. Inside it was finished in boards, rough sawn but evenly fitted into place. There was an old table, old chairs, a very old cook stove, pans hanging to nails on the walls. Parrell beckoned Thunstone to where a picture was tacked to a wall.

"It's her," he said.

The photograph was cheap, and some slipshod studio artist had touched it up with colors. But Thunstone could see what sort of woman Lill Warran had been. The picture was half length, and she wore a snug dress with large flower figuring. She smiled into the camera, with the wide full mouth of which he had heard. Her eyes were slanting, mocking and lustrous. Her head was proud on fine shoulders. Round and deep was the bosom into which a silver bullet had been sent by the old deer rifle of Taylor Howatt.

"You see why I loved her," said Parrell.

"I see," Thunstone assured him.

Parrell cooked for them. There was corn bread and syrup, and a plate of rib meat, hearty fare. Despite his sorrow, Parrell ate well of his own cooking. When the meal was finished, Parrell bowed and mumbled an old country blessing. They went out into the yard. Parrell walked slowly to the grave of Lill Warran and gazed down at it. Thunstone moved in among the trees, saw something that grew, and stooped to gouge it out.

"What you gathering?" called Parrell.

"Just an odd little growth," Thunstone called back, and pulled another. They were the roots called throughout the south by the name of John the Conqueror, great specifics against enchantment. Thunstone filled his pockets with them, and walked back to join Parrell.

"I'm glad you came along, Mr. Thunstone," said Parrell. His opposum face was touched with a shy smile. "I've lived alone for two years, but never so lonely as the last week."

Together they entered the house, Parrell found and lighted an oil lamp, and immediately Thunstone felt the impact of eyes from across the room. Swiftly facing that way, he gazed into the face of the portrait of Lill Warran. The pictured smile seemed to taunt and defy him, and to invite him as well. What had the man leered at the court house? *You'd slap a mortgage on your immortal soul to get a kiss.* That picture was enough to convince Thunstone that better men than pitiful, spindling Pos Parrell could find Lill Warran herself irresistible.

"I'll make you up a pallet bed here," offered Parrell.

"You needn't bother for me," Thunstone said, but Parrell opened a battered old wooden chest and brought out a quilt, another. As he spread them out, Thunstone recognized the ancient and famous patterns of the quilt work. Kentucky

Blazing Star, that was one of them. Another was True Love Fancy.

"My old mamma made them," Parrell informed him.

Parrell folded the quilts into a pallet along the wall. "Sure you'll be all right? You won't prefer to take my bed."

"I've slept a lot harder than what you're fixing for me," Thunstone quickly assured him.

They sat at a table and talked. Parrell's thoughts were still for his lost love. He spoke of her, earnestly, revealingly. Once or twice Thunstone suspected him of trying for poetic speech.

"I would look at her," said Parrell, "and it was like hearing, not seeing."

"Hearing what?"

"Hearing—well, more than anything else it was like the sound of a fiddle, played prettier than you ever heard. Prettier than I can ever play."

Thunstone had seen the battered fiddle-case on a hand-hewn shelf beside the door of the rear room which was apparently Parrell's sleeping quarters, but he had not mentioned it. "Suppose you play us something now," he suggested.

Parrell swallowed. "Play music? With her lying out there in her grave?"

"She wouldn't object, if she knew. Playing the fiddle gives you pleasure, doesn't it?"

Parrell seemed to need no more bidding. He rose, opened the case and brought out the fiddle. It was old and dark, and he turned it with fingers diffidently skillful. Thunstone looked at him. "Where did you get it? The fiddle, I mean."

"Oh, my granddaddy inherited it to me. I was the onliest grandboy he had cared to learn."

"Where did he get it?"

"I don't rightly know how to tell you that. I always heard a foreigner fellow—I mean a sure-enough foreigner from Europe or some place, not just somebody from some other part of the country—gave it to my granddaddy, or either traded it to him."

Thunstone knew something about violins, and judged that this one was worth a sum that would surprise Parrell, if no more than mentioned. Thunstone did not mention any sum. He only said, "Play something, why not?"

Parrell grinned, showing his lean teeth. He tucked the instrument against his jowl and played. He was erratic but vigorous; with training, he might have been brilliant. The music soared, wailed, thundered and died down. "That was interesting," said Thunstone. "What was it?"

"Just something I sort of figured out for myself," said Parrell apologetically. "I do that once in a while, but not lots. Folks would rather hear the old songs—things they know, like 'Arkansas Traveler' and 'Fire in the Mountains.' I generally play my own stuff to myself, alone here in the evenings." Parrell laid down the instrument. "My fiddle's kept me company, sometimes at night when I wished Lill was with me."

"Did you ever know," said Thunstone, "why we have so many fiddles in the American country localities?"

"Never heard that I recollect."

"In the beginnings of America," Thunstone told him, "frontier homes were lonely and there were wild beasts around. Wolves, mostly."

"Not now," put in Parrell. "Remember that crazy yarn Taylor Howatt told about shooting at a wolf, and there hasn't been a wolf around here since I don't know when."

"Maybe not now, but there were wolves in the old days. And the strains of fiddle music hurt the ears of the wolves and kept them away."

"There may be a lot in what you say," nodded Parrell, and put his instrument back into its box. "Listen, I'm tired. I've not slept fit for a dog these past six nights. But now, with you here, talking sense like you have—" Parrell paused, stretched and yawned. "If it's all right with you, I'll go sleep a while."

"Good night, Parrell," said Thunstone, and watched his host go into the rear room and close the door.

*   *   *

Then Thunstone went outside. It was quiet and starry, and
the moon rose, half of its disk gleaming pale. He took from
his pockets the roots of John the Conqueror, placing one on
the sill above the door, another above the front window, and
so on around the shanty. Returning, he entered the front room
again, turned up the lamp a trifle and spread out a piece of
paper. He produced a pen and began to write:
My Dear de Grandin:

I know your investigations kept you from coming here with
me, but I wonder if this thing isn't more interesting, if not
more important, than what you chose to stay and do in New
Jersey.

The rumors about Lill Warran, as outlined to you in the
letter I wrote this morning, are mostly confirmed. Here,
however, are the new items I've uncovered:

Strong evidence of the worst type of grimoire. I refer to one
with white, red and black sections. Since it's mentioned in
this case, I incline to believe there was one—these country
folk could hardly make up such a grimoire out of their heads.
Lill Warran, it seems, had a copy, which later vanished from
a locked drawer. Naturally! Or, super-naturally!

Presence of a werewolf. One Taylor Howatt was sure
enough to make himself a silver bullet, and to use it effec-
tively. He fired at a hairy, point-eared monster, and it was
Lill Warran they picked up dead. This item naturally suggests
the next.

*Nobody knows the person or persons who turned Lill Warran
twice out of her grave.* Most people of the region are rather
smugly pleased at the report that Lill Warran wasn't allowed
rest in consecrated churchyard soil, and Pos Parrell, grief-
stricken, has buried her in his yard, where he intends that she
will have peace. But, de Grandin, you will already have
guessed the truth they have failed even to imagine: if Lill
Warran was indeed a werewolf—and the black section of the
grimoire undoubtedly told her how to be one at will—if, I
say, Lill Warran was a werewolf. . . .

Thunstone sat up in the chair, the pen in his fingers. Somebody, or something, moved stealthily in the darkness outside.

There was a tapping whisper at the screen Pos Parrell had nailed over the window. Thunstone grimly forbore to glance. He made himself yawn, a broad hand covering his mouth— the reflex gesture, he meditated as he yawned, born of generations past who feared lest the soul might be snatched through the open mouth by a demon. Slowly he capped his pen, and laid it upon the unfinished letter to de Grandin. He rose, stretched and tossed aside his leather jacket. He stopped and pretended to untie his shoes, but did not take them off. Finally, cupping his palm around the top of the lamp chimney, he blew out the light. He moved to where Parrell had spread the pallet of quilts and lay down upon them. He began to breathe deeply and regularly. One hand, relaxed in its seeming, rested within an inch of the sword cane.

The climax of the adventure was upon him, he knew very well; but in the moments to follow he must possess himself with calm, must appear to be asleep in a manner to deceive the most skeptical observer.

Thus determined, he resolutely relaxed, from the toe-joints up. He let his big jaw go slack, his big hands curl open. He continued to breathe deeply and regularly, like a sleeper. Hardest of all was the task of conquering the swift race of heart and pulse, but John Thunstone had learned how to do that, too, because of necessity many times before. So completely did he contrive to pretend slumber that his mind went dreamy and vague around the edges. He seemed to float a little free of the pallet, to feel awareness at not too great a distance of the gates of dreamland.

But his ears were tuned to search out sounds. And outside in the dark the unknown creature continued its stealthy round.

It paused—just in front of the door, as John Thunstone judged. It knew that the root of John the Conqueror lay there, an obstacle; but not an obstacle that completely baffled. Such a herb, to turn back what Thunstone felt sure was besieging the dark cabin, would need to be wolfbane or garlic: or, for what grew naturally in these parts of the world, French lilac. John the Conqueror—Big John or Little John, as woodland gatherers defined the two varieties—was only "used to win," and might not assure victory. All it could do, certainly, was slow up the advance of the besieger.

Under his breath, very soft and very low, John Thunstone began to mutter a saying taught him by a white magician in a faraway city, half a prayer and half a spell against evil enemies:

"Two wicked eyes have overshadowed us, but two holy eyes are fixed upon us; the eyes of Saint Dunstan, who smote and shamed the devil. Beware, wicked one; beware twice, wicked one; beware thrice. . . ."

In the next room, Thunstone could hear sounds. They were sounds of dull, careful pecking. They came from the direction in which, as he had seen, was set the closed casement window of Pos Parrell's sleeping chamber.

With the utter silence he knew how to keep, Thunstone rolled from his pallet, lying for a moment face down on the floor. He drew up one knee and both hands, and rose to his full height. In one hand he brought along the sword cane.

The pecking sound persisted as he slid one foot along the rough planks of the floor, praying that no creak would sound. He managed a step, another, a third. He was at the door leading to the next room.

His free hand groped for a knob. There was none, only a latch string. Thunstone pulled, and the door sagged silently open.

He looked into a room, the dimness of which was washed by light from the moon outside. In the window, silhouetted against the four panes, showed the outline of head and shoulders. A tinkling whisper, and one of the panes fell inward, to shatter musically on the boards below. Something had picked away the putty. A dark arm crept in, weaving like a snake, to fumble at the catch. A moment later the window was open, and something thrust itself in, made the passage and landed on the floor.

The moonlight gave him a better look at the shape as it rose from all fours and faced toward the cot where Pos Parrell lay, silent and slack as though he were drugged.

John Thunstone knew that face from the picture in the room where he had slept. It had the slanted, lustrous eyes, the cloud of hair—not clubbed, but hanging in a great thunder cloud on either side of the face. And the wide, full mouth did not smile, but quivered as by some overwhelming pulse.

"Pos," whispered the mouth of Lill Warran.

She wore a white robelike garment, such as is put on dead women in that country. Its wide, winglike sleeves swaddled her arms, but it fell free of the smooth, pale shoulders, the fine upper slope of the bosom. Now as in life, Lill Warran was a forbiddingly beautiful creature. She seemed to sway, to float toward Parrell.

"You love me," she breathed at him.

The sleeper stirred for the first time. He turned toward her, a hand moved sleepily, almost as though it beckoned her. Lill Warran winnowed to the very bedside.

"Stop where you are!" called John Thunstone, and strode into the room, and toward the bed.

She paused, a hand on the blanket that covered Parrell. Her face turned toward Thunstone, the moonlight playing upon it. Her mocking smile possessed her lips.

"You were wise enough to guess most of me," she said. "Are you going to be fool enough to try to stop what is bound to happen?"

"You won't touch him," said Thunstone.

She chuckled. "Don't be afraid to shout. You cannot waken Pos Parrell tonight—not while I stand here. He loves me. He always loved me. The others loved and then hated. But he loves me—though he thinks I am dead—"

She sounded archaic, she sounded measured and stilted, as though she quoted ill-rehearsed lines from some old play. That was in order, Thunstone knew.

"He loves you, that's certain," agreed Thunstone. "That means you recognize his helplessness. You think that his love makes him your easy prey. You didn't reckon with me."

"Who are you?"

"My name is John Thunstone."

Lill Warran glared, her lips writhed back. She seemed as though she would spit.

"I've heard that name. John Thunstone! Shall I not dispose of you, right now and at once, you fool?"

She took a step away from the bed. Her hands lifted, the winglike sleeves slipped back from them. She crooked her fingers, talon fashion, and Thunstone saw the length and sharpness of her nails.

Lill Warran laughed.

"Fools have their own reward. Destruction!"

Thunstone stood with feet apart. The cane lay across his body, its handle in his right fist, the fingers of his left hand clasping around the lower shank that made a sheath.

"You have a stick," said Lill Warran. "Do you think you can beat me away, like a dog?"

"I do."

"You cannot even move, John Thunstone!" Her hands weaved in the air, like the hands of a hypnotist. "You're a toy for me! I remember hearing a poem once: 'A fool there was—' " She paused, laughing.

"Remember the title of that poem?" he said, almost sweetly, and she screamed, like the largest and loudest of bats, and leaped.

In that instant, Thunstone cleared the long silver rapier from its hiding, and, as swiftly as she, extended his arm like a fencer in riposte.

Upon the needle-pointed blade, Lill Warran skewered herself. He felt the point slip easily, smoothly, into the flesh of her bosom. It grated on a bone somewhere, then slid past and through. Lill Warran's body slammed to the very hilt, and for a moment she was no more than arm's length from him. Her eyes grew round, her mouth opened wide, but only a whisper of breath came from it.

Then she fell backward, slack as an empty garment, and as Thunstone cleared his blade she thudded on the floor and lay with her arms flung out to right and left, as though crucified.

From his hip pocket Thunstone fished a handkerchief and wiped way the blood that ran from point to base of the silver weapon forged centuries before by Saint Dunstan, patron of those who face and fight creatures of evil.

To his lips came the prayer engraved upon the blade, and he repeated it aloud: "*Sic pereant omnes inimici tui, Domine . . . So perish all thine enemies, O God.*"

"Huh?" sleepily said Pos Parrell, and sat up on his cot. He strained his eyes in the dimness. "What you say, Mister? What's happened?"

Thunstone moved toward the bureau, sheathing his silver blade. He struck a match, lifted the chimney from the lamp on the bureau and lighted it. The room filled with the warm glow from the wick.

Parrell sprang out of bed. "Hey, look. The window's open—it's broke in one pane. Who done that?"

"Somebody from outside," said Thunstone, standing still to watch.

Parrell turned and stared at what was on the floor. "It's Lill!" he bawled in a quivering voice. "Sink their rotten souls to hell, they come dug her up again and throwed her in here!"

"I don't think so," said Thunstone, and lifted the lamp. "Take a good look."

Moving, he shed light down upon the quiet form of Lill Warran. Parrell knelt beside her, his trembling hands touching the dark stain on her bosom.

"Blood!" he gulped. "That's fresh blood. Her wound was bleeding, right now. She wasn't dead down there in the grave!"

"No," agreed Thunstone quietly. "She wasn't dead down there in the grave. But she's dead now."

Parrell examined her carefully, miserably. "Yes, sir. She's dead now. She won't rise up no more."

"No more," agreed Thunstone again. "And she got out of her grave by her own strength. Nobody dug her up, dead or alive."

Parrell stared from where he knelt. Wonder and puzzlement touched his grief-lined, sharp-snouted face.

"Come out and see," invited Thunstone, and lifted the lamp from where it stood on the bureau. He walked through the front room and out of the door. Parrell tramped at his heels.

The night was quiet, with so little breeze that the flame of the lamp barely flickered. Straight to the graveside Thunstone led Parrell, stopped there and held the lamp high over the freshly opened hole.

"Look, Parrell," Thunstone bade him. "That grave was opened from inside, not outside."

Parrell stooped and stared. One hand crept up and wiped the low, slanting brow.

"You're right, I guess," said Parrell slowly. "It looks like what a fox does when he breaks through at the end of his digging—the dirt's flung outward from below, only bigger'n a fox's hole." Parrell straightened up. His face was like sick tallow in the light of the lamp. "Then it's true, though it looks right pure down impossible. She was in there, alive, and she got out tonight."

"She got out the other two nights," said Thunstone. "I don't think I can explain to you exactly why, but night time was the time of her strength. And each time she came here to you—walked or crept all the way. Each time, again, she could move no more when it was dawn."

"Lill came to me!"

"You loved her, didn't you? That's why she came to you."

Parrell turned toward the house. "And she must have loved me," he whispered, "to come to me out of the grave.

Tonight, she didn't have so far to go. If she'd stayed alive—''

Thunstone started back to the house. "Don't think about that, Parrell. She's certainly dead now, and what she would have done if she'd stayed alive isn't for us to think about.''

Parrell made no reply until they had once more entered the front door and walked through to where Lill Warran lay as they had left her. In the light of the lamp Thunstone carried her face was clearly defined.

It was a calm face, a face at peace and a little sorrowful. Yes, a sweet face. Lill Warran may not have looked like that in life, or in life-in-death, but now she was completely dead, she was of a gentle, sleeping beauty. Thunstone could see how Parrell, or any other man, might love a face like that.

"And she came to me, she loved me," breathed Parrell again.

"Yes, she loved you," nodded Thunstone. "In her own way she did love you. Let's take her back to her grave.''

Between them they carried her out and to the hole. At its bottom was the simple coffin of pine planks, its lid thrown outward and upward from its burst fastenings. Thunstone and Parrell put the body into the coffin, straightened its slack limbs and lowered the lid. Parrell brought a spade and a shovel, and they filled and smoothed the grave.

"I'm going to say my little verse again," said Parrell. Standing with head bowed, he mumbled the lines:

"The raven crow is a coal, coal black,
   The jay is a purple blue,
   If ever I forget my own fair love,
   Let my heart melt away like dew."

He looked up at Thunstone, tears streaming down his face. "Now she'll rest in peace.''

"That's right. She'll rest in peace. She won't rise again."

"Listen, you mind going back to the house? I'll just watch here till morning. You don't think that'll hurt, do you?''

Thunstone smiled.

"No, it won't hurt. It will be perfectly all right. Because nothing whatever will disturb you."

"Or her," added Parrell.

"Or her," nodded Thunstone. "She won't be disturbed. Just keep remembering her as somebody who loved you, and whose rest will never be interrupted again."

Back in the house, Thunstone brought the lamp to the table where he had interrupted his letter to de Grandin. He took his pen and began writing again:

I was interrupted by events that brought this adventure to a good end. And maybe I'll wait until I see you before I tell you that part of it.

But to finish my earlier remarks:

If Lill Warran was a werewolf, and killed in her werewolf shape, it follows as a commonplace that she became a vampire after death. You can read as much in Montague Summers, as well as the work of your countryman, Cyprien Robert.

And as a vampire, she would and did return, in a vampire's travesty of affection, to the one living person whose heart still turned to her.

Because I half suspected all this from the moment I got wind of the story of Lill Warran, I brought with me the silver blade forged for just such battles by Saint Dunstan, and it was my weapon of victory.

He finished and folded the letter. Outside, the moon brightened the quiet night, in which it seemed no evil thing could possibly stir.

FRITZ LIEBER

The Girl
with the Hungry Eyes

All right, I'll tell you why the Girl gives me the creeps. Why
I can't stand to go down town and see the mob slavering up at
her on the tower, with that pop bottle or pack of cigarettes or
whatever it is beside her. Why I hate to look at magazines
any more because I know she'll turn up somewhere in a
brassiere or a bubble bath. Why I don't like to think of
millions of Americans drinking in that poisonous half-smile.
It's quite a story—more story than you're expecting.

No, I haven't suddenly developed any long-haired indigna-
tion at the evils of advertising and the national glamour-girl
complex. That'd be a laugh for a man in my racket, wouldn't
it? Though I think you'll agree there's something a little
perverted about trying to capitalize on sex that way. But it's
okay with me. And I know we've had the Face and the Body
and the Look and what not else, so why shouldn't someone
come along who sums it all up so completely, that we have to
call her the Girl and blazon her on all the billboards from
Times Square to Telegraph Hill?

But the Girl isn't like any of the others. She's unnatural.
She's morbid. She's unholy.

Oh, these are modern times, you say, and the sort of thing
I'm hinting at went out with witchcraft. But you see I'm not

altogether sure myself what I'm hinting at, beyond a certain point. There are vampires and vampires, and not all of them suck blood.

And there were the murders, if they were murders. Besides, let me ask you this. Why, when America is obsessed with the Girl, don't we find out more about her? Why doesn't she rate a *Time* cover with a droll biography inside? Why hasn't there been a feature in *Life* or *The Post?* A profile in the *New Yorker?* Why hasn't *Charm* or *Mademoiselle* done her career saga? Not ready for it? Nuts!

Why haven't the movies snapped her up? Why hasn't she been on "Information, Please?" Why don't we see her kissing candidates at political rallies? Why isn't she chosen queen of some sort of junk or other at a convention?

Why don't we read about her tastes and hobbies, her views of the Russian situation? Why haven't the columnists interviewed her in a kimono on the top floor of the tallest hotel in Manhattan and told us who her boy friends are?

Finally—and this is the real killer—why hasn't she ever been drawn or painted?

Oh, no she hasn't. If you knew anything about commercial art you'd know that. Every blessed one of those pictures was worked up from a photograph. Expertly? Of course. They've got the top artists on it. But that's how it's done.

And now I'll tell you the why of all that. It's because from the top to the bottom of the whole world of advertising, news, and business, there isn't a solitary soul who knows where the Girl came from, where she lives, what she does, who she is, even what her name is.

You heard me. What's more, not a single solitary soul ever sees her—except one poor damned photographer, who's making more money off her than he ever hoped to in his life and who's scared and miserable as Hell every minute of the day.

No, I haven't the faintest idea who he is or where he has his studio. But I know there has to be such a man and I'm morally certain he feels just like I said.

Yes, I might be able to find her, if I tried. I'm not sure

though—by now she probably has other safeguards. Besides, I don't want to.

Oh, I'm off my rocker, am I? That sort of thing can't happen in the Era of the Atom? People can't keep out of sight that way, not even Garbo?

Well I happen to know they can, because last year I was that poor damned photographer I was telling you about. Yes, last year, when the Girl made her first poisonous splash right here in this big little city of ours.

Yes, I know you weren't here last year and you don't know about it. Even the Girl had to start small. But if you hunted through the files of the local newspapers, you'd find some ads, and I might be able to locate you some of the old displays—I think Lovelybelt is still using one of them. I used to have a mountain of photos myself, until I burned them.

Yes, I made my cut off her. Nothing like what that other photographer must be making, but enough so it still bought this whisky. She was funny about money. I'll tell you about that.

But first picture me then. I had a fourth-floor studio in that rathole the Hauser Building, not far from Ardleigh Park.

I'd been working at the Marsh-Mason studios until I'd gotten my bellyful of it and decided to start in for myself. The Hauser building was awful—I'll never forget how the stairs creaked—but it was cheap and there was a skylight.

Business was lousy. I kept making the rounds of all the advertisers and agencies, and some of them didn't object to me too much personally, but my stuff never clicked. I was pretty near broke. I was behind on my rent. Hell, I didn't even have enough money to have a girl.

It was one of those dark, gray afternoons. The building was very quiet—I'd just finished developing some pix I was doing on speculation for Lovelybelt Girdles and Budford's Pool and Playground. My model had left. A Miss Leon. She was a civics teacher at one of the high schools and modeled for me on the side, just lately on speculation, too. After one look at the prints, I decided that Miss Leon probably wasn't just what Lovelybelt was looking for—or my photography either. I was about to call it a day.

And then the street door slammed four stories down and there were steps on the stairs and she came in.

She was wearing a cheap, shiny black dress. Black pumps. No stockings. And except that she had a gray cloth coat over one of them, those skinny arms of hers were bare. Her arms are pretty skinny, you know, or can't you see things like that any more?

And then the thin neck, the slightly gaunt, almost prim face, the tumbling mass of dark hair, and looking out from under it the hungriest eyes in the world.

That's the real reason she's plastered all over the country today, you know—those eyes. Nothing vulgar, but just the same they're looking at you with a hunger that's all sex and something more than sex. That's what everybody's been looking for since the Year One—something a little more than sex.

Well, boys, there I was, alone with the Girl, in an office that was getting shadowy, in a nearly empty building. A situation that a million male Americans have undoubtedly pictured to themselves with various lush details. How was I feeling? Scared.

I know sex can be frightening. That cold heart-thumping when you're alone with a girl and feel you're going to touch her. But if it was sex this time, it was overlaid with something else.

At least I wasn't thinking about sex.

I remember that I took a backward step and that my hand jerked so that the photos I was looking at sailed to the floor.

There was the faintest dizzy feeling like something was being drawn out of me. Just a little bit.

That was all. Then she opened her mouth and everything was back to normal for a while.

"I see you're a photographer, mister," she said. "Could you use a model?"

Her voice wasn't very cultivated.

"I doubt it," I told her, picking up the pix. You see, I wasn't impressed. The commercial possibilities of her eyes hadn't registered on me yet, by a long shot. "What have you done?"

Well, she gave me a vague sort of story and I began to check her knowledge of model agencies and studios and rates and what not and pretty soon I said to her, "Look here, you never modeled for a photographer in your life. You just walked in here cold."

Well, she admitted that was more or less so.

All along through our talk I got the idea she was feeling her way, like someone in a strange place. Not that she was uncertain of herself, or of me, but just of the general situation.

"And you think anyone can model?" I asked her pityingly.

"Sure," she said.

"Look," I said, "a photographer can waste a dozen negatives trying to get one halfway human photo of an average woman. How many do you think he'd have to waste before he got a real catchy, glamorous photo of her?"

"I think I could do it," she said.

Well, I should have kicked her out right then. Maybe I admired the cool way she stuck to her dumb little guns. Maybe I was touched by her underfed look. More likely I was feeling mean on account of the way my pictures had been snubbed by everybody and I wanted to take it out on her by showing her up.

"Okay, I'm going to put you on the spot," I told her. "I'm going to try a couple of shots of you. Understand it's strictly on spec. If somebody should ever want to use a photo of you, which is about one chance in two million, I'll pay you regular rates for your time. Not otherwise."

She gave me a smile. The first. "That's swell by me," she said.

Well, I took three or four shots, close-ups of her face since I didn't fancy her cheap dress, and at least she stood up to my sarcasm. Then I remembered I still had the Lovelybelt stuff and I guess the meanness was still working in me because I

handed her a girdle and told her to go behind the screen and
get into it and she did, without getting flustered as I'd expected, and since we'd gone that far, I figured we might as
well shoot the beach scene to round it out, and that was that.

All this time I wasn't feeling anything particular one way
or the other, except every once in a while I'd get one of those
faint dizzy flashes and wonder if there was something wrong
with my stomach or if I could have been a bit careless with
my chemicals.

Still, you know, I think the uneasiness was in me all the
while.

I tossed her a card and pencil. "Write your name and
address and phone," I told her and made for the dark-room.

A little later she walked out. I didn't call any good-byes. I
was irked because she hadn't fussed around or seemed anxious about her poses, or even thanked me, except for that one
smile.

I finished developing the negatives, made some prints,
glanced at them, decided they weren't a great deal worse than
Miss Leon. On an impulse I slipped them in with the pictures
I was going to take on the rounds next morning.

By now I'd worked long enough, so I was a bit fagged and
nervous, but I didn't dare waste enough money on liquor to
help that. I wasn't very hungry. I think I went to a cheap
movie.

I didn't think of the Girl at all, except maybe to wonder
faintly why in my present womanless state I hadn't made a
pass at her. She had seemed to belong to a—well, distinctly
more approachable social strata than Miss Leon. But then, of
course, there were all sorts of arguable reasons for my not
doing that.

Next morning I made the rounds. My first step was Munsch's
Brewery. They were looking for a "Munsch Girl." Papa
Munsch had a sort of affection for me, though he razzed my
photography. He had a good natural judgment about that, too.
Fifty years ago he might have been one of the shoe-string
boys who made Hollywood.

Right now he was out in the plant pursuing his favorite occupation. He put down the beaded schooner, smacked his lips, gabbled something technical to someone about hops, wiped his hands on the big apron he was wearing, and grabbed my thin stack of pictures.

He was about halfway through, making noises with his tongue and teeth, when he came to her. I kicked myself for even having stuck her in.

"That's her," he said. "The photography's not so hot, but that's the girl."

It was all decided. I wonder now why Papa Munsch sensed what the Girl had right away, while I didn't. I think it was because I saw her first in the flesh, if that's the right word.

At the time I just felt faint.

"Who is she?" he said.

"One of my new models," I tried to make it casual.

"Bring her out tomorrow morning," he told me. "And your stuff. We'll photograph her here."

"Here, don't look so sick," he added. "Have some beer."

Well, I went away telling myself it was just a fluke, so that she'd probably blow it tomorrow with her inexperience, and so on.

Just the same, when I reverently laid my next stack of pictures on Mr. Fitch, of Lovelybelt's, rose-colored blotter, I had hers on top.

Mr Fitch went through the motions of being an art critic. He leaned over backwards, squinted his eyes, waved his long fingers, and said, "Hmm. What do you think, Miss Willow? Here, in this light, of course, the photograph doesn't show the bias cut. And perhaps we should use the Lovelybelt Imp instead of the Angel. Still, the girl. . . . Come over here, Binns." More finger-waving. "I want a married man's reaction."

He couldn't hide the fact that he was hooked.

Exactly the same thing happened at Budford's Pool and Playground, except that Da Costa didn't need a married man's say-so."

"Hot stuff," he said, sucking his lips. "Oh boy, you photographers!"

I hot-footed it back to the office and grabbed up the card I'd given her to put down her name and address.

It was blank.

I don't mind telling you that the next five days were about the worst I ever went through, in an ordinary way. When next morning rolled around and I still hadn't got gold of her, I had to start stalling.

"She's sick," I told Papa Munsch over the phone.

"She at a hospital?" he asked me.

"Nothing that serious," I told him.

"Get her out here then. What's a little headache?"

"Sorry, I can't."

Papa Munsch got suspicious. "You really got this girl?"

"Of course I have."

"Well, I don't know. I'd think it was some New York model, except I recognized your lousy photography."

I laughed.

"Well look, you get her here tomorrow morning, you hear?"

"I'll try."

"Try nothing. You get her out here."

He didn't know half of what I tried. I went around to all the model and employment agencies. I did some slick detective work at the photographic and art studios. I used up some of my last dimes putting advertisements in all three papers. I looked at high school yearbooks and at employee photos in local house organs. I went to restaurants and drugstores, looking at waitresses, and to dime stores and department stores, looking at clerks. I watched the crowds coming out of movie theaters. I roamed the streets.

Evenings, I spent quite a bit of time along Pick-up Row. Somehow that seemed the right place.

The fifth afternoon I knew I was licked. Papa Munsch's deadline—he'd given me several, but this was it—was due to run out at six o'clock. Mr. Fitch had already canceled.

I was at the studio window, looking out at Ardleigh Park.
She walked in.

I'd gone over this moment so often in my mind that I had
no trouble putting on my act. Even the faint dizzy feeling
didn't throw me off.

"Hello," I said, hardly looking at her.

"Hello," she said.

"Not discouraged yet?"

"No." It didn't sound uneasy or defiant. It was just a
statement.

I snapped a look at my watch, got up and said curtly,
"Look here, I'm going to give you a chance. There's a client
of mine looking for a girl your general type. If you do a real
good job you might break into the modeling business."

"We can see him this afternoon if we hurry," I said. I
picked up my stuff. "Come on. And next time if you expect
favors, don't forget to leave your phone number."

"Uh, uh," she said, not moving.

"What do you mean?" I said.

"I'm not going out to see any client of yours."

"The hell you aren't," I said. "You little nut, I'm giving
you a break."

She shook her head slowly. "You're not fooling me, baby,
you're not fooling me at all. They want me." And she gave
me the second smile.

At the time I thought she must have seen my newspaper
ad. Now I'm not so sure.

"And now I'll tell you how we're going to work," she
went on. "You aren't going to have my name or address or
phone number. Nobody is. And we're going to do all the
pictures right here. Just you and me."

You can imagine the roar I raised at that. I was everything—
angry, sarcastic, patiently explanatory, off my nut, threaten-
ing, pleading.

I would have slapped her face off, except it was photographic capital.

In the end all I could do was phone Papa Munsch and tell

him her conditions. I knew I didn't have a chance, but I had
to take it.

He gave me a really angry bawling out, said "no" several
times and hung up.

It didn't worry her. "We'll start shooting at ten o'clock
tomorrow," she said.

It was just like her, using that corny line from the movie
magazines.

About midnight Papa Munsch called me up.

"I don't know what insane asylum you're renting this girl
from," he said, "but I'll take her. Come round tomorrow
morning and I'll try to get it through your head just how I
want the pictures. And I'm glad I got you out of bed!"

After that it was a breeze. Even Mr. Fitch reconsidered and
after taking two days to tell me it was quite impossible, he
accepted the conditions too.

Of course you're all under the spell of the Girl, so you
can't understand how much self-sacrifice it represented on
Mr. Fitch's part when he agreed to forego supervising the
photography of my model in the Lovelybelt Imp or Vixen or
whatever it was we finally used.

Next morning she turned up on time according to her
schedule, and we went to work. I'll say one thing for her, she
never got tired and she never kicked at the way I fussed over
shots. I got along okay, except I still had that feeling of
something being shoved away gently. Maybe you've felt it
just a little, looking at her picture.

When we finished I found out there were still more rules. It
was about the middle of the afternoon. I started with her to
get a sandwich and coffee.

"Uh, uh," she said, "I'm going down alone. And look,
baby, if you ever try to follow me, if you ever so much as
stick your head out of that window when I go, you can hire
yourself another model."

You can imagine how all this crazy stuff strained my
temper—and my imagination. I remember opening the window after she was gone—I waited a few minutes first—and

standing there getting some fresh air and trying to figure out what could be behind it, whether she was hiding from the police, or was somebody's ruined daughter, or maybe had got the idea it was smart to be temperamental, or more likely Papa Munsch was right and she was partly nuts.

But I had my pictures to finish up.

Looking back it's amazing to think how fast her magic began to take hold of the city after that. Remembering what came after, I'm frightened of what's happening to the whole country—and maybe the world. Yesterday I read something in *Time* about the Girl's picture turning up on billboards in Egypt.

The rest of my story will help show you why I'm frightened in that big, general way. But I have a theory, too, that helps explain, though it's one of those things that's beyond that "certain point." It's about the Girl. I'll give it to you in a few words.

You know how modern advertising gets everybody's mind set in the same direction, wanting the same things, imagining the same things. And you know the psychologists aren't so skeptical of telepathy as they used to be.

Add up the two ideas. Suppose the identical desires of millions of people focused on one telepathic person. Say a girl. Shaped her in their image.

Imagine her knowing the hiddenmost hungers of millions of men. Imagine her seeing deeper into those hungers than the people that had them, seeing the hatred and the wish for death behind the lust. Imagine her shaping herself in that complete image, keeping herself as aloof as marble. Yet imagine the hunger she might feel in answer to their hunger.

But that's getting a long way from the facts of my story. And some of those facts are darn solid. Like money. We made money.

That was the funny thing I was going to tell you. I was afraid the Girl was going to hold me up. She really had me over a barrel, you know.

But she didn't ask for anything but the regular rates. Later on I insisted on pushing more money at her, a whole lot. But she always took it with that same contemptuous look, as if she were going to toss it down the first drain when she got outside.

Maybe she did.

At any rate, I had money. For the first time in months I had money enough to get drunk, buy new clothes, take taxicabs. I could make a play for any girl I wanted to. I only had to pick.

And so of course I had to go and pick. . . .

But first let me tell you about Papa Munsch.

Papa Munsch wasn't the first of the boys to try to meet my model but I think he was the first to really go soft on her. I could watch the change in his eyes as he looked at her pictures. They began to get sentimental, reverent. Mama Munsch had been dead for two years.

He was smart about the way he planned it. He got me to drop some information which told him when she came to work, and then one morning, he came pounding up the stairs a few minutes before.

"I've got to see her, Dave," he told me.

I argued with him, I kidded him, I explained he didn't know just how serious she was about her crazy ideas. I even pointed out he was cutting both our throats. I·even amazed myself by bawling him out.

He didn't take any of it in his usual way. He just kept repeating, "But Dave, I've got to see her."

The street door slammed.

"That's her," I said, lowering my voice. "You've got to get out."

He wouldn't, so I shoved him in the dark-room, "And keep quiet," I whispered. "I'll tell her I can't work today."

I knew he'd try to look at her and probably come bustling in, but there wasn't anything else I could do.

The footsteps came to the fourth floor. But she never showed at the door. I got uneasy.

"Get the bum out of here!" she yelled suddenly from beyond the door. Not very loud, but in her commonest voice.

"I'm going up to the next landing," she said. "And if that fat-bellied bum doesn't march straight down to the street, he'll never get another picture of me except spitting in his lousy beer."

Papa Munsch came out of the dark-room. He was white. He didn't look at me as he went out. He never looked at her pictures in front of me again.

That was Papa Munsch. Now it's me I'm telling about. I talked around the subject with her, I hinted, eventually I made my pass.

She lifted my hand off her as if it were a damp rag.

"No, baby," she said. "This is working time."

"But afterwards . . ." I pressed.

"The rules still hold." And I got what I think was the fifth smile.

It's hard to believe, but she never budged an inch from that crazy line. I mustn't make a pass at her in the office, because our work was very important and she loved it and there mustn't be any distractions. And I couldn't see her anywhere else, because if I tried to, I'd never snap another picture of her—and all this with more money coming in all the time and me never so stupid as to think my photography had anything to do with it.

Of course I wouldn't have been human if I hadn't made more passes. But they always got the wet-rag treatment and there weren't any more smiles.

I changed. I went sort of crazy and light-headed—only sometimes I felt my head was gong to burst. And I started to talk to her all the time. About myself.

It was like being in a constant delirium that never interfered with business. I didn't pay any attention to the dizzy feeling. It seemed natural.

I'd walk around and for a moment the reflector would look like a sheet of white-hot steel, or the shadows would seem like armies of moths, or the camera would be a big black coal car. But the next instant they'd come all right again.

I think sometimes I was scared to death of her. She'd seem the strangest, most horrible person in the world. But other times. . . .

And I talked. It didn't matter what I was doing—lighting her, posing her, fussing with props, snapping my pictures—or where she was—on the platform, behind the screen, relaxing with a magazine—I kept up a steady gab.

I told her everything I knew about myself. I told her about my first girl. I told her about my brother Bob's bicycle. I told her about running away on a freight, and the licking Pa gave me when I came home. I told her about shipping to South America and the blue sky at night. I told her about Betty. I told her about my mother dying of cancer. I told her about being beaten up in a fight in an alley behind a bar. I told her about Mildred. I told her about the first picture I ever sold. I told her how Chicago looked from a sailboat. I told her about the longest drunk I was ever on. I told her about Marsh-Mason. I told her about Gwen. I told her about how I met Papa Munsch. I told her about hunting her. I told her about how I felt now.

She never paid the slightest attention to what I said. I couldn't even tell if she heard me.

It was when we were getting our first nibble from national advertisers that I decided to follow her when she went home.

Wait, I can place it better than that. Something you'll remember from the out-of-town papers—those maybe murders I mentioned. I think there were six.

I say "maybe" because the police could never be sure they weren't heart attacks. But there's bound to be suspicion when attacks happen to people whose hearts have been okay, and always at night when they're alone and away from home and there's a question of what they were doing.

The six deaths created one of those "mystery poisoner" scares. And afterwards there was a feeling that they hadn't really stopped, but were being continued in a less suspicious way.

That's one of the things that scares me now.

But at that time my only feeling was relief that I'd decided to follow her.

I made her work until dark one afternoon. I didn't need any excuses, we were snowed under with orders. I waited until the street door slammed, then I ran down. I was wearing rubber-soled shoes. I'd slipped on a dark coat she'd never seen me in, and a dark hat.

I stood in the doorway until I spotted her. She was walking by Ardleigh Park toward the heart of town. It was one of those warm fall nights. I followed her on the other side of the street. My idea for tonight was just to find out where she lived. That would give me a hold on her.

She stopped in front of a display window of Everley's department store, standing back from the flow. She stood there looking in.

I remembered we'd done a big photograph of her for Everley's, to make a flat model for a lingerie display. That was what she was looking at.

At the time it seemed all right to me that she should adore herself, if that was what she was doing.

When people passed she'd turn away a little or drift back further into the shadows.

Then a man came by alone. I couldn't see his face very well, but he looked middle-aged. He stopped and stood looking in the window.

She came out of the shadows and stepped up beside him.

How would you boys feel if you were looking at a poster of the Girl and suddenly she was there beside you, her arm linked with yours?

This fellow's reaction showed plain as day. A crazy dream had come to life for him.

They talked for a moment. Then he waved a taxi to the curb. They got in and drove off.

I got drunk that night. It was almost as if she'd known I

was following her and had picked that way to hurt me. Maybe she had. Maybe this was the finish.

But the next morning she turned up at the usual time and I was back in the delirium, only now with some new angles added.

That night when I followed her she picked a spot under a street lamp, opposite one of the Munsch Girl billboards.

Now it frightens me to think of her lurking that way.

After about twenty minutes a convertible slowed down going past her, backed up, swung into the curb.

I was closer this time. I got a good look at the fellow's face. He was a little younger, about my age.

Next morning the same face looked up at me from the front page of the paper. The convertible had been found parked on a side street. He had been in it. As in the other maybe-murders, the cause of death was uncertain.

All kinds of thoughts were spinning in my head that day, but there were only two things I knew for sure. That I'd got the first real offer from a national advertiser, and that I was going to take the Girl's arm and walk down the stairs with her when we quit work.

She didn't seem surprised. "You know what you're doing?" she said.

"I know."

She smiled. "I was wondering when you'd get around to it."

I began to feel good. I was kissing everything good-bye, but I had my arm around hers.

It was another of those warm fall evenings. We cut across into Ardleigh Park. It was dark there, but all around the sky was a sallow pink from the advertising signs.

We walked for a long time in the park. She didn't say anything and she didn't look at me, but I could see her lips twitching and after a while her hand tightened on my arm.

We stopped. We'd been walking across the grass. She dropped down and pulled me after her. She put her hands on my shoulders. I was looking down at her face. It was the faintest sallow pink from the glow in the sky. The hungry eyes were dark smudges.

I was fumbling with her blouse. She took my hand away, not like she had in the studio. "I don't want that," she said.

First I'll tell you what I did afterwards. Then I'll tell you why I did it. Then I'll tell you what she said.

What I did was run away. I don't remember all of that because I was dizzy, and the pink sky was swinging against the dark trees. But after a while I staggered into the lights of the street. The next day I closed up the studio. The telephone was ringing when I locked the door and there were unopened letters on the floor. I never saw the Girl again in the flesh, if that's the right word.

I did it because I didn't want to die. I didn't want the life drawn out of me. There are vampires and vampires, and the ones that suck blood aren't the worst. If it hadn't been for the warning of those dizzy flashes, and Papa Munsch and the face in the morning paper, I'd have gone the way the others did. But I realized what I was up against while there was still time to tear myself away. I realized that wherever she came from, whatever shaped her, she's the quintessence of the horror behind the bright billboard. She's the smile that tricks you into throwing away your money and your life. She's the eyes that lead you on and on, and then show you death. She's the creature you give everything for and never really get. She's the being that takes everything you've got and gives nothing in return. When you yearn toward her face on the billboards, remember that. She's the lure. She's the bait. She's the Girl.

And this is what she said, "I want you. I want your high spots. I want everything that's made you happy and everything that's hurt you bad. I want your first girl. I want that shiny bicycle. I want that licking. I want that pinhole camera. I want Betty's legs. I want the blue sky filled with stars. I want your mother's death. I want your blood on the cobble-

stones. I want Mildred's mouth. I want the first picture you
sold. I want the lights of Chicago. I want the gin. I want
Gwen's hands. I want your wanting me. I want your life.
Feed me, baby, feed me.''

JULIAN HAWTHORNE

Ken's Mystery

One cool October evening—it was the last day of the month,
and unusually cool for the time of year—I made up my mind
to go and spend an hour or two with my friend Keningale.
Keningale was an artist (as well as a musical amateur and
poet), and had very delightful studio built onto his house, in
which he was wont to sit of an evening. The studio had a
cavernous fireplace, designed in imitation of the old-fashioned
fireplaces of Elizabethan manor-houses, and in it, when the
temperature out-doors warranted, he would build up a cheer-
ful fire of dry logs. It would suit me particularly well, I
thought, to go and have a quiet pipe and chat in front of that
fire with my friend.

I had not had such a chat for a very long time—not, in
fact, since Keningale (or Ken, as his friends called him) had
returned from his visit to Europe the year before. He went
abroad, as he affirmed at the time, "for purposes of study,"
whereat we all smiled, for Ken, as far as we knew him, was
more likely to do anything else than to study. He was a young
fellow of buoyant temperament, lively and social in his habits, of a brilliant and versatile mind, and possessing an income of twelve or fifteen thousand dollars a year; he could
sing, play, scribble, and paint very cleverly, and some of his

heads and figure-pieces were really well done, considering that he never had any regular training in art; but he was not a worker. Personally he was fine-looking, of good height and figure, active, healthy, and with a remarkably fine brow, and clear, full-gazing eye. Nobody was surprised at his going to Europe, nobody expected him to do anything there except amuse himself, and few anticipated that he would be soon again seen in New York. He was one of the sort that find Europe agree with them. Off he went, therefore; and in the course of a few months the rumor reached us that he was engaged to a handsome and wealthy New York girl whom he had met in London. This was nearly all we did hear of him until, not very long afterward, he turned up again on Fifth Avenue, to every one's astonishment; made no satisfactory answer to those who wanted to know how he happened to tire so soon of the Old World; while, as to the reported engagement, he cut short all allusion to that in so peremptory a manner as to show that it was not a permissible topic of conversation with him. It was surmised that the lady had jilted him; but, on the other hand, she herself returned home not a great while after, and, though she had plenty of opportunities she has never married to this day.

Be the rights of that matter what they may, it was soon remarked that Ken was no longer the careless and merry fellow he used to be; on the contrary, he appeared grave, moody, averse from general society, and habitually taciturn and undemonstrative even in the company of his most intimate friends. Evidently something had happened to him or he had done something. What? Had he committed a murder? or joined the Nihilists? or was his unsuccessful love affair at the bottom of it? Some declared that the cloud was only temporary, and would soon pass away. Nevertheless, up to the period of which I am writing, it had not passed away, but had rather gathered additional gloom, and threatened to become permanent.

Meanwhile I had met him twice or thrice at the club, at the opera, or in the street, but had as yet had no opportunity of regularly renewing my acquaintance with him. We had been on a footing of more than common intimacy in the old days, and I was not disposed to think that he would refuse to renew the former relations now. But what I had heard and myself seen of his changed condition imparted a stimulating tinge of suspense or curiosity to the pleasure with which I looked forward to the prospects of this evening. His house stood at a distance of two or three miles beyond the general range of habitations in New York at this time, and as I walked briskly along in the clear twilight air I had leisure to go over in my mind all that I had known of Ken and had divined of his character. After all, had there not always been something in his nature—deep down, and held in abeyance by the activity of his animal spirits—but something strange and separate, and capable of developing under suitable conditions into— into what? As I asked myself this question I arrived at his door; and it was with a feeling of relief that I felt the next moment the cordial grasp of his hand, and his voice bidding me welcome in a tone that indicated unaffected gratification at my presence. He drew me at once into the studio, relieved me of my hat and cane, and then put his hand on my shoulder.

"I am glad to see you," he repeated, with singular earnestness—"glad to see you and to feel you; and tonight of all nights in the year."

"Why tonight especially?"

"Oh, never mind. It's just as well, too, you didn't let me know beforehand you were coming; the unreadiness is all, to paraphrase the poet. Now, with you to help me, I can drink a glass of whisky and water and take a bit draw of the pipe. This would have been a grim night for me if I'd been left to myself."

"In such a lap of luxury as this, too!" said I, looking round at the glowing fireplace, the low, luxurious chairs, and all the rich and sumptuous fittings of the room. "I should have thought a condemned murderer might make himself comfortable here.''

"Perhaps; but that's not exactly my category at present. But have you forgotten what night this is? This November-eve, when, as tradition asserts, the dead arise and walk about, and fairies, goblins, and spiritual beings of all kinds have more freedom and power than on any other day of the year. One can see you've never been in Ireland.''

"I wasn't aware till now that you had been there, either.''

"Yes, I have been in Ireland. Yes—'' He paused, sighed, and fell into a reverie, from which, however, he soon roused himself by an effort, and went to a cabinet in a corner of the room for the liquor and tobacco. While he was thus employed I sauntered about the studio, taking note of the various beauties, grotesquenesses, and curiosities that it contained. Many things were there to repay study and arouse admiration; for Ken was a good collector, having excellent taste as well as means to back it. But, upon the whole, nothing interested me more than some studies of a female head, roughly done in oils, and, judging from the sequestered positions in which I found them, not intended by the artist for exhibition or criticism. There were three or four of these studies, all of the same face, but in different poses and costumes. In one the head was enveloped in a dark hood, overshadowing and partly concealing the features; in another she seemed to be peering duskily through a latticed casement, lit by a faint moonlight; a third showed her splendidly attired in evening costume, with jewels in her hair and ears, and sparkling on her snowy bosom. The expressions were as various as the poses; now it was demure penetration, now a subtle inviting glance, now burning passion, and again a look of elfish and elusive mockery. In whatever phase, the countenance possessed a singular and poignant fascination, not of beauty merely, though that was very striking, but of character and quality likewise.

"Did you find this model abroad?'' I inquired at length. "She has evidently inspired you, and I don't wonder at it.''

Ken, who had been mixing the punch, and had not noticed my movements, now looked up, and said: "I didn't mean those to be seen. They don't satisfy me, and I am going to destroy them; but I couldn't rest till I'd made some attempts to reproduce— What was it you asked? Abroad? Yes—or no. They were all painted here within the last six weeks."

"Whether they satisfy you or not, they are by far the best things of yours I have ever seen."

"Well, let them alone, and tell me what you think of this beverage. To my thinking, it goes to the right spot. It owes its existence to your coming here. I can't drink alone, and those portraits are not company, though, for aught I know, she might have come out of the canvas tonight and sat down in that chair." Then, seeing my inquiring look, he added, with a hasty laugh, "It's November-eve, you know, when anything may happen, provided it's strange enough. Well, here's to ourselves."

We each swallowed a deep draught of the smoking and aromatic liquor, and set down our glasses with approval. The punch was excellent. Ken now opened a box of cigars, and we seated ourselves before the fireplace.

"All we need now," I remarked, after a short silence, "is a little music. By-the-by, Ken, have you still got the banjo I gave you before you went abroad?"

He paused so long before replying that I supposed he had not heard my question. "I have got it," he said, at length, "but it will never make any more music."

"Got broken, eh? Can't it be mended? It was a fine instrument."

"It's not broken, but it's past mending. You shall see for yourself."

He arose as he spoke, and going to another part of the studio, opened a black oak coffer, and took out of it a long object wrapped up in a piece of faded yellow silk. He handed it to me, and when I had unwrapped it, there appeared a thing that might once have been a banjo, but had little resemblance to one now. It bore every sign of extreme age. The wood of the handle was honey-combed with the gnawing of worms, and dusty with dry-rot. The parchment head was green with mold, and hung in shriveled tatters. The hoop, which was of solid silver, was so blackened and tarnished that it looked like dilapidated iron. The strings were gone, and most of the tuning-screws had dropped out of their decayed sockets. Altogether it had the appearance of having been made before the Flood, and been forgotten in the forecastle of Noah's Ark ever since.

"It is a curious relic, certainly," I said. "Where did you come across it? I had no idea that the banjo was invented so long ago as this. It certainly can't be less than two hundred years old, and may be much older than that."

Ken smiled gloomily. "You are quite right," he said; "it is at least two hundred years old, and yet it is the very same banjo that you gave me a year ago."

"Hardly," I returned, smiling in my turn, "since that was made to my order with a view to presenting it to you."

"I know that; but the two hundred years have passed since then. Yes; it is absurd and impossible, I know, but nothing is truer. That banjo, which was made last year, existed in the sixteenth century, and has been rotting ever since. Stay. Give it to me a moment, and I'll convince you. You recollect that your name and mine, with the date, were engraved on the silver hoop?"

"Yes; and there was a private mark of my own there, also."

"Very well," said Ken, who had been rubbing a place on the hoop with a corner of the yellow silk wrapper; "look at that."

I took the decrepit instrument from him, and examined the spot which he had rubbed. It was incredible, sure enough; but there were the names and the date precisely as I had caused them to be engraved; and there, moreover, was my own private mark, which I had idly made with an old etching point not more than eighteen months before. After convincing myself that there was no mistake, I laid the banjo across my knees, and stared at my friend in bewilderment. He sat smoking with a kind of grim composure, his eyes fixed upon the blazing logs.

"I'm mystified, I confess," said I. "Come; what is the joke? What method have you discovered of producing the decay of centuries on this unfortunate banjo in a few months? And why did you do it? I have heard of an elixir to counteract the effects of time, but your recipe seems to work the other way—to make time rush forward at two hundred times his usual rate, in one place, while he jogs on at his usual gait elsewhere. Unfold your mystery, magician. Seriously, Ken, how on earth did the thing happen?"

"I know no more about it than you do," was his reply. "Either you and I and all the rest of the living world are insane, or else there has been wrought a miracle strange as any in tradition. How can I explain it? It is a common saying—a common experience, if you will—that we may, on certain trying or tremendous occasions, live years in one moment. But that's a mental experience, not a physical one, and one that applies, at all events, only to human beings, not to senseless things of wood and metal. You imagine the thing is some trick or jugglery. If it be, I don't know the secret of it. There's no chemical appliance that I ever heard of that will get a piece of solid wood into that condition in a few months, or a few years. And it wasn't done in a few years, or a few months either. A year ago to-day at this very hour that banjo was as sound as when it left the maker's hands, and twenty-four hours afterward—I'm telling you the simple truth—it was as you see it now."

The gravity and earnestness with which Ken made this astounding statement were evidently not assumed. He believed every word that he uttered. I knew not what to think. Of course my friend might be insane, though he betrayed none of the ordinary symptoms of mania; but, however that might be, there was the banjo, a witness whose silent testimony there was no gainsaying. The more I meditated on the matter the more inconceivable did it appear. Two hundred years—twenty-four hours; these were the terms of the proposed equation. Ken and the banjo both affirmed that the equation had been made; all worldly knowledge and experience affirmed it to be impossible. What was the explanation? What is time? What is life? I felt myself beginning to doubt the reality of all things. And so this was the mystery which my friend had been brooding over since his return from abroad? No wonder it had changed him. More to be wondered at was it that it had not changed him more.

"Can you tell me the whole story?" I demanded at length.

Ken quaffed another draught from his glass of whisky and water and rubbed his hand through his thick brown beard. "I have never spoken to any one of it heretofore," he said, "and I have never meant to speak of it. But I'll try and give you some idea of what it was. You know me better than any one else; you'll understand the thing as far as it can ever be understood, and perhaps I may be relieved of some of the oppression it has caused me. For it is rather a ghastly memory to grapple with alone, I can tell you."

Hereupon, without further preface, Ken related the following tale. He was, I may observe in passing, a naturally fine narrator. There were deep, lingering tones in his voice, and he could strikingly enhance the comic or pathetic effect of a sentence by dwelling here and there upon some syllable. His features were equally susceptible of humorous and of solemn expressions, and his eyes were in form and hue wonderfully adapted to showing great varities of emotion. Their mournful aspect was extremely earnest and affecting; and when Ken was giving utterance to some mysterious passage of the tale they had a doubtful, melancholy, exploring look which appealed irresistibly to the imagination. But the interest of his story was too pressing to allow of noticing these incidental embellishments at the time, though they doubtless had their influence upon me all the same.

"I left New York on an Inman Line steamer, you remember," began Ken, "and landed at Havre. I went the usual round of sight-seeing on the Continent, and got round to

London in July, at the height of the season. I had good introductions, and met any number of agreeable and famous people. Among others was a young lady, a countrywoman of my own—you know whom I mean—who interested me very much and before her family left London she and I were engaged. We parted there for the time, because she had the Continental trip still to make, while I wanted to take the opportunity to visit the north of England and Ireland. I landed at Dublin about the 1st of October, and, zigzagging about the country, I found myself in County Cork about two weeks later.

"There is in that region some of the most lovely scenery that human eyes ever rested on, and it seems to be less known to tourists than many places of infinitely less picturesque value. A lonely region too: during my rambles I met not a single stranger like myself, and few enough natives. It seems incredible that so beautiful a country should be so deserted. After walking a dozen Irish miles you come across a group of two or three one-roomed cottages, and, like as not, one or more of these will have the roof off and the walls in ruins. The few peasants whom one sees, however, are affable and hospitable, especially when they hear you are from that terrestrial heaven whither most of their friends and relatives have gone before them. They seem simple and primitive enough at first sight, and yet they are as strange and incomprehensible a race as any in the world. They are as superstitious, as credulous of marvels, fairies, magicians, and omens, as the men whom St. Patrick preached to, and at the same time they are shrewd, skeptical, sensible, and bottomless liars. Upon the whole, I met with no nation on my travels whose company I enjoyed so much, or who inspired me with so much kindliness, curiosity, and repugnance.

"At length I got to a place on the sea-coast, which I will not further specify than to say that it is not many miles from Ballymacheen, on the south shore. I have seen Venice and Naples, I have driven along the Cornice Road, I have spent a month at our own Mount Desert, and I say that all of them together are not so beautiful as this glowing, deep-hued, soft-gleaming, silvery-lighted, ancient harbor and town, with the tall hills crowding round it and the black cliffs and headlands planting their iron feet in the blue, transparent sea. It is a very old place, and has had a history which it has outlived ages since. It may once have had two or three thousand inhabitants; it has scarce five or six hundred today. Half the houses are in ruins or have disappeared; many of the remainder are standing empty. All the people are poor, most of them abjectly so; they saunter about with bare feet and uncovered heads, the women in quaint black or dark-blue cloaks, the men in such anomalous attire as only an Irishman knows how to get together, the children half naked. The only comfortable-looking people are the monks and the priests, and the soldiers in the fort. For there is a fort there, constructed on the huge ruins of one which may have done duty in the rein of Edward the Black Prince, or earlier, in whose mossy embrasures are mounted a couple of cannon, which occasionally sent a practice-shot or two at the cliff on the other side of the harbor. The garrison consists of a dozen men and three or four officers and non-commissioned officers. I suppose they are relieved occasionally, but those I saw seemed to have become component parts of their surroundings.

"I put up at a wonderful little old inn, the only one in the place, and took my meals in a dining-saloon fifteen feet by nine, with a portrait of George I (a print varnished to preserve it) hanging over the mantel-piece. On the second evening after dinner a young gentleman came in—the dining-saloon being public property of course—and ordered some bread and cheese and a bottle of Dublin stout. We presently fell into talk; he turned out to be an officer from the fort, Lieutenant O'Connor, and a fine young specimen of the Irish soldier he was. After telling me all he knew about the town, the surrounding country, his friends, and himself, he intimated a readiness to sympathize with whatever tale I might choose to pour into his ear; and I had pleasure in trying to rival his own outspokenness. We became excellent friends; we had up a half-pint of Kinahan's whisky, and the lieutenant expressed himself in terms of high praise of my countrymen, my country, and my own particular cigars. When it became time for him to depart I accompanied him—for there was a splendid moon abroad—and bade him farewell at the fort entrance, having promised to come over the next day and make the acquaintance of the other fellows. 'And mind your eye, now, going back, my dear boy,' he called out, as I turned my face homeward. 'Faith, 'tis a spooky place, that graveyard, and you'll as likely meet the black woman there as anywhere else!'

"The graveyard was a forlorn and barren spot on the hill-side, just the hither side of the fort; thirty or forty rough head-stones, few of which retained any semblance of the perpendicular, while many were so shattered and decayed as to seem nothing more than irregular natural projections from the ground. Who the black woman might be I knew not, and did not stay to inquire. I had never been subject to ghostly apprehensions, and as a matter of fact, though the path I had to follow was in places very bad going, not to mention a haphazard scramble over a ruined bridge that covered a deep-lying brook, I reached my inn without any adventure whatever.

"The next day I kept my appointment at the fort, and found no reason to regret it; and my friendly sentiments were abundantly reciprocated, thanks more especially, perhaps, to the success of my banjo, which I carried with me, and which was as novel as it was popular with those who listened to it. The chief personages in the social circle besides my friend the lieutenant were Major Molloy, who was in command, a racy and juicy old campaigner, with a face like a sunset, and the surgeon, Dr. Dudeen, a long, dry, humorous genius, with a wealth of anecdotical and traditional lore at his command that I have never seen surpassed. We had a jolly time of it, and it was the precursor of many more like it. The remains of October slipped away rapidly, and I was obliged to remember that I was a traveler in Europe, and not a resident in Ireland. The major, the surgeon, and the lieutenant all protested cordially against my proposed departure, but, as there was no help for it, they arranged a farewell dinner to take place in the fort on All-halloween.

"I wish you could have been at that dinner with me! It was the essence of Irish good-fellowship. Dr. Dudeen was in great force; the major was better than the best of Lever's novels; the lieutenant was overflowing with hearty good-humor, merry chaff, and sentimental rhapsodies anent this or the other pretty girl of the neighborhood. For my part I made the banjo ring as it had never rung before, and the others joined in the chorus with a mellow strength of lungs such as you don't often hear outside of Ireland. Among the stories that Dr. Dudeen regaled us with was one about the Kern of Querin and his wife, Ethelind Fionguala—which being interpreted signifies 'the white-shouldered.' The lady, it appears, was originally betrothed to one O'Connor (here the lieutenant smacked his lips), but was stolen away on the wedding night by a party of vampires, who, it would seem, were at that period a prominent feature among the troubles of Ireland. But as they were bearing her along—she being unconscious—to that supper where she was not to eat but to be eaten, the young Kern of Querin, who happened to be out duck-shooting, met the party, and emptied his gun at it. The vampires fled, the Kern carried the fair lady, still in a state of insensibility, to his house. 'And by the same token, Mr. Keningale,' observed the doctor, knocking the ashes out of his pipe, 'ye're after passing that very house on your way here. The one with the dark archway underneath it, and the big mullioned window at the corner, ye recollect, hanging over the street as I might say—'

" 'Go 'long wid the house, Dr. Dudeen, dear,' interrupted the lieutenant; 'sure can't you see we're all dying to know what happened to sweet Miss Fionguala, God be good to her, when I was after getting her safe upstairs—'

" 'Faith, then, I can tell ye that myself, Mr. O'Connor,' exclaimed the major, imparting a rotary motion to the remnants of whisky in his tumbler. ' 'Tis a question to be solved on general principles, as Colonel O'Halloran said that time he was asked what he'd do if he'd been the Dook o' Wellington, and the Prussians hadn't come up in the nick o' time at Waterloo. 'Faith,' says the colonel, 'I'll tell ye—'

" 'Arrah, then, major, why would ye be interruptin' the doctor, and Mr. Keningale there lettin' his glass stay empty till he hears— The Lord save us! the bottle's empty!'

"In the excitement consequent upon this discovery, the thread of the doctor's story was lost; and before it could be recovered the evening had advanced so far that I felt obliged to withdraw. It took some time to make my proposition heard and comprehended; and a still longer time to put it in execution; so that it was fully midnight before I found myself standing in the cool pure air outside the fort, with the farewells of my boon companions ringing in my ears.

"Considering that it had been rather a wet evening indoors, I was in a remarkably good state of preservation, and I therefore ascribed it rather to the roughness of the road than to the smoothness of the liquor, when, after advancing a few rods, I stumbled and fell. As I picked myself up I fancied I had heard a laugh, and supposed that the lieutenant, who had accompanied me to the gate, was making merry over my mishap; but on looking round I saw that the gate was closed and no one was visible. The laugh, moreover, had seemed to be close at hand, and to be even pitched in a key that was rather feminine than masculine. Of course I must have been deceived; nobody was near me: my imagination had played me a trick, or else there was more truth than poetry in the tradition that Halloween is the carnival-time of disembodied spirits. It did not occur to me at the time that a stumble is held by the superstitious Irish to be an evil omen, and had I remembered it it would only have been to laugh at it. At all events, I was physically none the worse for my fall, and I resumed my way immediately.

"But the path was singularly difficult to find, or rather the path I was following did not seem to be the right one. I did not recognize it; I could have sworn (except I knew the contrary) that I had never seen it before. The moon had risen, though her light was yet obscured by clouds, but neither my immediate surroundings nor the general aspect of the region appeared familiar. Dark, silent hillsides mounted up on either hand, and the road, for the most part, plunged downward, as if to conduct me into the bowels of the earth. The place was alive with strange echoes, so that at times I seemed to be walking through the midst of muttering voices and mysterious whispers, and a wild, faint sound of laughter seemed ever and anon to reverberate among the passes of the hills. Currents of colder air sighing up through narrow defiles and dark crevices touched my face as with airy fingers. A certain feeling of anxiety and insecurity began to take possession of me, though there was no definable cause for it, unless that I might be belated in getting home. With the perverse instinct of those who are lost I hastened my steps, but was impelled now and then to glance back over my shoulder, with a sensation of being pursued. But no living creature was in sight. The moon, however, had now risen higher, and the clouds that were drifting slowly across the sky flung into the naked valley dusky shadows, which occasionally assumed shapes that looked like the vague semblance of gigantic human forms.

"How long I had been hurrying onward I know not, when, with a kind of suddenness, I found myself approaching a graveyard. It was situated on the spur of a hill, and there was no fence around it, nor anything to protect it from the incursions of passers-by. There was something in the general appearance of this spot that made me half fancy I had seen it before; and I should have taken it to be the same that I had often noticed on my way to the fort, but that the latter was only a few hundred yards distant therefrom, whereas I must have traversed several miles at least. As I drew near, moreover, I observed that the head-stones did not appear so ancient and decayed as those of the other. But what chiefly attracted my attention was the figure that was leaning or half sitting upon one of the largest of the upright slabs near the road. It was a female figure draped in black, and a closer inspection—for I was soon within a few yards of her—showed that she wore the calla, or long hooded cloak, the most common as well as the most ancient garment of Irish women, and doubtless of Spanish origin.

"I was a trifle startled by this apparition, so unexpected as it was, and so strange did it seem that any human creature should be at that hour of the night in so desolate and sinister a place. Involuntarily I paused as I came opposite her, and gazed at her intently. But the moonlight fell behind her, and the deep hood of her cloak so completely shadowed her face that I was unable to discern anything but the sparkle of a pair of eyes, which appeared to be returning my gaze with much vivacity.

" 'You seem to be at home here,' I said, at length. 'Can you tell me where I am?'

"Hereupon the mysterious personage broke into a light laugh, which, though in itself musical and agreeable, was of a timber and intonation that caused my heart to beat faster than my late pedestrian exertions warranted; for it was the identical laugh (or so my imagination persuaded me) that had echoed in my ears as I arose from my tumble an hour or two ago. For the rest, it was the laugh of a young woman, and presumably of a pretty one; and yet it had a wild, airy, mocking quality, that seemed hardly human at all, or not, at any rate, characteristic of a being of affections and limitations like unto ours. But this impression of mine was fostered, no doubt, by the unusual and uncanny circumstances of the occasion.

" 'Sure, sir,' said she, 'you're at the grave of Ethelind Fionguala.'

"As she spoke she rose to her feet, and pointed to the inscription on the stone. I bent forward, and was able, without much difficulty, to decipher the name, and a date which indicated that the occupant of the grave must have entered the disembodied state between two and three centuries ago.

" 'And who are you?' was my next question.

" 'I'm called Elsie,' she replied. 'But where would your honor be going November-eve?'

"I mentioned my destination, and asked her whether she could direct me thither.

" 'Indeed, then, 'tis there I'm going myself,' Elsie replied; 'and if your honor'll follow me, and play me a tune on the pretty instrument, 'tisn't long we'll be on the road.'

"She pointed to the banjo which I carried wrapped up under my arm. How she knew that it was a musical instrument I could not imagine; possibly, I thought, she may have seen me playing on it as I strolled about the environs of the town. Be that as it may, I offered no opposition to the bargain, and further intimated that I would reward her more substantially on our arrival. At that she laughed again, and made a peculiar gesture with her hand above her head. I uncovered my banjo, swept my fingers across the strings, and struck into a fantastic dance-measure, to the music of which we proceeded along the path. Elsie slightly in advance, her feet keeping time to the airy measure. In fact, she trod so lightly, with an elastic, undulating movement, that with a little more it seemed as if she might float onward like a spirit. The extreme whiteness of her feet attracted my eye, and I was surprised to find that instead of being bare, as I had supposed, these were encased in white satin slippers quaintly embroidered with gold thread.

" 'Elsie, said I, lengthening my steps so as to come up with her, 'where do you live, and what do you do for a living?'

" 'Sure, I live by myself,' she answered; 'and if you'd be after knowing how, you must come and see for yourself.'

" 'Are you in the habit of walking over the hills at night in shoes like that?'

" 'And why would I not?' she asked, in her turn. 'And where did your honor get the pretty gold ring on your finger?'

"The ring, which was of no great intrinsic value, had struck my eye in an old curiosity-shop in Cork. It was an antique of very old-fashioned design, and might have belonged (as the vender assured me was the case) to one of the early kings or queens of Ireland.

" 'Do you like it?' said I.

" 'Will your honor be after making a present of it to Elsie?' she returned, with an insinuating tone and turn of the head.

" 'Maybe I will, Elsie, on one condition. I am an artist; I make pictures of people. If you will promise to come to my studio and let me paint your portrait, I'll give you the ring, and some money besides.'

" 'And will you give me the ring now?' said Elsie.

" 'Yes, if you'll promise.'

" 'And will you play the music to me?' she continued.

" 'As much as you like.'

" 'But maybe I'll not be handsome enough for ye,' said she, with a glance of her eyes beneath the dark hood.

" 'I'll take the risk of that,' I answered, laughing, 'though, all the same, I don't mind taking a peep beforehand to remember you by.' So saying, I put forth a hand to draw back the concealing hood. But Elsie eluded me, I scarce know how, and laughed a third time, with the same airy, mocking cadence.

" 'Give me the ring first, and then you shall see me,' she said, coaxingly.

" 'Stretch out your hand, then,' returned I, removing the ring from my finger. 'When we are better acquainted, Elsie, you won't be so suspicious.'

"She held out a slender, delicate hand, on the forefinger of which I slipped the ring. As I did so, the folds of her cloak fell a little apart, affording me a glimpse of a white shoulder and of a dress that seemed in that deceptive semi-darkness to be wrought of rich and costly material; and I caught, too, or so I fancied, the frosty sparkle of precious stones.

" 'Arrah, mind where ye tread!' said Elsie, in a sudden, sharp tone.

"I looked round, and became aware for the first time that we were standing near the middle of a ruined bridge which spanned a rapid stream that flowed at a considerable depth below. The parapet of the bridge on one side was broken down, and I must have been, in fact, in imminent danger of stepping over into empty air. I made my way cautiously across the decaying structure; but, when I turned to assist Elsie, she was nowhere to be seen.

"What had become of the girl? I called, but no answer came. I gazed about on every side, but no trace of her was visible. Unless she had plunged into the narrow abyss at my feet, there was no place where she could have concealed herself—none at least that I could discover. She had vanished, nevertheless; and since her disappearance must have been premeditated, I finally came to the conclusion that it was useless to attempt to find her. She would present herself again in her own good time, or not at all. She had given me the slip very cleverly, and I must make the best of it. The adventure was perhaps worth the ring.

"On resuming my way, I was not a little relieved to find that I once more knew where I was. The bridge that I had just crossed was none other than the one I mentioned some time back; I was within a mile of the town, and my way lay clear before me. The moon, moreover, had now quite dispersed the clouds, and shone down with exquisite brilliance. Whatever her other failings, Elsie had been a trustworthy guide; she had brought me out of the depth of elf-land into the material world again. It had been a singular adventure, certainly, and I mused over it with a sense of mysterious pleasure as I sauntered along, humming snatches of airs, and accompanying myself on the strings. Hark! what light step was that behind me? It sounded like Elsie's; but no, Elsie was not there. The same impression or hallucination, however, recurred several times before I reached the outskirts of the town—the tread of an airy foot behind or beside my own. The fancy did not make me nervous; on the contrary, I was pleased with the notion of being thus haunted, and gave myself up to a romantic and genial vein of reverie.

"After passing one or two roofless and moss-grown cottages, I entered the narrow and rambling street which leads through the town. This street a short distance down widens a little, as if to afford the wayfarer space to observe a remarkable old house that stands on the northern side. The house was built of stone, and in a noble style of architecture; it reminded me somewhat of certain palaces of the old Italian nobility that I had seen on the Continent, and it may very probably have been built by one of the Italian or Spanish immigrants of the sixteenth or seventeenth century. The molding of the projecting windows and arched doorway was richly carved, and upon the front of the building was an escutcheon wrought in high relief, though I could not make out the purport of the device. The moonlight falling upon this picturesque pile enhanced all its beauties, and at the same time made it seem like a vision that might dissolve away when the light ceased to shine. I must often have seen the house before, and yet I retained no definite recollection of it; I had never until now examined it with my eyes open, so to speak. Leaning against the wall on the opposite side of the street, I contemplated it for a long while at my leisure. The window at the corner was really a very fine and massive affair. It projected over the pavement below, throwing a heavy shadow aslant; the frames of the diamond-paned lattices were heavily mullioned. How often in past ages had that lattice been pushed open by some fair hand, revealing the charming countenances of his high-born mistress! Those were brave days. They had passed away long since. The great house had stood empty for who could tell how many years; only bats and vermin were its inhabitants. Where now were those who had built it? and who were they? Probably the very name of them was forgotten.

"As I continued to stare upward, however, a conjecture presented itself to my mind which rapidly ripened into a conviction. Was not this the house that Dr. Dudeen had described that very evening as having been formerly the abode of the Kern of Querin and his mysterious bride? There was the projecting window, the arched doorway. Yes, beyond a doubt this was the very house. I emitted a low exclamation of renewed interest and pleasure, and my speculations took a still more imaginative, but also a more definite turn.

"What had been the fate of that lovely lady after the Kern had brought her home insensible in his arms? Did she recover, and were they married and made happy ever after; or had the sequel been a tragic one? I remembered to have read that the victims of vampires generally became vampires themselves. Then my thoughts went back to that grave on the hill-side. Surely that was unconsecrated ground. Why had they buried her there? Ethelind of the white shoulder! Ah! why not not I lived in those days; or why might not some magic cause them to live again for me? Then would I seek this street at midnight, and standing here beneath her window, I would lightly touch the strings of my bandore until the casement opened cautiously and she looked down. A sweet vision indeed! And who prevented my realizing it? Only a matter of a couple of centuries or so. And was time, then, at which poets and philosophers sneer, so rigid and real a matter that a little faith and imagination might not overcome it? At all events, I had my banjo, the bandore's legitimate and lineal descendant, and the memory of Fionguala should have the love-ditty.

"Hereupon, having retuned the instrument, I launched forth into an old Spanish love-song, which I had met with in some moldy library during my travels, and had set to music of my own. I sang low, for the deserted street re-echoed the lightest sound, and what I sang must reach only my lady's ears. The words were warm with the fire of the ancient Spanish chivalry, and I threw into their expression all the passion of the lovers of romance. Surely Fionguala, the white-shouldered, would hear, and awaken from her sleep of centuries, and come to be latticed casement and look down! Hist! see yonder! What light—what shadow is that that seems to flit from room to room within the abandoned house, and now approaches the mullioned window? Are my eyes dazzled by the play of the moonlight, or does the casement move—does it open? Nay, this is no delusion; there is no error of the senses here. There is simply a woman, young, beautiful, and richly attired, bending forward from the window, and silently beckoning me to approach.

"Too much amazed to be conscious of amazement, I advanced until I stood directly beneath the casement, and the lady's face, as she stooped toward me, was not more than twice a man's height from my own. She smiled and kissed her finger-tips; something white fluttered in her hand, then fell through the air to the ground at my feet. The next moment she had withdrawn, and I heard the lattice close.

"I picked up what she had let fall; it was a delicate lace handkerchief, tied to the handle of an elaborately wrought bronze key. It was evidently the key of the house, and invited me to enter. I loosened it from the handkerchief, which bore a faint, delicious perfume, like the aroma of flowers in an ancient garden, and turned to the arched doorway. I felt no misgiving, and scarcely any sense of strangeness. All was as I had wished it to be, and as it should be; the medieval age was alive once more, and as for myself, I almost felt the velvet cloak hanging from my shoulder and the long rapier dangling at my belt. Standing in front of the door I thrust the key into the lock, turned it, and felt the bolt yield. The next instant the door was opened, apparently from within; I stepped across the threshold, the door closed again, and I was alone in the house, and in darkness.

"Not alone, however! As I extended my hand to grope my way it was met by another hand, soft, slender, and cold, which insinuated itself gently into mine and drew me forward. Forward I went, nothing loath; the darkness was impenetrable, but I could hear the light rustle of a dress close to me, and the same delicious perfume that had emanated from the handkerchief enriched the air that I breathed, while the little hand that clasped and was clasped by my own alternately tightened and half relaxed the hold of its soft cold fingers. In this manner, and treading lightly, we traversed that I presumed to be a long, irregular passageway, and ascended a staircase. Then another corridor, until finally we

paused, a door opened, emitting a flood of soft light, into
which we entered, still hand in hand. The darkness and the
doubt were at an end.

"The room was of imposing dimensions, and was furnished and decorated in a style of antique splendor. The walls
were draped with mellow hues of tapestry; clusters of candles
burned in polished silver sconces, and were reflected and
multiplied in tall mirrors placed in the four corners of the
room. The heavy beams of the dark oaken ceiling crossed
each other in squares, and were laboriously carved; the curtains and the drapery of the chairs were of heavy-figured
damask. At one end of the room was a broad ottoman, and in
front of it a table, on which was set forth, in massive silver
dishes, a sumptuous repast, with wines in crystal beakers. At
the side was a vast and deep fireplace, with space enough on
the broad hearth to burn whole trunks of trees. No fire,
however, was there, but only a great heap of dead embers;
and the room, for all its magnificence, was cold—cold as a
tomb, or as my lady's hand—and it sent a subtle chill creeping to my heart.

"But my lady! how fair she was! I gave but a passing
glance at the room; my eyes and my thoughts were all for
her. She was dressed in white, like a bride; diamonds sparkled in her dark hair and on her snowy bosom; her lovely
face and slender lips were pale, and all the paler for the dusky
glow of her eyes. She gazed at me with a strange, elusive
smile; and yet there was, in her aspect and bearing, something familiar in the midst of strangeness, like the burden of a
song heard long ago and recalled among other conditions and
surroundings. It seemed to me that something in me recognized her and knew her, had known her always. She was the
woman of whom I had dreamed, whom I had beheld in
visions, whose voice and face had haunted me from boyhood
up. Whether we had ever met before, as human beings meet,
I knew not; perhaps I had been blindly seeking her all over
the world, and she had been awaiting me in this splendid room,
sitting by those dead embers until all the warmth had gone

out of her blood, only to be restored by the heat with which my love might supply her.

"'I thought you had forgotten me,' she said, nodding as if in answer to my thought. 'The night was so late—our one night of the year! How my heart rejoiced when I heard your dear voice singing the song I know so well! Kiss me—my lips are cold!'

"Cold indeed they were—cold as the lips of death. But the warmth of my own seemed to revive them. They were now tinged with a faint color, and in her cheeks also appeared a delicate shade of pink. She drew fuller breath, as one who recovers from a long lethargy. Was it my life that was feeding her? I was ready to give her all. She drew me to the table and pointed to the viands and the wine.

"'Eat and drink,' she said. 'You have traveled far, and you need food.'

"'Will you eat and drink with me?' said I, pouring out the wine.

"'You are the only nourishment I want,' was her answer. 'This wine is thin and cold. Give me wine as red as your blood and as warm, and I will drain a goblet to the dregs.'

"At these words, I know not why, a slight shiver passed through me. She seemed to gain vitality and strength at every instant, but the chill of the great room stuck into me more and more.

"She broke into a fantastic flow of spirits, clapping her hands, and dancing about me like a child. Who was she? And was I myself, or was she mocking me when she implied that we had belonged to each other of old? At length she stood still before me, crossing her hands over her breast. I saw upon the forefinger of her right hand the gleam of an antique ring.

"'Where did you get that ring?' I demanded.

"She shook her head and laughed. 'Have you been faithful?' she asked. 'It is my ring; it is the ring that unites us; it is the ring you gave when you loved me first. It is the ring of the Kern—the fairy ring, and I am your Ethelind—Ethelind Fionguala.'

" 'So be it,' I said, casting aside all doubt and fear, and yielding myself wholly to the spell of her inscrutable eyes and wooing lips. 'You are mine, and I am yours, and let us be happy while the hours last.'

" 'You are mine, and I am yours,' she repeated, nodding her head with an elfish smile. 'Come and sit beside me, and sing that sweet song again that you sang to me so long ago. Ah, now I shall live a hundred years.'

"We seated ourselves on the ottoman, and while she nestled luxuriously among the cushions, I took my banjo and sang to her. The song and the music resounded through the lofty room, and came back in throbbing echoes. And before me as I sang I saw the face and form of Ethelind Fonguala, in her jeweled bridal dress, gazing at me with burning eyes. She was pale no longer, but ruddy and warm, and life was like a flame within her. It was I who had become cold and bloodless, yet with the last life that was in me I would have sung to her of love that can never die. But at length my eyes grew dim, the room seemed to darken, the form of Ethelind alternately brightened and waxed indistinct, like the last flickerings of a fire; I swayed toward her, and felt myself lapsing into unconsciousness, with my head resting on her white shoulder."

Here Keningale paused a few moments in his story, flung a fresh log upon the fire, and then continued:

"I awoke, I know not how long afterward. I was in a vast, empty room in a ruined building. Rotten shreds of drapery depended from the walls, and heavy festoons of spiders' webs gray with dust covered the windows, which were destitute of glass or sash; they had been boarded up with rough planks which had themselves become rotten with age, and admitted through their holes and crevices pallid rays of light and chilly draughts of air. A bat, disturbed by these rays or by my own movement, detached himself from his hold on a remnant of moldy tapestry near me, and after circling dizzily around my head, wheeled the flickering noiselessness of his flight into a darker corner. As I arose unsteadily from the heap of miscellaneous rubbish on which I had been lying, something which had been resting across my knees fell to the floor with a rattle. I picked it up, and found it to be my banjo—as you see it now.

"Well, that is all I have to tell. My health was seriously impaired; all the blood seemed to have been drawn out of my veins; I was pale and haggard, and the chill— Ah, that chill," murmured Keningale, drawing nearer to the fire, and spreading out his hands to catch the warmth— "I shall never get over it; I shall carry it to my grave."

SEABURY QUINN

Restless Souls

"Ten thousand small green devils! What a night; what an odious night!" Jules de Grandin paused beneath the theater's porte-cochère and scowled ferociously at the pelting rain.

"Well, summer's dead and winter hasn't quite come," I reminded soothingly. "We're bound to have a certain amount of rain in October. The autumnal equinox—"

"May Satan's choicest imps fly off with the autumnal equinox!" the little Frenchman interrupted. "*Morbleu,* it is that I have seen no sun since God alone knows when; besides that, I am most abominably hungry!"

"That condition, at least, we can remedy," I promised, nudging him from the awning's shelter toward my parked car. "Suppose we stop at the Café Bacchanale? They usually have something good to eat."

"Excellent, capital," he agreed enthusiastically, skipping nimbly into the car and rearranging the upturned collar of his raincoat. "You are a true philosopher, *mon vieux.* Always you tell me that which I most wish to hear."

They were having a hilarious time at the cabaret, for it was the evening of October 31, and the management had put on a special Halloween celebration. As we passed the velvet rope that looped across the entrance to the dining room a burst of Phrygian music greeted us, and a dozen agile young women in abbreviated attire were performing intricate gyrations under the leadership of an apparently boneless damsel whose costume was principally composed of strands of jangling hawk-bells threaded round her neck and wrists and ankles.

"Welsh rabbit?" I suggested. They make a rather tasty one here." He nodded almost absent-mindedly as he surveyed a couple eating at a nearby table.

At last, just as the waiter brought our boiling-hot refreshment: "Regard them, if you will, Friend Trowbridge," he whispered. "Tell me what, if anything, you make of them."

The girl was, as the saying goes, "a knockout." Tall, lissome, lovely to regard, she wore a dinner dress of simple black without a single hint of ornament except a single strand of small matched pearls about her slim and rather long throat. Her hair was bright chestnut, almost copper-colored, and braided round her small head in a Grecian coronal, and in its ruddy frame her face was like some strange flower on a tall stalk. Her darkened lids and carmined mouth and pale cheeks made an interesting combination.

As I stole a second glance at her it seemed to me she had a vague yet unmistakable expression of invalidism. Nothing definite, merely the combination of certain factors which pierced the shell of my purely masculine admiration and struck response from my years of experience as a medical practitioner—a certain blueness of complexion which meant "interesting pallor" to the layman but spelled imperfectly oxidized blood to the physician; a slight tightening of the muscles about the mouth which gave her lovely pouting lips a pathetic droop; and a scarcely perceptible retraction at the junction of cheek and nose which meant fatigue of nerves or muscles, possibly both.

Idly mingling admiration and diagnosis, I turned my glance upon her escort, and my lips tightened slightly as I made a mental note: "Golddigger!" The man was big-boned and coarse-featured, bullet-headed and thick-necked, and had the pasty, toad-belly complexion of one who drinks too much and sleeps and exercises far too little. He hardly changed expression as the girl talked eagerly in a hushed whisper. His whole attitude was one of proprietorship, as if she were his thing and chattel, bought and paid for, and constantly his fishy eyes roved round the room and rested covetously on attractive women supping at the other tables.

"I do not like it, me," de Grandin's comment brought my wandering attention back. "It is both strange and queer; it is not right."

"Eh?" I returned. "Quite so; I agree with you. It's shameful for a girl like that to sell—or maybe only rent—herself to such a creature—"

"*Non, non,*" he interrupted testily. "I have no thought of censoring their morals, such are their own affair. It is their treatment of the food that intrigues me."

"Food?" I echoed.

"*Oui-da,* food. On three distinct occasions they have ordered refreshment, yet each time they allowed it to grow cold; let it remain untouched until the *garçon* carried it away. I ask you, is that right?"

"Why—er—" I temporized, but he hurried on.

"Once as I watched I saw the woman make as though to lift a goblet to her lips, but the gesture of her escort halted her; she set the beverage down untasted. What sort of people ignore wine—the living soul of the grape?"

"Well, are you going to investigate?" I asked, grinning. I knew his curiosity was well-nigh as boundless as his self-esteem, and should not have been too greatly surprised if he had marched to the strange couple's table and demanded an explanation.

"Investigate?" he echoed thoughtfully. "U'm. Perhaps I shall."

He snapped the pewter lid of his beer-mug back, took a long, pensive draught, then leant forward, small round eyes unwinkingly on mine. "You know what night this is?" he demanded.

"Of course, it's Halloween. All the little devils will be out stealing garden gates and knocking at front doors—"

"Perhaps the larger devils will be abroad, too."

"Oh, come, now," I protested, "you're surely not serious—"

"By blue, I am," he affirmed solemnly. *"Regardez, s'il vous plaît."* He nodded toward the pair at the adjoining table.

Seated directly opposite the strange couple was a young man occupying a table by himself. He was a good-looking, sleek-haired youngster of the sort to be found by scores on any college campus. Had de Grandin brought the same charge of food wastage against him that he had leveled at the other two he would have been equally justified, for the boy left an elaborate order practically untasted while his infatuated eyes devoured every line of the girl at the next table.

As I turned to look at him I noted from the corner of my eye that the girl's escort nodded once in the same direction, then rose and left the table abruptly. I noticed as he walked toward the door that his walk was more like the rapid amble of an animal than the step of a man.

The girl half turned as she was left alone and under lowered lashes looked at the young man so indifferently that there was no mistaking her intent.

De Grandin watched with what seemed bleak disinterest as the young man rose to join her, and save for an occasional covert glance paid no attention as they exchanged the inane amenities customary in such cases, but when they rose to leave a few minutes later he motioned me to do likewise. "It is of importance that we see which way they go," he told me earnestly.

"Oh, for goodness' sake, be sensible!" I chided. "Let them flirt if they want to. I'll warrant she's in better company now than she came in with—"

"Précisément, exactly, quite so!" he agreed. "It is of that 'better company' I think when I have the anxiety."

"H'm, that *was* a tough-looking customer she was with," I conceded. "And for all her innocent-looking prettiness she might be the bait in a badger-game—"

"A badger-game? *Mais oui,* my friend. A game-of-the-badger in which the stakes are infinitely high!" Of the ornate doorman he demanded, "That couple, that young man and woman—they did go what wáy, *Monsieur le Concierge?*"

"Huh?"

"The young man and young woman—you saw them depart? We would know their direction—" a crumpled dollar bill changed hands, and the doorman's memory revived miraculously.

"Oh, them. Yeah, I seen 'em. They went down th' street that-a-way in a big black taxi. Little English feller drivin' 'em. Looked like th' feller's made a mash. He'll *get* mashed, too, if th' tough bimbo 'at brought th' broad in ketches 'im messin' round with her. That gink's one awful mean-lookin' bozo, an'—"

"Assuredly," de Grandin agreed. "And this Monsieur le Gink of whom you speak, he went which way, if you please?"

"He come outer here like a bat outer hell 'bout ten minutes ago. Funny thing 'bout him, too. He was walkin' down th' street, an' I was watchin' him, not special, but just lookin' at him, an' I looked away for just a minute, an' when I looked back he was gone. He wasn't more'n half way down th' block when I last seen him, but when I looked again he wasn't there. Dam' if I see how he managed to get round th' corner in that time."

"I think that your perplexity is justified," de Grandin answered as I brought the car to a stop at the curb, then, to me: "Hasten, Friend Trowbridge. "I would that we get them in sight before they are lost in the storm."

It was a matter of only a few minutes to pick up the tail light of the big car in which the truants sped toward the outskirts of town. Occasionally we lost them, only to catch them again almost immediately, for their route led straight out Orient Boulevard toward the Old Turnpike. "This is the craziest thing we've ever done," I grumbled. "There isn't any more chance that we'll catch them than—Great Scott, they've stopped!''

Improbably, the big car had drawn up at the imposing Canterbury Gate of Shadow Lawn Cemetery.

De Grandin leant forward in his seat like a jockey in the saddle. "Quick, hurry, make all speed, my friend!" he besought. "We must catch them before they alight!"

Try as I would my efforts were futile. Only an empty limousine and a profanely bewildered chauffeur awaited us when we drew up at the burying ground, our engine puffing like a winded horse.

"Which way, my friend—where did they go?" de Grandin vaulted from the car before we had come to a full stop.

"Inside th' graveyard!" answered the driver. "What th' hell d'ye know about that? Bringin' me way out here where th' devil says 'Good Night!' an' leavin' me as flat as a dam' pancake." His voice took on a shrill falsetto in imitation of a woman's. " 'You needn't wait for us, driver, we'll not be comin' back,' she says. Good God A'mighty, who th' hell but dead corpses goes into th' cemet'ry an' don't come back?"

"Who, indeed?" the Frenchman echoed, then, to me: "Come, Friend Trowbridge, we must hasten, we must find them all soon, or it is too late!"

Solemn as the purpose to which it was dedicated, the burial park stretched dark and forbidding about us as we stepped through the grille in the imposing stone gateway. The curving graveled avenues, bordered with double rows of hemlocks, stretched away like labyrinthine mazes, and the black turf with its occasional corrugations of mounded graves or decorations of pallid marble, sloped upward from us, seemingly to infinity.

Like a terrier on the scent de Grandin hurried forward, bending now and then to pass beneath the downward-swaying bough of some rain-laden evergreen, then hurrying still faster.

"You know this place, Friend Trowbridge?" he demanded during one of his brief halts.

"Better than I want to," I admitted. "I've been here to several funerals."

"Good!" he returned. "You can tell me then where is the—how do you call him?—the receiving vault?"

"Over there, almost in the center of the park," I answered, and he nodded understandingly, then took up his course, almost at a run.

Finally we reached the squat gray-stone receiving mausoleum, and he tried one of the heavy doors after another. "A loss!" he announced disappointedly as each of the tomb's great metal doors defied his efforts. "It seems we must search elsewhere."

He trotted to the open space reserved for parking funeral vehicles and cast a quick appraising look about, arrived at a decision and started like a cross-country runner down the winding road that led to a long row of family mausoleums. At each he stopped, trying the strong metal gratings at its entrance, peering into its gloomy interior with the aid of his pocket flashlight.

Tomb after tomb we visited, till both my breath and patience were exhausted. "What's all this nonsense?" I demanded. "What're you looking for—"

"That which I fear to find," he panted, casting the beam of his light about. "If we are balked?—*ah?* Look, my friend, look and tell me what it is you see."

In the narrow cone of light cast by his small electric torch I descried a dark form draped across the steps of a mausoleum. "Wh—why, it's a man!" I exclaimed.

"I hope so," he replied. "It may be we shall find the mere relic of one, but—ah? So. He is still breathing."

Taking the flashlight from him I played its ray on the still form stretched upon the tomb steps. It was the young man we had seen leave the café with the strange woman. On his forehead was a nasty cut, as though from some blunt instrument swung with terrific force—a blackjack, for instance.

Quickly, skillfully, de Grandin ran his supple, practiced hands over the youngster's body, pressed his fingers to his pulse, bent to listen at his chest. "He lives," he announced at the end of his inspection, "but his heart, I do not like it. Come; let us take him hence, my friend."

"And now, *mon brave*," he demanded half an hour later when we had revived the unconscious man with smelling salts and cold applications, "perhaps you will be good enough to tell us why you left the haunts of the living to foregather with the dead?"

The patient made a feeble effort to rise from the examination table, gave it up as too difficult and sank back. "I thought I *was* dead," he confessed.

"U'm?" the Frenchman regarded him narrowly. "You have not yet answered our question, young Monsieur."

The boy made a second attempt to rise, and an agonized expression spread over his face, his hand shot up to his left breast, and he fell back, half-lolling, half-writhing on the table.

"Quick, Friend Trowbridge, the amyl nitrate, where is it?" de Grandin asked.

"Over there," I waved my hand toward the medicine cabinet. "You'll find some three-minim capsules in the third bottle."

In a moment he secured the pearly little pellets, crushed one in his handkerchief and applied it to the fainting boy's nostrils. "Ah, that is better, *n'est-ce-pas*, my poor one?" he asked.

"Yes, thanks," the other replied, taking another deep inhalation of the powerful restorative, "much better." Then, "How'd you know what to give me? I didn't think—"

"My friend," the Frenchman interrupted with a smile. "I was practicing the treatment of angina pectoris when you were still unthought of. Now, if you are sufficiently restored, you will please tell us why you left the Café Bacchanale, and what occurred thereafter. We wait."

Slowly, assisted by de Grandin on one side, and me on the other, the young man descended from the table and seated himself in an easy chair. "I'm Donald Rochester," he introduced himself, "and this was to have been my last night on earth."

"Ah?" Jules de Grandin murmured.

"Six months ago," the young man continued, "Dr. Simmons told me I had angina pectoris. My case was pretty far advanced when he made his diagnosis, and he gave me only a little while to live. Two weeks ago he told me I'd be lucky to see the month out, and the pain was getting more severe and the attacks more frequent; so today I decided to give myself one last party, then go home and make a quick, clean job of it."

"Damn!" I muttered. I knew Simmons, a pompous old ass, but a first-rate diagnostician and a good heart man, though absolutely brutal with his patients.

"I ordered the sort of meal they haven't allowed me in the last half year," Rochester went on, "and was just about to start enjoying it when—when I saw her come in. "Did"—he turned from de Grandin to me as if expecting greater understanding from a fellow countryman—"did you see her, too?" An expression of almost religious rapture overspread his face.

"Perfectly, *mon vieux*," de Grandin returned. "We all saw her. Tell us more."

"I always thought this talk of love at first sight was a lot of tripe, but I'm cured now. I even forgot my farewell meal, couldn't see or think of anything but her. If I'd had even two more years to live, I thought, nothing could have kept me from hunting her out and asking her to marry—"

"*Précisément*, assuredly, quite so," the Frenchman interrupted testily. "We do concede that you were fascinated, Monsieur; but, for the love of twenty thousand pale blue monkeys, I entreat you tell us what you did, not what you thought."

"I just sat and goggled at her, sir. Couldn't do anything else. When that big brute she was with got up and left and she smiled at me, this poor old heart of mine almost blinked out, I tell you. When she smiled a second time there wasn't enough chain in the country to keep me from her.

"You'd have thought she'd known me all her life, the way she fell in step when we went out of the café. She had a big black car waiting outside and I climbed right in with her. Before I knew it, I was telling her who I was, how long I had to live, and how my only regret was losing her, just when I'd found her. I— "

"*Parbleu*, you told her that?"

"I surely did, and a lot more—blurted out that I loved her before I knew what I was about."

"And she— "

"Gentlemen, I'm not sure whether I ought to have delirium or not with this disease, but I'm pretty sure I've had a touch of something. Now, I want you to know I'm not crazy before I tell you the rest; but I might have had a heart attack or something, then fallen asleep and dreamed it."

"Say on, Monsieur," de Grandin ordered rather grimly. "We listen."

"Very well. When I said I loved her that girl just put her hands up to her eyes—like this—as if to wipe away some unshed tears. I half-expected she'd be angry, or maybe giggle, but she didn't. All she said was, 'Too late—oh, too late!'

" 'I know it is,' I answered. 'I've already told you I'm as good as dead, already but I can't go west without telling you how I feel.'

"Then she said, 'Oh, no, it's not that, my dear. That's not at all what I meant. For I love you, too, though I've no right to say so—I've no right to love anyone—it's too late for me, too.'

"After that I just took her in my arms and held her tight, and she sobbed as if her heart would break. Finally I asked her to make me a promise. "I'll rest better in my grave if I know you'll never go out with that ugly brute I saw you with tonight,' I told her, and she let out a little scream and cried harder than ever.

"Then I had the awful thought that maybe she was married to him, and that was what she meant when she said it was too late. So I asked her point blank.

"She said something devilish queer then. She told me, 'I must go to him whenever he wants me. Though I hate him as you can never understand; when he calls I have to go. This is the first time I've ever gone with him, but I must go again, and again, and again!" She kept screaming the word till I stopped her mouth with kisses.

"Presently the car stopped and we got out. We were at some sort of park, I think, but I was so engrossed in helping her compose herself I didn't notice much of anything.

"She led me through a big gate and down a winding road. At last we stopped before some sort of lodgehouse, and I took her in my arms for one last kiss.

"I don't know whether the rest of it really happened or whether I passed out and dreamed it. What I *thought* happened was this: instead of putting her lips against mine, she put them *around* them and seemed to draw the very breath out of my lungs. I could feel myself go faint, like a swimmer caught in the surf and mauled and pounded till the breath's knocked out of him, and my eyes seemed blinded with a sort of mist; then everything went sort o' dark green round me, and I began sagging at the knees. I could still feel her arms round me, and remember being surprised at her strength, but it seemed as if she'd transferred her lips to my throat. I kept getting weaker and weaker with a sort of languorous ecstasy, if that means anything to you. Rather like sinking to sleep in a soft dry bed with a big drink of brandy tucked under your belt after you're dog-tired with cold and exposure. Next thing I knew I'd toppled over and fallen down the steps with no more strength in my knees than a rag doll has. I must have got an awful crack on the head when I went down, for I passed out completely, and the next thing I remember was waking to find you gentlemen working over me. Tell me, did I dream it all? I'm—just—about—played—out.''

The sentence trailed off slowly, as if he were falling to sleep, and his head dropped forward while his hand slipped nervelessly from his lap, trailing flaccidly to the floor.

"Has he gone?" I whispered as de Grandin sprang across the room and ripped his collar open.

"Not quite," he answered. "More amyl nitrate, if you please; he will revive in a moment, but go home he shall not unless he promises not to destroy himself. *Mon Dieu*, destroyed he would be, body and soul, were he to put a bullet through his brain before—ah-*ha?* Behold, Friend Trowbridge, it is even as I feared!"

Against the young man's throat there showed two tiny perforated wounds, as though a fine needle had been thrust through a fold of skin.

"H'm," I commented. "If there were four of them I'd say a snake had bitten him."

"She has! Name of a little blue man, she has!" he retorted. "A serpent more virulent and subtle than any which goes on its belly has sunk her fangs in him; he is envenomed surely as if he'd had been the victim of a cobra's bite; but by the wings of Jacob's Angel we shall thwart her, my friend. We shall show her Jules de Grandin must be reckoned with— her and that fish-eyed paramour of hers as well, or may I eat stewed turnips for my Christmas dinner and wash them down with ditch-water!"

It was a serious face he showed at breakfast the next day. "You have perhaps a half hour's liberty this morning?" he asked as he drained his fourth cup of coffee.

"H'm, I suppose so. Anything special you'd like to do?"

"There is, indeed. I should like to go again to Shadow Lawn Cemetery. I would examine it by daylight, if you please."

"Shadow Lawn?" I echoed in amazement. "What in this world—"

"Only partially," he interrupted. "Unless I am much more mistaken than I think our business has as much to do with the next world as this. Come; you have your patients to attend, I have my duties to perform. Let us go."

The rain had vanished with the night and a bright November sun was shining when we reached the graveyard. Making straight for the tomb where we had found young Rochester the night before, de Grandin halted and inspected it carefully. On the lintel of the massive doorway he invited my attention to the single incised word:

HEATHERTON

"U'm?" he nursed his narrow pointed chin between a thoughtful thumb and forefinger. "That name I must remember, Friend Trowbridge."

Inside the tomb, arranged in two superimposed rows, were the crypts containing the remains of deceased Heathertons, each sealed by a white marble slab set with cement in a bronze frame, a two-lined legend telling the name and vital data of the occupant. The withering remains of a wreath clung by a knot or ribbon to the bronze ring-bolt ornamenting the marble panel of the farthest crypt, and behind the desiccating circle of roses and ruscus leaves I made out:

ALICE HEATHERTON
Sept. 28, 1906   Oct. 2, 1928

"You see?" he asked.

"I see a girl named Alice Heatherton died a month ago at the age of twenty-two," I admitted, "but what that has to do with last night is more than I can—"

"Of course," he broke in with a chuckle somehow lacking merriment. "But certainly. There are many things you do not see, my old one, and there are many more at which you blink your eyes, like a child passing over the unpleasant pages of a picture book. Now, if you will be so kind as to leave me, I shall interview *Monsieur l'Intendant* of this so lovely park, and several other people as well. If possible I shall return in time for dinner, but"—he raised his shoulders in a fatalistic shrug—"at times we must forego a meal in deference to duty. Yes, it is unfortunately so."

The consommé had grown cold and the roast lamb kiln-dried in the oven when the stutter of my study telephone called me. "Trowbridge, my friend," de Grandin's voice, shrill with excitement, came across the wire, "meet me at Adelphi Mansions quickly as you can. I would have you for witness!"

"Witness?" I echoed. "What—" A sharp click notified me he had hung up and I was left bewildered at the unresponsive instrument.

He was waiting for me at the entrance of the fashionable apartment house when I arrived, and refused to answer my impatient questions as he dragged me through the ornate entrance and down the rug-strewn foyer to the elevators. As the car shot upward he reached in his pocket and produced a shiny thumb-smudged photograph. "This I begged from *le Journal*," he explained. "They had no further use for it."

"Good heavens!" I exclaimed as I looked at the picture. "Wh—why, it's—"

"Assuredly it is," he answered in a level tone. "It is the girl we saw last night beyond a doubt; the girl whose tomb we visited this morning; the girl who gave the kiss of death to the young Rochester."

"But that's impossible. She's—"

His short laugh interrupted. "I was convinced you would say just that, Friend Trowbridge. Come, let us hear what Madame Heatherton can tell us."

A trim Negro maid in black-and-white uniform answered our summons and took our cards to her mistress. As she left the rather sumptuous reception room I glanced covetously about, noting rugs from China and the Near East, early American mahogany and an elaborately wrought medieval tapestry depicting a scene from the *Nibelungenlied* with its legend in formal Gothic text: *"Hic Siegriedum Aureum Occidunt*—Here They Slay Siegfried the Golden."

"Dr. Trowbridge? Dr. de Grandin?" the soft, cultured voice recalled me from my study of the fabric as an imposing white-haired lady entered.

"Madame, a thousand pardons for this intrusion!" de Grandin clicked his heels together and bowed stiffly from the hips. "Believe me, we have no desire to trespass on your privacy, but a matter of the most importance brings us. You will forgive me if I inquire of the circumstances of your daughter's death, for I am of the *Sûreté* of Paris, and make investigation as a scientific research."

Mrs. Heatherton was, to use an overworked expression, a "perfect lady." Nine women out of ten would have frozen at de Grandin's announcement, but she was the tenth. The direct glance the little Frenchman gave her and his evident sincerity, combined with perfect manners and immaculate dress, carried conviction. "Please be seated, gentlemen," she invited. "I cannot see where my poor child's tragedy can interest an officer of the Paris secret police, but I've no objection to telling all I can; you could get a garbled version from the newspapers anyway.

"Alice was my youngest child. She and my son Ralph were two years apart, almost to the day. Ralph graduated from Cornell year before last, majoring in civil engineering, and went to Florida to take charge of some construction work. Alice died while visiting him."

"But—forgive my seeming rudeness, Madame—your son, is not he also deceased?"

"Yes," our hostess assented. "He is dead, also. They died almost together. There was a man down there, a fellow townsman of ours, Joachim Palenzeke—not the sort of person one knows—but Ralph's superior in the work. He had something to do with promoting the land development, I believe. When Alice went to visit Ralph this person presumed on his position and the fact that we were all from Harrisonville, and attempted to force his attentions on her.''

"One sees. And then?'' de Grandin prompted softly.

"Ralph resented his overtures. Palenzeke made some insulting remarks—some scurrilous allusions to Alice and me, I've been told—and they fought. Ralph was a small man, but a thoroughbred. Palenzeke was almost a giant, but a throughgoing coward. When Ralph began to get the better of him he drew a pistol and fired five shots into my poor son's body, Ralph died the next day after hours of terrible suffering.

"His murderer fled to the swamps where it would be difficult to track him with hounds, and according to some squatters he committed suicide, but there must have been some mistake, for—'' she broke off, pressing her crumpled handkerchief to her mouth, as if to force back the sobs.

De Grandin reached from his chair and patted her hand gently, as if consoling a child. "Dear lady,'' he murmured, "I am distressed, believe me, but also please believe me when I say I do not ask these so heart-breaking questions idly. Tell me, if you will, why you believe the story of this vile miscreant's suicide an error.''

"Because—because he was seen again! He killed Alice!''

"*Nom d'un nom!* Do you say so!'' His comment was a suppressed shout. "Tell me, tell me, Madame, how came this vileness about? This is of the great importance; this explains much which was inexplicable. Say on, *chére Madame*, I implore you!''

"Alice was prostrated at the tragedy of Ralph's murder— somehow, she seemed to think she was responsible for it— but in a few days she recovered enough to make preparations to return home with his body.

"There was no railway nearer than fifteen miles, and she wanted to catch an early train, so she set out by motor the night before her train was due. As she drove through a length of lonely, unlighted road between two stretches of undrained swampland someone emerged from the tall reeds—we have the chauffeur's statement for this—and leaped upon the running-board. He struck the driver senseless with a single blow, but not before he had been recognized. It was Joachim Palenzeke. The car ran into the swamp when the driver lost consciousness, but fortunately for him the mud was deep enough to stall the machine, though not deep enough to engulf it. He recovered in a short time and raised the alarm.

"A sheriff's posse found them both next morning. Palenzeke had apparently slipped in the bog while trying to escape and been drowned. Alice was dead—from shock, the doctors said. Her lips were terribly bruised, and there was a wound on her throat, though not serious enough to have caused death; and she had been—"

"Enough! No more, Madame, I entreat you! *Sang de Saint Denis,* is Jules de Grandin a monster that he should roll a stone upon a mother's breaking heart? *Dieu de Dieu, non!* But tell me, if you can, and then I shall ask you no more— what became of this ten-thousand-times-damned—your parden, Madame!—this so execrable *cochon* of Palenzeke?"

"They brought him home for burial," Mrs. Heatherton replied softly. "His family is very wealthy. Some of them were bootleggers during prohibition, some are real estate speculators, some are politicians. He had the most elaborate funeral ever seen in the local Greek Orthodox Church—they say the flowers alone cost more than five thousand dollars— but Father Apostolakos refused to say Mass over him, merely recited a short prayer, and denied him burial in the consecrated part of the church cemetery."

"Ah!" de Grandin looked meaningly at me, as if to say, "I told you as much!"

"This may interest you, too, though I don't know," Mrs. Heatherton added: "A friend of mine who knows a reporter on the *Journal*—newspapermen know everything," she added with simple naïveté—"told me that the coward really must have tried suicide and failed, for there was a bullet-mark on his temple, though of course it couldn't have been fatal, since they found him drowned in the swamp. Do you suppose he could have wounded himself purposely where those swamp-dwellers could see, so that the story of his suicide would get about and the officers stop looking for him?''

''Quite possibly,'' de Grandin agreed as he rose. ''Madame, we are your debtors more than you suspect, and though you cannot know it, we have saved you at least one pang this night. *Adieu, chère Madame,* and may the good God watch over you—and yours.'' He laid his lips to her fingers and bowed himself from the room.

As we passed through the outer door we caught the echo of a sob and Mrs. Heatherton's despairing cry: ''Me and mine— there are no 'mine.' All, all are gone!''

''*La pauvre!*'' de Grandin murmured as he closed the door softly. ''All the more reason for *le bon Dieu's* watchfulness, though she knows it not!''

''Now what?'' I demanded, dabbing furtively at my eyes with my handkerchief.

The Frenchman made no effort to conceal his tears. They trickled down his face as if he had been a half-grown schoolboy. ''Go home, my friend,'' he ordered. ''Me, I shall consult the priest of that Greek Church. From what I hear of him he must be a capital fellow. I think he will give credence to my story. If not, *parbleu,* we must take matters into our own hands. Meantime, crave humble pardon from the excellent Nora for having neglected her dinner and ask that she prepare some slight refreshment, then be ready to accompany me again when we shall have regaled ourselves. *Nom d'un canard vert,* we have a busy night before us, my old and rare!''

It was nearly midnight when he returned, but from the sparkle in his eyes I knew he had successfully attended to some of his ''offices.''

''*Barbe d'une chèvre,*'' he exclaimed as he disposed of his sixth cold lamb sandwich and emptied his eighth glass of Ponte Canet, ''that Father Apostolakos is no man's fool, my friend. He is no empty-headed modern who knows so much that he knows nothing; a man versed in the occult may talk freely with him and be understood. Yes. He will help us.''

"U'm?" I commented noncommittally, my mouth half-filled with lamb sandwich.

"Precisely," he agreed, refilling his glass and lifting another sandwich from the tray. "Exactly, my friend. The good *papa* is supreme in matters ecclesiastical, and tomorrow he will give the necessary orders without so much as 'by your leave' from the estimable ex-bootleggers, real estate dealers and politicians who compose the illustrious Palenzeke clan. The sandwiches are all gone, and the bottle empty? Good, then let us be upon our way."

"Where?" I demanded.

"To the young Monsieur Rochester's. Me, I would have further talk with that one."

As we left the house I saw him transfer a small oblong packet from his jacket to his overcoat. "What's that?" I asked.

"A thing the good father lent me. I hope we shall have no occasion to use it, but it will prove convenient if we do."

A light mist, dappled here and there with chilling rain, was settling in the streets as we set off for Rochester's. Half an hour's cautious driving brought us to the place, and as we drew up at the curb the Frenchman pointed to a lighted window on the seventh floor. "That burns in his suite," he informed me. "Can it be he entertains at this hour?"

The night elevator operator snored in a chair in the lobby, and, guided by de Grandin's cautious gesture, I followed his lead up the stairs. "We need not announce our coming," he whispered as we rounded the landing on the sixth floor. "It is better that we come as a surprise, I think."

Another flight we climbed silently, and paused before the door of Rochester's apartment. De Grandin rapped once softly, repeated the summons more authoritatively, and was about to try the knob when we heard footsteps beyond the panels.

Young Rochester wore a silk robe over his pajamas, his hair was somewhat disarranged, but he looked neither sleepy nor particularly pleased to see us.

"We are unexpected it seems," de Grandin announced, "but we are here, nevertheless. Be kind enough to stand aside and let us enter, if you please."

"Not now," the young man refused. "I can't see you now. If you'll come back tomorrow morning—"

"This is tomorrow morning, *mon vieux*," the little Frenchman interrupted. "Midnight struck an hour ago." He brushed past our reluctant host and hurried down the long hall to the living room.

The room was tastefully furnished in typically masculine style, heavy chairs of hickory and maple, Turkish carpets, a table with a shaded lamp, a long couch piled with pillows before the fireplace in which a bed of cannel coal glowed in a brass grate. An after-tang of cigarette smoke hung in the air, but mingled with it was the faint, provocative scent of heliotrope.

De Grandin paused upon the threshold, threw his head back and sniffed like a hound at fault. Directly opposite the entrance was a wide arch closed by two Paisley shawls hung lambrequinwise from a brass rod, and toward this he marched, his right hand in his topcoat pocket, the ebony cane which I knew concealed a sword blade held lightly in his left.

"De Grandin!" I cried in shocked protest, aghast at his air of proprietorship.

"Don't" Rochester called warningly. "You mustn't——"

The hangings at the archway parted and a girl stepped from between them. The long, close-clinging gown of purple tissue she wore was almost as diaphanous as smoke, and through it we could see the white outlines of her body. Her copper-colored hair flowed in a cloven tide about her face and over smooth bare shoulders. Halted in the act of stepping, one small bare foot showed its blue-veined whiteness in sharp silhouette against the rust-red of the Bokhara rug.

As her eyes met de Grandin she paused with a sibilant intake of breath, and her eyes widened with a look of fright. It was no shame-faced glance she gave him; no expression of confusion at detected guilt or brazen attempt at facing out a hopelessly embarrassing situation. Rather, it was the look of one in dire peril, such a look as she might have given a rattlesnake writhing toward her.

"So!" she breathed, and I could see the thin stuff of her gown grow tight across her breasts. "So you know! I was afraid you would, but—" She broke off as he took another step toward her and swerved until his right-hand coat pocket was within arm's length of her.

"*Mais oui, mais oui, Mademoiselle la Morte,*" he returned, bowing ceremoniously, but not removing his hand from his pocket. "I know, as you say. The question now arises, 'What shall we do about it?' "

"See here," Rochester flung himself between them, "what's the meaning of this unpardonable intrusion—"

The little Frenchman turned to him, a look of mild inquiry on his face. "*You* demand an explanation? If explanations are in order—"

"See here, damn you, I'm my own man, and not accountable to anyone. Alice and I love each other. She came to me tonight of her own free will—"

"*En vérité?*" the Frenchman interrupted. "How did she come, Monsieur?"

The young man seemed to catch his breath like a runner struggling to regain his wind at the end of a hard course. "I—I went out for a little while," he faltered, "and when I came back—"

"My poor one." de Grandin broke in sympathetically. "You do lie like a gentleman, but also you lie very poorly. You are in need of practice. Attend me, I will tell you how she came: this night, I do not know exactly when, but well after sundown, you heard a knock-rap at your window or door, and when you looked out, *voilà,* there was the so lovely *demoiselle*. You thought you dreamed, but once again the pretty fingers tap-tapped at the window pane, and the soft lovely eyes looked love at you, and you opened your door or window and made her enter, content to entertain the dream of her, since there was no chance of her coming in the flesh. Tell me, young

Monsieur, and you, too, lovely Mademoiselle, do I not recite the facts?''

Rochester and the girl stared at him in amazement. Only the quivering of the young man's eyelids and the trembling of the girl's sensitive lips gave testimony he had spoken accurately.

For a moment there was a tense, vibrant silence; then with a little gasping cry the girl lurched forward on soft, soundless feet and dropped to her knees before de Grandin. "Have pity—be merciful!'' she begged. "Be merciful to me as you may one day hope for mercy. It's such a little thing I ask. You know *what* I am; do you also know who I am, and why I am now—now the accused thing you see?'' She buried her face in her hands. "Oh, it's cruel—too cruel!'' she sobbed. "I was so young; my whole life lay before me. I'd never known real love until it was too late. You can't be so unkind as to drive me back now; you *can't!*''

"*Ma pauvre!*'' de Grandin laid his hand upon the girl's bowed, shining head. "My innocent, poor lamb who met the butcher ere you had the lambkin's right to play! I know all there is to know of you. Your sainted mother told me far more than she dreamed this evening. I am not cruel, my little lovely one: I am all sympathy and sorrow, but life is cruel and death is even crueler. Also, you now what the inevitable end must be if I forebear to do my duty. If I could work a miracle I would roll back the gates of death and bid you live and love until your natural time had come to die, but—''

"I don't care what the end must be!'' the girl blazed, sinking back until she sat upon the upturned soles of her bare feet. "I only know that I've been cheated out of every woman's birthright. I've found love now and I want it; I want it! He's mine, I tell you, mine—'' She cowered, groveling before him. "Think what a little thing I'm asking!'' Inching forward on her knees she took his hand in both of hers and fondled it against her cheek. "I'm asking just a little drop of blood now and then; just a little, tiny drop to keep my body whole and beautiful. If I were like other women and Donald were my lover he'd be glad to give me a transfusion—to give me a whole pint or quart of his blood any time I needed it. Is it so much, then, when I ask only an occasional drop? Just a drop now and then, and once in a while a draft of living breath from his lungs to—''

''To slay his poor sick body, then destroy his young, clean soul!'' the Frenchman interrupted softly. ''It is not of the living that I think so much, but of the dead. Would you deny him quiet rest in his grave when he shall have lost his life because of you? Would you refuse him peaceful sleep until the dawn of God's Great Tomorrow?''

''O-o-oh!'' the cry wrung from her writhing lips was like the wail of a lost spirit. ''You're right—it is his soul we must protect. I'd kill that, too, as mine was killed that night in the swamps. Oh, pity, pity me, dear Lord! Thou who didst heal the lepers and despised not the Magdalen, have pity on me, the soiled, the unclean!''

Scalding tears of agony fell between the fingers of her long, almost transparent hands as she had them before her eyes. Then: ''I am ready,'' she announced, seeming to find courage for complete renunciation. ''Do what you must to me. If it must be the knife and stake, strike quickly. I shall not scream or cry, if I can help it.''

For a long moment he looked in her face as he might have looked in the casket of a dear friend. ''*Ma pauvre,*'' he murmured compassionately. ''My poor, brave, lovely one!''

Abruptly he turned to Rochester. ''Monsieur,'' he announced sharply. ''I would examine you. I would determine the state of your health.''

We stared at him astounded as he proceeded to strip back the young man's pajama jacket and listen carefully at his chest, testing by percussion, counting the pulse action, then feeling slowly up and down the arm. ''U'm,'' he remarked judicially at the end of the examination, ''you are in bad condition, my friend. With medicines, careful nursing, and more luck than the physician generally has, we might keep you alive another month. Again, you might drop over any moment. But in all my life I have never given a patient his death warrant with more happiness.''

Two of us looked at him in mute wonder; it was the girl who understood. ''You mean,'' she trilled, laughter and a light the like of which there never was on land or sea breaking in her eyes, ''you mean that I can have him till—''

He grinned at her delightedly. There was a positively gleeful chuckle in his voice as he replied: ''Precisely, exactly, quite so, Mademoiselle.'' Turning from her he addressed Rochester.

''You and Mademoiselle Alice are to love each other as much as you please while life holds out. And afterwards''—he stretched his hand out to grasp the girl's fingers—''afterwards I shall do the needful—for you both. Ha, *Monsieur Diable,* I have tricked you nicely; Jules de Grandin has made one great fool of hell!'' He threw his head back and assumed an attitude of defiance, eyes flashing, lips twitching with excitement and elation.

The girl bent forward, took his hand and covered it with kisses. ''Oh, you're kind—kind!'' she sobbed brokenly. ''No other man in all the world knowing what you know, would have done what you have done!''

''*Mais non, mais certainement non, Mademoiselle,*'' he agreed imperturbably. ''You do forget that I am Jules de Grandin.

''Come, Trowbridge, my friend,'' he admonished ''we obtrude her most unwarrantably. What have we, who drained the purple wine of youth long years ago, to do with those who laugh and love the night away? Let us go.''

Hand in hand, the lovers followed us to the hall, but as we paused upon the threshold—''

Rat-tat-tat! something struck the fog-glazed window, and as I wheeled in my tracks I felt the breath go hot in my throat. Beyond the window, seemingly adrift in the fog, there was a human form. A second glance told me it was the brutal-faced man we had seen at the café the previous night.

But now his ugly, evil face was like the devil's, not merely a wicked man's.

"*Eh bien*, Monsieur, is it you indeed?" de Grandin asked nonchalantly. "I thought you might appear, so I am ready for you.

"Do not invite him in," he called the sharp command to Rochester. "He cannot come in unbidden. Hold your beloved, place your hand or lips against her mouth, lest she who is his thing and chattel, however unwillingly, give him permission to enter. Remember, he cannot cross the sill without the invitation of someone in this room!"

Flinging up the sash he regarded the apparition sardonically. "What have you to say, *Monsieur le Vampire*, before I send you hence?" he asked.

The thing outside mouthed at us, very fury robbing it of words. At last: "She's mine!" it shrieked. "I made her what she is, and she belongs to me. I'll have her, and that dough-faced, dying thing she holds in her arms, too. All, all of you are mine! I shall be king, I shall be emperor of the dead! Not you nor any mortal can stop me. I am all-powerful, supreme, I am—"

"You are the greatest liar outside burning hell," de Grandin cut in icily. "As for your power and your claims, Monsieur Monkey-Face, tomorrow you shall have nothing, not even so much as a little plot of earth to call a grave. Meanwhile, behold this, devil's spawn; behold and be afraid!"

Whipping his hand from his topcoat pocket he produced a small flat case like the leather containers sometimes used for holding photographs, pressed a concealed spring and snapped back its top. For a moment the thing in the night gazed at the object with stupefied, unbelieving horror; then with a wild cry fell backward, its uncouth motion somehow reminding me of a hooked bass.

"You do not like it, I see," the Frenchman mocked. "*Parbleu*, you stinking truant from the charnel-house, let us see what nearer contact will effect!" He stretched his hand out till the leather-cased object almost touched the phantom face outside the window.

A wild, inhuman screech echoed, and as the demon face retreated we saw a weal of red across its forehead, as if the Frenchman had scored it with a hot iron.

"Close the windows, *mes amis*," he ordered casually as though nothing hideous hovered outside. "Shut them tight and hold each other close until the morning comes and shadows flee away. *Bonne nuit!*"

"For heaven's sake," I besought as we began our homeward drive, "what's it all mean? You and Rochester called that girl Alice, and she's the speaking image of the girl we saw in the café last night. But Alice Heatherton is dead. Her mother told us how she died this evening; we saw her tomb this morning. Are there two Alice Heathertons, or is this girl her double—"

"In a way," he answered. "It was Alice Heatherton we saw back there, my friend, yet not the Alice Heatherton of whom her mother spoke this evening, nor yet the one whose tomb we saw this morning."

"For God's sake," I burst out, "stop this damned double-talk! Was or was it not Alice Heatherton—"

"Be patient, my old one," he counseled. "At present I can not tell you, but later I will have a complete explanation—I hope."

Daylight was just breaking when his pounding on my bedroom door roused me from comalike sleep. "Up, Friend Trowbridge!" he shouted, punctuating his summons with another knock. "Up and dress as quickly as may be. We must be off at once. Tragedy has overtaken them!"

Scarcely knowing what I did I stumbled from the bed, felt my way into my clothes and, sleep still filming my eyes, descended to the lower hall where he waited in a perfect frenzy of excitement.

"What's happened?" I asked as we started for Rochester's.

"The worst," he answered. "Ten minutes ago I was awak-

ened by the telephone. 'It is for Friend Trowbridge,' I told
me. 'Some patient with the *mal de l' estomac* desires a little
paregoric and much sympathy. I shall not waken him, for he
is all tired with the night's exertions.'' But still the bell kept
ringing, and so I answered it. My friend, it was Alice. *Hélas*,
as strong as her love was, her bondage was still stronger. But
when the harm was done she had the courage to call us.
Remember that when you come to judge her.''

I would have paused for explanation, but he waved me on
impatiently. ''Make haste; oh, hurry, hurry!'' he urged. ''We
must go to him at once. Perhaps it is even now too late.''

There was no traffic in the streets, and we made the run to
Rochester's apartment in record time. Almost before we realized it we were at his door once more, and this time de
Grandin stood upon no ceremony. Flinging the door open he
raced down the hall and into the living room, pausing at the
threshold with a sharp indrawn breath. ''So!'' he breathed.
''He was most thorough, that one.''

The place was a shambles. Chairs were overturned, pictures hung awry, bits of broken bric-à-brac were strewn
about, the long throw-cover of the center table had been
jerked off, overturning the lamp and scattering ashtrays and
cigarette boxes indiscriminately.

Donald Rochester lay on the rug before the dead fire, one
leg bent queerly under him, his right arm stretched out flaccidly along the floor and bent at a sharp right angle at the
wrist.

The Frenchman crossed the room at a run, unclasping the
lock of his kit as he leaped. Dropping to his knees he listened
intently at the young man's chest a moment, then stripped
back his sleeve, swabbed his arm with alcohol and thrust the
needle of his hypodermic through a fold of skin. ''It is a
desperate chance I take,'' he muttered as he drove the plunger
home, ''but the case is urgent; *le bon Dieu* knows how
urgent.''

Rochester's eyelids fluttered as the powerful stimulant took
effect. He moaned and turned his head with great effort, but

made no move to rise. As I knelt beside de Grandin and helped him raise the injured man I understood the cause of his lethargy. His spine had been fractured at the fourth dorsal vertebra, paralysis resulting.

"Monsieur," the little Frenchman whispered softly,, "you are going fast. Your minutes are now more than numbered on the circle of the watch-face. Tell us, tell us quickly, what occurred." Once more he injected stimulant into Rochester's arm.

The young man wet his blued lips with the tip of his tongue, attempted a deep breath, but found the effort too great. "It was he—the fellow you scared off last night," he whispered hoarsely.

"After you'd gone Alice and I lay on the hearth rug, counting our minutes together as a miser counts his gold. I heaped coals on the fire, for she was chilled, but it didn't seem to do any good. Finally she began to pant and choke, and I let her draw breath from me. That revived her a little, and when she'd sucked some blood from my throat she seemed almost herself again, though I could feel no movement of her heart as she lay against me.

"It must have been just before daybreak—I don't know just when, for I'd fallen asleep in her arms—when I heard a clattering at the window, and someone calling to be let in. I remembered your warning, and tried to hold Alice, but she fought me off. She ran to the window and flung it up as she called, 'Enter, master; there is none to stop you now.'

"He made straight for me, and when she realized what he was about she tried to stop him, but he flung her aside as if she were a rag doll—took her by the hair and dashed her against the wall. I heard her bones crack as she struck it.

"I grappled with him, but I was no more his match than a three-year-old child was mine. He threw me down and broke my arms and legs with his feet. The pain was terrible. Then he grabbed me up and hurled me to the floor again, and after that I felt no pain, except this dreadful headache. I couldn't move, but I was conscious, and the last thing I remember was seeing Alice stepping out the window with him, hand in hand. She didn't even look back.''

He paused a moment, fighting desperately for breath, then, still lower, "Oh, Alice—how could you? And I loved you so!''

"Peace, my poor one,'' bade de Grandin. "She did not do it of her own accord. That fiend holds her in bondage she cannot resist. She is his thing and chattel more completely than ever black slave belonged to his master. Hear me; go with this thought uppermost in your mind: She loved you, she loves you. It is because she called us we are here now, and her last word was one of love for you. Do you hear me? Do you understand? 'Tis sad to die, *mon pauvre,* but surely it is something to die loving and beloved. Many a man lives out his whole life without as much, and many there are who would trade a whole span of four score gladly for five little minutes of the ecstasy that was yours last night.

"Monsieur Rochester—do you hear me?'' he spoke sharply, for the young man's face was taking on the grayness of impending death.

"Ye-es. She loves me—she loves me. Alice!'' With the name sighing on his lips his facial muscles loosened and his eyes took on the glazed, unwinking stare of eyes that see no more.

De Grandin gently drew the lids across the sightless eyes and raised the fallen jaw, then set about straightening the room with methodical haste. "As a licensed practitioner you will sign the death certificate,'' he announced matter-of-factly. "Our young friend suffered from angina pectoris. This morning he had an attack, and after calling us fell from the chair on which he stood to reach his medicine, thereby fracturing several bones. He told us this when we arrived to find him dying. You understand?''

"I'm hanged if I do,'' I denied. "You know as well as I—''

"That the police would have awkward questions to address to us,'' he reminded me. "We were the last ones to see him alive. Do you conceive that they would credit what we said if we told them the truth?''

Much as I disliked it, I followed his orders to the letter and the boy's body was turned over to the ministrations of Mortician Martin within an hour.

As Rochester had been an orphan without known family de Grandin assumed the role of next friend, made all arrangements for the funeral, and gave orders that the remains be cremated without delay, the ashes to be turned over to him for final disposition.

Most of the day was taken up in making these arrangements and in my round of professional calls. I was thoroughly exhausted by four o'clock in the afternoon, but de Grandin, hustling, indefatigable, seemed fresh as he had been at daybreak.

"Not yet, my friend," he denied as I would have sunk into the embrace of an easy chair, "there is yet something to be done. Did not you hear my promise to the never-quite-to-be-sufficiently anathematized Palenzeke last night?''

"Eh, your promise?''

"*Précisément*. We have one great surprise in store for that one.''

Grumbling, but with curiosity that overrode my fatigue, I drove him to the little Greek Orthodox parsonage. Parked at the door was the severely plain black service wagon of a funeral director, its chauffeur yawning audibly at the delay in getting through his errand.

De Grandin ran lightly up the steps, gained admission and returned in a few minutes with the venerable priest arrayed in full canonicals. "*Allons mon enfant*," he told the chauffeur, "be on your way; we follow.''

Even when the imposing granite walls of the North Hudson Crematory loomed before us I failed to understand his hardly suppressed glee.

All arrangements had apparently been made. In the little chapel over the retort Father Apostolakos recited the orthodox burial office, and the casket sank slowly from view on the concealed elevator provided for conveying it to the incineration chamber below.

The aged priest bowed courteously to us and left the building, seating himself in my car, and I was about to follow when de Grandin motioned to me imperatively. "Not yet, Friend Trowbridge," he told me. "Come below and I will show you something."

We made our way to the subterranean chamber where incineration took place. The casket rested on a low wheeled truck before the yawning cavern of the retort, but de Grandin stopped the attendants as they were about to roll it into place. Tiptoeing across the tiled floor he bent above the casket, motioning me to join him.

As I paused beside him I recognized the heavy, evil features of the man we had first seen with Alice, the same bestial, furious face which had mouthed curses at us outside Rochester's window the night before. I would have drawn back, but the Frenchman clutched me firmly by the elbow, drawing me still nearer the body.

"*Tiens, Monsieur le Cadavre,*" he whispered as he bent above the dead thing, "what think you of this, *hein?* You who would be king and emperor of the dead, you who boasted that no power on earth could balk you—did not Jules de Grandin promise you that you should have nothing, not even one poor plot of earth to call a grave? *Pah,* murderer and ravisher of women, man-killer, where is now your power? Go—go through the furnace fire to hell-fire, and take this with you!" He pursed his lips and spat full in the cold upturned visage of the corpse.

It might have been a trick of overwrought nerves or an optical illusion produced by the electric lights, but I still believe I saw the dead, long-buried body writhe in its casket and a look of terrible, unutterable hate disfigure the waxen features.

He stepped back, nodding to the attendants, and the casket slid noiselessly into the retort. A whirring sounded as the pressure pump was started, and in a moment came the subdued roar of oil-flames shooting from the burners.

He raised his narrow shoulders in a shrug. "*C'est une affaire finie.*"

It was somewhat after midnight when we made our way once more to Shadow Lawn Cemetery. Unerringly as though going to an appointment de Grandin led the way to the Heatherton family mausoleum, let himself through the massive bronze gates with a key he had procured somewhere, and ordered me to stand guard outside.

Lighted by a flash of his electric torch he entered the tomb, a long cloth-covered parcel clasped under his arm. A moment later I heard the clink of metal on metal, the sound of some heavy object being drawn across the floor; then, as I grew half-hysterical at the long-continued silence, there came the short, half-stifled sound of a gasping cry, the sort of cry a patient in the dental chair gives when a tooth is extracted without anesthetic.

Another period of silence, broken by the rasp of heavy objects being moved, and the Frenchman emerged from the tomb, tears streaming down his face. "Peace," he announced chokingly. "I brought her peace, Friend Trowbridge, but oh! how pitiful it was to hear her moan, and still more pitiful to see the lovely, live-seeming body shudder in the embrace of relentless death. It is not hard to see the living die, my old one, but the dead! *Mordieu,* my soul will be in torment every time I think of what I had to do tonight for mercy's sake!"

Jules de Grandin chose a cigar from the humidor and set it glowing with the precision that distinguished his every movement. "I grant you the events of the last three days have been decidedly queer," he agreed as he sent a cloud of fragrant smoke ceilingward. "But what would you? All that lies outside our everyday experience is queer. To one who has not studied biology the sight of an ameba beneath the microscope is queer; the Eskimos undoubtedly thought Monsieur Byrd's airplane queer; we think the sights which we have seen these nights queer. It is our luck—and all mankind's—that they are.

"To begin: just as there exist today certain protozoa which are probably identical with the earliest forms of life on earth, so there are still, though constantly diminishing in numbers, certain holdovers of ancient evil. Time was when earth swarmed with them—devils and devilkins, imps, satyrs and demons, elementals, werewolves and vampires. All once were numerous; all, perhaps, exist in considerable numbers to this day, though we know them not, and most of us never so much as hear of them. It is with the vampire that we had to deal this time. You know him, no?

"Strictly, he is an earthbound soul, a spirit which because of manifold sins and wickedness is bound to the world wherein it once worked evil and cannot take itself to its proper place. He is in India in considerable numbers, also in Russia, Hungary, Romania and throughout the Balkans—wherever civilization is very old and decadent, there he seems to find a favorable soil. Sometimes he steals the body of one already dead; sometimes he remains in the body which he had in life, and then he is most terrible of all, for he needs nourishment for that body, but not such nourishment as you or I take. No, he subsists on the life-force of the living, imbibed through their blood, for the blood is the life. He must suck the breath from those who live, or he cannot breathe; he must drink their blood, or he dies of starvation. And here is where the danger rises: a suicide, one who dies under a curse, *or one who has been innoculated with the vampire virus* by having his blood sucked by a vampire, becomes a vampire after death. Innocent of all wrong he may be, often is, yet he is doomed to tread the earth by night, preying ceaselessly upon the living, ever recruiting the grisly ranks of his tribe. You apprehend?

"Consider this case: This *sacré* Palenzeke, because of his murder and suicide, perhaps partly because of his Slavic ancestry, maybe also because of his many other sins, became a vampire when he killed himself to death. Madame Heatherton's informant was correct, he had destroyed himself; but his evil body and more evil soul remained in partnership, ten thousand times a greater menace to mankind than when they had been partners in their natural life.

"Enjoying the supernatural power of his life-in-death, he rose from the swamplands, waylaid Mademoiselle Alice, assaulted her chauffeur, then dragged her off into the bog to work his evil will on her, gratifying at once his bestial lust, his vampire's thirst for blood and his revenge for her rejection of his wooing. When he had killed her, he had made her such a thing as he was. More, he had gained dominion over her. She was his toy, his plaything, his automaton, without will or volition of her own. What he commanded she must do, however much she hated doing it. You will recall, perhaps, how she told the young Rochester that she must go out with the villain, although she hated him? Also, how she bade him enter the apartment where she and her beloved lay in love's embrace, although his entrance meant her lover's undoing?

"Now, if the vampire added all the powers of living men to his dead powers we should have no defense, but fortunately he is subject to unbreakable laws. He can not independently cross the thread of a running stream, he must be carried; he can not enter any house or dwelling until invited by someone therein; he can fly through the air, enter at keyholes and window-chinks, or through the crack of the door, but he can move about only at night—between sunset and cock-crow. From sunrise to dark he is only a corpse, helpless as any other, and must lie corpse-dead in his tomb. At much times he can easily be slain, but only in certain ways. First, if his heart be pierced by a stake of ash and his head severed from his body, he is dead in good earnest, and can no more rise to plague us. Second, if he can be completely burned to ashes he is no more, for fire cleanses all things.

"Now, with this information, fit together the puzzle that so mystifies you: the other night at the Café Bacchanale I liked the looks of that one not at all. He had the face of a dead man and the look of a born villain, as well as the eye of a fish. Of his companion I thoroughly approved, though she, too, had an otherworldly look. Wondering about them, I watched them from my eye's tail, and when I observed that they ate nothing I thought it not only strange, but menacing. Normal people do not do such things; abnormal people usually are dangerous.

"When Palenzeke left the young woman, after indicating she might flirt with the young Rochester, I liked the look of things a little less. My first thought was that it might be a game of decoy and robbery—how do you call him?—the game of the badger? Accordingly, I thought it best to follow them to see what we should see. *Eh bien*, my friend, we saw a plenty, *n'est-ce-pas?*

"You will recall young Rochester's experience in the cemetery. As he related it to us I saw at once what manner of foeman we must grapple with, though at that time I did not know how innocent Mademoiselle Alice was. Our information from Madame Heatherton confirmed my worst fears. What we behold at Rochester's apartment that night proved all I had imagined, and more.

"But me, I had not been idle meantime. Oh, no. I had seen the good Father Apostolakos, and told him what I had learned. He understood at once, and made immediate arrangements to have Palenzeke's foul body exhumed and taken to the crematory for incineration. He also lent me a sacred *ikon*, the blessed image of a saint whose potency to repel demons had more than once been proved. Perhaps you noticed how Mademoiselle Alice shrank from me when I approached her with the relic in my pocket? And how the restless soul of Palenzeke flinched from it as flesh recoils from white-hot iron?

"Very well. Rochester loved this woman already dead. He himself was moribund. Why not let him taste of love with the shade of the woman who returned his passion for the few days he had yet to live? When he died, as die he must, I was prepared to treat his poor clay so that, though he were already half a vampire from the vampire's kisses on his throat, he could yet do no harm. You know I have done so. The cleansing fire has rendered Palenzeke impotent. Also, I had pledged myself to do as much for the poor, lovely, sinned-against Alice when her brief aftermath of earthly happiness should have expired. You heard me promise her, and I have kept my word.

"I could not bear to hurt her needlessly, so when I went to her with stake and knife tonight I took also a syringe loaded with five grains of morphine and gave her an injection before I began my work. I do not think she suffered greatly. Her moan of dissolution and the torsion of her poor body as the stake pierced through her heart, they were but reflex acts, not signs of conscious misery."

"But look here," I objected, "if Alice were a vampire, as you say, and able to float about after dark, how comes it that she lay in her casket when you went there tonight?"

"Oh, my friend," tears welled up in his eyes, "she waited for me. We had a definite engagement; the poor one lay in her casket, awaiting the knife and stake which should set her free from bondage. She—she smiled at me and pressed my hand when I had dragged her from the tomb!"

He wiped his eyes and poured an ounce or so of cognac into a bud-shaped inhaler. "To you, young Rochester, and to your lovely lady," he said as he raised the glass in salute. "Though there be neither marrying nor giving in marriage where you are, may your restless souls find peace and rest eternally—together."

The fragile goblet shattered as he tossed it, emptied, into the fireplace.

AUGUST DERLETH

The Drifting Snow

Aunt Mary's advancing footsteps halted suddenly, short of the table, and Clodetta turned to see what was keeping her. She was standing very rigidly, her eyes fixed upon the French windows just opposite the door through which she had entered, her cane held stiffly before her.

Clodetta shot a quick glance across the table toward her husband, whose attention had also been drawn to his aunt; his face vouchsafed her nothing. She turned again to find that the old lady had transferred her gaze to her, regarding her stonily and in silence. Clodetta felt uncomfortable.

"Who withdrew the curtains from the west windows?"

Clodetta flushed, remembering. "I did, Aunt. I'm sorry. I forgot about your not wanting them drawn away."

The old lady made an odd grunting sound, shifting her gaze once again to the French windows. She made a barely perceptible movement, and Lisa ran forward from the shadow of the hall, where she had been regarding the two at table with stern disapproval. The servant went directly to the west windows and drew the curtains.

Aunt Mary came slowly to the table and took her place at its head. She put her cane against the side of her chair, pulled at the chain about her neck so that her lorgnette lay in her lap, and looked from Clodetta to her nephew, Ernest.

Then she fixed her gaze on the empty chair at the foot of the table, and spoke without seeming to see the two beside her.

"I told both of you that none of the curtains over the west windows was to be withdrawn after sundown, and you must have noticed that none of those windows has been for one instant uncovered at night. I took especial care to put you in rooms facing east, and the sitting-room is also in the east."

"I'm sure Clodetta didn't mean to go against your wishes, Aunt Mary," said Ernest abruptly.

"No, of course not, Aunt."

The old lady raised her eyebrows, and went on impassively. "I didn't think it wise to explain why I made such a request. I'm not going to explain. But I do want to say that there is a very definite danger in drawing away the curtains. Ernest has heard that before, but you, Clodetta, have not."

Clodetta shot a startled glance at her husband.

The old lady caught it, and said, "It's all very well to believe that my mind's wandering or that I'm getting eccentric, but I shouldn't advise you to be satisfied with that."

A young man came suddenly into the room and made for the seat at the foot of the table, into which he flung himself with an almost inaudible greeting to the other three.

"Late again, Henry," said the old lady.

Henry mumbled something and began hurriedly to eat. The old lady sighed, and began presently to eat also, whereupon Clodetta and Ernest did likewise. The old servant, who had continued to linger behind Aunt Mary's chair, now withdrew, not without a scornful glance at Henry.

Clodetta looked up after a while and ventured to speak, "You aren't as isolated as I thought you might be up here, Aunt Mary."

"We aren't, my dear, what with telephones and cars and all. But only twenty years ago it was quite a different thing, I can tell you." She smiled reminiscently and looked at Ernest.

"Your grandfather was living then, and many's the time he was snowbound with no way to let anybody know."

"Down in Chicago when they speak of 'up north' or the 'Wisconsin woods' it seems very far away," said Clodetta.

"Well, it *is* far away," put in Henry abruptly. "And, Aunt, I hope you've made some provision in case we're locked in here for a day or two. It looks like snow outside, and the radio says a blizzard's coming."

The old lady grunted and looked at him. "Ha, Henry— you're overly concerned, it seems to me. I'm afraid you've been regretting this trip ever since you set foot in my house. If you're worrying about a snowstorm, I can have Sam drive you down to Wausau, and you can be in Chicago tomorrow."

"Of course not."

Silence fell, and presently the old lady called gently, "Lisa," and the servant came into the room to help her from her chair, though, as Clodetta had previously said to her husband, "She didn't need help."

From the doorway, Aunt Mary bade them all goodnight, looking impressively formidable with her cane in one hand and her unopened lorgnette in the other, and vanished into the dusk of the hall, from which her receding footsteps sounded together with those of the servant, who was seldom seen away from her. These two were alone in the house most of the time, and only very brief periods when the old lady had up her nephew Ernest, "Dear John's boy," or Henry, of whose father the old lady never spoke, helped to relieve the pleasant somnolence of their quiet lives. Sam, who usually slept in the garage, did not count.

Clodetta looked nervously at her husband, but it was Henry who said what was uppermost in their thoughts.

"I think she's losing her mind," he declared matter-of-factly. Cutting off Clodetta's protest on her lips, he got up and went into the sitting-room, from which came presently the strains of music from the radio.

Clodetta fingered her spoon idly and finally said, "I do think she is a little queer, Ernest."

Ernest smiled tolerantly. "No, I don't think so. I've an idea why she keeps the west windows covered. My grandfather died out there—he was overcome by the cold one night, and froze on the slope of the hill. I don't rightly know how it happened—I was away at the time. I suppose she doesn't like to be reminded of it."

"But where's the danger she spoke of, then?"

He shrugged. "Perhaps it lies in her—she might be affected and affect us in turn." He paused for an instant, and finally added, "I suppose she *does* seem a little strange to you—but she was like that as long as I can remember; next time you come, you'll be used to it."

Clodetta looked at her husband for a moment before replying. At last she said. "I don't think I like the house, Ernest."

"Oh, nonsense, darling." He started to get up, but Clodetta stopped him.

"Listen, Ernest, I remembered perfectly well Aunt Mary's not wanting those curtains drawn away—but I just felt I had to do it. I didn't want to but—*something made me do it.*" Her voice was unsteady.

"Why, Clodetta," he said, faintly alarmed. "Why didn't you tell me before?"

She shrugged. "Aunt Mary might have thought I'd gone woolgathering."

"Well, it's nothing serious, but you've let it bother you a little and that isn't good for you. Forget it; think of something else. Come and listen to the radio."

They rose and moved toward the sitting-room together. At the door Henry met them. He stepped aside a little, saying, "I might have known we'd be marooned up here," and adding, as Clodetta began to protest, "We're going to be, all right. There's a wind coming up and it's beginning to snow, and I know what that means." He passed them and went into the deserted dining-room, where he stood a moment looking at the too long table. Then he turned aside and went over to the French windows, from which he drew away the curtains and stood there peering out into the darkness. Ernest saw him standing at the window, and protested from the sitting-room.

"Aunt Mary doesn't like those windows uncovered, Henry."

Henry half turned and replied, "Well *she* may think it's dangerous, but I can risk it."

Clodetta, who had been staring beyond Henry into the night through the French windows, said suddenly, "Why, there's someone out there!"

Henry looked quickly through the glass and replied, "No, that's the snow; it's coming down heavily, and the wind's drifting it this way and that." He dropped the curtains and came away from the windows.

Clodetta said uncertainly, "Why, I could have sworn I saw someone out there, walking past the window."

"I suppose it does look that way from here," offered Henry, who had come back into the sitting-room. "But personally, I think you've let Aunt Mary's eccentricities impress you too much."

Ernest made an impatient gesture at this, and Clodetta did not answer. Henry sat down before the radio and began to move the dial slowly. Ernest had found himself a book, and was becoming interested, but Clodetta continued to sit with her eyes fixed upon the still slowly moving curtains cutting off the French windows. Presently she got up and left the room, going down the long hall into the east wing, where she tapped gently upon Aunt Mary's door.

"Come in," called the old lady.

Clodetta opened the door and stepped into the room where Aunt Mary sat in her dressing-robe, her dignity, in the shape of her lorgnette and cane, resting respectively on her bureau and in the corner. She looked surprisingly benign, as Clodetta at once confessed.

"Ha, thought I was an ogre in disguise, did you?" said the old lady, smiling in spite of herself. "I'm really not, you see, but I have a sort of bogey about the west windows, as you have seen."

"I wanted to tell you something about those windows,

Aunt Mary,'' said Clodetta. She stopped suddenly. The expression on the old lady's face had given way to a curiously dismaying one. It was not anger, not distaste—it was a lurking suspense. Why, the old lady was afraid!

"What?" she asked Clodetta shortly.

"I was looking out—just for a moment or so—and I thought I saw someone out there."

"Of course, you didn't, Clodetta. Your imagination, perhaps, or the drifting snow."

"My imagination? Maybe. But there was no wind to drift the snow, though one has come up since."

"I've often been fooled that way, my dear. Sometimes I've gone out in the morning to look for footprints—there weren't any, ever. We're pretty far away from civilization in a snowstorm, despite our telephones and radios. Our nearest neighbor is at the foot of the long, sloping rise—over three miles away—and all wooded land between. There's no highway nearer than that."

"I was so clear. I could have sworn to it."

"Do you want to go out in the morning and look?" asked the old lady shortly.

"Of course not."

"Then you didn't see anything?"

It was half question, half demand. Clodetta said. "Oh, Aunt Mary, you're making an issue of it now."

"Did you or didn't you in your own mind see anything, Clodetta?"

"I guess I didn't, Aunt Mary."

"Very well. And now do you think we might talk about something more pleasant?"

"Why, I'm sure—I'm sorry, Aunt. I didn't know that Ernest's grandfather had died out there"

"Ha, he's told you that, has he? Well?"

"Yes, he said that was why you didn't like the slope after sunset—that you didn't like to be reminded of his death."

The old lady looked at Clodetta impassively. "Perhaps he'll never know how near right he was."

"What do you mean, Aunt Mary?"

"Nothing for you to know, my dear." She smiled again, her sternness dropping from her. "And now I think you'd better go, Clodetta; I'm tired."

Clodetta rose obediently and made for the door, where the old lady stopped her. "How's the weather?"

"It's snowing—hard, Henry says—and blowing."

The old lady's face showed her distaste at the news. "I don't like to hear that, not at all. Suppose someone should look down that slope tonight?" She was speaking to herself, having forgotten Clodetta at the door. Seeing her again abruptly, she said, "But you don't know, Clodetta. Good night."

Clodetta stood with her back against the closed door, wondering what the old lady could have meant. *But you don't know, Clodetta.* That was curious. For a moment or two the old lady had completely forgotten her.

She moved away from the door, and came upon Ernest just turning into the east wing.

"Oh, there you are," he said. "I wondered where you had gone."

"I was talking a bit with Aunt Mary."

"Henry's been at the west windows again—and now *he* thinks there's someone out there."

Clodetta stopped short. "Does he really think so?"

Ernest nodded gravely. "But the snow's drifting frightfully, and I can imagine how that suggestion of yours worked on his mind."

Clodetta turned and went back along the hall. "I'm going to tell Aunt Mary."

He started to protest, but to no avail, for she was already tapping on the old lady's door, was indeed opening the door and entering the room before he could frame an adequate protest.

"Aunt Mary," she said, "I didn't want to disturb you again, but Henry's been at the French windows in the dining-room, and he says he's seen someone out there."

The effect on the old lady was magical. "He's seen them!"

she exclaimed. Then she was on her feet, coming rapidly over to Clodetta. "How long ago?" she demanded, seizing her almost roughly by the arms. "Tell me, quickly. How long ago did he see them?"

Clodetta's amazement kept her silent for a moment, but at last she spoke, feeling the old lady's keen eyes staring at her. "It was some time ago, Aunt Mary, after supper."

The old lady's hands relaxed, and with it her tension. "Oh," she said, and turned and went back slowly to her chair, taking her cane from the corner where she had put it for the night.

"Then there *is* someone out there?" challenged Clodetta, when the old lady had reached her chair.

For a long time, it seemed to Clodetta, there was no answer. Then presently the old lady began to nod gently, and a barely audible "Yes" escaped her lips

"Then we had better take them in, Aunt Mary."

The old lady looked at Clodetta earnestly for a moment; then she replied, her voice firm and low, her eyes fixed upon the wall beyond. "We can't take them in, Clodetta—because they're not alive."

At once Henry's words came flashing into Clodetta's memory—"She's losing her mind"—and her involuntary start betrayed her thought.

"I'm afraid I'm not mad, my dear—I hoped at first I might be, but I wasn't. I'm not, now. There was only one of them out there at first—the girl; Father is the other. Quite long ago, when I was young, my father did something which he regretted all his days. He had a too strong temper, and it maddened him. One night he found out that one of my brothers—Henry's father—had been very familiar with one of the servants, a very pretty girl, older than I was. He thought she was to blame, though she wasn't, and he didn't find out until too late. He drove her from the house, then and there. Winter had not yet set in, but it was quite cold, and she had some five miles to go to her home. We begged Father not to send her away—though we didn't now what was wrong then—but he paid no attention to us. The girl had to go.

"Not long after she had gone, a biting wind came up, and close upon it a fierce storm. Father had already repented his hasty action, and sent some of the men to look for the girl. They didn't find her, but in the morning she was found frozen to death on the long slope of the hill to the west."

The old lady sighed, paused a moment, and went on. "Years later—she came back. She came in a snowstorm, as she went; but she had become vampiric. We all saw her. We were at supper table, and Father saw her first. The boys had already gone upstairs, and Father and the two of us girls, my sister and I, did not recognize her. She was just a dim shape floundering about in the snow beyond the French windows. Father ran out to her, calling to us to send the boys after him. We never saw him alive again. In the morning we found him in the same spot where years before the girl had been found. He, too, had died of exposure.

"Then, a few years after—she returned with the snow, and she brought him along; he, too, had become vampiric. They stayed until the last snow, always trying to lure someone out there. After that, I knew, and had the windows covered during the winter nights, from sunset to dawn, because they never went beyond the west slope.

"Now you know, Clodetta."

Whatever Clodetta was going to say was cut short by running footsteps in the hall, a hasty rap, and Ernest's head appearing suddenly in the open doorway."

"Come on, you two," he said, almost gaily, "There *are* people out on the west slope—a girl and an old man—and Henry's gone out to fetch them in!"

Then, triumphant, he was off. Clodetta came to her feet, but the old lady was before her, passing her and almost running down the hall, calling loudly for Lisa, who presently appeared in nightcap and gown from her room.

"Call Sam, Lisa," said the old lady, "and send him to me in the dining-room."

She ran on into the dining-room, Clodetta close on her heels. The French windows were open, and Ernest stood on the snow-covered terrace beyond, calling his cousin. The old lady went directly over to him, even striding into the snow to his side, though the wind drove the snow against her with great force. The wooded western slope was lost in a snow-fog; the nearest trees were barely discernible.

"Where could they have gone?" Ernest said, turning to the old lady, whom he had thought to be Clodetta. Then, seeing that it was the old lady, he said, "Why, Aunt Mary—and so little on, too! You'll catch your death of cold."

"Never mind, Ernest," said the old lady. "I'm all right. I've had Sam get up to help you look for Henry—but I'm afraid you won't find him."

"He can't be far; he just went out."

"He went before you saw where; he's far enough gone."

Sam came running into the blowing snow from the dining room, muffled in a greatcoat. He was considerably older than Ernest, almost the old lady's age. He shot a questioning glance at her and asked, "Have they come again?"

Aunt Mary nodded. "You'll have to look for Henry. Ernest will help you. And remember, don't separate. And don't go far from the house."

Clodetta came with Ernest's overcoat, and together the two women stood there, watching them until they were swallowed up in the wall of driven snow. Then they turned slowly and went back into the house.

The old lady sank into a chair facing the windows. She was pale and drawn, and looked, as Clodetta said afterwards, "as if she'd fallen together." For a long time she said nothing. Then, with a gentle little sigh, she turned to Clodetta and spoke.

"Now there'll be three of them out there."

Then, so suddenly that no one knew how it happened, Ernest and Sam appeared beyond the windows, and between them they dragged Henry. The old lady flew to open windows, and the three of them, cloaked in snow, came into the room.

"We found him—but the cold's hit him pretty hard, I'm afraid," said Ernest.

The old lady sent Lisa for cold water, and Ernest ran to get himself other clothes. Clodetta went with him, and in their rooms told him what the old lady had related to her.

Ernest laughed. "I think you believed that, didn't you, Clodetta? Sam and Lisa do, I know, because Sam told me the story long ago. I think the shock of Grandfather's death was too much for all three of them."

"But the story of the girl, and then——"

"That part's true, I'm afraid. A nasty story, but it did happen."

"But those people Henry and I saw!" protested Clodetta weakly.

Ernest stood without movement. "That's so," he said, "I saw them, too. Then they're out there yet, and we'll have to find them!" He took up his overcoat again, and went from the room, Clodetta protesting in a shrill unnatural voice. The old lady met him at the door of the dining-room, having overheard Clodetta pleading with him. "No, Ernest—you can't go out there again," she said. "There's no one out there."

He pushed gently into the room and called to Sam, "Coming, Sam? There are still two of them out there—we almost forgot them."

Sam looked at him strangely. "What do you mean?" he demanded roughly. He looked challengingly at the old lady, who shook her head.

"The girl and the old man, Sam. We've got to get them, too."

"Oh, *them*," said Sam. "They're dead!"

"Then I'll go out alone," said Ernest.

Henry came to his feet suddenly, looking dazed. He walked forward a few steps, his eyes traveling from one to the other of them yet apparently not seeing them. He began to speak abruptly, in an unnatural child-like voice.

"*The snow*," he murmured, "*the snow—the beautiful hands, so little, so lovely—her beautiful hands—and the snow, the beautiful lovely snow, drifting and falling about her. . . .*"

He turned slowly and looked toward the French windows, the others following his gaze. Beyond was a wall of white, where the snow was drifting against the house. For a moment Henry stood quietly watching; then suddenly a white figure came forward from the snow—a young girl, cloaked in long snow-whips, her glistening eyes strangely fascinating.

The old lady flung herself forward, her arms outstretched to cling to Henry, but she was too late. Henry had run toward the windows, had opened them, and even as Clodetta cried out, had vanished into the wall of snow beyond.

Then Ernest ran forward, but the old lady threw her arms around him and held him tightly, murmuring, "You shall not go! Henry is gone beyond our help!"

Clodetta came to help her, and Sam stood menacingly at the French windows, now closed against the wind and the sinister snow. So they held him, and would not let him go.

"And tomorrow," said the old lady in a harsh whisper, "we must go to their graves and stake them down. We should have gone before."

In the morning they found Henry's body crouched against the bole of an ancient oak, where two others had been found years before. There were almost obliterated marks of where something had dragged him, a long, uneven swath in the snow, and yet no footprints, only strange, hollowed places along the way as if the wind had whirled the snow away, and only the wind.

But on his skin were signs of the snow vampire—the delicate small prints of a young girl's hands.

MANLY WADE WELLMAN

When it was Moonlight

Let my heart be still a moment,
and this mystery explore.
                              The Raven

His hand, as slim as a white claw, dipped a quillful of ink and wrote in one corner of the page the date—3rd March 1842.

THE PREMATURE BURIAL
by Edgar A. Poe

He hated his middle name, the name of his miserly and spiteful stepfather. For a moment he considered crossing out even the initial; then he told himself that he was only woolgathering, putting off the drudgery of writing. And write he must, or starve—the Philadelphia *Dollar Newspaper* was clamoring for the story he had promised. Well, today he had heard a tag of gossip—his mother-in-law had it from a neighbor—that revived in his mind a subject always fascinating.

He began rapidly, to write, in a fine copperplate hand:

There are certain themes of which the interest is
all-absorbing, but which are entirely too horrible for the
purposes of legitimate fiction . . .

This would really be an essay, not a tale, and he could do
it justice. Often he thought of the whole world as a vast fat
cemetery, close set with tombs in which not all the occupants
were at rest—too many struggled unavailingly against their
smothering shrouds, their locked and weighted coffin lids.
What were his own literary labors, he mused, but a struggle
against being shut down and throttled by a society as heavy
and grim and senseless as clods heaped by a sexton's spade?

He pause, and went to the slate mantelshelf for a candle.
His kerosene lamp had long ago been pawned, and it was
dark for mid afternoon, even in March. Elsewhere in the
house his mother-in-law swept busily, and in the room next to
his sounded the quiet breathing of his invalid wife. Poor
Virginia slept, and for the moment knew no pain. Returning
with his light, he dipped more ink and continued down the
sheet:

To be buried while alive is, beyond question, the
most terrific of these extremes which has ever fallen to
the lot of mere mortality. That it has frequently, very
frequently, fallen will scarcely be denied . . .

Again his dark imagination savored the tale he had heard
that day. It had happened here in Philadelphia, in this very
quarter, less than a month ago. A widower had gone, after
weeks of mourning, to his wife's tomb, with flowers. Stooping to place them on the marble slab, he had heard noise
beneath. At once joyful and aghast, he fetched men and
crowbars, and recovered the body, all untouched by decay.
At home that night, the woman returned to consciousness.

So said the gossip, perhaps exaggerated, perhaps not. And
the house was only six blocks away from Spring Garden
Street, where he sat.

Poe fetched out his notebooks and began to marshal bits of narrative for his composition—a gloomy tale of resurrection in Baltimore, another from France, a genuinely creepy citation from the *Chirurgical Journal* of Leipzig; a sworn case of revival, by electrical impulses, of a dead man in London. Then he added an experience of his own, romantically embellished, a dream adventure of his boyhood in Virginia. Just as he thought to make an end, he had a new inspiration.

Why not learn more about that reputed Philadelphia burial and the one who rose from seeming death? It would point up his piece, give it a timely local climax, ensure acceptance—he could hardly risk a rejection. Too, it would satisfy his own curiosity. Laying down the pen, Poe got up. From a peg he took his wide black hat, his old military cloak that he had worn since his ill-fated cadet days at West Point. Huddling it round his slim little body, he opened the front door and went out.

March had come in like a lion and, lion-like, roared and rampaged over Philadelphia. Dry, cold dust blew up into Poe's full gray eyes, and he hardened his mouth under the gay dark mustache. His shins felt goosefleshy; his striped trousers were unseasonably thin and his shoes badly needed mending. Which way lay his journey?

He remembered the name of the street, and something about a ruined garden. Eventually he came to the place, or what must be the place—the garden was certainly ruined, full of dry, hardy weeds that still stood in great ragged clumps after the hard winter. Poe forced open the creaky gate, went up the rough-flagged path to the stoop. He saw a bronzed nameplate—"Gauber," it said. Yes, that was the name he had heard. He swung the knocker loudly, and thought he caught a whisper of movement inside. But the door did not open.

"Nobody lives there, Mr. Poe," said someone from the street. It was a grocery boy, with a heavy basket on his arm. Poe left the doorstep. He knew the lad; indeed he owed the grocer eleven dollars.

"Are you sure?" Poe prompted.

"Well"—and the boy shifted the weight of his burden—"if anybody lived here, they'd buy from our shop, wouldn't they? And I'd deliver, wouldn't I? But I've had this job for six months, and never set foot inside that door."

Poe thanked him and walked down the street, but did not take the turn that would lead home. Instead he sought the shop of one Pemberton, a printer and a friend, to pass the time of day and ask for a loan.

Pemberton could not lend even one dollar—times were hard—but he offered a drink of Monongahela whiskey, which Poe forced himself to refuse; then a supper of crackers, cheese and garlic sausage, which Poe thankfully shared. At home, unless his mother-in-law had begged or borrowed from the neighbors, would be only bread and molasses. It was past sundown when the writer shook hands with Pemberton, thanked him with warm courtesy for his hospitality, and ventured into the evening.

Thank Heaven, it did not rain. Poe was saddened by storms. The wind had abated and the March sky was clear save for a tiny fluff of scudding cloud and a banked dark line at the horizon, while up rose a full moon the color of frozen cream. Poe squinted from under his hat brim at the shadow-pattern on the disc. Might he not write another story of a lunar voyage—like the one about Hans Pfaal, but dead serious this time? Musing thus, he walked along the dusk-filling street until he came again opposite the ruined garden, the creaky gate, and the house with the doorplate marked: "Gauber."

Hello, the grocery boy had been wrong. There was light inside the front window, water-blue light—or was there? Anyway, motion—yes, a figure stooped there, as if to peer out at him.

Poe turned in at the gate, and knocked at the door once again.

Four or five moments of silence; then he heard the old lock grating. The door moved inward, slowly and noisily. Poe fancied that he had been wrong about the blue light, for he saw only darkness inside. A voice spoke:

"Well, sir."

The two words came huskily but softly, as though the door-opener scarcely breathed. Poe swept off his broad black hat and made one of his graceful bows.

"If you will pardon me. . . ." He paused, not knowing whether he addressed man or woman. "This is the Gauber residence?"

"It is," was the reply, soft, hoarse and sexless. "Your business, sir?"

Poe spoke with official crispness; he had been a sergeant-major of artillery before he was twenty-one, and knew how to inject the proper note. "I am here on public duty," he announced. "I am a journalist, tracing a strange report."

"Journalist?" repeated his interrogator. "Strange report? Come in, sir."

Poe complied, and the door closed abruptly behind him, with a rusty snick of the lock. He remembered being in jail once, and how the door of his cell had slammed just so. It was not a pleasant memory. But he saw more clearly, now he was inside—his eyes got used to the tiny trickle of moonlight.

He stood in a dark hallway, all paneled in wood, with no furniture, drapes or pictures. With him was a woman, in full skirt and down-drawn lace cap, a woman as tall as he and with intent eyes that glowed as from within. She neither moved nor spoke, but waited for him to tell her more of his errand.

Poe did so, giving his name and, stretching a point, claiming to be a sub-editor of the *Dollar Newspaper*, definitely assigned to the interview. "And now, madam, concerning this story that is rife concerning a premature burial. . . ."

She had moved very close, but as his face turned toward her she drew back. Poe fancied that his breath had blown her away like a feather; then, remembering Pemberton's garlic sausage, he was chagrined. To confirm his new thought, the woman was offering him wine—to sweeten his breath.

"Would you take a glass of canary, Mr Poe?" she invited, and opened a side door. He followed her into a room papered in pale blue. Moonglow, drenching it, reflected from that paper and seemed an artificial light. That was what he had seen from outside. From an undraped table his hostess lifted bottle, poured wine into a metal goblet and offered it.

Poe wanted that wine, but had recently promised his sick wife, solemnly and honestly, to abstain from even a sip of the drink that so easily upset him. Through thirsty lips he said: "I thank you kindly, but I am a temperance man."

"Oh," and she smiled. Poe saw white teeth. Then: "I am Elva Gauber—Mrs. John Gauber. The matter of which you ask I cannot explain clearly, but it is true. My husband was buried, in the Eastman Luterhan Churchyard. . . ."

"I had heard, Mrs. Gauber, that the burial concerned a woman."

"No, my husband. He had been ill. He felt cold and quiet. A physician, a Dr. Mecham, pronounced him dead, and he was interred beneath a marble slab in his family vault." She sounded weary, but her voice was calm. "This happened shortly after the New Year. On Valentine's Day, I brought flowers. Beneath his slab he stirred and struggled. I had him brought forth. And he lives—after a fashion—today."

"Lives today?" repeated Poe. "In this house?"

"Would you care to see him? Interview him?"

Poe's heart raced, his spine chilled. It was his peculiarity that such sensations gave him pleasure. "I would like nothing better," he assured her, and she went to another door, an inner one.

Opening it, she paused on the threshold, as though summoning her resolution for a plunge into cold, swift water. Then she started down a flight of steps.

Poe followed, unconsciously drawing the door shut behind him.

The gloom of midnight, or prison—yes, of the tomb—fell at once upon those stairs. He heard Elva Gauber gasp:

"No—the moonlight—let it in. . . ." And then she fell, heavily and limply, rolling downstairs.

Aghast, Poe quickly groped his way after her. She lay

against a door at the foot of the flight, wedged against the panel. He touched her—she was cold and rigid, without motion or elasticity of life. His thin hand groped for and found the knob of the lower door, flung it open. More dim reflected moonlight, and he made shift to drag the woman into it.

Almost at once she sighed heavily, lifted her head, and rose. "How stupid of me," she apologized hoarsely.

"The fault was mine," protested Poe. "Your nerves, your health, have naturally suffered. The sudden dark—the closeness—overcame you." He fumbled in his pocket for a tinderbox. "Suffer me to strike a light."

But she held out a hand to stop him. "No, no. The moon is sufficient." She walked to a small, oblong pane set in the wall. Her hands, thin as Poe's own, with long grubby nails, hooked on the sill. Her face, bathed in the full light of the moon, strengthened and grew calm. She breathed deeply, almost voluptuously. "I am quite recovered," she said. "Do not fear for me. You need not stand so near, sir."

He had forgotten that garlic odor, and drew back contritely. She must be as sensitive to the smell as . . . as . . . what was it that was sickened and driven by garlic? Poe could not remember, and he took time to note that they were in a basement, stone-walled and with a floor of dirt. In one corner water seemed to drip, forming a dank pool of mud. Close to this set into the wall, showed a latched trap-door of planks, thick and wide, cleated cross-wise, as though to cover a window. But no window would be set so low. Everything smelt earthy and close, as though fresh air had been shut out for decades.

"Your husband is here?" he inquired.

"Yes." She walked to the shutter-like trap, unlatched it and drew it open.

The recess beyond was as black as ink, and from it came a feeble mutter. Poe followed Elva Gauber, and strained his eyes. In a little stone-flagged nook a bed had been made up. Upon it lay a man, stripped almost naked. His skin was as white as dead bone, and only his eyes, now opening, had life. He gazed at Elva Gauber and past her at Poe.

"Go away," he mumbled.

"Sir," ventured Poe formally. "I have come to hear of how you came to life in the grave. . . .

"It's a lie," broke in the man on the pallet. He writhed halfway to a sitting posture, laboring upward as against a crushing weight. The wash of moonlight showed how wasted and fragile he was. His face stared and snarled bare-toothed, like a skull. "A lie, I say!" he cried, with a sudden strength that might well have been his last. "Told by this monster who is not—my wife. . . ."

The shutter-trap slammed upon his cries. Elva Gauber faced Poe, withdrawing a pace to avoid his garlic breath.

"You have seen my husband," she said. "Was it a pretty sight, sir?"

He did not answer, and she moved across the dirt to the stair doorway. "Will you go up first?" she asked. "At the top, hold the door open, that I may have"—she said "life," or, perhaps, "light." Poe could not be sure which.

Plainly she, who had almost welcomed his intrusion at first, now sought to lead him away. Her eyes, compelling as shouted commands, were fixed upon him. He felt their power, and bowed to it.

Obediently he mounted the stairs, and stood with the upper door wide. Elva Gauber came up after him. At the top her eyes again seized his. Suddenly Poe knew more than ever before about the mesmeric impulses he loved to write about. "I hope," she said measuredly, "that you have not found your visit fruitless. I live here alone—seeing nobody, caring for the poor thing that was once my husband, John Gauber. My mind is not clear. Perhaps my manners are not good. Forgive me, and good night."

Poe found himself ushered from the house and outside the wind was howling once again. The front door closed behind him, and the lock grated.

The fresh air, the whip of gale in his face, and the absence of Elva Gauber's impelling gaze suddenly brought him back, as though from sleep, to a realization of what had happened—or what had not happened.

He had come out, on this uncomfortable March evening to investigate the report of a premature burial. He had seen a ghastly sick thing, that had called the gossip a lie. Somehow, then, he had been drawn abruptly away—stopped from full study of what might be one of the strangest adventures it was ever a writer's good fortune to know. Why was he letting things drop at this state?

He decided not to let them drop. That would be worse than staying away altogether.

He made up his mind, formed quickly a plan. Leaving the doorstep, he turned from the gate, slipped quickly around the house. He knelt by the foundation at the side, just where a small oblong pane was set flush with the ground.

Bending his head, he found that he could see plainly inside, by reason of the flood of moonlight—a phenomenon, he realized, for generally an apartment was disclosed only by light within. The open doorway to the stairs, the swamp mess of mud in the corner, the out-flung trapdoor, were discernible. And something stood or huddled at the exposed niche—something that bent itself upon and above the frail white body of John Gauber.

Full skirt, white cap—it was Elva Gauber. She bent herself down, her face was touching the face or shoulder of her husband.

Poe's heart, never the healthiest of organs, began to drum and race. He pressed closer to the pane, for a better glimpse of what went on in the cellar. His shadow cut away some of the light. Elva Gauber turned to look.

Her face was as pale as the moon itself. Like the moon, it was shadowed in irregular patches. She came quickly, almost running, toward the pane where Poe crouched. He saw her, plainly and at close hand.

Dark, wet, sticky stains lay upon her mouth and cheeks. Her tongue roved out, licking at the stains——

Blood!

Poe sprang up and ran to the front of the house. He forced his thin, trembling fingers to seize the knocker, to swing it heavily again and again. When there was no answer, he pushed heavily against the door itself—it did not give. He moved to a window, rapped on it, pried at the sill, lifted his fist to smash the glass.

A silhouette moved beyond the pane, and threw it up. Something shot out at him like a pale snake striking—before he could move back, fingers had twisted in the front of his coat. Elva Gauber's eyes glared into his.

Her cap was off, her dark hair fallen in disorder. Blood still smeared and dewed her mouth and jowls.

"You have pried too far," she said, in a voice as measured and cold as the drip from icicles. "I was going to spare you, because of the odor about you that repelled me—the garlic. I showed you a little, enough to warn any wise person, and let you go. Now . . ."

Poe struggled to free himself. Her grip was immovable, like the clutch of a steel trap. She grimaced in triumph, yet she could not quite face him—the garlic still clung to his breath.

"Look in my eyes," she bade him. "Look—you cannot refuse, you cannot escape. You will die, with John—and the two of you, dying, shall rise again like me. I'll have two fountains of life while you remain—two companions after you die."

"Woman," said Poe, fighting against her stabbing gaze, "you are mad."

She snickered gustily. "I am sane, and so are you. We both know that I speak the truth. We both know the futility of your struggle." Her voice rose a little. "Through a chink in the tomb, as I lay dead, a ray of moonlight streamed and struck my eyes. I woke. I struggled. I was set free. Now at night, when the moon shines—Ugh! Don't breathe that herb in my face!"

She turned her head away. At that instant it seemed to Poe

that a curtain of utter darkness fell and with it sank down the form of Elva Gauber.

He peered in the sudden gloom. She was collapsed across the window sill, like a discarded puppet in its booth. Her hand still twisted in the bosom of his coat, and he pried himself loose from it, finger by steely, cold finger. Then he turned to flee from this place of shadowed peril to body and soul.

As he turned, he saw whence had come the dark. A cloud had come up from its place on the horizon—the fat, sooty bank he had noted there at sundown—and now it obscured the moon. Poe paused, in mid-retreat, gazing.

His thoughtful eye gauged the speed and size of the cloud. It curtained the moon, would continue to curtain it for—well, ten minutes. And for that ten minutes Elva Gauber would lie motionless, lifeless. She had told the truth about the moon giving her life. Hadn't she fallen like one slain on the stairs when they were darkened? Poe began grimly to string the evidence together.

It was Elva Gauber, not her husband, who had died and gone to the family vault. She had come back to life, or a mockery of life, by touch of the moon's rays. Such light was an unpredictable force—it made dogs howl, it flogged madmen to violence, it brought fear, or black sorrow, or ecstasy. Old legends said that it was the birth of fairies, the transformation of werewolves, the motive power of broom-riding witches. It was surely the source of the strength and evil animating what had been the corpse of Elva Gauber—and he, Poe, must not stand there dreaming.

He summoned all the courage that was his, and scrambled in at the window through which clumped the woman's form. He groped across the room to the cellar door, opened it and went down the stairs, through the door at the bottom, and into the stone-walled basement.

It was dark, moonless still. Poe paused only to bring forth his tinder box, strike a light and kindle the end of a tightly twisted linen rag. It gave a feeble steady light, and he found his way to the shutter, opened it and touched the naked, wasted shoulder of John Gauber.

"Get up," he said. "I've come to save you."

The skull-face feebly shifted its position to meet his gaze. The man managed to speak, moaningly:

"Useless. I can't move—unless she lets me. Her eyes keep me here—half-alive. I'd have died long ago, but somehow. . . ."

Poe thought of a wretched spider, paralyzed by the sting of a mud-wasp, lying helpless in its captive's close den until the hour of feeding comes. He bent down, holding his blazing tinder close. He could see Gauber's neck, and it was a mass of soft tiny puncture wounds, some of them still beaded with blood drops fresh or dried. He winced, but bode firm in his purpose.

"Let me guess the truth," he said quickly. "Your wife was brought home from the grave, came back to a seeming of life. She put a spell on you, or played a trick—made you a helpless prisoner. That isn't contrary to nature, that last. I've studied mesmerism."

"It's true," John Gauber mumbled.

"And nightly she comes to drink your blood?"

Gauber weakly nodded. "Yes. She was beginning just now, but ran upstairs. She will be coming back."

"Good," said Poe bleakly. "Perhaps she will come back to more than she expects. Have you ever heard of vampires? Probably not, but I have studied them, too. I began to guess, I think, when first she was so repelled by the odor of garlic. Vampires lie motionless by day and walk and feed at night. They are creatures of the moon—their food is blood. Come."

Poe broke off, put out his light, and lifted the man in his arms. Gauber was as light as a child. The writer carried him to the slanting shelter of the closed-in staircase, and there set him against the wall. Over him Poe spread his old cadet cloak. In the gloom, the gray of the cloak harmonized with the gray of the wall stones. The poor fellow would be well hidden.

Next Poe flung off his coat, waist-coat and shirt. Heaping his clothing in a deeper shadow of the stairway, he stood up, stripped to the waist. His skin was almost as bloodlessly pale as Gauber's, his chest and arms almost as gaunt. He dared believe that he might pass momentarily for the unfortunate man.

The cellar sprang full of light again. The cloud must be passing from the moon. Poe listened. There was a dragging sound above, then footsteps.

Elva Gauber, the blood drinker by night, had revived.

Now for it. Poe hurried to the niche, thrust himself in and pulled the trapdoor shut after him.

He grinned, sharing a horrid paradox with the blackness around him. He had heard all the fabled ways of destroying vampires—transfixing stakes, holy water, prayer, fire. But he, Edgar Allan Poe, had evolved a new way. Myriads of tales whispered frighteningly of fiends lying in wait for normal men, but who ever heard of a normal man lying in wait for a fiend? Well, he had never considered himself normal, in spirit, or brain, or taste.

He stretched out, feet together, hands crossed on his bare midriff. Thus it would be in the tomb, he found himself thinking. To his mind came a snatch of poetry by a man named Bryant, published long ago in a New England review—"Breathless darkness, and the narrow house." It was breathless and dark enough in this hole, Heaven knew, and narrow as well. He rejected, almost hysterically, the implication of being buried. To break the ugly spell, that daunted him where thought of Elva Gauber failed, he turned sideways to face the wall, his naked arm lying across his cheek and temple.

As his ear touched the musty bedding, it brought to him once again the echo of footsteps, footsteps descending stairs. They were rhythmic, confident. They were eager.

Elva Gauber was coming to seek again her interrupted repast.

Now she was crossing the floor. She did not pause or turn aside—she had not noticed her husband, lying under the cadet cloak in the shadow of the stairs. The noise came straight to the trapdoor, and he heard her fumbling for the latch.

Light, blue as skimmed milk, poured into his nook. A shadow fell in the midst of it, full upon him. His imagination, ever outstripping reality, whispered that the shadow had weight, like lead—oppressive, baleful.

"John," said the voice of Elva Gauber in his ear, "I've come back. You know why—you know what for." Her voice sounded greedy, as though it came through loose, trembling lips. "You're my only source of strength now. I thought tonight, that a stranger—but he got away. He had a cursed odor about him, anyway."

Her hand touched the skin of his neck. She was prodding him, like a butcher fingering a doomed beast.

"Don't hold yourself away from me, John," she was commanding, in a voice of harsh mockery. "You know it won't do any good. This is the night of the full moon, and I have power for anything, anything!" She was trying to drag his arm away from his face. "You won't gain by——" She broke off, aghast. Then, in a wild-dry-throated scream:

"You're not John!"

Poe whipped over on his back, and his bird-claw hands shot out and seized her—one hand clinching upon her snaky disorder of dark hair, the other digging its fingertips into the chill flesh of her arm.

The scream quivered away into a horrible breathless rattle. Poe dragged his captive violently inward, throwing all his collected strength into the effort. Her feet were jerked from the floor and she flew into the recess, hurtling above and beyond Poe's recumbent body. She struck the inner stones with a crashing force that might break bones, and would have collapsed upon Poe; but, at the same moment, he had released her and slid swiftly out upon the floor of the cellar.

With frantic haste he seized the edge of the back-flung trapdoor. Elva Gauber struggled up on hands and knees, among the tumbled bedclothes in the niche; then Poe had slammed the panel shut.

She threw herself against it from within, yammering and wailing like an animal in a trap. She was almost as strong as he, and for a moment he thought that she would win out of niche. But, sweating and wheezing, he bore against the planks with his shoulder, bracing his feet against the earth. His fingers found the latch, lifted it, forced it into place.

"Dark," moaned Elva Gauber from inside. "Dark—no moon——" Her voice trailed off.

Poe went to the muddy pool in the corner, thrust in his hands. The mud was slimy but workable. He pushed a double handful of it against the trapdoor, sealing cracks and edges. Another handful, another. Using his palms like trowels, he coated the boards with thick mud.

"Gauber," he said breathlessly, "how are you?"

"All right—I think." The voice was strangely strong and clear. Looking over his shoulder, Poe saw that Gauber had come upright of himself, still pale but apparently steady. "What are you doing?" Gauber asked.

"Walling her up," jerked out Poe, scooping still more mud. "Walling her up forever, with her evil."

He had a momentary flash of inspiration, a symbolic germ of a story; in it a man sealed a woman into such a nook of the wall, and with her an embodiment of active evil—perhaps in the form of a black cat.

Pausing at last to breathe, deeply, he smiled to himself. Even in the direst of danger, the most heart-breaking moment of toil and fear, he must ever be coining new plots for stories.

"I cannot thank you enough," Gauber was saying to him. "I feel that all will be well—if only she stays there."

Poe put his ear to the wall. "Not a whisper of motion, sir. She's shut off from moonlight—from life and power. Can you help me with my clothes? I feel terribly chilled.

His mother-in-law met him on the threshold when he returned to the house in Spring Garden Street. Under the white widow's cap, her strong-boned face was drawn with worry.

"Eddie, are you ill?" She was really asking if he had been drinking. A look reassured her. "No," she answered herself, "but you've been away from home so long. And you're dirty, Eddie—filthy. You must wash."

He let her lead him in, pour hot water into a basin. As he scrubbed himself, he formed excuses, a banal lie about a long walk for inspiration, a moment of dizzy weariness, a stumble into a mud puddle.

"I'll make you some nice hot coffee, Eddie," his mother-in-law offered.

"Please," he responded, and went back to his own room with the slate mantelpiece. Again he lighted the candle, sat down and took up his pen.

His mind was embellishing the story inspiration that had come to him at such a black moment, in the cellar of the Gauber house. He'd work on that tomorrow. The *United States Saturday Post* would take it, he hoped. Title? He would call it simply "The Black Cat."

But to finish the present task! He dipped his pen in ink. How to begin? How to end? How, after writing and publishing such an account, to defend himself against the growing whisper of his insanity?

He decided to forget it, if he could—at least to seek healthy company, comfort, quiet—perhaps even to write some light verse, some humorous articles and stories. For the first time in his life, he had had enough of the macabre.

Quickly he wrote a final paragraph:

There are moments when, even to the sober eye of Reason, the word of our sad Humanity may assume the semblance of a Hell—but the imagination of man is no Carathis, to explore with impunity its every cavern. Alas! The grim legion of sepulchral terrors cannot be regarded as altogether fanciful—but, like the Demons in whose company Afrasiab made his voyage down the Oxus, they must sleep, or they will devour us—they must be suffered to slumber, or we will perish.

That would do for the public, decided Edgar Allan Poe. In any case, it would do for the Philadelphia *Dollar Newspaper*.

His mother-in-law brought in the coffee.

MARY WILKINS FREEMAN

Luella Miller

Close to the village street stood the one-story house in which
Luella Miller, who had an evil name in the village, had
dwelt. She had been dead for years, yet there were those in
the village who, in spite of the clearer light which comes on a
vantage-point from a long-past danger, half believed in the
tale which they had heard from their childhood. In their
hearts, although they scarcely would have owned it, was a
survival of the wild horror and frenzied fear of their ancestors
who had dwelt in the same age with Luella Miller. Young
people even would stare with a shudder at the old house as
they passed, and children never played around it as was their
wont around an untenanted building. Not a window in the old
Miller house was broken: the panes reflected the morning
sunlight in patches of emerald and blue, and the latch of the
sagging front door was never lifted, although no bolt secured
it. Since Luella Miller had been carried out of, the house had
had no tenant except one friendless old soul who had no
choice between that and the far-off shelter of the open sky.
This old woman, who had survived her kindred and friends,
lived in the house one week, then one morning no smoke
came out of the chimney, and a body of neighbors, a score
strong, entered and found her dead in her bed. There were

dark whispers as to the cause of her death, and there were those who testified to an expression of fear so exalted that it showed forth the state of the departing soul upon the dead face. The old woman had been hale and hearty when she entered the house, and in seven days she was dead; it seemed that she had fallen a victim to some uncanny power. The minister talked in the pulpit with covert severity against the sin of superstition; still the belief prevailed. Not a soul in the village but would have chosen the almshouse rather than that dwelling. No vagrant, if he heard the tale, would seek shelter beneath that old roof, unhallowed by nearly half a century of superstitious fear.

There was only one person in the village who had actually known Luella Miller. That person was a woman well over eighty, but a marvel of vitality and unextinct youth. Straight as an arrow, with the spring of one recently let loose from the bow of life, she moved about the streets, and she always went to church rain or shine. She had never married, and had lived alone for years in a house across the road from Luella Miller's.

This woman had none of the garrulousness of age, but never in all her life had she ever held her tongue for any will save her own, and she never spared the truth when she essayed to present it. She it was who bore testimony to the life, evil, though possibly wittingly or designedly so, of Luella Miller, and to her personal appearance. When this old woman spoke—and she had the gift of description, although her thoughts were clothed in the rude vernacular of her native village—one could seem to see Luella Miller as she had really looked. According to this woman, Lydia Anderson by name, Luella Miller had been a beauty of a type rather unusual in New England. She had been a slight, pliant sort of creature, as ready with a strong yielding to fate and as unbreakable as a willow. She had glimmering lengths of straight, fair hair, which she wore softly looped around a long, lovely face. She had blue eyes full of soft pleading, little slender, clinging hands, and a wonderful grace of motion and attitude.

"Luella Miller used to sit in a way nobody else could if they sat up and studied a week of Sundays," said Lydia Anderson, "and it was a sight to see her walk. If one of them willows over there on the edge of the brook could start up and get its roots free of the ground, and move off, it would go just the way Luella Miller used to. She had a green shot silk she used to wear, too, and a hat with green ribbon streamers, and a lace veil blowing across her face and out sideways, and a green ribbon flyin' from her waist. That was what she came out bride in when she married Erastus Miller. Her name before she was married was Hill. There was always a sight of "l's" in her name, married or single. Erastus Miller was good lookin', too, better lookin' than Luella. Sometimes I used to think that Luella wa'n't so handsome after all. Erastus just about worshiped her. I used to know him pretty well. He lived next door to me, and we went to school together. Folks used to say he was waitin' on me, but he wa'n't. I never thought he was except once or twice when he said things that some girls might have suspected meant somethin'. That was before Luella came here to teach the district school. It was funny how she came to get it, for folks said she hadn't any education, and that one of the big girls, Lottie Henderson, used to do all the teachin' for her, while she sat back and did embroidery work on a cambric pocket-handkerchief. Lottie Henderson was a real smart girl, a splendid scholar, and she just set her eyes by Luella, as all the girls did. Lottie would have made a real smart woman, but she died when Luella had been here about a year—just faded away and died: nobody knew what ailed her. She dragged herself to that schoolhouse and helped Luella teach till the very last minute. The committee all knew how Luella didn't do much of the work herself, but they winked at it. It wa'n't long after Lottie died that Erastus married her. I always thought he hurried it up because she wa'n't fit to teach. One of the big boys used to help her after Lottie died, but he hadn't much government, and the school didn't do very well, and Luella might have had to give it up, for the committee couldn't have shut their eyes to things much longer. The boy that helped her was a real honest, innocent sort of fellow, and he was a good scholar, too. Folks said he overstudied, and that was the reason he was took crazy the year after Luella married, but I don't know. And I don't know what made Erastus Miller go into consumption of the blood the year after he was married: consumption wa'n't in his family. He just grew weaker and weaker, and went almost bent double when he tried to wait on Luella, and he spoke feeble, like an old man. He worked terrible hard till the last trying to save up a little to leave Luella. I've seen him out in the worst storms on a wood-sled—he used to cut and sell wood—and he was hunched up on top lookin' more dead than alive. Once I couldn't stand it: I went over and helped him pitch some wood on the cart—I was always strong in my arms. I wouldn't stop for all he told me to, and I guess he was glad enough for the help. That was only a week before he died. He fell on the kitchen floor while he was gettin' breakfast. He always got the breakfast and let Luella lay abed. He did all the sweepin' and the washin' and the ironin' and most of the cookin'. He couldn't bear to have Luella lift her finger, and she let him do for her. She lived like a queen for all the work she did. She didn't even do her sewin'. She said it made her shoulder ache to sew, and poor Erastus' sister Lily used to do all her sewin'. She wa'n't able to, either; she was never strong in her back, but she did it beautifully. She had to, to suit Luella, she was so dreadful particular. I never saw anythin' like the fagottin' and hemstitchin' that Lily Miller did for Luella. She made all Luella's weddin' outfit, and that green silk dress, after Maria Babbit cut it. Maria she cut it for nothin', and she did a lot more cuttin' and fittin' for nothin' for Luella, too. Lily Miller went to live with Luella after Erastus died. She gave up her home, though she was real attached to it and wa'n't a mite afraid to stay alone. She rented it and she went to live with Luella right away after the funeral.''

Then this old woman, Lydia Anderson, who remembered Luella Miller, would go on to relate the story of Lily Miller.

It seemed that on the removal of Lily Miller to the house of her dead brother, to live with his widow, the village people first began to talk. This Lily Miller had been hardly past her first youth, and a most robust and blooming woman, rosy-cheeked, with curls of strong, black hair overshadowing round, candid temples and bright dark eyes. It was not six months after she had taken up her residence with her sister-in-law that her rosy color faded and her pretty curves became wan hollows. White shadows began to show in the black rings of her hair, and the light died out of her eyes, her features sharpened, and there were pathetic lines at her mouth, which yet wore always an expression of utter sweetness and even happiness. She was devoted to her sister; there was no doubt that she loved her with her whole heart, and was perfectly content in her service. It was her sole anxiety lest she should die and leave her alone.

"The way Lily Miller used to talk about Luella was enough to make you mad and enough to make you cry," said Lydia Anderson. "I've been in there sometimes toward the last when she was too feeble to cook and carried her some blanc-mange or custard—somethin' I thought she might relish, and she'd thank me, and when I asked her how she was, say she felt better than she did yesterday, and asked me if I didn't think she looked better, dreadful pitiful, and say poor Luella had an awful time takin' car of her and doin' the work—she wa'n't strong enough to do anything'—when all the time Luella wa'n't liftin' her finger and poor Lily didn't get any care except what the neighbors gave her, and Luella eat up everythin' that was carried in for Lily. I had it real straight that she did. Luella used to just sit and cry and do nothin'. She did act real fond of Lily, and she pined away considerable, too. There was those that thought she'd go into a decline herself. But after Lily died, her Aunt Abby Mixter came, and then Luella picked up and grew as fat and rosy as ever. But poor Aunt Abby begun to droop just the way Lily had, and I guess somebody wrote to her married daughter, Mrs. Sam Abbot, who lived in Barre, for she wrote her

mother that she must leave right away and come and make
her a visit, but Aunt Abby wouldn't go. I can see her now.
She was a real good lookin' woman, tall and large, with a
big, square face and a high forehead that looked of itself kind
of benevolent and good. She just tended out on Luella as if
she had been a baby, and when her married daughter sent for
her she wouldn't stir one inch. She'd always thought a lot of
her daughter, too, but she said Luella needed her and her
married daughter didn't. Her daughter kept writin' and writin',
but it didn't do any good. Finally she came, and when she
saw how bad her mother looked, she broke down and cried
and all but went on her knees to have her come away. She
spoke her mind out to Luella, too. She told her that she'd
killed her husband and everybody that had anythin' to do with
her, and she'd thank her to leave her mother alone. Luella
went into hysterics, and Aunt Abby was so frightened that
she called me after her daughter went. Mrs. Sam Abbot she
went away fairly cryin' out loud in the buggy, the neighbors
heard her, and well she might, for she never saw her mother
again alive. I went in that night when Aunt Abby called for
me, standin' in the door with her little green-checked shawl
over her head. I can see her now. 'Do come over here, Miss
Anderson,' she sung out, kind of gasping for breath. I didn't
stop for anythin'. I put over as fast as I could, and when I got
there, there was Luella laughin' and cryin' all together, and
Aunt Abby trying to hush her, and all the time she herself
was white as a sheet and shakin' so she could hardly stand.
'For the land sakes, Mrs. Mixter,' says I, 'you look worse
than she does. You ain't' fit to be up out of your bed.'

  "Oh, there ain't anythin' the matter with me,' says she.
Then she went on talkin' to Luella. 'There, there, don't,
don't, poor little lamb,' says she. 'Aunt Abby is here. She
ain't goin' away and leave you. Don't, poor little lamb.'

  " 'Do leave her with me, Mrs. Mixter, and you get back to
bed,' says I, for Aunt Abby had been layin' down considerable lately, though somehow she contrived to do the work.

" 'I'm well enough,' says she. 'Don't you think she had better have the doctor, Miss Anderson?'

" 'The doctor,' says I, 'I think *you* had better have the doctor. I think you need him much worse than some folks I could mention.' And I looked right straight at Luella Miller laughin' and cryin' and goin' on as if she was the center of all creation. All the time she was actin' so—seemed as if she was too sick to sense anythin'—she was keepin' a sharp lookout as to how we took it out of the corner of one eye. I see her. You could never cheat me about Luella Miller. Finally I got real mad and I run home and I got a bottle of valerian I had, and I poured some boilin' hot water on a handful of catnip, and I mixed up that catnip tea with most half a wineglass of valerian, and I went with it over to Luella's. I marched right up to Luella, a-holdin' out that cup, all smokin'. 'Now' says I, 'Luella Miller, *you swaller this!*'

" 'What is—what is it, oh, what is it?' she sort of screeches out. Then she goes off a-laughin' enough to kill.

" 'Poor lamb, poor little lamb,' says Aunt Abby, standin' over her, all kind of tottery, and tryin' to bathe her head with camphor.

" '*You swaller this right down,*' says I. And I didn't waste any ceremony. I just took hold of Luella Miller's chin and I tipped her head back, and I caught her mouth open with laughin', and I clapped that cup to her lips, and I fairly hollered at her: 'Swaller, swaller, swaller!' and she gulped it right down. She had to, and I guess it did her good. Anyhow, she stopped cryin' and laughin' and let me put her to bed, and she went to sleep like a baby inside of half an hour. That was more than poor Aunt Abby did. She lay awake all that night and I stayed with her, though she tried not to have me; said she wa'n't sick enough for watchers. But I stayed, and I made some good cornmeal gruel and I fed her a teaspoon every little while all night long. It seemed to me as if she was jest dyin' from bein' all wore out. In the mornin' as soon as it was light I run over to the Bisbees and sent Johnny Bisbee for the doctor. I told him to tell the doctor to hurry, and he come pretty quick. Poor Aunt Abby didn't seem to know much of anythin' when he got there. You couldn't hardly tell she breathed, she was so used up. When the doctor had gone, Luella came into the room lookin' like a baby in her ruffled nightgown. I can see her now. Her eyes were as blue and her face all pink and white like a blossom, and she looked at Aunt Abby in the bed sort of innocent and surprised. 'Why,' says she, 'Aunt Abby ain't got up yet?'

" 'No, she ain't,' says I, pretty short.

" 'I thought I didn't smell the coffee,' says Luella.

" 'Coffee,' says I. 'I guess if you have coffee this mornin' you'll make it yourself.'

" 'I never made the coffee in all my life,' says she, dreadful astonished. 'Erastus always made the coffee as long as he lived, and then Lily she made it, and then Aunt Abby made it. I don't believe I *can* make the coffee, Miss Anderson.'

" 'You can make it or go without, jest as you please,' says I.

" 'Ain't Aunt Abby goin' to get up?' says she.

" 'I guess she won't get up,' says I, 'sick as she is.' I was gettin' madder and madder. There was somethin' about that little pink-and-white thing standin' there and talkin' about coffee, when she had killed so many better folks than she was, and had jest killed another, that made me feel 'most as if I wished somebody would up and kill her before she had a chance to do any more harm.

" 'Is Aunt Abby sick?' says Luella, as if she was sort of aggrieved and injured.

" 'Yes,' says I, 'she's sick, and she's goin' to die, and then you'll be left alone, and you'll have to do for yourself and wait on yourself, or do without things.' I don't know but I was sort of hard, but it was the truth, and if I was any harder than Luella Miller had been I'll give up. I ain't never been sorry that I said it. Well, Luella, she up and had hysterics again at that, and I just let her have 'em. All I did was to bundle her into the room on the other side of the entry where Aunt Abby couldn't hear her, if she wa'n't past it—I don't know but she was—and set her down hard in a chair and told her not to come back into the other room, and she minded. She had her hysterics in there till she got tired. When she found out that nobody was comin' to coddle her and do for her she stopped. At least I suppose she did. I had all I could do with poor Aunt Abby tryin' to keep the breath of life in her. The doctor had told me that she was dreadful low, and give me some very strong medicine to give to her in drops real often, and told me real particular about the nourishment. Well, I did as he told me real faithful till she wa'n't able to swaller any longer. Then I had her daughter sent for. I had begun to realize that she wouldn't last any time at all. I hadn't 'realized it before, though I spoke to Luella the way I did. The doctor he came, and Mrs. Sam Abbot, but when she got there it was too late; her mother was dead. Aunt Abby's daughter just give one look at her mother layin' there, then she turned sort of sharp and sudden and looked at me.

" 'Where is she?' says she, and I knew she meant Luella.

" 'She's out in the kitchen,' says I. 'She's too nervous to see folks die. She's afraid it will make her sick.'

"The Doctor he speaks up then. He was a young man. Old Doctor Park had died the year before, and this was a young fellow just out of college. 'Mrs. Miller is not strong,' says he, kind of severe, 'and she is quite right in not agitating herself.'

" 'You are another, young man; she's got her pretty claw on you,' thinks I, but I didn't say anythin' to him. I just said over to Mrs. Sam Abbot that Luella was in the kitchen, and Mrs. Sam Abbot she went out there, and I went, too, and I never heard anythin' like the way she talked to Luella Miller. I felt pretty hard to Luella myself, but this was more than I ever would have dared to say. Luella she was too scared to go into hysterics. She jest flopped. She seemed to jest shrink away to nothin' in that kitchen chair, with Mrs. Sam Abbot standin' over her and talkin' and tellin' her the truth. I guess the truth was most too much for her and no mistake, because

Luella presently actually did faint away, and there wa'n't any sham about it, the way I always suspected there was about them hysterics. She fainted dead away and we had to lay her flat on the floor, and the Doctor he came runnin' out and he said somethin' about a weak heart dreadful fierce to Mrs. Sam Abbot, but she wa'n't a mite scared. She faced him jest as white as even Luella was layin' there lookin' like death and the Doctor feelin' of her pulse.

" 'Weak heart,' says she, 'weak heart; weak fiddlesticks! There ain't nothin' weak about that woman. She's got strength enough to hang onto other folks till she kills 'em. Weak? It was my poor mother that was weak: this woman killed her as sure as if she had taken a knife to her.'

"But the Doctor he didn't pay much attention. He was bendin' over Luella layin' there with her yellow hair all streamin' and her pretty pink-and-white face all pale, and her blue eyes like stars gone out, and he was holdin' onto her hand and smoothin' her forehead, and tellin' me to get the brandy in Aunt Abby's room, and I was sure as I wanted to be that Luella had got somebody else to hang onto, now Aunt Abby was gone, and I thought of poor Erastus Miller, and I sort of pitied the poor young Doctor, led away by a pretty face, and I made up my mind I'd see what I could do.

"I waited till Aunt Abby had been dead and buried about a month, and the Doctor was goin' to see Luella steady and folks were beginnin' to talk; then one evenin', when I knew the Doctor had been called out of town and wouldn't be round, I went over to Luella's. I found her all dressed up in a blue muslin with white polka dots on it, and her hair curled jest as pretty, and there wa'n't a young girl in the place could compare with her. There was somethin' about Luella Miller seemed to draw the heart right out of you, but she didn't draw it out of *me*. She was settin' rocking in the chair by her sittin'-room window, and Maria Brown had gone home. Maria Brown had been in to help her, or rather to do the work, for Luella wa'n't helped when she didn't do anythin'. Maria Brown was real capable and she didn't have any ties; she wa'n't married, and lived alone, so she'd offered. I couldn't see why she should do the work any more than Luella; she wa'n't any too strong; but she seemed to think she could and Luella seemed to think so, too, so she went over and did all the work—washed, and ironed, and baked, while Luella sat and rocked. Maria didn't live long afterward. She began to fade away just the same fashion the others had. Well, she was warned, but she acted real mad when folks said anythin': said Luella was a poor, abused woman, too delicate to help herself, and they'd ought to be ashamed, and if she died helpin' them that couldn't help themselves she would—and she did.

'' 'I s'pose Maria has gone home,' says I to Luella, when I had gone in and sat down opposite her.

'' 'Yes, Maria went half an hour ago, after she had got supper and washed the dishes,' says Luella, in her pretty way.

'' 'I suppose she has got a lot of work to do in her own house tonight,' says I, kind of bitter, but that was all thrown away on Luella Miller. It seemed to her right that other folks that wa'n't any better able than she was herself should wait on her, and she couldn't get it through her head that anybody should think it *wa'n't* right.

'' 'Yes,' says Luella, real sweet and pretty, 'yes, she said she had to do her washin' tonight. She has let it go for a fortnight along of comin' over here.'

'' 'Why don't she stay home and do her washin' instead of comin' over here and doin' *your* work, when you are just as well able, and enough sight more so, than she is to do it?' says I.

''Then Luella she looked at me like a baby who has a rattle shook at it. She sort of laughed as innocent as you please. 'Oh, I can't do the work myself, Miss Anderson,' says she. 'I never did. Maria *has* to do it.'

''Then I spoke out: 'Has to do it!' says I. 'Has to do it!' She don't have to do it, either. Maria Brown has her own home and enough to live on. She ain't beholden to you to come over here and slave for you and kill herself!'

"Luella she jest set and stared at me for all the world like a doll-baby that was so abused that it was comin' to life.

" 'Yes,' says I, 'she's killin' herself. She's goin' to die just the way Erastus did, and Lily, and your Aunt Abby. You're killin' her jest as you did them. I don't know what there is about you, but you seem to bring a curse,' says I. 'You kill everybody that is fool enough to care anythin' about you and do for you.'

"She stared at me and she was pretty pale.

" 'And Maria ain't the only one you're goin' to kill,' says I. 'You're goin' to kill Doctor Malcom before you're done with him.'

"Then a red color came flamin' all over her face. 'I ain't goin' to kill him, either,' says she, and she begun to cry.

" 'Yes, you *be!*' says I. Then I spoke as I had never spoke before. You see, I felt it on account of Erastus. I told her that she hadn't any business to think of another man after she'd been married to one that had died for her: that she was a dreadful woman; and she was, that's true enough, but sometimes I have wondered lately if she knew it—if she wa'n't like a baby with scissors in its hand cuttin' everybody without knowin' what it was doin'.

"Luella she kept gettin' paler and paler, and she never took her eyes off my face. There was somethin' awful about the way she looked at me and never spoke one word. After awhile I quit talkin' and I went home. I watched that night, but her lamp went out before nine o'clock, and when Doctor Malcom came drivin' past and sort of slowed up he see there wa'n't any light and he drove along. I saw her sort of shy out of meetin' the next Sunday, too, so he shouldn't go home with her, and I begun to think mebbe she did have some conscience after all. It was only a week after that that Maria Brown died—sort of sudden at the last, though everybody had seen it was comin'. Well, then there was a good deal of feelin' and pretty dark whispers. Folks said the days of witchcraft had come again, and they were pretty shy of Luella. She acted sort of offish to the Doctor and he didn't go there, and there wa'n't anybody to do anythin' for her. I don't know how she *did* get along. I wouldn't go in there and offer to help her—not because I was afraid of dyin' like the rest, but I thought she was just as well able to do her own work as I was to do it for her, and I thought it was about time that she did it and stopped killin' other folks. But it wa'n't very long before folks began to say that Luella herself was goin' into a decline jest the way her husband, and Lily, and Aunt Abby and the others had, and I saw myself that she looked pretty bad. I used to see her goin' past from the store with a bundle as if she could hardly crawl, but I remembered how Erastus used to wait and 'tend when he couldn't hardly put one foot before the other, and I didn't go out to help her.

"But at last one afternoon I saw the Doctor come drivin' up like mad with his medicine chest, and Mrs. Babbit came in after supper and said that Luella was real sick.

" 'I'd offer to go in and nurse her,' says she, 'but I've got my children to consider, and mebbe it ain't true what they say, but it's queer how many folks that have done for her have died.'

"I didn't say anythin', but I considered how she had been Erastus's wife and how he had set his eyes by her, and I made up my mind to go in the next mornin', unless she was better, and see what I could do; but the next mornin' I see her at the window, and pretty soon she came steppin' out as spry as you please, and a little while afterward Mrs. Babbit came in and told me that Doctor had got a girl from out of town, a Sarah Jones, to come there, and she said she was pretty sure that the Doctor was goin' to marry Luella.

"I saw him kiss her in the door that night myself, and I knew it was true. The woman came that afternoon, and the way she flew around was a caution. I don't believe Luella had swept since Maria died. She swept and dusted, and washed and ironed; wet clothes and dusters and carpets were flyin' over there all day, and every time Luella set her foot out when the Doctor wa'n't there there was that Sarah Jones helpin' of her up and down the steps, as if she hadn't learned to walk.

"Well, everybody knew that Luella and the Doctor were goin' to be married, but it wa'n't long before they began to talk about his lookin' so poorly, jest as they had about the others; and they talked about Sarah Jones, too.

"Well, the Doctor did die, and he wanted to be married first, so as to leave what little he had to Luella, but he died before the minister could get there, and Sarah Jones died a week afterward.

"Well, that wound up everything for Luella Miller. Not another soul in the whole town would lift a finger for her. There got to be a sort of panic. Then she began to droop in good earnest. She used to have to go to the store herself, for Mrs. Babbit was afraid to let Tommy go for her, and I've seen her goin' past and stoppin' every two or three steps to rest. Well, I stood it as long as I could, but one day I see her comin' with her arms full and stoppin' to lean against the Babbit fence, and I run out and took her bundles and carried them to her house. Then I went home and never spoke one word to her though she called after me dreadful kind of pitiful. Well, that night I was taken sick with a chill, and I was sick as I wanted to be for two weeks. Mrs. Babbit had seen me run out to help Luella and she came in and told me I was goin' to die on account of it. I didn't know whether I was or not, but I considered I had done right by Erastus's wife.

"That last two weeks Luella she had a dreadful hard time, I guess. She was pretty sick, and as near as I could make out nobody dared go near her. I don't know as she was really needin' anythin' very much, for there was enough to eat in her house and it was warm weather, and she made out to cook a little flour gruel every day, I know, but I guess she had a hard time, she that had been so petted and done for all her life.

"When I got so I could go out, I went over there one morning. Mrs. Babbit had just come in to say she hadn't seen any smoke and she didn't know but it was somebody's duty to go in, but she couldn't help thinkin' of her children, and I got right up, though I hadn't been out of the house for two weeks, and I went in there, and Luella she was layin' on the bed, and she was dyin'.

"She lasted all that day and into the night. But I sat there after the new doctor had gone away. Nobody else dared to go there. It was about midnight that I left her for a minute to run home and get some medicine I had been takin', for I begun to feel rather bad.

"It was a full moon that night, and just as I started out of my door to cross the street back to Luella's, I stopped short, for I saw something."

Lydia Anderson at this juncture always said with a certain defiance that she did not expect to be believed, and then proceeded in a hushed voice:

"I saw what I saw, and I know I saw it, and I will swear on my death bed that I saw it. I saw Luella Miller and Erastus Miller, and Lily, and Aunt Abby, and Maria, and the Doctor, and Sarah, all goin' out of her door, and all but Luella shone white in the moonlight, and they were all helpin' her along till she seemed to fairly fly in the midst of them. Then it all disappeared. I stood a minute with my heart poundin', then I went over there. I thought of goin' for Mrs. Babbit, but I thought she'd be afraid. So I went alone, though I knew what had happened. Luella was layin' real peaceful, dead on her bed."

This was the story that the old woman, Lydia Anderson, told, but the sequel was told by the people who survived her, and this is the tale which has become folklore in the village.

Lydia Anderson died when she was eighty-seven. She had continued wonderfully hale and hearty for one of her years until about two weeks before her death.

One bright moonlight evening she was sitting beside a window in her parlor when she made a sudden exclamation, and was out of the house and across the street before the neighbor who was taking care of her could stop her. She followed as fast as possible and found Lydia Anderson stretched on the ground before the door of Luella Miller's deserted house, and she was quite dead.

The next night there was a red gleam of fire athwart the moonlight and the old house of Luella Miller was burned to the ground. Nothing is now left of it except a few old cellar stones and a lilac bush, and in summer a helpless trail of morning glories among the weeds, which might be considered emblematic of Luella herself.

RICHARD MATHESON

Dress of White Silk

Quiet is here and all in me.

Granma locked me in my room and wont let me out. Because its happened she says. I guess I was bad. Only it was the dress. Mommas dress I mean. She is gone away forever. Granma says your momma is in heaven. I dont know how. Can she go in heaven if she's dead?

Now I hear granma. She is in mommas room. She is putting mommas dress down the box. Why does she always? And locks it too. I wish she didn't. Its a pretty dress and smells sweet so. And warm. I love to touch it against my cheek. But I cant never again. I guess that is why granma is mad at me.

But I amnt sure. All day it was only like everyday. Mary Jane came over to my house. She lives across the street. Everyday she comes to my house and play. Today she was.

I have seven dolls and a fire truck. Today granma said play with your dolls and it. Dont you go inside your mommas room now she said. She always says it. She just means not mess up I think. Because she says it all the time. Dont go in your mommas room. Like that.

But its nice in mommas room. When it rains I go there. Or when granma is doing her nap I do. I dont make noise. I just

267

sit on the bed and touch the white cover. Like when I was only small. The room smells like sweet.

I make believe momma is dressing and I am allowed in. I smell her white silk dress. Her going out for night dress. She called it that I dont remember when.

I hear it moving if I listen hard. I make believe to see her sitting at the dressing table. Like touching on perfume or something I mean. And see her dark eyes. I can remember.

Its so nice if it rains and I see eyes on the window. The rain sounds like a big giant outside. He says shushshush so every one will be quiet. I like to make believe that in mommas room.

What I like almost best is sit at mommas dressing table. It is like pink and big and smells sweet too. The seat in front has a pillow sewed in it. There are bottles and bottles with bumps and have colored perfume in them. And you can see almost your whole self in the mirror.

When I sit there I make believe to be momma. I say be quiet mother I am going out and you can not stop me. It is something I say I dont know why like hear it in me. And oh stop your sobbing mother they will not catch me I have my magic dress.

When I pretend I brush my hair long. But I only use my own brush from my room. I didnt never use mommas brush. I dont think granma is mad at me for that because I never use mommas brush. I wouldnt never.

Sometimes I did open the box up. Because I know where granma puts the key. I saw her once when she wouldnt know I saw her. She puts the key on the hook in mommas closet. Behind the door I mean.

I could open the box lots of times. Thats because I like to look at mommas dress. I like best to look at it. It is so pretty and feels soft and like silky. I could touch it for a million years.

I kneel on the rug with roses on it. I hold the dress in my arms and like breathe from it. I touch it against my cheek. I wish I could take it to sleep with me and hold it. I like to.

Now I cant. Because granma says. And she says I should burn it up but I loved her so. And she cries about the dress.

I wasnt never bad with it. I put it back neat like it was never touched. Granma never knew. I laughed that she never knew before. But she knows now I did it I guess. And shell punish me. What did it hurt her? Wasnt it my mommas dress?

What I like the real best in mommas room is look at the picture of momma. It has a gold thing around it. Frame is what granma says. It is on the wall on top the bureau.

Momma is pretty. Your momma was pretty granma says. Why does she? I see momma there smiling on me and she *is* pretty. For always.

Her hair is black. Like mine. Her eyes are even pretty like black. Her mouth is red so red. I like the dress and its the white one. It is all down on her shoulders. Her skin is white almost white like the dress. And so too are her hands. She is so pretty. I love her even if she is gone away forever I love her so much.

I guess I think thats what made me bad. I mean to Mary Jane.

Mary Jane came from lunch like she does. Granma went to do her nap. She said dont forget now no going in your mommas room. I told her no granma. And I was saying the truth but then Mary Jane and I was playing fire truck. Mary Jane said I bet you haven't no mother I bet you made up it all she said.

I got mad at her. I have a momma I know. She made me mad at her to say I made up it all. She said Im a liar. I mean about the bed and the dressing table and the picture and the dress even and every thing.

I said well Ill show you smarty.

I looked into granmas room. She was doing her nap still. I went down and said Mary Jane to come on because granma wont know.

She wasn't so smart after then. She giggled like she does. Even she made a scaredy noise when she hit into the table in the hall upstairs. I said youre a scaredy cat to her. She said back well *my* house isnt so dark like this. Like that was so much.

We went in mommas room. It was more dark than you could see. So I took back the curtains. Just a little so Mary Jane could see. I said this is my mommas room I suppose I made up it all.

She was by the door and she wasnt smart then either. She didnt say any word. She looked around the room. She jumped when I got her arm. Well come on I said.

I sat on the bed and said this is my mommas bed see how soft it is. She didnt say nothing. Scaredy cat I said. Am not she said like she does.

I said to sit down how can you tell if its soft if you dont sit down. She sat down by me. I said feel how soft it is. Smell how like sweet it is.

I closed my eyes but funny it wasnt like always. Because Mary Jane was there. I told her to stop feeling the cover. You said to she said. Well stop it I said.

See I said and I pulled her up. Thats the dressing table. I took her and brought her there. She said let go. It was so quiet and like always. I started to feel bad. Because Mary Jane was there. Because it was in my mommas room and momma wouldnt like Mary Jane there.

But I had to show her the things because. I showed her the mirror. We looked at each other in it. She looked white. Mary Jane is a scaredy cat I said. Am not am not she said anyway nobodys house is so quiet and dark inside. Anyway she said it smells.

I got mad at her. No it doesnt smell I said. Does so she said you said it did. I got madder too. It smells like sugar she said. It smells like sick people in your mommas room.

Dont say my mommas room is like sick people I said to her.

Well you didnt show me no dress and youre lying she said there isnt no dress. I felt all warm inside so I pulled her hair. Ill show you I said and dont never say Im a liar again.

She said Im going home and tell my mother on you. You are not I said youre going to see my mommas dress and youll better not call me a liar.

I made her stand still and I got the key off the hook. I kneeled down. I opened the box with the key.

Mary Jane said pew that smells like garbage.

I put my nails in her and she pulled away and got mad. Dont you pinch me she said and she was all red. Im telling my mother on you she said. And anyway its not a white dress its dirty and ugly she said.

Its not dirty I said. I said it so loud I wonder why granma didnt hear. I pulled out the dress from the box. I held it up to show her how its white. It fell open like the rain whispering and the bottom touched on the rug.

It is too white I said all white and clean and silky.

No she said she was so mad and red it has a hole in it. I got more madder. If my momma was here shed show you I said. You got no momma she said all ugly. I hate her.

I have. I said it way loud. I pointed my finger to mommas picture. Well who can see in this stupid dark room she said. I pushed her hard and she hit against the bureau. See then I said mean look at the picture. Thats my momma and shes the most beautiful lady in the whole world.

Shes ugly she has funny hands Mary Jane said. She hasnt I said shes the most beautiful lady in the world!

Not not she said *she has buck teeth*.

I dont remember then. I think like the dress moved in my arms. Mary Jane screamed. I dont remember what. It got dark and the curtains were closed I think. I couldnt see anyway. I couldnt hear nothing except buck teeth funny hands buck teeth funny hands even when no one was saying it.

There was something else because I think I heard some one call *dont let her say that!* I couldnt hold to the dress. And I had it on me I cant remember. Because I was like grown up strong. But I was a little girl still I think. I mean outside.

I think I was terrible bad then.

Granma took me away from there I guess. I dont know. She was screaming god help us its happened its happened. Over and over. I dont know why. She pulled me all the way here to my room and locked me in. She wont let me out. Well Im not so scared. Who cares if she locks me in a million billion years? She doesnt have to even give me supper. Im not hungry anyway.

Im full.

TANITH LEE

Red as Blood

The beautiful Witch Queen flung open the ivory case of the magic mirror. Of dark gold the mirror was, dark gold as the hair of the Witch Queen that poured down her back. Dark gold the mirror was, and ancient as the seven stunted black trees growing beyond the pale blue glass of the window.

"*Speculum, speculum,*" said the Witch Queen to the magic mirror. "*Dei gratia.*"

"*Volente Deo. Audio.*"

"Mirror," said the Witch Queen. "Whom do you see?"

"I see you, mistress," replied the mirror. "And all in the land. But one."

"Mirror, mirror, who is it you do not see?"

"I do not see Bianca."

The Witch Queen crossed herself. She shut the case of the mirror and, walking slowly to the window, looked out at the old trees through the panes of pale blue glass.

Fourteen years ago, another woman had stood at this window, but she was not like the Witch Queen. The woman had black hair that fell to her ankles; she had a crimson gown, the girdle worn high beneath her breasts, for she was far gone with child. And this woman had thrust open the glass casement on the winter garden, where the old trees crouched in

273

the snow. Then, taking a sharp bone needle, she had thrust it
into her finger and shaken three bright drops on the ground.
"Let my daughter have," said the woman, "hair black as
mine, black as the wood of these warped and arcane trees.
Let her have skin like mine, white as this snow. And let her
have my mouth, red as my blood." And the woman had
smiled and licked at her finger. She had a crown on her head;
it shone in the dusk like a star. She never came to the window
before dusk; she did not like the day. She was the first
Queen, and she did not possess a mirror.

The second Queen, the Witch Queen, knew all this. She
knew how, in giving birth, the first Queen had died. Her
coffin had been carried into the cathedral and masses had
been said. There was an ugly rumor—that a splash of holy
water had fallen on the corpse and the dead flesh had smoked.
But the first Queen had been reckoned unlucky for the kingdom. There had been a strange plague in the land since she
came there, a wasting disease for which there was no cure.

Seven years went by. The King married the second Queen,
as unlike the first as frankincense to myrrh.

"And this is my daughter," said the King to his second
Queen.

There stood a little girl child, nearly seven years of age.
Her black hair hung to her ankles, her skin was white as
snow. Her mouth was red as blood, and she smiled with it.

"Bianca," said the King, "you must love your new
mother."

Bianca smiled radiantly. Her teeth were bright as sharp
bone needles.

"Come," said the Witch Queen, "come, Bianca. I will
show you my magic mirror."

"Please, Mama," said Bianca softly, "I do not like mirrors."

"She is modest," said the King. "And delicate. She never
goes out by day. The sun distresses her."

That night, the Witch Queen opened the case of her mirror.

"Mirror, whom do you see?"

"I see you, mistress. And all in the land. But one."

"Mirror, mirror, who is it you do not see?"

"I do not see Bianca."

The second Queen gave Bianca a tiny crucifix of golden filigree. Bianca would not accept it. She ran to her father and whispered: "I am afraid. I do not like to think of Our Lord dying in agony on His cross. She means to frighten me. Tell her to take it away."

The second Queen grew wild white roses in her garden and invited Bianca to walk there after sundown. But Bianca shrank away. She whispered to her father: "The thorns will tear me. She means me to be hurt."

When Bianca was twelve years old, the Witch Queen said to the King, "Bianca should be confirmed so that she may take Communion with us."

"This may not be," said the King. "I will tell you, she has not even been christened, for the dying word of my first wife was against it. She begged me, for her religion was different from ours. The wishes of the dying must be respected."

"Should you not like to be blessed by the church," said the Witch Queen to Bianca. "To kneel at the golden rail before the marble altar. To sing to God, to taste the ritual bread and sip the ritual wine."

"She means me to betray my true mother," said Bianca to the King. "When will she cease tormenting me?"

The day she was thirteen, Bianca rose from her bed, and there was a red stain there, like a red, red flower.

"Now you are a woman," said her nurse.

"Yes," said Bianca. And she went to her true mother's jewel box, and out of it she took her mother's crown and set it on her head.

When she walked under the old black trees in the dusk, the crown shone like a star.

The wasting sickness, which had left the land in peace for thirteen years, suddenly began again, and there was no cure.

*　　*　　*

The Witch Queen sat in a tall chair before a window of pale green and dark white glass, and in her hands she held a Bible bound in rosy silk.

"Majesty," said the huntsman, bowing very low.

He was a man, forty years old, strong and handsome, and wise in the hidden lore of the forests, the occult lore of the earth. He would kill too, for it was his trade, without faltering. The slender fragile deer he could kill, and the moonwinged birds, and the velvet hares with their sad, foreknowing eyes. He pitied them, but pitying, he killed them. Pity could not stop him. It was his trade.

"Look in the garden," said the Witch Queen.

The hunter looked through a dark white pane. The sun had sunk, and a maiden walked under a tree.

"The Princess Bianca," said the huntsman.

"What else?" asked the Witch Queen.

The huntsman crossed himself.

"By Our Lord, Madam, I will not say."

"But you know."

"Who does not?"

"The King does not."

"Or he does."

"Are you a brave man?" asked the Witch Queen.

"In the summer, I have hunted and slain boar. I have slaughtered wolves in winter."

"But are you brave enough?"

"If you command it, Lady," said the huntsman, "I will try my best."

The Witch Queen opened the Bible at a certain place, and out of it she drew a flat silver crucifix, which had been resting against the words: *Thou shalt not be afraid for the terror by night. . . . Nor for the pestilence that walketh in darkness*.

The huntsman kissed the crucifix and put it about his neck, beneath his shirt.

"Approach," said the Witch Queen, "and I will instruct you in what to say."

Presently, the huntsman entered the garden, as the stars were burning up in the sky. He strode to where Bianca stood under a stunned dwarf tree, and he kneeled down.

"Princess," he said. "Pardon me, but I must give you ill tidings."

"Give them then," said the girl, toying with the long stem of a wan, night-growing flower which she had plucked.

"Your stepmother, that accursed, jealous witch, means to have you slain. There is no help for it but you must fly the palace this very night. If you permit, I will guide you to the forest. There are those who will care for you until it may be safe for you to return."

Bianca watched him, but gently, trustingly.

"I will go with you, then," she said.

They went by a secret way out of the garden, through a passage under the ground, through a tangled orchard, by a broken road between great overgrown hedges.

Night was a pulse of deep, flickering blue when they came to the forest. The branches of the forest overlapped and intertwined like leading in a window, and the sky gleamed dimly through like panes of blue-colored glass.

"I am weary," sighed Bianca. "May I rest a moment?"

"By all means," said the huntsman. "In the clearing there, foxes come to play by night. Look in that direction, and you will see them."

"How clever you are," said Bianca. "And how handsome."

She sat on the turf, and gazed at the clearing.

The huntsman drew his knife silently and concealed it in the folds of his cloak. He stopped above the maiden.

"What are you whispering?" demanded the huntsman, laying his hand on her wood-black hair.

"Only a rhyme my mother taught me."

The huntsman seized her by the hair and swung her about so her white throat was before him, stretched ready for the knife. But he did not strike, for there in his hand he held the dark golden locks of the Witch Queen, and her face laughed up at him and she flung her arms about him, laughing.

"Good man, sweet man, it was only a test of you. Am I not a witch? And do you not love me?"

The huntsman trembled, for he did love her, and she was pressed so close her heart seemed to beat within his own body.

"Put away the knife. Throw away the silly crucifix. We have no need of these things. The King is not one half the man you are."

And the huntsman obeyed her, throwing the knife and crucifix far off among the roots of the trees. He gripped her to him, and she buried her face in his neck, and the pain of her kiss was the last thing he felt in this world.

The sky was black now. The forest was blacker. No foxes played in the clearing. The moon rose and made white lace through the boughs, and through the backs of the huntsman's empty eyes. Bianca wiped her mouth on a dead flower.

"Seven asleep, seven awake," said Bianca. "Wood to wood. Blood to blood. Thee to me."

There came a sound like seven huge rendings, distant by the length of several trees, a broken road, an orchard, and underground passage. Then a sound like seven huge single footfalls. Nearer. And nearer.

Hop, hop, hop, hop. Hop, hop, hop.

In the orchard, seven black shudderings.

On the broken road, between the high hedges, seven black creepings.

Brush crackled, branches snapped.

Through the forest, into the clearing, pushed seven warped, misshapen, hunched-over, stunted things. Woody-black mossy fur woody-black bald masks. Eyes like glittering cracks, mouths like moist caverns. Lichen beards. Fingers of twiggy gristle. Grinning. Kneeling. Faces pressed to the earth.

"Welcome," said Bianca.

The Witch Queen stood before a window of glass like diluted wine. She looked at the magic mirror.

"Mirror. Whom do you see?"

"I see you, mistress. I see a man in the forest. He went hunting, but not for deer. His eyes are open, but he is dead. I see all in the land. But one."

The Witch Queen pressed her palms to her ears.

Outside the window the garden lay, empty of its seven black and stunted dwarf trees.

"Bianca," said the Queen.

The windows had been draped and gave no light. The light spilled from a shallow vessel, light in a sheaf, like the pastel wheat. It glowed upon four swords that pointed east and west, that pointed north and south.

Four winds had burst through the chamber, and three arch-winds. Cool fires had risen, and parched oceans, and the gray-silver powders of Time.

The hands of the Witch Queen floated like folded leaves on the air, and through dry lips the Witch Queen chanted.

"Pater omnipotens, mittere digneris sanctum Angelum tuum de Infernis."

The light faded, and grew brighter.

There, between the hilts of the four swords, stood the Angel Lucefiel, somberly gilded, his face in shadow, his golden wings spread and blazing at his back.

"Since you have called me, I know your desire. It is a comfortless wish. You ask for pain."

"You speak of pain, Lord Lucefiel, who suffer the most merciless pain of all. Worse than the nails in the feet and wrists. Worse than the thorns and the bitter cup and the blade in the side. To be called upon for evil's sake, which I do not, comprehending your true nature, son of God, brother of The Son."

"You recognize me, then. I will grant what you ask."

And Lucefiel (by some named Satan, Rex Mundi, but nevertheless the left hand, the sinister hand of God's design) wrenched lightning from the ether and cast it at the Witch Queen.

It caught her in the breast. She fell.

The sheaf of light towered and lit the golden eyes of the
Angel, which were terrible, yet luminous with compassion,
as the swords shattered and he vanished.

The Witch Queen pulled herself from the floor of the
chamber, no longer beautiful, a withered, slobbering hag.

Into the core of the forest, even at noon, the sun never
shone. Flowers propagated in the grass, but they were colorless. Above, the black-green roof hung down nets of thick,
green twilight through which albino butterflies and moths
feverishly drizzled. The trunks of the trees were smooth as
the stalks of underwater weeds. Bats flew in the daytime,
and birds who believed themselves to be bats.

There was a sepulcher, dripped with moss. The bones had
been rolled out, had rolled around the feet of seven twisted
dwarf trees. They looked like trees. Sometimes they moved.
Sometimes something like an eye glittered, or a tooth, in the
wet shadows.

In the shade of the sepulcher door sat Bianca, combing her
hair.

A lurch of motion disturbed the thick twilight.

The seven trees turned their heads.

A hag emerged from the forest. She was crook-backed and
her head was poked forward, predatory, withered, and almost
hairless, like a vulture's.

"Here we are at last," grated the hag, in a vulture's voice.

She came closer, and cranked herself down on her knees,
and bowed her face into the turf and the colorless flowers.

Bianca sat and gazed at her. The hag lifted herself. Her
teeth were yellow palings.

"I bring you the homage of witches, and three gifts," said
the hag.

"Why should you do that?"

"Such a quick child, and only fourteen years old. Why?
Because we fear you. I bring you gifts to curry favor."

Bianca laughed. "Show me."

The hag made a pass in the green air. She held a silken cord worked curiously with plaited human hair.

"Here is a girdle which will protect you from the devices of priests, from crucifix and chalice and the accursed holy water. In it are notted the tresses of a virgin, and of a woman no better than she should be, and of a woman dead. And here—" a second pass and a comb was in her hand, lacquered blue over green—"a comb from the deep sea, a mermaid's trinket, to charm and subdue. Part your locks with this, and the scent of ocean will fill men's nostrils and the rhythm of the tides their ears, the tides that bind men like chains. Last," added the hag, "that old symbol of wickedness, the scarlet fruit of Eve, the apple red as blood. Bite, and the understanding of sin, which the serpent boasted of, will be made to known to you." And the hag made her last pass in the air and extended the apple, with the girdle and the comb, toward Bianca.

Bianca glanced at the seven stunted trees.

"I like her gifts, but I do not quite trust her."

The bald masks peered from their shaggy beardings. Eyelets glinted. Twiggy claws clacked.

"All the same," said Bianca. "I will let her tie the girdle on me, and comb my hair herself."

The hag obeyed, simpering. Like a toad she waddled to Bianca. She tied on the girdle. She parted the ebony hair. Sparks sizzled, white from the girdle, peacock's eye from the comb.

"And now, hag, take a little bite of the apple."

"It will be my pride," said the hag, "to tell my sisters I shared this fruit with you." And the hag bit into the apple, and mumbled the bite noisily, and swallowed, smacking her lips.

Then Bianca took the apple and bit into it.

Bianca screamed—and choked.

She jumped to her feet. Her hair whirled about her like a storm cloud. Her face turned blue, then slate, then white again. She lay on the pallid flowers, neither stirring nor breathing.

The seven dwarf trees rattled their limbs and their bear-shaggy heads, to no avail. Without Bianca's art they could not hop. They strained their claws and ripped at the hag's sparse hair and her mantle. She fled between them. She fled into the sunlit acres of the forest, along the broken road, through the orchard, into a hidden passage.

The hag reentered the palace by the hidden way, and the Queen's chamber by a hidden stair. She was bent almost double. She held her ribs. With one skinny hand she opened the ivory case of the magic mirror.

Speculum, speculum. Dei gratia. Whom do you see?''

''I see you, mistress. And all in the land. And I see a coffin.''

''Whose corpse lies in the coffin?''

''That I cannot see. It must be Bianca.''

The hag, who had been the beautiful Witch Queen, sank into her tall chair before the window of pale, cucumber green and dark white glass. Her drugs and potions waited, ready to reverse the dreadful conjuring of age the Angel Lucefiel had placed on her, but she did not touch them yet.

The apple had contained a fragment of the flesh of Christ, the sacred wafer, the Eucharist.

The Witch Queen drew her Bible to her and opened it randomly.

And read, with fear, the word: *Resurcat.*

It appeared like glass, the coffin, milky glass. It had formed this way. A thin white smoke had risen from the skin of Bianca. She smoked as a fire smokes when a drop of quenching water falls on it. The piece of Eucharist had stuck in her throat. The Eucharist, quenching water to her fire, caused her to smoke.

Then the cold dews of night gathered, and the colder atmospheres of midnight. The smoke of Bianca's quenching froze about her. Frost formed in exquisite silver scroll-work all over the block of misty ice that contained Bianca.

Bianca's frigid heart could not warm the ice. Nor the sunless, green twilight of the day.

You could just see her, stretched in the coffin, through the glass. How lovely she looked, Bianca. Black as ebony, white as snow, red as blood.

The trees hung over the coffin. Years passed. The trees sprawled about the coffin, cradling it in their arms. Their eyes wept fungus and green resin. Green amber drops hardened like jewels in the coffin of glass.

"Who is that lying under the trees?" the Prince asked, as he rode into the clearing.

He seemed to bring a golden moon with him, shining about his golden head, on the golden armor and the cloak of white satin blazoned with gold and blood and ink and sapphire. The white horse trod on the colorless flowers, but the flowers sprang up again when the hoofs had passed. A shield hung from the saddle-bow, a strange shield. From one side it had a lion's face, but from the other, a lamb's face.

The trees groaned, and their heads split on huge mouths.

"Is this Bianca's coffin?" asked the Prince.

"Leave her with us," said the seven trees. They hauled at their roots. The ground shivered. The coffin of ice-glass gave a great jolt, and a crack bisected it.

Bianca coughed.

The jolt had precipitated the piece of Eucharist from her throat.

Into a thousand shards the coffin shattered, and Bianca sat up. She stared at the Prince, and she smiled.

"Welcome, beloved," said Bianca.

She got to her feet, and shook out her hair, and began to walk toward the Prince on the pale horse.

But she seemed to walk into a shadow, into a purple room, then into a crimson room whose emanations lanced her like knives. Next she walked into a yellow room where she heard the sound of crying, which tore her ears. All her body seemed

stripped away; she was a beating heart. The beats of her heart
became two wings. She flew. She was a raven, then an owl.
She flew into a sparkling pane. It scorched her white. Snow
white. She was a dove.

She settled on the shoulder of the Prince and hid her head
under her wing. She had no longer anything black about her,
and nothing red.

"Begin again now, Bianca," said the Prince. He raised her
from his shoulder. On his wrist there was a mark. It was like
a star. Once a nail had been driven in there.

Bianca flew away, up through the roof of the forest. She
flew in at a delicate wine window. She was in the palace. She
was seven years old.

The Witch Queen, her new mother, hung a filigree crucifix
around her neck.

"Mirror," said the Witch Queen. "Whom do you see?"

"I see you, mistress," replied the mirror. "And all in the
land. I see Bianca."

SHERIDAN LeFANU

Carmilla

I
An Early Fright

In Styria, we, though by no means magnificent people, inhabit a castle, or schloss. A small income, in that part of the world, goes a great way. Eight or nine hundred a year does wonders. Scantily enough ours would have answered among wealthy people at home. My father is English, and I bear an English name, although I never saw England. But here, in this lonely and primitive place, where everything is so marvelously cheap, I really don't see how ever so much more money would at all materially add to our comforts, or even luxuries.

My father was in the Austrian service, and retired upon a pension and his patrimony, and purchased this feudal residence, and the small estate on which it stands, a bargain.

Nothing can be more picturesque or solitary. It stands on a slight eminence in a forest. The road, very old and narrow, passes in front of its drawbridge, never raised in my time, and its moat, stocked with perch, and sailed over by many swans, and floating on its surface white fleets of water-lilies.

Over all this the schloss shows its many-windowed front; its towers, and its Gothic chapel.

The forest opens in an irregular and very picturesque glade before its gate, and at the right a steep Gothic bridge carries

the road over a stream that winds in deep shadow through the
wood.

I have said that this is a very lonely place. Judge whether I
say truth. Looking from the hall door toward the road, the
forest in which our castle stands extends fifteen miles to the
right, and twelve to the left. The nearest inhabited village is
about seven of your English miles to the left. The nearest
inhabited schloss of any historic associations, is that of old
General Spielsdorf, nearly twenty miles away to the right.

I have said "the nearest *inhabited* village," because there
is, only three miles westward, that is to say in the direction of
General Spielsdorf's schloss, a ruined village, with its quaint
little church, now roofless, in the aisle of which are the
moldering tombs of the proud family of Karnstein, now
extinct, who once owned the equally desolate château which,
in the thick of the forest, overlooks the silent ruins of the
town.

Respecting the cause of the desertion of this striking and
malancholy spot, there is a legend which I shall relate to you
another time.

I must tell you now how very small is the party who
constitute the inhabitants of our castle. I don't include servants, or those dependents who occupy rooms in the buildings attached to the schloss. Listen, and wonder! My father,
who is the kindest man on earth, but growing old; and I, at
the date of my story, only nineteen. Eight years have passed
since then. I and my father constituted the family at the
schloss. My mother, a Styrian lady, died in my infancy, but I
had a good-natured governess, who had been with me from, I
might almost say, my infancy. I could not remember the time
when her fat, benignant face was not a familiar picture in my
memory. This was Madame Perrodon, a native of Berne,
whose care and good nature in part supplied to me the loss of
my mother, whom I do not even remember, so early I lost
her. She made a third at our little dinner party. There was a
fourth, Mademoiselle De Lafontaine, a lady such as you
term, I believe, a "finishing governess." She spoke French

and German, Madame Perrodon French and broken English, to which my father and I added English, which, partly to prevent its becoming a lost language among us, and partly from patriotic motives, we spoke every day. The consequence was a Babel, at which strangers used to laugh, and which I shall make no attempt to reproduce in this narrative. And there were two or three young lady friends besides, pretty nearly of my own age, who were occasional visitors, for longer or shorter terms; and these visits I sometimes returned.

These were our regular social resources; but of course there were chance visits from "neighbors" of only five or six leagues distance. My life was, notwithstanding; rather a solitary one, I can assure you.

My gouvernantes had just so much control over me as you might conjecture such sage persons would have in the case of a rather spoiled girl, whose only parent allowed her pretty nearly her own way in everything.

The first occurrence in my existence, which produced a terrible impression upon my mind, which, in fact, never has been effaced, was one of the very earliest incidents of my life which I can recollect. Some people will think it so trifling that it should not be recorded here. You will see, however, by-and-by, why I mention it. The nursery, as it was called, though I had it all to myself, was a large room in the upper story of the castle, with a steep oak roof. I can't have been more than six years old, when one night I awoke, and looking around the room from my bed, failed to see the nursery-maid. Neither was my nurse there; and I thought myself alone. I was not frightened, for I was one of those happy children who are studiously kept in ignorance of ghost stories, of fairy tales, and of all such lore as makes us cover up our heads when the door creaks suddenly, or the flicker of an expiring candle makes the shadow of a bed-post dance upon the wall, nearer to our faces. I was vexed and insulted at finding myself, as I conceived, neglected, and I began to whimper, preparatory to a hearty bout of roaring; when to my surprise,

I saw a solemn, but very pretty face looking at me from the side of the bed. It was that of a young lady who was kneeling, with her hands under the coverlet. I looked at her with a kind of pleased wonder, and ceased whimpering. She caressed me with her hands, and lay down beside me on the bed, and drew me toward her, smiling; I felt immediately delightfully soothed, and fell asleep again. I was wakened by a sensation as if two needles ran into my breast very deep at the same moment, and I cried loudly. The lady started back, with her eyes fixed on me, and then slipped down upon the floor, and, as I thought, hid herself under the bed.

I was now for the first time frightened, and I yelled with all my might and main. Nurse, nursery-maid, housekeeper, all came running in, and hearing my story, they made light of it, soothing me all they could meanwhile. But, child as I was, I could perceive that their faces were pale with an unwonted look of anxiety, and I saw them look under the bed, and about the room, and peep under tables and pluck open cupboards; and the housekeeper whispered to the nurse: "Lay your hand along that hollow in the bed; some one *did* lie there, so sure as you did not; the place is still warm."

I remember the nursery-maid petting me, and all three examining my chest, where I told them I felt the puncture, and pronouncing that there was no sign visible that any such thing had happened to me.

The housekeeper and the two other servants who were in charge of the nursery, remained sitting up all night; and from that time a servant always sat up in the nursery until I was about fourteen.

I was very nervous for a long time after this. A doctor was called in, he was pallid and elderly. How well I remember his long saturnine face, slightly pitted with smallpox, and his chestnut wig. For a good while, every second day, he came and gave me medicine, which of course I hated.

The morning after I saw this apparition I was in a state of terror, and could not bear to be left alone, daylight though it was, for a moment.

I remember my father coming up and standing at the bedside, and talking cheerfully, and asking the nurse a number of questions, and laughing very heartily at one of the answers; and patting me on the shoulder, and kissing me, and telling me not to be frightened, that it was nothing but a dream and could not hurt me.

But I was not comforted, for I knew the visit of the strange woman was *not* a dream; and I was *awfully* frightened.

I was a little consoled by the nursery-maid's assuring me that it was she who had come and looked at me, and lain down beside me in the bed, and that I must have been half-dreaming not to have known her face. But this, though supported by the nurse, did not quite satisfy me.

I remembered, in the course of that day, a venerable old man, in a black cassock, coming into the room with the nurse and housekeeper, and talking a little to them, and very kindly to me; his face was very sweet and gentle, and he told me they were going to pray, and joined my hands together, and desired me to say, softly, while they were praying, "Lord hear all good prayers for us, for Jesus' sake." I think these were the very words, for I often repeated them to myself, and my nurse used for years to make me say them in my prayers.

I remembered so well the thoughtful sweet face of that white-haired old man, in his black cassock, as he stood in that rude, lofty, brown room, with the clumsy furniture of a fashion three hundred years old, about him, and the scanty light entering its shadowy atmosphere through the small lattice. He kneeled, and the three women with him, and he prayed aloud with an earnest quavering voice for, what appeared to me, a long time. I forget all my life preceding that event, and for some time after it is all obscure also, but the scenes I have just described stand out vivid as the isolated pictures of the phantasmagoria surrounded by darkness.

II

A Guest

I am now going to tell you something so strange that it will require all your faith in my veracity to believe my story. It is not only true, nevertheless, but truth of which I have been an eye-witness.

It was a sweet summer evening, and my father asked me, as he sometimes did, to take a little ramble with him along that beautiful forest vista which I have mentioned as lying in front of the schloss.

"General Spielsdorf cannot come to us so soon as I had hoped," said my father, as we pursued our walk.

He was to have paid us a visit of some weeks, and we had expected his arrival next day. He was to have brought with him a young lady, his niece and ward, Mademoiselle Rheinfeldt, whom I had never seen, but whom I had heard described as a very charming girl, and in whose society I had promised myself many happy days. I was more disappointed than a young lady living in a town, or a bustling neighborhood can possibly imagine. This visit, and the new acquaintance it promised, had furnished my day dream for many weeks.

"And how soon does he come?" I asked.

"Not till autumn. Not for two months, I dare say," he answered. "And I am very glad now, dear, that you never knew Mademoiselle Rheinfeldt."

"And why?" I asked, both mortified and curious.

"Because the poor young lady is dead," he replied. "I quite forgot I had not told you, but you were not in the room when I received the General's letter this evening."

I was very much shocked. General Spielsdorf had mentioned in his first letter, six or seven weeks before, that she was not so well as he would wish her, but there was nothing to suggest the remotest suspicion of danger.

"Here is the General's letter," he said, handing it to me.

"I am afraid he is in great affliction; the letter appears to me to have been written very nearly in distraction."

We sat down on a rude bench, under a group of magnificent lime-trees. The sun was setting with all its melancholy splendor behind the sylvan horizon, and the stream that flows beside our home, and passes under the steep old bridge I have mentioned, wound through many a group of noble trees, almost at our feet, reflecting in its current the fading crimson of the sky. General Spielsdorf's letter was so extraordinary, so vehement, and in some places so self-contradictory, that I read it twice over—the second time aloud to my father—and was still unable to account for it, except by supposing that grief had unsettled his mind.

It said, "I have lost my darling daughter, for as such I loved her. During the last days of dear Bertha's illness I was not able to write to you. Before then I had no idea of her danger. I have lost her, and now learn *all*, too late. She died in the peace of innocence, and in the glorious hope of a blessed futurity. The fiend who betrayed our infatuated hospitality has done it all. I thought I was receiving into my house innocence, gaiety, a charming companion for my lost Bertha. Heavens! what a fool have I been! I thank God my child died without a suspicion of the cause of her sufferings. She is gone without so much as conjecturing the nature of her illness, and the accursed passion of the agent of all this misery. I devote my remaining days to tracking and extinguishing a monster. I am told I may hope to accomplish my righteous and merciful purpose. At present there is scarcely a gleam of light to guide me. I curse my conceited incredulity, my despicable affectation of superiority, my blindness, my obstinacy—all—too late. I cannot write or talk collectedly now. I am distracted. So soon as I shall have a little recovered, I mean to devote myself for a time to inquiry, which may possibly lead me as far as Vienna. Some time in the autumn, two months hence, or earlier if I live, I will see you—that is, if you permit me; I will then tell you all that I scarce dare put upon paper now. Farewell. Pray for me, dear friend."

In these terms ended this strange letter. Though I had never seen Bertha Rheinfeldt my eyes filled with tears at the sudden intelligence; I was startled as well as profoundly disappointed.

The sun had now set, and it was twilight by the time I had returned the General's letter to my father.

I was a soft clear evening, and we loitered, speculating upon the possible meanings of the violent and incoherent sentences which I had just been reading. We had nearly a mile to walk before reaching the road that passes the schloss in front, and by that time the moon was shining brilliantly. At the drawbridge we met Madame Perrodon and Mademoiselle De Lafontaine, who had come out, without their bonnets, to enjoy the exquisite moonlight.

We heard their voices gabbling in animated dialogue as we approached. We joined them at the drawbridge, and turned about to admire with them the beautiful scene.

The glade through which we had just walked lay before us. At our left the narrow road wound away under clumps of lordly trees, and was lost to sight amid the thickening forest. At the right the same road crosses the steep and picturesque bridge, near which stands a ruined tower which once guarded that pass; and beyond the bridge an abrupt eminence rises, covered with trees, and showing in the shadows some gray ivy-clustered rocks.

Over the sward and low grounds a thin film of mist was stealing, like smoke, marking the distances with a transparent veil; and here and there we could see the river faintly flashing in the moonlight.

No softer, sweeter scene could be imagined. The news I had just heard made it melancholy; but nothing could disturb its character of profound serenity, and the enchanted glory and vagueness of the prospect.

My father, who enjoyed the picturesque, and I, stood looking in silence over the expanse beneath us. The two good governesses, standing a little way behind us, discoursed upon the scene, and were eloquent upon the moon.

Madame Perrodon was fat, middle-aged, and romantic, and

talked and sighed poetically. Mademoiselle De Lafontaine—in right of her father, who was a German, assumed to be psychological, metaphysical, and something of a mystic—now declared that when the moon shone with a light so intense it was well known that it indicated a special spiritual activity. The effect of the full moon in such a state of brilliancy was manifold. It acted on dreams, it acted on lunacy, it acted on nervous people; it had marvelous physical influences connected with life. Mademoiselle related that her cousin, who was mate of a merchant ship, having taken a nap on deck on such a night lying on his back, with his face full in the light on the moon, had wakened, after a dream of an old woman clawing him by the cheek, with his features horribly drawn to one side; and his countenance had never quite recovered its equilibrium.

"The moon, this night," she said, "is full of idyllic and magnetic influence—and see, when you look behind you at the front of the schloss how all its windows flash and twinkle with that silvery splendor, as if unseen hands had lighted up the rooms to receive fairy guests."

There was indolent states of the spirits in which, indisposed to talk ourselves, the talk of others is pleasant to our listless ears; and I gazed on, pleased with the tinkle of the ladies' conversation.

"I have got into one of my moping moods tonight," said my father, after a silence, and quoting Shakespeare, whom, by way of keeping up our English, he used to read aloud, he said:

> " 'In truth I know not why I am so sad:
> It wearies me; you say it wearies you;
> But how I got it—came by it.'

"I forgot the rest. But I feel as if some great misfortune were hanging over us. I suppose the poor General's afflicted letter has had something to do with it."

At this moment the unwonted sound of carriage wheels and many hoofs upon the road, arrested our attention.

They seemed to be approaching from the high ground overlooking the bridge, and very soon the equipage emerged from that point. Two horsemen first crossed the bridge, then came a carriage drawn by four horses, and two men rode behind.

It seemed to be the traveling carriage of a person of rank; and we were all immediately absorbed in watching that very unusual spectacle. It became, in a few moments, greatly more interesting, for just as the carriage had passed the summit of the steep bridge, one of the leaders, taking fright, communicated his panic to the rest, and after a plunge or two, the whole team broke into a wild gallop together, and dashing between the horsemen who rode in front, came thundering along the road toward us with the speed of a hurricane.

The excitement of the scene was made more painful by the clear, long-drawn screams of a female voice from the carriage window.

We all advanced in curiosity and horror; my father in silence, the rest with various ejaculations of terror.

Our suspense did not last long. Just before you reach the castle drawbridge, on the route they were coming, there stands by the roadside a magnificent lime-tree, on the other stands an ancient stone cross, at sight of which the horses, now going at a pace that was perfectly frightful, swerved so as to bring the wheel over the projecting roots of the tree.

I knew what was coming. I covered my eyes, unable to see it out, and turned my head away; at the same moment I heard a cry from my lady-friends, who had gone on a little.

Curiosity opened my eyes, and I saw a scene of utter confusion. Two of the horses were on the ground, the carriage lay upon its side with two wheels in the air; the men were busy removing the traces, and a lady, with a commanding air and figure had got out, and stood with clasped hands, raising the handkerchief that was in them every now and then to her eyes. Through the carriage door was now lifted a young lady, who appeared to be lifeless. My dear old father was already beside the elder lady, with his hat in his hand, evidently tendering his aid and the resources of his schloss. The lady did not appear to hear him, or to have eyes for anything but the slender girl who was being placed against the slope of the bank.

I approached; the young lady was apparently stunned, but she was certainly not dead. My father, who piqued himself on being something of a physician, had just had his fingers on her wrist and assured the lady, who declared herself her mother, that her pulse, though faint and irregular, was undoubtedly still distinguishable. The lady clasped her hands and looked upward, as if in a momentary transport of gratitude; but immediately she broke out again in that theatrical way which is, I believe, natural to some people.

She was what is called a fine looking woman for her time of life, and must have been handsome; she was tall, but not thin, and dressed in black velvet, and looked rather pale, but with a proud and commanding countenance, though now agitated strangely.

"Was ever being so born to calamity?" I heard her say, with clasped hands, as I came up. "Here am I, on a journey of life and death, in prosecuting which to lose an hour is possibly to lose all. My child will not have recovered sufficiently to resume her route for who can say how long. I must leave her; I cannot, dare not, delay. How far on, sir, can you tell, is the nearest village? I must leave her there; and shall not see my darling, or even hear of her till my return, three months hence."

I plucked my father by the coat, and whispered earnestly in his ear: "Oh! papa, pray ask her to let her stay with us—it would be so delightful. Do, pray."

"If Madame will entrust her child to the care of my daughter, and of her good gouvernante, Madame Perrodon, and permit her to remain as our guest, under my charge, until her return, it will confer a distinction and an obligation upon us, and we shall treat her with all the care and devotion which so sacred a trust deserves.''

"I cannot do that, sir, it would be to task your kindness and chivalry too cruelly,'' said the lady, distractedly.

"It would, on the contrary, be to confer on us a very great kindness at the moment when we most need it. My daughter has just been disappointed by a cruel misfortune, in a visit from which she had long anticipated a great deal of happiness. If you confide this young lady to our care it will be her best consolation. The nearest village on your route is distant, and affords no such inn as you could think of placing your daughter at; you cannot allow her to continue her journey for any considerable distance without danger. If, as you say, you cannot suspend your journey, you must part with her to-night, and nowhere could you do so with more honest assurances of care and tenderness than here.''

There was something in this lady's air and appearance so distinguished, and even imposing, and in her manner so engaging, as to impress one, quite apart from the dignity of her equipage, with a conviction that she was a person of consequence.

By this time the carriage was replaced in its upright position, and the horses, quite tractable, in the traces again.

The lady threw on her daughter a glance which I fancied was not quite so affectionate as one might have anticipated from the beginning of the scene; then she beckoned slightly to my father, and withdrew two or three steps with him out of hearing; and talked to him with a fixed and stern countenance, not at all like that with which she had hitherto spoken.

I was filled with wonder that my father did not seem to perceive the change, and also unspeakably curious to learn what it could be that she was speaking, almost in his ear, with so much earnestness and rapidity.

Two or three minutes at most I think she remained thus employed, then she turned, and a few steps brought her to where her daughter lay, supported by Madame Perrodon. She kneeled beside her for a moment and whispered, as Madame supposed, a little benediction in her ear; then hastily kissing her she stepped into her carriage, the door was closed, the footmen in stately liveries jumped up behind, the outriders spurred on, the postillions cracked their whips, the horses plunged and broke suddenly into a furious canter that threatened soon again to become a gallop, and the carriage whirled away, followed at the same rapid pace by the two horsemen in the rear.

III

We Compare Notes

We followed the *cortège* with our eyes until it was swiftly lost to sight in the misty wood; and the very sound of the hoofs and the wheels died away in the silent night air.

Nothing remained to assure us that the adventure had not been an illusion of a moment but the young lady, who just at that moment opened her eyes. I could not see, for her face was turned from me, but she raised her head, evidently looking about her, and I heard a very sweet voice ask complainingly. "Where is mamma?"

Our good Madame Perrodon answered tenderly, and added some comfortable assurances.

I then heard her ask:

"Where am I? What is this place?" and after that she said, "I don't see the carriage; and Matska, where is she?"

Madame answered all her questions in so far as she understood them; and gradually the young lady remembered how the misadventure came about, and was glad to hear that no one in, or in attendance on, the carriage was hurt; and on learning that her mamma had left her here, till her return in about three months, she wept.

I was going to add my consolations to those of Madame Perrodon when Mademoiselle De Lafontaine placed her hand upon my arm, saying:.

"Don't approach, one at a time is as much as she can at present converse with; a very little excitement would possibly overpower her now."

As soon as she is comfortably in bed, I thought, I will run up to her room and see her.

My father in the meantime had sent a servant on horseback for the physician, who lived about two leagues away; and a bedroom was being prepared for the young lady's reception.

The stranger now rose, and leaning on Madame's arm, walked slowly over the drawbridge and into the castle gate.

In the hall, servants waited to receive her, and she was conducted forthwith to her room.

The room we usually sat in as our drawing-room is long, having four windows, that looked over the moat and draw-bridge, upon the forest scene I have just described.

It is furnished in old carved oak, with large carved cabi-nets, and the chairs are cushioned with crimson Utrecht vel-vet. The walls are covered with tapestry, and surrounded with great gold frames, the figures being as large as life, in ancient and very curious costume, and the subjects represented are hunting, hawking, and generally festive. It is not too stately to be extremely comfortable; and here we had our tea, for with his usual patriotic learnings he insisted that the national beverage should make its appearance regularly with our cof-fee and chocolate.

We sat here this night, and with candles lighted, were talking over the adventure of the evening.

Madame Perrodon and Mademoiselle De Lafontaine were both of our party. The young stranger had hardly lain down in her bed when she sank into a deep sleep; and those ladies had left her in the care of a servant.

"How do you like our guest?" I asked, as soon as Ma-dame entered. "Tell me all about her?"

"I like her extremely," answered Madame, "she is, I almost think, the prettiest creature I ever saw; about your age, and so gentle and nice."

"She is absolutely beautiful," threw in Mademoiselle, who had peeped for a moment into the stranger's room.

"And such a sweet voice!" added Madame Perrodon.

"Did you remark a woman in the carriage, after it was set up again, who did not get out," inquired Mademoiselle, "but only looked from the window?"

"No, we had not seen her."

Then she described a hideous black woman, with a sort of colored turban on her head, and who was gazing all the time from the carriage window, nodding and grinning derisively toward the ladies, with gleaming eyes and large white eye-balls, and her teeth set as if in fury.

"Did you remark what an ill-looking pack of men the servants were?" asked Madame.

"Yes," said my father, who had just come in, "ugly, hang-dog looking fellows, as ever I beheld in my life. I hope they mayn't rob the poor lady in the forest. They are clever rogues, however; they got everything to rights in a minute."

"I dare say they are worn out with too long traveling," said Madame. "Besides looking wicked, their faces were so strangely lean, and dark, and sullen. I am very curious, I own; but I dare say the young lady will tell us all about it tomorrow, if she is sufficiently recovered."

"I don't think she will," said my father, with a mysterious smile, and a little nod of his head, as if she knew more about it than he cared to tell us.

This made us all the more inquisitive as to what had passed between him and the lady in the black velvet, in the brief but earnest interview that had immediately preceded her departure.

We were scarcely alone, when I entreated him to tell me. He did not need much pressing.

"There is no particularly reason why I should not tell you. She expressed a reluctance to trouble us with the care of her daughter, saying she was in delicate health, and nervous, but not subject to any kind of seizure—she volunteered that—nor to any illusion; being, in fact, perfectly sane."

"How very odd to say all that!" I interpolated. "It was so unnecessary."

"At all events it *was* said," he laughed, "and as you wish to know all that passed, which was indeed very little, I tell you. She then said, 'I am making a long journey of *vital* importance—she emphasized the word—rapid and secret; I shall return for my child in three months; in the meantime, she will be silent as to who we are, whence we come, and whither we are traveling.' That is all she said. She spoke very pure French. When she said the word 'secret,' she paused for a few seconds, looking sternly, her eyes fixed on mine. I fancy she makes a great point of that. You saw how quickly she was gone. I hope I have not done a very foolish thing, in taking charge of the young lady."

For my part, I was delighted. I was longing to see and talk to her; and only waiting till the doctor should give me leave. You, who live in towns, can have no idea now great an event the introduction of a new friend is, in such a solitude as surrounded us.

The doctor did not arrive till nearly one o'clock; but I could no more have gone to my bed and slept, then I could have overtaken, on foot, the carriage in which the princess in black velvet had driven away.

When the physician came down into the drawing-room, it was to report very favorably upon his patient. She was now sitting up, her pulse quite regular, apparently perfectly well. She had sustained no injury, and the little shock to her nerves had passed away quite harmlessly. There could be no harm certainly in my seeing her, if we both wished it; and, with this permission, I sent, forthwith, to know whether she would allow me to visit her for a few minutes in her room.

The servant returned immediately to say that she desired nothing more.

You may be sure I was not long in availing myself of this permission.

Our visitor lay in one of the handsomest rooms in the schloss. It was, perhaps, a little stately. There was a somber piece of tapestry opposite the foot of the bed, representing Cleopatra with the asps to her bosom; and other solemn classic scenes were displayed, a little faded, upon the other walls. But there was gold carving, and rich and varied color enough in the other decorations of the room, to more than redeem the gloom of the old tapestry.

There were candles at the bed-side. She was sitting up; her slender pretty figure enveloped in the soft silk dressing-gown, embroidered with flowers, and lined with thick quilted silk, which her mother had thrown over her feet as she lay upon the ground.

What was it that, as I reached the bed-side and had just begun my little greeting, struck me dumb in a moment, and made me recoil a step or two from before her? I will tell you.

I saw the very face which had visited me in my childhood at night, which remained so fixed in my memory, and on which I had for so many years so often ruminated with horror, when no one suspected of what I was thinking.

It was pretty, even beautiful; and when I first beheld it, wore the same melancholy expression.

But this almost instantly lighted into a strange fixed smile of recognition.

There was a silence of fully a minute, and then at length *she* spoke; *I* could not.

"How wonderful!" she exclaimed. "Twelve years ago, I saw your face in a dream, and it has haunted me ever since."

"Wonderful indeed!" I repeated, overcoming with an effort the horror that had for a time suspended my utterness. "Twelve years ago, in vision or reality, *I* certainly saw you. I could not forget your face. It has remained before my eyes ever since."

Her smile had softened. Whatever I had fancied strange in it, was gone, and it and her dimpling cheeks were now delightfully pretty and intelligent.

I felt reassured, and continued more in the vein which hospitality indicated, to bid her welcome, and to tell her how much pleasure her accidental arrival had given us all, and especially what a happiness it was to me.

I took her hand as I spoke. I was a little shy, as lonely people are, but the situation made me eloquent, and even bold. She pressed my hand, she laid hers upon it, and her eyes glowed, as, looking hastily into mine, she smiled again, and blushed.

She answered my welcome very prettily. I sat down beside her, still wondering, and she said:

"I must tell you my vision about you; it is so very strange that you and I should have had, each of the other so vivid a dream, that each should have seen, I you and you me, looking as we do now, when of course we both were mere children. I was a child, about six years old, and I awoke from a confused and troubled dream, and found myself in a room, unlike my nursery, wainscoted clumsily in some dark wood, and with cupboards and bedsteads, and chairs, and benches placed about it. The beds were, I thought, all empty, and the room itself without anyone but myself in it; and I, after looking about me for some time, and admiring especially an iron candlestick with two branches, which I should certainly know again, crept under one of the beds to reach the window; but as I got from under the bed, I heard someone crying; and looking up, while I was still upon my knees, I saw *you*— most assuredly you—as I see you now; a beautiful young lady, with golden hair and large blue eyes, and lips—your lips—you, as you are here. Your looks won me; I climbed on the bed and put my arms about you, and I think we both fell asleep. I was aroused by a scream; you were sitting up screaming. I was frightened, and slipped down upon the ground and, it seemed to me, lost consciousness for a moment; and when I came to myself, I was again in my nursery at home. Your face I have never forgotten since. I could not be misled by mere resemblance. You *are* the lady whom I saw then."

It was now my turn to relate my corresponding vision, which I did, to the undisguised wonder of my new acquaintance.

"I don't know which should be most afraid of the other," she said, again smiling—"If you were less pretty I think I should be very much afraid of you, but being as you are, and you and I both so young, I feel only that I have made your acquaintance twelve years ago, and have already a right to your intimacy; at all events it does seem as if we were destined, from our earliest childhood, to be friends. I wonder whether you feel as strangely drawn toward me as I do to you; I have never had a friend—shall I find one now?" She sighed, and her fine dark eyes gazed passionately on me.

Now the truth is, I felt rather unaccountably toward the beautiful stranger. I did feel, as she said, "drawn toward her," but there was also something of repulsion. In this ambiguous feeling, however, the sense of the attraction immensely prevailed. She interested and won me; she was so beautiful and so indescribably engaging.

I perceived now something of languor and exhaustion stealing over her, and hastened to bid her good night.

"The doctor thinks," I added, "that you ought to have a maid to sit up with you tonight; one of ours is waiting, and you will find her a very useful and quiet creature."

"How kind of you, but I could not sleep. I never could with an attendant in the room. I shan't require any assistance—and, shall I confess my weakness, I am haunted with a terror of robbers. Our house was robbed once, and two servants murdered, so I always lock my door. It has become a habit—and you look so kind I know you will forgive me. I see there is a key in the lock."

She held me close in her pretty arms for a moment and whispered in my ear, "Good night, darling, it is very hard to part with you, but good night; tomorrow, but not early, I shall see you again."

She sank back on the pillow with a sigh, and her fine eyes followed me with a fond and melancholy gaze, and she murmured again "Good night, dear friend."

Young people like, and even love, on impulse. I was flattered by the evident, though as yet undeserved, fondness

she showed me. I liked the confidence with which she at once
received me. She was determined that we should be very near
friends.

Next day came and we met again. I was delighted with my
companion; that is to say, in many respects.

Her looks lost nothing in daylight—she was certainly the
most beautiful creature I had ever seen, and the unpleasant
remembrance of the face presented in my early dream, had
lost the effect of the first unexpected recognition.

She confessed that she had experienced a similar shock on
seeing me, and precisely the same faint antipathy that had
mingled with my admiration of her. We now laughed together
over our momentary horrors.

IV

Her Habits—A Saunter

I told you that I was charmed with her in most particulars.

There were some that did not please me so well.

She was above the middle height of women. I shall begin
by describing her. She was slender, and wonderfully graceful. Except that her movements were languid—*very* languid—
indeed, there was nothing in her appearance to indicate an
invalid. Her complexion was rich and brilliant; her features
were small and beautifully formed; her eyes large, dark, and
lustrous; her hair was quite wonderful, I never saw hair so
magnificently thick and long when it was down about her
shoulders; I have often placed my hands under it, and laughed
with wonder at its weight. It was exquisitely fine and soft,
and in color a rich very dark brown, with something of gold.
I loved to let it down, tumbling with its own weight, as, in
her room, she lay back in her chair talking in her sweet low
voice, I used to fold and braid it, and spread it out and play
with it. Heavens! If I had but known all!

I said there were particulars which did not please me. I

have told you that her confidence won me the first night I saw her; but I found that she exercised with respect to herself, her mother, her history, everything in fact connected with her life, plans, and people, an ever wakeful reserve. I dare say I was unreasonable, perhaps I was wrong; I dare say I ought to have respected the solemn injunction laid upon my father by the stately lady in black velvet. But curiosity is a restless and unscrupulous passion, and no one girl can endure, with patience, that hers should be baffled by another. What harm could it do anyone to tell me what I so ardently desired to know? Had she no trust in my good sense or honor? Why would she not believe me when I assured her, so solemnly, that I would not divulge one syllable of what she told me to any mortal breathing.

There was a coldness, it seemed to me, beyond her years, in her smiling melancholy persistant refusal to afford me the last ray of light.

I cannot say we quarreled upon this point, for she would not quarrel upon any. It was, of course, very unfair of me to press her, very ill-bred, but I really could not help it; and I might just as well have let it alone.

What she did tell me amounted, in my unconscionable estimation—to nothing.

It was all summed up in three very vague disclosures:

First—Her name was Carmilla.

Second—Her family was very ancient and noble.

Third—Her home lay in the direction of the west.

She would not tell me the name of her family, nor their armorial bearings, nor the name of their estate, nor even that of the country they lived in.

You are not to suppose that I worried her incessantly on these subjects. I watched opportunity, and rather insinuated than urged my inquiries. Once or twice, indeed, I did attack her more directly. But no matter what my tactics, utter failure was invariably the result. Reproaches and caresses were all lost upon her. But I must add this, that her evasion was conducted with so pretty a melancholy and deprecation, with so many, and even passionate declarations of her liking for me, and trust in my honor, and with so many promises that I should at last know all, that I could not find it in my heart long to be offended with her.

She used to place her pretty arms about my neck, draw me to her, and laying her cheek to mine, murmur with her lips near my ear, "Dearest, your little heart is wounded; think me not cruel because I obey the irresistible law of my strength and weakness; if your dear heart is wounded, my wild heart bleeds with yours. In the rapture of my enormous humiliation I live in your warm life, and you shall die—die, sweetly die—into mine. I cannot help it; as I draw near to you, you, in your turn, will draw near to others, and learn the rapture of that cruelty, which yet is love; so, for a while, seek to know no more of me and mine, but trust me with all your loving spirit."

And when she had spoken such a rhapsody, she would press me more closely in her trembling embrace, and her lips in soft kisses gently glow upon my cheek.

Her agitations and her language were unintelligible to me.

From these foolish embraces, which were not of very frequent occurrence, I must allow, I used to wish to extricate myself; but my energies seemed to fail me. Her murmured words sounded like a lullaby in my ear, and soothed my resistance into a trance, from which I only seemed to recover myself when she withdrew her arms.

In these mysterious moods I did not like her. I experienced a strange tumultuous excitement that was pleasurable, ever and anon, mingled with a vague sense of fear and disgust. I had no distinct thought about her while such scenes lasted, but I was conscious of a love growing into adoration, and also of abhorrence. This I know is paradox, but I can make no other attempt to explain the feeling.

I now write, after an interval of more than ten years, with a trembling hand, with a confused and horrible recollection of certain occurrences and situations, in the ordeal through which I was unconsciously passing; though with a vivid and very sharp remembrance of the main current of my story. But, I suspect, in all lives there are certain emotional scenes, those in which our passions have been most wildly and terribly roused, that are of all others the most vaguely and dimly remembered.

Sometimes after an hour of apathy, my strange and beautiful companion would take my hand and hold it with a fond pressure, renewed again and again; blushing softly, gazing in my face with languid and burning eyes, and breathing so fast that her dress rose and fell with the tumultuous respiration. It was like the ardor of a lover; it embarrassed me; it was hateful and yet overpowering; and with gloating eyes she drew me to her, and her hot lips traveled among my cheek in kisses; and she would whisper, almost in sobs, "You are mine, you *shall* be mine, you and I are one for ever." Then she threw herself back in her chair, with her small hands over her eyes, leaving me trembling.

"Are we related," I used to ask; "what can you mean by all this? I remind you perhaps of some one whom you love; but you must not, I hate it; I don't know you—I don't know myself when you look so and talk so."

She used to sigh at my vehemence, then turn away and drop my hand.

Respecting these very extraordinary manifestations I strove in vain to form any satisfactory theory—I could not refer them to affectation or trick. It was unmistakably the momentary breaking out of suppressed instinct and emotion. Was she, notwithstanding her mother's volunteered denial, subject to brief visitations of insanity; or was there here a disguise and a romance? I had read in old story books of such things. What if a boyish lover had found his way into the house, and sought to prosecute his suit in masquerade, with the assistance of a clever old adventuress. But there were many things against this hypothesis, highly interesting as it was to my vanity.

I could boast of no little attentions such as masculine gallantry delights to offer. Between these passionate moments there were long intervals of common-place, of gaiety, of brooding melancholy, during which, except that I detected her eyes so full of melancholy fire, following me, at times I might have been as nothing to her. Except in these brief periods of mysterious excitement her ways were girlish; and there was always a languor about her, quite incompatible with a masculine system in a state of health.

In some respects her habits were odd. Perhaps not so singular in the opinion of a town lady like you, as they appeared to us rustic people. She used to come down very late, generally not till one o'clock, she would then take a cup of chocolate, but eat nothing; we then went out for a walk, which was a mere saunter, and she seemed, almost immediately, exhausted, and either returned to the schloss or sat on one of the benches that were placed, here and there, among the trees. This was a bodily languor in which her mind did not sympathize. She was always an animated talker, and very intelligent.

She sometimes alluded for a moment to her own home, or mentioned an adventure or situation, or an early recollection, which indicated a people of strange manners, and described customs of which we knew nothing. I gathered from these chance hints that her native country was much more remote than I had at first fancied.

As we sat thus one afternoon under the trees a funeral passed us by. It was that of a pretty young girl, whom I had often seen, the daughter of one of the rangers of the forest. The poor man was walking behind the coffin of his darling; she was his only child, and he looked quite heartbroken. Peasants walking two-and-two came behind, they were singing a funeral hymn.

I rose to mark my respect as they passed, and joined in the hymn they were very sweetly singing.

My companion shook me a little roughly, and I turned surprised.

She said brusquely, "Don't you perceive how discordant that is?"

"I think it very sweet, on the contrary," I answered, vexed at the interruption, and very uncomfortable, lest the people who composed the little procession should observe and resent what was passing.

I resumed, therefore, instantly, and was again interrupted. "You pierce my ears," said Carmilla, almost angrily, and stopping her ears with her tiny fingers, "Besides, how can you tell that your religion and mine are the same; your forms wound me, and I hate funerals. What a fuss! Why *you* must die—*everyone* must die; and all are happier when they do. Come home."

"My father has gone on with the clergyman to the churchyard. I thought you knew she was to be buried today."

"*She?* I don't trouble my head about peasants. I don't know who she is," answered Carmilla, with a flash from her fine eyes.

"She is the poor girl who fancied she saw a ghost a fortnight ago, and has been dying ever since, till yesterday, when she expired."

"Tell me nothing about ghosts. I shan't sleep tonight if you do."

"I hope there is no plague or fever coming; all this looks very like it," I continued. "The swinehead's young wife died only a week ago, and she thought something seized her by the throat as she lay in her bed, and nearly strangled her. Papa says such horrible fancies do accompany some forms of fever. She was quite well the day before. She sank afterward, and died before a week."

"Well, *her* funeral is over, I hope, and *her* hymn sung; and our ears shan't be tortured with that discord and jargon. It has made me nervous. Sit down here, beside me; sit close; hold my hand; press it hard—hard—harder."

We had moved a little back, and had come to another seat.

She sat down. Her face underwent a change that alarmed and even terrified me for a moment. It darkened, and became horribly livid; her teeth and hands were clenched, and she frowned and compressed her lips, while she stared down upon the ground at her feet, and trembled all over with a continued shudder as irrepressible as ague. All her energies seemed strained to suppress a fit, with which she was then breathlessly tugging; and at length a low convulsive cry of suffering broke from her, and gradually the hysteria subsided. "There! That comes of strangling people with hymns!" she said at last. "Hold me, hold me still. It is passing away."

And so gradually it did; and perhaps to dissipate the somber impression which the spectacle had left upon me, she became unusually animated and chatty; and so we got home.

This was the first time I had seen her exhibit any definable symptoms of that delicacy of health which her mother had spoken of. It was the first time, also, I had seen her exhibit anything like temper.

Both passed away like a summer cloud; and never but once afterward did I witness on her part a momentary sign of anger. I will tell you how it happened.

She and I were looking out of one of the long drawing-room windows, when there entered the courtyard, over the drawbridge, a figure of a wanderer whom I knew very well. He used to visit the schloss generally twice a year.

It was the figure of a hunchback, with the sharp lean features that generally accompany deformity. He wore a pointed black beard, and he was smiling from ear to ear, showing his white fangs. He was dressed in buff, black, and scarlet, and crossed with more straps and belts than I could count, from which hung all manner of things. Behind, he carried a magic-lantern, and two boxes, which I well knew, in one of which was a salamander, and in the other a mandrake. These monsters used to make my father laugh. They were compounded of parts of monkeys, parrots, squirrels, fish, and hedgehogs, dried and stitched together with great neatness and startling effect. He had a fiddle, a box of conjuring apparatus, a pair of foils and masks attached to his belt, several other mysterious cases dangling about him, and a black staff with copper ferrules in his hand. His companion was a rough spare dog, that followed at his heels, but stopped short, suspiciously at the drawbridge, and in a little while began to howl dismally.

In the meantime, the mountebank, standing in the midst of the courtyard, raised his grotesque hat, and made us a very ceremonious bow, paying his compliments very volubly in execrable French, and German not much better. Then, disengaging his fiddle, he began to scrape a lively air, to which he sang with merry discord, dancing with ludicrous airs and activity, that made me laugh, in spite of the dog's howling.

Then he advanced to the window with many smiles and salutations, and his hat in his left hand, his fiddle under his arm, and with a fluency that never took breath, he gabbled a long advertisement of all his accomplishments, and the resources of the various arts which he placed at our service, and the curiosities and entertainments which it was in his power, at our bidding, to display.

"Will your ladyships be pleased to buy an amulet against the oupire, which is going like the wolf, I hear, through these woods," he said, dropping his hat on the pavement. "They are dying of it right and left, and here is a charm that never fails; only pinned to the pillow, and you may laugh in his face."

These charms consisted of oblong slips of vellum, with cabalistic ciphers and diagrams upon them.

Carmilla instantly purchased one, and so did I.

He was looking up, and we were smiling down upon him, amused; at least, I can answer for myself. His piercing black eye, as he looked up in our faces, seemed to detect something that fixed for a moment his curiosity.

In an instant he unrolled a leather case, full of all manner of odd little steel instruments.

"See here, my lady," he said, displaying it, and addressing me, "I profess, among other things less useful, the art of dentistry. Plague take the dog!" he interpolated. "Silence, beast! He howls so that your ladyships can scarcely hear a word. Your noble friend, the young lady at your right, has the sharpest tooth—long, thin, pointed, like an awl, like a needle; ha, ha! With my sharp and long sight, as I look up, I have seen it distinctly; now if it happens to hurt the young lady, and I think it must, here am I, here are my file, my punch, my nippers; I will make it round and blunt, if her ladyship pleases; no longer the tooth of a fish, but of a beautiful young lady as she is. Hey? Is the young lady displeased? Have I been too bold? Have I offended her?"

The young lady, indeed, looked very angry as she drew back from the window.

"How does that mountebank insult us so? Where is your father? I shall demand redress from him. My father would have had the wretch tied up to the pump, and flogged with a cart-whip, and burnt to the bones with the castle brand!"

She retired from the window a step or two, and sat down, and had hardly lost sight of the offender, when her wrath subsided as suddenly as it had risen, and she gradually recovered her usual tone, and seemed to forget the little hunchback and his follies.

My father was out of spirits that evening. On coming in he told us that there had been another case very similar to the two fatal ones which had lately occurred. The sister of a young peasant on his estate, only a mile away, was very ill, had been, as she described it, attacked very nearly in the same way, and was now slowly but steadily sinking.

"All this," said my father, "is strictly referable to natural causes. These poor people infect one another with their superstitions, and so repeat in imagination the images of terror that have infested their neighbors."

"But that very circumstance frightens one horribly," said Carmilla.

"How so?" inquired my father.

"I am so afraid of fancying I see such things; I think it would be as bad as reality."

"We are in God's hands; nothing can happen without his permission, and all will end well for those who love him. He is our faithful creator; He had made us all, and will take care of us."

"Creator! *Nature!*" said the young lady in answer to my gentle father. "And this disease that invades the country is natural. Nature. All things proceed from Nature—don't they? All things in the heaven, in the earth, and under the earth, act and live as Nature ordains? I think so."

"The doctor said he would come here today," said my father, after a silence. "I want to know what he thinks about it, and what he thinks we had better do."

"Doctors never did me any good," said Carmilla.

"Then you have been ill?" I asked.

"More ill than ever you were," she answered.

"Long ago?"

"Yes, a long time. I suffered from this very illness; but I forget all my pain and weakness, and they were not so bad as are suffered in other diseases."

"You were very young then?"

"I dare say; let us talk no more of it. You would not wound a friend?" She looked languidly in my eyes, and passed her arm round my waist lovingly, and led me out of the room. My father was busy over some papers near the window.

"Why does your papa like to frighten us?" said the pretty girl, with a sigh and a little shudder.

"He doesn't, dear Carmilla, it is the very furthest thing from his mind."

"Are you afraid, dearest?"

"I should be very much if I fancied there was any real danger of my being attacked as those poor people were."

"You are afraid to die?"

"Yes, every one is."

"But to die as lovers may—to die together, so that they may live together. Girls are caterpillars while they live in the world, to be finally butterflies when the summer comes; but in the meantime there are grubs and larvae, don't you see—each with their peculiar propensities, necessities and structure. So says Monsieur Buffon, in his big book, in the next room."

Later in the day the doctor came, and was closeted with papa from some time. He was a skillful man, of sixty and upward, he wore powder, and shaved his pale face as smooth as a pumpkin. He and papa emerged from the room together, and I heard papa laugh, and say as they came out:

"Well, I do wonder at a wise man like you. What do you say to hippogriffs and dragons?"

The doctor was smiling, and made answer, shaking his head—

"Nevertheless life and death are mysterious states, and we know little of the resources of either."

And so they walked on, and I heard no more. I did not then know what the doctor had been broaching, but I think I guess it now.

V

A Wonderful Likeness

This evening there arrived from Gratz the grave, dark-faced son of the picture cleaner, with a horse and cart laden with two large packing cases, having many pictures in each. It was a journey of ten leagues, and whenever a messenger arrived at the schloss from our little capital of Gratz, we used to crowd about him in the hall, to hear the news.

This arrival created in our secluded quarters quite a sensation. The cases remained in the hall, and the messenger was taken charge of by the servants till he had eaten his supper. Then with assistants, and armed with hammer, ripping-chisel, and turnscrew, he met us in the hall, where we had assembled to witness the unpacking of the cases.

Carmilla sat looking listlessly on, while one after the other the old pictures, nearly all portraits, which had undergone the process of renovation, were brought to light. My mother was of an old Hungarian family, and most of these pictures, which were about to be restored to their places, had come to us through her.

My father had a list in his hand, from which he read, as the artist rummaged out the corresponding numbers. I don't know that the pictures were very good, but they were, undoubtedly, very old, and some of them very curious also. They had, for the most part, the merit of being now seen by me, I may say, for the first time; for the smoke and dust of time had all but obliterated them.

"There is a picture that I have not seen yet," said my father. "In one corner, at the top of it, is the name, as well as I could read, 'Marcia Karnstein,' and the date '1698'; and I am curious to see how it has turned out."

I remembered it; it was a small picture, about a foot and a half high, and nearly square, without a frame; but it was so blackened by age that I could not make it out.

The artist now produced it, with evident pride. It was quite beautiful; it was startling; it seemed to live. It was the effigy of Carmilla!

"Carmilla, dear, here is an absolute miracle. Here you are, living, smiling, ready to speak, in this picture. Isn't it beautiful, papa? And see, even the little mole on her throat."

My father laughed, and said "Certainly it is a wonderful likeness," but he looked away, and to my surprise seemed but little struck by it, and went on talking to the picture cleaner, who was also something of an artist, and discoursed with intelligence about the portraits or other works, which his art had just brought into light and color, while *I* was more and more lost in wonder the more I looked at the picture.

"Will you let me hang this picture in my room, papa?" I asked.

"Certainly, dear," said he, smiling, "I'm very glad you think it so like. It must be prettier even than I thought it, if it is."

The young lady did not acknowledge this pretty speech, did not seem to hear it. She was leaning back in her seat, her

fine eyes under their long lashes gazing on me in contemplation, and she smiled in a kind of rapture.

"And now you can read quite plainly the name that is
written in the corner. It is not Marcia; it looks as if it was
done in gold. The name is Mircalla, Countess Karnstein, and
this is a little coronet over it, and underneath A.D. 1698. I am
descended from the Karnsteins; that is, mamma was."

"Ah!" said the lady, languidly, "so am I, I think, a very
long descent, very ancient. Are they any Karnsteins living
now?"

"None who bear the name, I believe. The family were
ruined, I believe, in some civil wars, long ago, but the ruins
of the castle are only about three miles away."

"How interesting!" she said, languidly. "But see what
beautiful moonlight!" She glanced through the hall-door,
which stood a little open. "Suppose you take a little ramble
round the court, and look down at the road and river."

"It is so like the night you came to us," I said.

She sighed, smiling.

She rose, and each with her arm about the other's waist,
we walked out upon the pavement.

In silence, slowly we walked down to the drawbridge,
where the beautiful landscape opened before us.

"And so you were thinking of the night I came here?" she
almost whispered. "Are you glad I came?"

"Delighted, dear Carmilla," I answered.

"And you asked for the picture you think like me, to hang
in your room," she murmured with a sigh, as she drew her
arm closer about my waist, and let her pretty head sink upon
my shoulder.

"How romantic you are, Carmilla," I said. "Whenever
you tell me your story, it will be made up chiefly of some one
great romance."

She kissed me silently.

"I am sure, Carmilla, you have been in love; that there is,
at this moment, an affair of the heart going on."

"I have been in love with no one, and never shall," she whispered, "unless it should be with you."

How beautiful she looked in the moonlight.

Shy and strange was the look with which she quickly hid her face in my neck and hair, with tumultuous sighs, that seemed almost to sob, and pressed in mine a hand that trembled.

Her soft cheek was glowing against mine. "Darling, darling," she murmured, "I live in you; and you would die for me, I love you so."

I started from her.

She was gazing on me with eyes from which all fire, all meaning had flown, and a face colorless and apathetic.

"Is there a chill in the air, dear?" she said drowsily. "I almost shiver; have I been dreaming? Let us come in. Come; come; come in."

"You look ill, Carmilla; a little faint. You certainly must take some wine," I said.

"Yes, I will, I'm better now. I shall be quite well in a few minutes. Yes, do give me a little wine," answered Carmilla, as we approached the door. "Let us look again for a moment; it is the last time, perhaps, I shall see the moonlight with you."

"How do you feel now, Carmilla? Are you really better?" I asked.

I was beginning to take alarm, lest she should have been stricken with the strange epidemic that they said had invaded the country about us.

"Papa would be grieved beyond measure," I added, "if he thought you were ever so little ill, without immediately letting us know. We have a very skillful doctor near this, the physician who was with papa today."

"I'm sure he is. I know how kind you all are; but, dear child, I am quite well again. There is nothing ever wrong with me, but a little weakness. People say I am languid; I am incapable of exertion; I can scarcely walk as far as a child of three years old; and every now and then the little strength I have falters, and I become as you have just seen me. But after all I am very easily set up again; in a moment I am perfectly myself. See how I have recovered.''

So, indeed, she had; and she and I talked a great deal, and very animated she was; and the remainder of that evening passed without any recurrence of what I called her infatuations. I mean her crazy talk and looks, which embarrassed, and even frightened me.

But there occurred that night an event which gave my thoughts quite a new turn, and seemed to startle even Carmilla's languid nature into momentary energy.

VI

A Very Strange Agony

When we got into the drawing-room, and had sat down to our coffee and chocolate, although Carmilla did not take any, she seemed quite herself again, and Madame, and Mademoiselle De Lafontaine, joined us, and made a little card party, in the course of which papa came in for what he called his ''dish of tea.''

When the game was over he sat down beside Carmilla on the sofa, and asked her, a little anxiously, whether she had heard from her mother since her arrival.

She answered ''No.''

He then asked whether she knew where a letter would reach her at present.

''I cannot tell,'' she answered ambiguously, ''but I have been thinking of leaving you; you have been already too hospitable and too kind to me. I have given you an infinity of trouble, and I should wish to take a carriage tomorrow, and post in pursuit of her; I know where I shall ultimately find her, although I dare not yet tell you.''

''But you must not dream of any such thing,'' exclaimed my father, to my great relief. ''We can't afford to lose you so, and I won't consent to your leaving us, except under the care of your mother, who was so good as to consent to your remaining with us till she should herself return. I should be quite happy if I knew that you heard from her; but this evening the accounts of the progress of the mysterious disease that has invaded our neighborhood, grow even more alarming; and my beautiful guest, I do feel the responsibility, unaided by advice from your mother, very much. But I shall do my best; and one thing is certain, that you must not think of leaving us without her distinct direction to that effect. We should suffer too much in parting from you to consent to it easily."

"Thank you, sir, a thousand times for your hospitality," she answered, smiling bashfully. "You have all been too kind to me; I have seldom been so happy in all my life before, as in your beautiful château, under your care, and in the society of your dear daughter."

So he gallantly, in his old-fashioned way, kissed her hand, smiling and pleased at her little speech.

I accompanied Carmilla as usual to her room, and sat and chatted with her while she was preparing for bed.

"Do you think," I said at length, "that you will ever confide fully in me?"

She turned round smiling, but made no answer, only continued to smile on me.

"You won't answer that?" I said. "You can't answer pleasantly; I ought not to have asked you."

"You were quite right to ask me that, or anything. You do not know how dear you are to me, or you could not think any confidence too great to look for. But I am under vows, no nun half so awfully, and I dare not tell my story yet, even to you. The time is very near when you shall know everything. You will think me cruel, very selfish, but love is always selfish; the more ardent the more selfish. How jealous I am you cannot know. You must come with me, loving me to death; or else hate me and still come with me, and *hating* me through death and after. There is no such word as indifference in my apathetic nature."

"Now, Carmilla, you are going to talk your wild nonsense again," I said hastily.

"Not I, silly little fool as I am, and full of whims and fancies; for your sake I'll talk like a sage. Were you ever at a ball?"

"No; how you do run on. What is it like? How charming it must be."

"I almost forget, it is years ago."

I laughed.

"You are not so old. Your first ball can hardly be forgotten yet."

"I remember everything about it—with an effort. I see it all, as divers see what is going on above them, through a medium, dense, rippling, but transparent. There occurred that night what has confused the picture, and made its colors faint. I was all but assassinated in my bed, wounded *here*," she touched her breast, "and never was the same since."

"Were you near dying?"

"Yes, very—a cruel love—strange love, that would have taken my life. Love will have its sacrifices. No sacrifice without blood. Let us go to sleep now; I feel so lazy. How can I get up just now and lock my door?"

She was lying with her tiny hands buried in her rich wavy hair, under her cheek, her little head upon the pillow, and her glittering eyes followed me wherever I moved, and a kind of shy smile that I could not decipher.

I bid her good night, and crept from the room with an uncomfortable sensation.

I often wondered whether our pretty guest ever said her prayers. *I* certainly had never seen her upon her knees. In the morning she never came down until long after our family prayers were over, and at night she never left the drawing-room to attend our brief evening prayers in the hall.

If it had not been that it had casually come out in one of our careless talks that she had been baptized, I should have doubted her being a Christian. Religion was a subject on which I had never heard her speak a word. If had known the world better, this particular neglect or antipathy would not have so much surprised me.

The precautions of nervous people are infectious, and persons of a like temperament are pretty sure, after a time, to imitate them. I had adopted Carmilla's habit of locking her bedroom door, having taken into my head all her whimsical alarms about midnight invaders and prowling assassins. I had also adopted her precaution of making a brief search through her room, to satisfy herself that no lurking assassin or robber was "ensconced."

These wise measures taken, I got into my bed and fell asleep. A light was burning in my room. This was an old habit, of very early date, and which nothing could have tempted me to dispense with.

Thus fortified I might take my rest in peace. But dreams come through stone walls, light up dark rooms, or darken light ones, and their persons make their exits and their entrances as they please, and laugh at locksmiths.

I had a dream that night that was the beginning of a very strange agony.

I cannot call it a nightmare, for I was quite conscious of being asleep. But I was equally conscious of being in my room, and lying in bed, precisely as I actually was. I saw, or fancied I saw, the room and its furniture just as I had seen it last, except that it was very dark, and I saw something moving round the foot of the bed, which at first I could not accurately distinguish. But I soon saw that it was a sooty-black animal that resembled a monstrous cat. It appeared to me about four or five feet long, for it measured fully the length of the hearthrug as it passed over it; and it continued to-ing and fro-ing with the lithe, sinister restlessness of a beast in a cage. I could not cry out, although as you may suppose, I was terrified. Its pace was growing faster, and the room rapidly darker and darker, and at length so dark that I could no longer see anything of it but its eyes. I felt it spring lightly on the bed. The two broad eyes approached my face, and suddenly I felt a stinging pain as if two large needles darted, an inch or two apart, deep into my breast. I waked with a scream. The room was lighted by the candle that burnt there all through the night, and I saw a female figure standing at the foot of the bed, a little at the right side. It was in a dark loose dress, and its hair was down and covered its shoulders. A block of stone could not have been more still. There was not the slightest stir of respiration. As I stared at it, the figure appeared to have changed its place, and was now nearer the door; then, close to it, the door opened, and it passed out.

I was now relieved, and able to breathe and move. My first thought was that Carmilla had been playing me a trick, and that I had forgotten to secure my door. I hastened to it, and found it locked as usual on the inside. I was afraid to open it—I was horrified. I sprang into my bed and covered my head up in the bedclothes, and lay there more dead than alive till morning.

VII
Descending

It would be vain my attempting to tell you the horror with which, even now, I recall the occurrence of that night. It was no such transitory terror as a dream leaves behind it. It seemed to deepen by time, and communicated itself to the room and the very furniture that had encompassed the apparition.

I could not bear next day to be alone for a moment. I should have told papa, but for two opposite reasons. At one time I thought he would laugh at my story, and I could not bear its being treated as a jest; and at another, I thought he might fancy that I had been attacked by the mysterious complaint which had invaded our neighborhood. I had myself no misgivings of the kind, and as he had been rather an invalid for some time, I was afraid of alarming him.

I was comfortable enough with my good-natured companions, Madame Perrodon, and the vivacious Mademoiselle Lafontaine. They both perceived that I was out of spirits and nervous, and at length I told them what lay so heavy at my heart.

Mademoiselle laughed, but I fancied that Madame Perrodon looked anxious.

"By-the-by" said Mademoiselle, laughing, "the long lime-tree walk, behind Carmilla's bedroom-window, is haunted!"

"Nonsense," exclaimed Madame, who probably thought the theme rather inopportune, "and who tells the story, my dear?"

"Martin says that he came up twice, when the old yard-gate was being repaired, before sunrise, and twice saw the same female figure walking down the lime-tree avenue."

"So he well might, as long as there are cows to milk in the river fields," said Madame.

"I daresay; but Martin chooses to be frightened, and never did I see fool *more* frightened."

"You must not say a word about it to Carmilla, because she can see down that walk from her room window," I interposed, "and she is, if possible, a greater coward than I."

Carmilla came down rather later than usual that day.

"I was so frightened last night," she said, so soon as were together," and I am sure I should have seen something dreadful if it had not been for that charm I bought from the poor little hunchback whom I called such hard names. I had a dream of something black coming round my bed, and I awoke in a perfect horror, and I really thought, for some seconds, I saw a dark figure near the chimney-piece, but I felt under my pillow for my charm, and the moment any fingers touched it, the figure disappeared, and I felt quite certain, only that I had it by me, that something frightful would have made its appearance, and, perhaps, throttled me, as it did those poor people we heard of."

"Well, listen to me," I began, and recounted my adventure, at the recital of which she appeared horrified.

"And had you the charm near you?" she asked, earnestly.

"No, I had dropped it into a china vase in the drawing-room, but I shall certainly take it with me tonight, as you have so much faith in it."

At this distance of time I cannot tell you, or even understand, how I overcame my horror so effectually as to lie alone in my room that night. I remember distinctly that I pinned the charm to my pillow. I fell asleep almost immediately, and slept even more soundly than usual all night.

Next night I passed as well. My sleep was delightfully deep and dreamless. But I wakened with a sense of lassitude and melancholy, which, however, did not exceed a degree that was almost luxurious.

"Well, I told you so," said Carmilla, when I described my quiet sleep, "I had such delightful sleep myself last night; I pinned the charm to the breast of my nightdress. It was too far away the night before. I am quite sure it was all fancy, except the dreams. I used to think that evil spirits made dreams, but our doctor told me it is no such thing. Only a fever passing by, or some other malady, as they often do, he said, knocks at the door, and not being able to get in, passes on, with that alarm."

"And what do you think the charm is?" said I.

"It has been fumigated or immersed in some drug, and is an antidote against the malaria," she answered.

"Then it acts only on the body?"

"Certainly; you don't suppose that evil spirits are frightened by bits of ribbon, or the perfumes of a druggist's shop? No, these complaints, wandering in the air, begin by trying the nerves, and so infect the brain, but before they can seize upon you, the antidote repels them. That I am sure is what the charm has done for us. It is nothing magical, it is simply natural."

I should have been happier if I could have quite agreed with Carmilla, but I did my best, and the impression was a little losing its force.

For some nights I slept profoundly; but still every morning

I felt the same lassitude, and a languor weighed upon me all day. I felt myself a changed girl. A strange melancholy was stealing over me, a melancholy that I would not have interrupted. Dim thoughts of death began to open, and an idea that I was slowly sinking took gentle, and, somehow, not unwelcome, possession of me. If it was sad, the tone of mind which this induced was also sweet. Whatever it might be, my soul acquiesced in it.

I would not admit that I was ill, I would not consent to tell my papa, or to have the doctor sent for.

Carmilla became more devoted to me than ever, and her strange paroxysms of languid adoration more frequent. She used to gloat on me with increasing ardor the more my strength and spirits waned. This always shocked me like a momentary glare of insanity.

Without knowing it, I was now in a pretty advanced stage of the strangest illness under which mortal ever suffered. There was an unaccountable fascination in its earlier symptoms that more than reconciled me to the incapacitating effect of that stage of the malady. This fascination increased for a time, until it reached a certain point, when gradually a sense of the horrible mingled itself with it, deepening, as you shall hear, until it discolored and perverted the whole state of my life.

The first change I experienced was rather agreeable. It was very near the turning point from which began the descent of Avernus.

Certain vague and strange sensations visited me in my sleep. The prevailing one was of that pleasant, peculiar cold thrill which we feel in bathing, when we move against the current of a river. This was soon accompanied by dreams that seemed interminable, and were so vague that I could never recollect their scenery and persons, or any one connected portion of their action. But they left an awful impression, and a sense of exhaustion, as if I had passed through a long period of great mental exertion and danger. After all these dreams there remained on waking a remembrance of having been in a place very nearly dark, and of having spoken to people whom I could not see; and especially of one clear voice, of a female's, very deep, that spoke as if at a distance, slowly, and producing always the same sensation of indescribable solemnity and fear. Sometimes there came a sensation as if a hand was drawn softly along my cheek and neck. Sometimes it was as if warm lips kissed me, and longer and more lovingly as they reached my throat, but there the caress fixed itself. My heart beat faster, my breathing rose and fell rapidly and full drawn; a sobbing, that rose into a sense of strangulation, supervened, and turned into a dreadful convulsion, in which my senses left me and I became unconscious.

It was now three weeks since the commencement of this unaccountable state. My sufferings had, during the last week, told upon my appearance. I had grown pale, my eyes were dilated and darkened underneath, and the languor which I had long felt began to display itself in my countenance.

My father asked me often whether I was ill; but, with an obstinacy which now seems to me unaccountable, I persisted in assuring him that I was quite well.

In a sense this was true. I had no pain. I could complain of no bodily derangement. My complaint seemed to be one of the imagination, or the nerves, and, horrible as my sufferings were, I kept them, with a morbid reserve, very nearly to myself.

It could not be that terrible complaint which the peasants called the oupire, for I had now been suffering for three weeks, and they were seldom ill for much more than three days, when death put an end to their miseries.

Carmilla complained of dreams and feverish sensations, but by no means of so alarming a kind as mine. I say that mine were extremely alarming. Had I been capable of comprehending my condition, I would have invoked aid and advice on my knees. The narcotic of an unsuspected influence was acting upon me, and my perceptions were benumbed.

I am going to tell you now of a dream that led immediately to an odd discovery.

One night, instead of the voice I was accustomed to hear in the dark, I heard one, sweet and tender, and at the same time terrible, which said, "Your mother warns you to beware of the assassin." At the same time a light unexpectedly sprang up, and I saw Carmilla, standing, near the foot of my bed, in her white nightdress, bathed, from her chin to her feet, in one great stain of blood.

I wakened with a shriek, possessed with the one idea that Carmilla was being murdered. I remember springing from my bed, and my next recollection is that of standing on the lobby, crying for help.

Madame and Mademoiselle came scurrying out of their rooms in alarm; a lamp burned always on the lobby, and seeing me, they soon learned the cause of my terror.

I insisted on our knocking at Carmilla's door. Our knocking was unanswered. It soon became a pounding and an uproar. We shrieked her name, but all was vain.

We all grew frightened, for the door was locked. We hurried back, in panic, to my room. There we rang the bell long and furiously. If my father's room had been at that side of the house we would have called him up at once to our aid. But, alas! he was quite out of hearing, and to reach him involved an excursion for which we none of us had courage.

Servants, however, soon came running up the stairs; I had got on my dressing-gown and slippers meanwhile, and my companions were already similarly furnished. Recognizing the voices of the servants on the lobby, we sallied out together; and having renewed, as fruitlessly, our summons at Carmilla's door, I ordered the men to force the lock. They did so, and we stood, holding our lights aloft, in the doorway, and so stared into the room.

We called her by name; but there was still no reply. We looked around the room. Everything was undisturbed. It was exactly in the state in which I had left it on bidding her good night. But Carmilla was gone.

VIII
Search

At sight of the room, perfectly undisturbed except for our violent entrance, we began to cool a little, and soon recovered our senses sufficiently to dismiss the men. It had struck Mademoiselle that possibly Carmilla had been wakened by the uproar at her door, and in her first panic had jumped from her bed, and hid herself in a press, or behind a curtain, from which she could not, of course, emerge until the majordomo and his myrmidons had withdrawn. We now recommenced our search, and began to call her by name again.

It was all to no purpose. Our perplexity and agitation increased. We examined the windows, but they were secured. I implored of Carmilla, if she had concealed herself, to play this cruel trick no longer—to come out, and to end our anxieties. It was all useless. I was by this time convinced that she was not in the room, nor in the dressing-room, the door of which was still locked on this side. She could not have passed it. I was utterly puzzled. Had Carmilla discovered one of those secret passages which the old housekeeper said were known to exist in the schloss, although the tradition of their exact situation had been lost? A little time would, no doubt, explain all—utterly perplexed as, for the present, we were.

It was past four o'clock, and I preferred passing the remaining hour of darkness in Madame's room. Daylight brought no solution of the difficulty.

The whole household, with my father at its head, was in a state of agitation next morning. Every part of the château was searched. The grounds were explored. Not a trace of the missing lady could be discovered. The stream was about to be dragged; my father was in distraction; what a tale to have to tell the poor girl's mother on her return. I, too, was almost beside myself, though my grief was quite of a different kind.

The morning was passed in alarm and excitement. It was now one o'clock, and still no tidings. I ran up to Carmilla's room, and found her standing at her dressing-table. I was astounded. I could not believe my eyes. She beckoned me to her with her pretty finger, in silence. Her face expressed extreme fear.

I ran to her in an ecstasy of joy; I kissed and embraced her again and again. I ran to the bell and rang it vehemently, to bring others to the spot, who might at once relieve my father's anxiety.

"Dear Carmilla, what has become of you all this time? We have been in agonies of anxiety about you," I exclaimed. "Where have you been? How did you come back?"

"Last night has been a night of wonders," she said.

"For mercy's sake, explain all you can."

"It was past two last night," she said, "when I went to sleep as usual in my bed, with my doors locked, that of the dressing-room, and that opening upon the gallery. My sleep was uninterrupted, and, so far as I know, dreamless; but I woke just now on the sofa in the dressing-room there, and I found the door between the rooms open, and the other door forced. How could all this have happened without my being wakened? It must have been accompanied with a great deal of noise, and I am particularly easily wakened; and how could I have been carried out of my bed without my sleep having been interrupted, I whom the slightest stir startles?"

By this time, Madame, Mademoiselle, my father, and a number of the servants were in the room. Carmilla was, of course, overwhelmed with inquiries, congratulations, and welcomes. She had but one story to tell, and seemed the least able of all the party to suggest any way of accounting for what had happened.

My father took a turn up and down the room, thinking. I saw Carmilla's eye follow him for a moment with a sly, dark glance.

When my father had sent the servants away, Mademoiselle having gone in search of a little bottle of valerian and salvolatile, and there being no one now in the room with Carmilla, except my father, Madame, and myself, he came to her thoughtfully, took her hand very kindly, led her to the sofa, and sat down beside her.

"Will you forgive me, my dear, if I risk a conjecture, and ask a question?"

"Who can have a better right?" she said. "Ask what you please, and I will tell you everything. But my story is simply one of bewilderment and darkness. I know absolutely nothing. Put any question you please. But you know, of course, the limitations mamma has placed me under."

"Perfectly, my dear child. I need not approach the topics on which she desires our silence. Now, the marvel of last night consists in your having been removed from your bed and your room, without being wakened, and this removal having occurred apparently while the windows were still secured, and the two doors locked upon the inside. I will tell you my theory, and first ask you a question."

Carmilla was leaning on her hand dejectedly; Madame and I were listening breathlessly.

"Now, my question is this. Have you ever been suspected of walking in your sleep?"

"Never, since I was very young indeed."

"But you did walk in your sleep when you were young?"

"Yes; I know I did. I have been told so often by my old nurse."

My father smiled and nodded.

"Well, what has happened is this. You got up in your sleep, unlocked the door, not leaving the key, as usual, in the lock, but taking it out and locking it on the outside; you again took the key out, and carried it away with you to some one of the five-and-twenty rooms on this floor, or perhaps upstairs or downstairs. There are so many rooms and closets, so much heavy furniture, and such accumulations of lumber, that it would require a week to search this old house thoroughly. Do you see, now, what I mean?"

"I do, but not all," she answered.

"And how, papa, do you account for her finding herself on

the sofa in the dressing-room, which we had searched so carefully?''

"She came there after you had searched it, still in her sleep, and at last awoke spontaneously, and was as much surprised to find herself where she was as any one else. I wish all mysteries were as easily and innocently explained as yours, Carmilla,'' he said, laughing. "And so we may congratulate ourselves on the certainty that the most natural explanation of the occurrence is one that involves no drugging, no tampering with locks, no burglars, or poisoners, or witches—nothing that need alarm Carmilla, or anyone else, for our safety.''

Carmilla was looking charmingly. Nothing could be more beautiful than her tints. Her beauty was, I think, enhanced by that graceful languor that was peculiar to her. I think my father was silently contrasting her looks with mine, for he said:

"I wish my poor Laura was looking more like herself''; and he sighed.

So our alarms were happily ended, and Carmilla restored to her friends.

IX

The Doctor

As Carmilla would not hear of an attendent sleeping in her room, my father arranged that a servant should sleep outside her door, so that she could not attempt to make another such excursion without being arrested at her own door.

That night passed quietly; and next morning early, the doctor, whom my father had sent for without telling me a word about it, arrived to see me.

Madame accompanied me to the library; and there the grave little doctor, with white hair and spectacles, whom I mentioned before, was waiting to receive me.

I told him my story, and as I proceeded he grew graver and graver

We were standing, he and I, in the recess of one of the windows, facing one another. When my statement was over, he leaned with his shoulders against the wall, and with his eyes fixed on me earnestly, with an interest in which was a dash of horror.

After a minute's reflection, he asked Madame if he could see my father.

He was sent for accordingly, and as he entered, smiling, he said:

"I dare say, doctor, you are going to tell me that I am an old fool for having brought you here; I hope I am."

But his smile faded into shadow as the doctor, with a very grave face, beckoned him to him.

He and the doctor talked for some time in the same recess where I had just conferred with the physician. It seemed an earnest and argumentative conversation. The room is very large, and I and Madame stood together, burning with curiosity, at the farther end. Not a word could we hear, however, for they spoke in a very low tone, and the deep recess of the window quiet concealed the doctor from view, and very nearly my father, whose foot, arm, and shoulder only could we see; and the voices were, I suppose, all the less audible for the sort of closet which the thick wall and window formed.

After a time my father's face looked into the room; it was pale, thoughtful, and, I fancied, agitated.

"Laura, dear, come here for a moment. Madame, we shan't trouble you, the doctor says, at present."

Accordingly I approached, for the first time a little alarmed; for, although I felt very weak, I did not feel ill; and strength, one always fancies, is a thing that may be picked up when we please.

My father held out his hand to me, as I drew near, but he was looking at the doctor, and he said:

"It certainly *is* very odd; I don't understand it quite.

Laura, come here, dear; now attend to Doctor Spielsberg, and recollect yourself."

"You mentioned a sensation like that of two needles piercing the skin, somewhere about your neck, on the night when you experienced your first horrible dream. Is there still any soreness?"

"None at all," I answered.

"Can you indicate with your finger about the point at which you think this occurred?"

"Very little below my throat—*here,*" I answered.

I wore a morning dress, which covered the place I pointed to.

"Now you can satisfy yourself," said the doctor. "You won't mind your papa's lowering your dress a very little. It is necessary, to detect a symptom of the complaint under which you have been suffering."

I acquiesced. It was only an inch or two below the edge of my collar.

"God bless me!—so it is," exclaimed my father, growing pale.

"You see it now with your own eyes," said the doctor, with a gloomy triumph.

"What is it?" I exclaimed, beginning to be frightened.

"Nothing, my dear young lady, but a small blue spot, about the size of the tip of your little finger; and now," he continued, turning to papa, "the question is what is best to be done?"

"Is there any danger?" I urged, in great trepidation.

"I trust not, my dear," answered the doctor. "I don't see why you should not recover. I don't see why you should not begin *immediately* to get better. That is the point at which the sense of strangulation begins?"

"Yes," I answered.

"And—recollect as well as you can—the same point was a kind of center of that thrill which you described just now, like the current of a cold stream running against you?"

"It may have been; I think it was."

"Ay, you see?" he added, turning to my father. "Shall I say a word to Madame?"

"Certainly," said my father.

He called Madame to him, and said:

"I find my young friend here far from well. It won't be of any great consequence, I hope; but it will be necessary that some steps be taken, which I will explain by-and-by; but in the meantime, Madame, you will be so good as not to let Miss Laura be alone for one moment. That is the only direction I need give for the present. It is indispensable."

"We may rely upon your kindness, Madame, I know," added my father.

Madame satisfied him eagerly.

"And you, dear Laura, I know you will observe the doctor's direction."

"I shall have to ask your opinion upon another patient, whose symptoms slightly resemble those of my daughter, that have just been detailed to you—very much milder in degree, but I believe quite of the same sort. She is a young lady—our guest; but as you say you will be passing this way again this evening, you can't do better than take your supper here, and you can then see her. She does not come down till the afternoon."

"I thank you," said the doctor. "I shall be with you, then, at about seven this evening."

And then they repeated their directions to me and to Madame, and with this parting charge my father left us, and walked out with the doctor; and I saw them pacing together up and down between the road and the moat, on the grassy platform in front of the castle, evidently absorbed in earnest conversation.

The doctor did not return. I saw him mount his horse there, take his leave, and ride away eastward through the forest.

Nearly at the same time I saw the man arrive from Dranfield with the letters, and dismount and hand the bag to my father.

In the meantime, Madame and I were both busy, lost in conjecture as to the reasons of the singular and earnest direc-

tion which the doctor and my father had concurred in imposing. Madame, as she afterward told me, was afraid the doctor
apprehended a sudden seizure, and that, without prompt assistance, I might either lose my life in a fit, or at least be
seriously hurt.

The interpretation did not strike me; and I fancied, perhaps
luckily for my nerves, that the arrangement was prescribed
simply to secure a companion, who would prevent my taking
too much exercise, or eating unripe fruit, or doing any of the
fifty foolish things to which young people are supposed to be
prone.

About half an hour after my father came in—he had a letter
in his hand—and said:

"This letter had been delayed; it is from General Spielsdorf.
He might have been here yesterday, he may not come till
tomorrow or he may be here today."

He put the open letter into my hand; but he did not look
pleased, as he used when a guest, especially one so much
loved as the General, was coming. On the contrary, he
looked as if he wished him at the bottom of the Red Sea.
There was plainly something on his mind which he did not
choose to divulge.

"Papa, darling, will you tell me this?" said I, suddenly
laying my hand on his arm, and looking, I am sure, imploringly
in his face.

"Perhaps," he answered, smoothing my hair caressingly
over my eyes.

"Does the doctor think me very ill?"

"No, dear; he thinks, if right steps are taken, you will be
quite well again, at least, on the high road to a complete
recovery, in a day or two," he answered, a little dryly. "I
wish our good friend, the General, had chosen any other
time; that is, I wish you had been perfectly well to receive
him."

"But do tell me, papa," I insisted, "*what* does he think is
the matter with me?"

"Nothing; you must not plague me with questions," he

answered, with more irritation than I ever remember him to
have displayed before; and seeing that I looked wounded, I
suppose, he kissed me, and added, "You shall know all
about it in a day or two; that is, all that *I* know. In the
meantime you are not to trouble your head about it."

He turned and left the room, but came back before I had
done wondering and puzzling over the oddity of all this; it
was merely to say that he was going to Karnstein, and had
ordered the carriage to be ready at twelve, and that I and
Madame should accompany him; he was going to see the
priest who lived near those picturesque grounds, upon business, and as Carmilla had never seen them, she could follow,
when she came down, with Mademoiselle, who would bring
materials for what you call a picnic, which might be laid for
us in the ruined castle.

At twelve o'clock, accordingly, I was ready, and not long
after, my father, Madame and I set out upon our projected
drive.

Passing the drawbridge we turn to the right, and follow the
road over the steep Gothic bridge, westward, to reach the
deserted village and ruined castle of Karnstein.

No sylvan drive can be fancied prettier. The ground breaks
into gentle hills and hollows, all clothed with beautiful wood,
totally destitute of the comparative formality which artificial
planting and early culture and pruning impart.

The irregularities of the ground often lead the road out of
its course, and cause it to wind beautifully round the sides of
broken hollows and the steeper sides of the hills, among
varieties of ground almost inexhaustible.

Turning one of these points, we suddenly encountered our
old friend, the General, riding toward us, attended by a
mounted servant. His portmanteaus were following in a hired
wagon, such as we term a cart.

The General dismounted as we pulled up, and, after the
usual greetings, was easily persuaded to accept the vacant
seat in the carriage and send his horse on with his servant to
the schloss.

X
Bereaved

It was about ten months since we had last seen him; but that time had sufficed to make an alteration of years in his appearance. He had grown thinner; something of gloom and anxiety had taken the place of that cordial serenity which used to characterize his features. His dark blue eyes, always penetrating, now gleamed with a sterner light from under his shaggy gray eyebrows. It was not such a change as grief alone usually induces, and angrier passions seemed to have had their share in bringing it about.

We had not long resumed our drive, when the General began to talk, with his usual soldierly directness, of the bereavement, as he termed it, which he had sustained in the death of his beloved niece and ward; and he then broke out in a tone of intense bitterness and fury, inveighing against the "hellish arts" to which she had fallen a victim, and expressing, with more exasperation than piety, his wonder that Heaven should tolerate so monstrous an indulgence of the lusts and malignity of hell.

My father, who saw at once that something very extraordinary had befallen, asked him, if not too painful to him, to detail the circumstances which he thought justified the strong terms in which he expressed himself.

"I should tell you all with pleasure," said the General, "but you would not believe me."

"Why should I not?" he asked.

"Because," he answered testily, "you believe in nothing but what consists with your own prejudices and illusions. I remember when I was like you, but I have learned better."

"Try me," said my father; "I am not such a dogmatist as you suppose. Besides which, I very well know that you generally require proof for what you believe, and am, therefore, very strongly predisposed to respect your conclusions."

"You are right in supposing that I have not been led lightly into a belief in the marvelous—for what I have experienced *is* marvelous—and I have been forced by extraordinary evidence to credit that which ran counter, diametrically, to all my theories. I have been made the dupe of a preternatural conspiracy."

Notwithstanding his professions of confidence in the General's penetration, I saw my father, at this point, glance at the General, with, as I thought, a marked suspicion of his sanity.

The General did not see it, luckily. He was looking gloomily and curiously into the glades and vistas of the woods that were opening before us.

"You are going to the Ruins of Karnstein?" he said. "Yes, it is a lucky coincidence; do you know I was going to ask you to bring me there to inspect them. I have a special object in exploring. There is a ruined chapel, ain't there, with a great many tombs of that extinct family?"

"So there are—highly interesting," said my father. "I hope you are thinking of claiming the title and estates?"

My father said this gaily, but the General did not recollect the laugh, or even the smile, which courtesy exacts for a friend's joke; on the contrary, he looked grave and even fierce, ruminating on a matter that stirred his anger and horror.

"Something very different," he said, gruffy. "I mean to unearth some of those fine people. I hope, by God's blessing, to accomplish a pious sacrilege here, which will relieve our earth of certain monsters, and enable honest people to sleep in their beds without being assailed by murderers. I have strange things to tell you, my dear friend, such as I myself would have scouted as incredible a few months since."

My father looked at him again, but this time not with a glance of suspicion—with an eye, rather, of keen intelligence and alarm.

"The house of Karnstein," he said, "has been long extinct: a hundred years at least. My dear wife was maternally descended from the Karnsteins. But the name and title have long ceased to exist. The castle is a ruin; the very village is deserted; it is fifty years since the smoke of a chimney was seen there; not a roof left.''

"Quite true. I have heard a great deal about that since I last saw you; a great deal that will astonish you. But I had better relate everything in the order in which it occurred," said the General. "You saw my dear ward—my child, I may call her. No creature could have been more beautiful, and only three months ago none more blooming.''

"Yes, poor thing! when I saw her last she certainly was quite lovely," said my father. "I was grieved and shocked more than I can tell you, my dear friend; I knew what a blow it was to you.''

He took the General's hand, and they exchanged a kind pressure. Tears gathered in the old soldier's eyes. He did not seek to conceal them. He said:

"We have been very old friends; I knew you would feel for me, childless as I am. She had become an object of very near interest to me, and repaid my care by an affection that cheered my home and made my life happy. That is all gone. The years that remain to me on earth may not be very long; but by God's mercy I hope to accomplish a service to mankind before I die, and to subserve the vengenance of Heaven upon the friends who have murdered my poor child in the spring of her hopes and beauty!''

"You said, just now, that you intended relating everything as it occurred," said my father. "Pray do; I assure you that it is not mere curiosity that prompts me.''

By this time we had reached the point at which the Drunstall road, by which the General had come, diverges from the road which we were traveling to Karnstein.

"How far is it to the ruins?" inquired the General, looking anxiously forward.

"About half a league," answered my father. "Pray let us hear the story you were so good as to promise.''

XI
The Story

"With all my heart," said the General, with an effort; and after a short pause in which to arrange his subject, he commenced one of the strangest narratives I ever heard.

"My dear child was looking forward with great pleasure to the visit you had been so good as to arrange for her to your charming daughter." Here he made me a gallant but melancholy bow. "In the meantime we had an invitation to my old friend the Count Carlsfeld, whose schloss is about six leagues to the other side of Karnstein. It was to attend the series of fêtes which, you remember, were given by him in honor of his illustrious visitor, the Grand Duke Charles."

"Yes; and very splendid, I believe, they were," said my father.

"Princely! But then his hospitalities are quite regal. He has Aladdin's lamp. The night from which my sorrow dates was devoted to a magnificent masquerade. The grounds were thrown open, the trees hung with colored lamps. There was such a display of fireworks as Paris itself had never witnessed. And such music—music, you know, is my weakness— such ravishing music! The finest instrumental band, perhaps, in the world, and the finest singers who could be collected from all the great operas in Europe. As you wandered through these fantastically illuminated grounds, the moon-lighted château throwing a rosy light from its long rows of windows, you would suddenly hear these ravishing voices stealing from the silence of some grove, or rising from boats upon the lake. I felt myself, as I looked and listened, carried back into the romance and poetry of my early youth.

"When the fireworks were ended, and the ball beginning, we returned to the noble suite of rooms that were thrown open to the dancers. A masked ball, you know, is a beautiful sight; but so brilliant a spectacle of the kind I never saw before.

"It was a very aristrocratic assembly. I was myself almost the only 'nobody' present.

"My dear child was looking quite beautiful. She wore no mask. Her excitement and delight added an unspeakable charm to her features, always lovely. I remarked a young lady, dressed magnificently, but wearing a mask, who appeared to me to be observing my ward with extraordinary interest. I had seen her, earlier in the evening, in the great hall, and again, for a few minutes, walking near us, on the terrace under the castle windows, similarly employed. A lady, also masked, richly and gravely dressed, and with a stately air, like a person of rank, accompanied her as a chaperon. Had the young lady not worn a mask, I could, of course, have been much more certain upon the question whether she was really watching my poor darling. I am now well assured that she was.

"We were now in one of the *salons*. My poor dear child had been dancing, and was resting a little in one of the chairs near the door; I was standing near. The two ladies I have mentioned had approached and the younger took the chair next my ward; while her companion stood beside me, and for a little time addressed herself, in a low tone, to her charge.

"Availing herself of the privilege of her mask, she turned to me, and in the tone of an old friend, and calling me by my name, opened a conversation with me, which piqued my curiosity a good deal. She referred to many scenes where she had met me—at Court, and at distinguished houses. She alluded to little incidents which I had long ceased to think of, but which, I found, had only lain in abeyance in my memory, for they instantly started into life at her touch.

"I became more and more curious to ascertain who she was, every moment. She parried my attempts to discover very adroitly and pleasantly. The knowledge she showed of many passages in my life seemed to me all but unaccountable; and she appeared to take a not unnatural pleasure in foiling my curiosity, and in seeing me flounder in my eager perplexity, from one conjecture to another.

"In the meantime the young lady, whom her mother called by the odd name of Millarca, when she once or twice addressed her, had, with the same ease and grace, got into conversation with my ward.

"She introduced herself by saying that her mother was a very old acquaintance of mine. She spoke of the agreeable audacity which a mask rendered practicable; she talked like a friend; she admired her dress, and insinuated very prettily her admiration of her beauty. She amused her with laughing criticisms upon the people who crowded the ballroom, and laughed at my poor child's fun. She was very witty and lively when she pleased, and after a time they had grown very good friends, and the young stranger lowered her mask, displaying a remarkably beautiful face. I had never seen it before, neither had my dear child. But though it was new to us, the features were so engaging, as well as lovely, that it was impossible not to feel the attraction powerfully. My poor girl did so. I never saw anyone more taken with another at first sight, unless, indeed, it was the stranger herself, who seemed quite to have lost her heart to her.

"In the meantime, availing myself of the license of a masquerade, I put not a few questions to the elder lady.

" 'You have puzzled me utterly,' I said, laughing. 'Is that not enough? Won't you, now, consent to stand on equal terms, and do me the kindness to remove your mask?'

" 'Can any request be more unreasonable?' she replied. 'Ask a lady to yield an advantage! Beside, how do you know you should recognize me? Years make changes.'

" ' "As you see," I said, with a bow, and, I suppose, a rather melancholy little laugh.

" 'As philosophers tell us,' she said; 'and how do you know that a sight of my face would help you?'

" 'I should take chance for that,' I answered. 'It is vain trying to make yourself out an old woman; your figure betrays you.'

" 'Years, nevertheless, have passed since I saw you, rather

since you saw me, for that is what I am considering. Millarca, there, is my daughter; I cannot then be young, even in the opinion of people whom time has taught to be indulgent, and I may not like to be compared with what you remember me. You have no mask to remove. You can offer me nothing in exchange.'

" 'My petition is to your pity, to remove it.'

" 'And mine to yours, to let it stay where it is,' she replied.

" 'Well, then, at least you will tell me whether you are French or German; you speak both languages so perfectly.'

" 'I don't think I shall tell you that, General; you intend a surprise, and are meditating the particular point of attack.'

" 'At all events, you won't deny this,' I said, 'that being honored by your permission to converse, I ought to know how to address you. Shall I say Madame la Comtesse?'

"She laughed, and she would, no doubt, have met me with another evasion—if, indeed, I can treat any occurrence in an interview every circumstance of which was pre-arranged, as I now believe, with the profoundest cunning, as liable to be modified by accident.

" 'As to that,' she began; but she was interrupted, almost as she opened her lips, by a gentleman, dressed in black, who looked particularly elegant and distinguished, with this drawback, that his face was the most deadly pale I ever saw, except in death. He was in no masquerade—in the plain evening dress of a gentleman; and he said, without a smile, but with a courtly unusually low bow:—

" 'Will Madame la Comtesse permit me to say a very few words which may interest her?'

"The lady turned quickly to him, and touched her lip in token of silence; she then said to me, 'Keep my place for me, General; I shall return when I have said a few words.'

"And with this injunction, playfully given, she walked a little aside with the gentleman in black, and talked for some minutes, apparently very earnestly. They then walked away slowly together in the crowd, and I lost them for some minutes.

"I spent the interval in cudgeling my brains for a conjecture as to the identity of the lady who seemed to remember me so kindly, and I was thinking of turning about and joining in the conversation between my pretty ward and the Countess' daughter, and trying whether, by the time she returned, I might not have a surprise in store for her, by having her name, title, château, and estates at my fingers' ends. But at this moment she returned, accompanied by the pale man in black, who said:

"'I shall return and inform Madame la Comtesse when her carriage is at the door.'

"He withdrew with a bow."

XII
A Petition

"'Then we are to lose Madame la Comtesse, but I hope only for a few hours,' I said, with a low bow.

"'It may be that only, or it may be a few weeks. It was very unlucky his speaking to me just now as he did. Do you now know me?'

"I assured her I did not.

"'You shall know me,' she said, 'but not at present. We are older and better friends than, perhaps, you suspect. I cannot yet declare myself. I shall in there weeks pass your beautiful schools, about which I have been making inquiries. I shall then look in upon you for an hour or two, and renew a friendship which I never think of without a thousand pleasant recollections. This moment a piece of news has reached me like a thunderbolt. I must set out now and travel by a devious route, nearly a hundred miles, with all the dispatch I can possibly make. My perplexities multiply. I am only deterred by the compulsory reserve I practice as to my name from

making a very singular request of you. My poor child has not
quite recovered her strength. Her horse fell with her, at a hunt
which she had ridden out to witness, her nerves have not yet
recovered the shock, and our physician says that she must on
no account exert herself for some time to come. We came
here, in consequence, by very easy stages—hardly six leagues
a day. I must now travel day and night, on a mission of life
and death—a mission the critical and momentous nature of
which I shall be able to explain to you when we meet, as I
hope we shall, in a few weeks, without the necessity of any
concealment.'

"She went on to make her petition, and it was in the tone
of a person from whom such a request amounted to confer-
ring, rather than seeking a favor. This was only in manner,
and, as it seemed, quite unconsciously. Than the terms in
which it was expressed, nothing could be more deprecatory.
It was simply that I would consent to take charge of her
daughter during her absence.

"This was, all things considered, a strange, not to say, an
audacious request. She in some sort disarmed me, by stating
and admitting everything that could be urged against it, and
throwing herself entirely upon my chivalry. At the same
moment, by a fatality that seems to have predetermined all
that happened, my poor child came to my side, and, in an
undertone, besought me to invite her new friend, Millarca, to
pay us a visit. She had just been sounding her, and thought, if
her mamma would allow her, she would like it extremely.

"At another time I should have told her to wait a little,
until, at least, we knew who they were. But I had not a
moment to think in. The two ladies assailed me together, and
I must confess the refined and beautiful face of the young
lady, about which there was something extremely engaging,
as well as the elegance and fire of high birth, determined me;
and, quite overpowered, I submitted, and undertook, too
easily, the care of the young lady, whom her mother called
Millarca.

"The Countess beckoned to her daughter, who listened

with grave attention while she told her, in general terms, how suddenly and peremptorily she had been summoned, and also of the arrangement she had made for her under my care, adding that I was one of her earliest and most valued friends.

"I made, of course, such speeches as the case seemed to call for, and found myself, on reflection, in a position which I did not half like.

"The gentleman in black returned, and very ceremoniously conducted the lady from the room.

"The demeanor of this gentleman was such as to impress me with the conviction that the Countess was a lady of very much more importance than her modest title alone might have led me to assume.

"Her last charge to me was that no attempt was to be made to learn more about her than I might have already guessed, until her return. Our distinguished host, whose guest she was, knew her reasons.

" 'But here,' she said, 'neither I nor my daughter could safely remain for more than a day. I removed my mask imprudently for a moment, about an hour ago, and, too late, I fancied you saw me. So I resolved to seek an opportunity of talking a little to you. Had I found that you *had* seen me, I should have thrown myself on your high sense of honor to keep my secret for some weeks. As it is, I am satisfied that you did not see me; but if you now *suspect*, or, on reflection, *should* suspect, who I am, I commit myself, in like manner, entirely to your honor. My daughter will observe the same secrecy, and I will know that you will, from time to time remind her, lest she should thoughtlessly disclose it.'

"She whispered a few words to her daughter, kissed her hurriedly twice, and went away, accompanied by the pale gentleman in black, and disappeared in the crowd.

" 'In the next room,' said Millarca, 'there is a window that looks upon the hall door. I should like to see the last of mamma, and to kiss my hand to her.'

"We assented, of course, and accompanied her to the window. We looked out, and saw a handsome old-fashioned carriage, with a troop of couriers and footmen. We saw the slim figure of the pale gentleman in black, as he held a thick velvet cloak, and placed it about her shoulders and threw the hood over her head. She nodded to him, and just touched his hand with hers. He bowed low repeatedly as the door closed, and the carriage began to move.

" 'She is gone,' said Millarca, with a sigh.

" 'She is gone,' I repeated to myself, for the first time—in the hurried moments that had elapsed since my consent—reflecting upon the folly of my act.

" 'She did not look up,' said the young lady, plaintively.

" 'The Countess had taken off her mask, perhaps, and did not care to show her face,' I said; 'and she could not know that you were in the window.'

"She sighed, and looked in my face. She was so beautiful that I relented. I was sorry I had for a moment repented of my hospitality, and I determined to make her amends for the unavowed churlishness of my reception.

"The young lady, replacing her mask, joined my ward in persuading me to return to the grounds, where the concert was soon to be renewed. We did so, and walked up and down the terrace that lies under the castle windows. Millarca became very intimate with us, and amused us with lively descriptions and stories of most of the great people whom we saw upon the terrace. I liked her more and more every minutes. Her gossip, without being ill-natured, was extremely diverting to me, who had been so long out of the great world. I thought what life she would give to our sometimes lonely evenings at home.

"This ball was not over until the morning sun had almost reached the horizon. It pleased the Grand Duke to dance till then, so loyal people could not go away, or think of bed.

"We had just got through a crowded saloon, when my ward asked me what had become of Millarca. I thought she had been by her side, and she fancied she was by mine. The fact was, we had lost her.

"All my efforts to find her were vain. I feared that she had mistaken, in the confusion of a momentary separation from us, other people for her new friends, and had, possibly, pursued and lost them in the extensive grounds which were thrown open to us.

"Now, in its full force, I recognized a new folly in my having undertaken the charge of a young lady without so much as knowing her name; and fettered as I was by promises, of the reasons for imposing which I knew nothing, I could not even point my inquiries by saying that the missing young lady was the daughter of the Countess who had taken her departure a few hours before.

"Morning broke. It was clear daylight before I gave up my search. It was not till near two o'clock next day that we heard anything of my missing charge.

"At about that time a servant knocked at my niece's door, to say that he had been earnestly requested by a young lady, who appeared to be in great distress, to make out where she could find the General Baron Spielsdorf and the young lady his daughter, in whose charge she had been left by her mother.

"There could be no doubt, notwithstanding the slight inaccuracy, that our young friend had turned up; and so she had. Would to heaven we had lost her!

"She told my poor child a story to account for her having failed to recover us for so long. Very late, she said, she had got to the housekeeper's bedroom in despair of finding us, and had then fallen into a deep sleep which, long as it was, had hardly sufficed to recruit her strength after the fatigues of the ball.

"That day Millarca came home with us. I was only too happy, after all, to have secured so charming a companion for my dear girl."

XIII
The Woodman

"There soon, however, appeared some drawbacks. In the first place, Millarca complained of extreme languor—the weakness that remained after her late illness—and she never emerged from her room till the afternoon was pretty far advanced. In the next place, it was accidentally discovered, although she always locked her door on the inside, and near disturbed the key from its place till she admitted the maid to assist at her toilet, that she was undoubtedly sometimes absent from her room in the very early morning, and at various times later in the day, before she wished it to be understood that she was stirring. She was repeatedly seen from the windows of the schloss, in the first faint gray of the morning, walking through the trees, in an easterly direction, and looking like a person in a trance. This convinced me that she walked in her sleep. But this hypothesis did not solve the puzzle. How did she pass out from her room, leaving the door locked on the inside? How did she escape from the house without unbarring door or window?

"In the midst of my perplexities, an anxiety of a far more urgent kind presented itself.

"My dear child began to lose her looks and health and that in a manner so mysterious, and even horrible, that I became thoroughly frightened.

"She was at first visited by appalling dreams; then, as she fancied, by a specter, sometimes resembling Millarca, sometimes in the shape of a beast, indistinctly seen, walking round the foot of her bed, from side to side. Lastly came sensations. One, not unpleasant, but very peculiar, she said, resembled the flow of an icy stream against her breast. At a later time, she felt something like a pair of large needles pierce her, a little below the throat, with a very sharp pain. A few nights after, followed a gradual and convulsive sense of strangulation; then came unconsciousness."

I could hear distinctly every word the kind old General was saying, because by this time we were driving upon the short grass that spreads on either side of the road as you approach the roofless village which had not shown the smoke of a chimney for more than half a century.

You may guess how strangely I felt as I heard my own symptoms so exactly described in those which had been experienced by the poor girl who, but for the catastrophe which followed, would have been at that moment a visitor at my father's château. You may suppose, also, how I felt as I heard him detail habits and mysterious peculiarities which were, in fact, those of our beautiful guest, Carmilla!

A vista opened in the forest; we were of a sudden under the chimneys and gables of the ruined village, and the towers and battlements of the dismantled castle, round which gigantic trees are grouped, overhung us from a slight eminence.

In a frightened dream I got down from the carriage, and in silence, for we had each abundant matter for thinking; we soon mounted the ascent, and were among the spacious chambers, winding stairs, and dark corridors of the castle.

"And this was once the palatial residence of the Karnsteins!" said the old General at length, as from a great window he looked out across the village, and saw the wide, undulating expanse of forest. "It was a bad family, and here its blood-stained annals were written," he continued. "It is hard that they should, after death, continue to plague the human race with their atrocious lusts. That is the chapel of the Karnsteins, down there."

He pointed down to the gray walls of the Gothic building, partly visible through the foliage, a little way down the steep. "And I hear the axe of a woodman," he added, "busy among the trees that surround it; he possibly may give us the information of which I am in search, and point out the grave of Mircalla, Countess of Karnstein. These rustics preserve the local traditions of great families, whose stories die out among the rich and titled as soon as the families themselves become extinct."

"We have a portrait, at home, of Mircalla, the Countess Karnstein; should you like to see it?" asked my father.

"Time enough, dear friend," replied the General. "I believe that I have seen the original; and one motive which has led me to you earlier than I at first intended, was to explore the chapel which we are now approaching."

"What! see the Countess Mircalla," exclaimed my father; "why, she has been dead more than a century!"

"Not so dead as you fancy, I am told," answered the General.

"I confess, General, you puzzle me utterly," replied my father, looking at him, I fancied, for a moment with a return of the suspicion I detected before. But although there was anger and detestation, at times, in the old General's manner, there was nothing flighty.

"There remains to me," he said, as we passed under the heavy arch of the Gothic church—for its dimensions would have justified its being so styled—"but one object which can interest me during the few years that remain to me on earth, and that is to wreak on her the vengeance which, I thank God, may still be accomplished by a mortal arm."

"What vengeance can you mean?" asked my father, in increasing amazement.

"I mean, to decapitate the monster," he answered, with a fierce flush, and a stamp that echoed mournfully through the hollow ruin, and his clenched hand was at the same moment raised, as if it grasped the handle of an axe, while he shook it ferociously in the air.

"What?" exclaimed my father, more than ever bewildered.

"To strike her head off."

"Cut her head off!"

"Aye, with a hatchet, with a spade, or with anything that can cleave through her murderous throat. You shall hear, " he answered, trembling with rage. And hurrying forward he said:

"That beam will answer for a seat; your dear child is

fatigued; let her be seated, and I will, in a few sentences, close my dreadful story."

The squared block of wood, which lay on the grass-grown pavement of the chapel, formed a bench on which I was very glad to seat myself, and in the meantime the General called to the woodman, who had been removing some boughs which leaned upon the old walls; and, axe in hand, the hardy old fellow stood before us.

He could not tell us anything of these monuments; but there was an old man, he said, a ranger of this forest, at present sojourning in the house of the priest, about two miles away, who could point out every monument of the old Karnstein family; and, for a trifle, he undertook to bring him back with him, if we would lend him one of our horses, in little more than half an hour.

"Have you been long employed about this forest?" asked my father of the old man.

"I have been a woodman here," he answered in his *patois*, "under the forester, all my days; so has my father before me, and so on, as many generations as I can count up. I could show you the very house in the village here, in which my ancestors lived."

"How came the village to be deserted?" asked the General.

"It was troubled by *revenants*, sir; several were tracked to their graves, there detected by the usual tests, and extinguished in the usual way, by decapitation, by the stake, and by burning; but not until many of the villagers were killed.

"But after all these proceedings according to law," he continued—"so many graves opened, and so many vampires deprived of their horrible animation—the village was not relieved. But a Moravian nobleman, who happened to be traveling this way, heard how matters were, and being skilled—as many people are in his country—in such affairs, he offered to deliver the village from its tormentor. He did so thus: There being a bright moon that night, he ascended, shortly after sunset, the towers of the chapel here, from whence he could distinctly see the churchyard beneath him;

you can see it from that window. From this point he watched until he saw the vampire come out of his grave, and place near it the linen clothes in which he had been folded, and then glide away toward the village to plague its inhabitants.

"The stranger, having seen all this, came down from the steeple, took the linen wrappings of the vampire, and carried them up to the top of the tower, which he again mounted. When the vampire returned from his prowlings and missed his clothes, he cried furiously to the Moravian, whom he saw at the summit of the tower, and who, in reply, beckoned him to ascend and take them. Whereupon the vampire, accepting his invitation, began to climb the steeple, and so soon as he had reached the battlements, the Moravian, with a stroke of his sword, clove his skull in twain, hurling him down to the churchyard, whither, descending by the winding stairs, the stranger followed and cut his head off, and the next day delivered it and the body to the villagers, who duly impaled and burnt them.

"This Moravian nobleman had authority from the then head of the family to remove the tomb of Mircalla, Countess Karnstein, which he did effectually, so that in a little while its site was quite forgotten."

"Can you point out where it stood?" asked the General, eagerly.

The forester shook his head, and smiled.

"Not a soul living could tell you that now," he said; "besides, they say her body was removed; but no one is sure of that either."

Having thus spoken, as time pressed, he dropped his axe and departed, leaving us to hear the remainder of the General's strange story.

XIV
The Meeting

"My beloved child," he resumed, "was now growing rapidly worse. The physician who attended her had failed to produce the slightest impression upon her disease, for such I then supposed it to be. He saw my alarm, and suggested a consultation. I called in an abler physician, from Gratz. Several days elapsed before he arrived. He was a good and pious, as well as a learned man. Having seen my poor ward together, they withdrew to my library to confer and discuss. I, from the adjoining room, where I awaited their summons, heard these two gentlemen's voices raised in something sharper than a strictly philosophical discussion. I knocked at the door and entered. I found the old physician from Gratz maintaining his theory. His rival was combating it with undisguised ridicule, accompanied with bursts of laughter. This unseemly manifestation subsided and the altercation ended on my entrance.

" 'Sir,' said my first physician, 'my learned brother seems to think that you want a conjuror, and not a doctor.'

" 'Pardon me,' said the old physician from Gratz, looking displeased, 'I shall state my own view of the case in my own way another time. I grieve, Monsieur le Général, that by my skill and science I can be of no use. Before I go I shall do myself the honor to suggest something to you.'

"He seemed thoughtful, and sat down at a table and began to write. Profoundly disappointed, I made my bow, and as I turned to go, the other doctor pointed over his shoulder to his companion who was writing, and then, with a shrug, significantly touched his forehead.

"This consultation, then, left me precisely where I was. I walked out into the grounds, all but distracted. The doctor from Gratz, in ten or fifteen minutes, overtook me. He apologized for having followed me, but said that he could not conscientiously take his leave without a few words more. He told me that he could not be mistaken; no natural disease exhibited the same symptoms; and that death was already very near. There remained, however, a day, or possibly two, of life. If the fatal seizure were at once arrested, with great care and skill her strength might possibly return. But all hung now upon the confines of the irrevocable. One more assault might extinguish the last spark of vitality which is, every moment, ready to die.

" 'And what is the nature of the seizure you speak of?' I entreated.

" 'I have stated all fully in this note, which I place in your hands upon the distinct condition that you send for the nearest clergyman, and open my letter in his presence, and on no account read it till he is with you; you would despise it else, and it is a matter of life and death. Should the priest fail you, then, indeed, you may read it.'

"He asked me, before taking his leave finally, whether I would wish to see a man curiously learned upon the very subject, which, after I had read his letter, would probably interest me above all others, and he urged me earnestly to invite him to visit him there; and so took his leave.

"The ecclesiastic was absent, and I read the letter by myself. At another time, or in another case, it might have excited my ridicule. But into what quackeries will not people rush for a last chance, where all accustomed means have failed, and the life of a beloved object is at stake?

"Nothing, you will say could be more absurd than the learned man's letter. It was monstrous enough to have consigned him to a madhouse. He said that the patient was suffering from the visits of a vampire! The punctures which she described as having occurred near the throat, were, he insisted, the insertion of those two long, thin, and sharp teeth which, it is well known, are peculiar to vampires; and there could be no doubt, he added, as to the well-defined presence of the small livid mark which all concurred in describing as that induced by the demon's lips, and every symptom described by the sufferer was in exact conformity with those recorded in every case of a similar visitation.

"Being myself wholly skeptical as to the existence of any such portent as the vampire, the supernatural theory of the good doctor furnished, in my opinion, but another instance of learning and intelligence oddly associated with some one hallucination. I was so miserable, however, that, rather than try nothing, I acted upon the instructions of the letter.

"I concealed myself in the dark dressing-room, that opened upon the poor patient's room, in which a candle was burning, and watched there till she was fast asleep. I stood at the door, peeking through the small crevice, my sword laid on the table beside me, as my directions prescribed, until, a little after one, I saw a large black object, very ill-defined, crawl, as it seemed to me, over the foot of the bed, and swiftly spread itself up to the poor girl's throat, where it swelled, in a moment, into a great, palpitating mass.

"For a few moments I had stood petrified. I now sprang forward, with my sword in my hand. The black creature suddenly contracted toward the foot of the bed, glided over it, and, standing on the floor about a yard below the foot of the bed, with a glare of skulking ferocity and horror fixed on me, I saw Millarca. Speculating I know not what, I struck at her instantly with my sword; but I saw her standing near the door, unscathed. Horrified, I pursued, and struck again. She was gone; and my sword flew to shivers against the door.

"I can't describe to you all that passed on that horrible night. The whole house was up and stirring. The specter Millarca was gone. But her victim was sinking fast, and before the morning dawned, she died."

The old General was agitated. We did not speak to him. My father walked to some little distance, and began reading the inscriptions on the tombstones; and thus occupied, he strolled into the door of a side-chapel to prosecute his researches. The General leaned against the wall, dried his eyes, and sighed heavily. I was relieved on hearing the voices of

Carmilla and Madame, who were at that moment approaching. The voices died away.

In this solitude, having just listened to so strange a story, connected, as it was, with the great and titled dead, whose monuments were moldering among the dust and ivy round us, and every incident of which bore so awfully upon my own mysterious case—in this haunted spot, darkened by the towering foliage that rose on every side dense and high above its noiseless walls—a horror began to steal over me, and my heart sank as I thought that my friends were, after all, not about to enter and disturb this triste and ominous scene.

The old General's eyes were fixed on the ground, as he leaned with his hand upon the basement of a shattered monument.

Under a narrow, arched doorway, surmounted by one of those demoniaeal grotesques in which the cynical and ghastly fancy of old Gothic carving delights, I saw very gladly the beautiful face and figure of Carmilla enter the shadowy chapel.

I was just about to rise and speak, and nodded smiling, in answer to her peculiarly engaging smile; when with a cry, the old man by my side caught up the woodman's hatchet, and started forward. On seeing him a brutalized change came over her features. It was an instantaneous and horrible transformation, as she made a crouching step backward. Before I could utter a scream, he struck at her with all his force, but she dived under his blow, and unscatched, caught him in her tiny grasp by the wrist. He struggled for a moment to release his arm, but his hand opened, the axe fell to the ground, and the girl was gone.

He staggered against the wall. His gray hair stood upon his head, and a moisture shone over his face, as if he were at the point of death.

The frightful scene had passed in a moment. The first thing I recollect after, is Madame standing before me, and impatiently repeating again and again, and question, "Where is Mademoiselle Carmilla?"

I answered at length. "I don't know—I can't tell—she

went there," and I pointed to the door through which Madame had just entered; "only a minute or two since."

"But I have been standing there, in the passage, ever since Mademoiselle Carmilla entered; and she did not return."

She then began to call "Carmilla," through every door and passage and from the windows, but no answer came.

"She called herself Carmilla?" asked the General, still agitated.

"Carmilla, yes," I answered.

"Aye," he said; "that is Millarca. That is the same person who long ago was called Mircalla, Countess Karnstein. Depart from this accursed ground, my poor child, as quickly as you can. Drive to the clergyman's house, and stay there till we come. Begone! May you never behold Carmilla more; you will not find her here."

XV
Ordeal and Execution

As he spoke one of the strangest looking men I ever beheld entered the chapel at the door through which Carmilla had made her entrance and her exit. He was tall, narrow-chested, stooping, with high shoulders, and dressed in black. His face was brown and dried in with deep furrows; he wore an oddly-shaped hat with a broad leaf. His hair, long and grizzled, hung on his shoulders. He wore a pair of gold spectacles, and walked slowly, with an odd shambling gait, with his face sometimes turned up to the sky, and sometimes bowed down toward the ground, seemed to wear a perpetual smile; his long thin arms were swinging, and his lank hands, in old black gloves ever so much too wide for them, waving and gesticulating in utter abstraction.

"The very man!" exclaimed the General, advancing with manifest delight. "My dear Baron, how happy I am to see you, I had no hope of meeting you so soon." He signed to

my father, who had by this time returned, and leading the
fantastic old gentleman, whom he called the Baron to meet
him. He introduced him formally, and they at once entered
into earnest conversation. The stranger took a roll of paper
from his pocket, and spread it on the worn surface of a tomb
that stood by. He had a pencil case in his fingers, with which
he traced imaginary lines from point to point on the paper,
which from their often glancing from it, together, at certain
points of the building, I concluded to be a plan of the chapel.
He accompanied, what I may term, his lecture, with occasional readings from a dirty little book, whose yellow leaves
were closely written over.

They sauntered together down the side aisle, opposite to
the spot where I was standing, conversing as they went; then
they began measuring distances by paces, and finally they all
stood together, facing a piece of the side-wall, which they
began to examine with great minuteness; pulling off the ivy
that clung over it, and rapping the plaster with the ends of
their sticks, scraping here, and knocking there. At length they
ascertained the existence of a broad marble tablet, with letters
carved in relief upon it.

With the assistance of the woodman, who soon returned, a
monumental inscription, and carved escutcheon, were disclosed. They proved to be those of the long lost monument of
Mircalla, Countess Karnstein.

The old General, though not I fear given to the praying
mood, raised his hands and eyes to heaven, in mute thanks-
giving for some moments.

"Tomorrow," I heard him say: "the commissioner will be
here, and the Inquisition will be held according to law."

Then turning to the old man with the gold spectacles,
whom I have described, he shook him warmly by both hands
and said:

"Baron, how can I thank you? How can we all thank you?
You will have delivered this region from a plague that has
scourged its inhabitants for more than a century. The horrible
enemy, thank God, is at last tracked."

My father led the stranger aside, and the General followed. I knew that he had led them out of hearing, that he might relate my case, and I saw them glance often quickly at me, as the discussion proceeded.

My father came to me, kissed me again and again, and leading me from the chapel, said:

"It is time to return, but before we go home, we must add to our party the good priest, who lives but a little way from this; and persuade him to accompany us to the schloss."

In this quest we were successful: and I was glad, being unspeakably fatigued when we reached home. But my satisfaction was changed to dismay, on discovering that there were no tidings of Carmilla. Of the scene that had occurred in the ruined chapel, no explanation was offered to me, and it was clear that it was a secret which my father for the present determined to keep from me.

The sinister absence of Carmilla made the remembrance of the scene more horrible to me. The arrangements for the night were singular. Two servants, and Madame were to sit up in my room that night; and the ecclesiastic with my father kept watch in the adjoining dressing-room.

The priest had performed certain solemn rites that night, the purport of which I did not understand any more than I comprehended the reason of this extraordinary precaution taken for my safety during sleep.

I saw all clearly a few days later.

The disappearance of Carmilla was followed by the discontinuance of my nightly sufferings.

You have heard, no doubt, of the appalling superstition that prevails in Upper and Lower Styria, in Moravia, Silesia, in Turkish Servia, in Poland, even in Russia; the superstition, so we must call it, of the Vampire.

If human testimony, taken with every care and solemnity, judicially, before commissions innumerable, each consisting of many members, all chosen for integrity and intelligence, and constituting reports more voluminous perhaps than exist upon any one other class of cases, is worth anything, it is difficult to deny, or even to doubt the existence of such a phenomenon as the Vampire.

For my part I have heard no theory by which to explain what I myself have witnessed and experienced, other than that supplied by the ancient and well-attested belief of the country.

The next day the formal proceedings took place in the Chapel of Karnstein. The grave of the Countess Mircalla was opened; and the General and my father recognized each his perfidious and beautiful guest, in the face now disclosed to view. The features, though a hundred and fifty years had passed since her funeral, were tinted with the warmth of life. Her eye were open; no cadaverous smell exhaled from the coffin. The two medical men, one officially present, the other on the part of the promoter of the inquiry, attested the marvelous fact that there was a faint but appreciable respiration, and a corresponding action of the heart. The limbs were perfectly flexible, the flesh elastic; and the leaden coffin floated with blood, in which to a depth of seven inches, the body lay immersed. Here then, were all the admitted signs and proofs of vampirism. The body, therefore, in accordance with the ancient practice, was raised, and a sharp stake driven through the heart of the vampire, who uttered a piercing shriek at the moment, in all respects such as might escape from a living person in the last agony. Then the head was struck off, and a torrent of blood flowed from the severed neck. The body and head was next placed on a pile of wood, and reduced to ashes, which were thrown upon the river and borne away, and that territory has never since been plagued by the visits of a vampire.

My father has a copy of the report of the Imperial Commission, with the signatures of all who were present at these proceedings, attached in verification of the statement. It is from this official paper that I have summarized my account of this last shocking scene.

XVI
Conclusion

I write all this you suppose with composure. But far from it; I cannot think of it without agitation. Nothing but your earnest desire so repeatedly expressed, could have induced me to sit down to a task that has unstrung my nerves for months to come, and reinduced a shadow of the unspeakable horror which years after my deliverance continued to make my days and nights dreadful, and solitude insupportably terrific.

Let me add a word or two about that quaint Baron Vordenburg, to whose curious lore we were indebted for the discovery of the Countess Mircalla's grave.

He had taken up his abode in Gratz, where, living upon a mere pittance, which was all that remained of him of the once princely estates of his family, in Upper Styria, he devoted himself to the minute and laborious investigation of the marvelously authenticated tradition of Vampirism. He had at his fingers' ends all the great and little works upon the subject. "Magia Posthuma," "Phlegon de Mirabilibus," "Augustinus de curâ pro Mortuis," "Philosophicae et Christianae Cogitationes de Vampiris," by John Christofer Herenberg; and a thousand others, among which I remember only a few of those which he lent to my father. He had a voluminous digest of all the judicial cases, from which he had extracted a system of principles that appear to govern—some always, and others occasionally only—the condition of the vampire. I may mention, in passing, that the deadly pallor attributed to that sort of *revenants*, is a mere melodramatic fiction. They present, in the grave, and when they show themselves in human society, the appearance of healthy life. When disclosed to light in their coffins, they exhibit all the symptoms that are enumerated as those which proved the vampire-life of the long-dead Countess Karnstein.

How they escape from their graves and return to them for certain hours every day without displacing the clay or leaving any trace of disturbance in the state of the coffin or the cerements, has always been admitted to be utterly inexplicable. The amphibious existence of the vampire is sustained by daily renewed slumber in the grave. Its horrible lust for living blood supplies the vigor of its waking existence. The vampire is prone to be fascinated with an engrossing vehemence, resembling the passion of love, by particular persons. In pursuit of these it will exercise inexhaustible patience and stratagem, for access to a particular object may be obstructed in a hundred ways. It will never desist until it has satiated its passion, and drained the very life of its coveted victim. But it will, in these cases, husband and protract its murderous enjoyment with the refinement of an epicure, and heighten it by the gradual approaches of an artful courtship. In these cases it seems to yearn for something like sympathy and consent. In ordinary ones it goes direct to its object, overpowers with violence, and strangles and exhausts often at a single feast.

The vampire is, apparently, subject, in certain situations, to special conditions. In the particular instance of which I have given you a relation, Mircalla seemed to be limited to a name which, if not her real one, should at least reproduce, without the omission or addition of a single letter, those, as we say, anagrammatically, which compose it. *Carmilla* did this; so did *Millarca*.

My father related to the Baron Vordenburg, who remained with us for two or three weeks after the expulsion of Carmilla, the story about the Moravian nobleman and the vampire at Karnstein churchyard, and then he asked the Baron how he had discovered the exact position of the long-concealed tomb of the Countess Mircalla? The Baron's grotesque features puckered up into a mysterious smile; he looked down, still smiling on his worn spectacle-case and fumbled with it. Then, looking up, he said:

"I have many journals, and other papers, written by that remarkable man; the most curious among them is one treating of the visit of which you speak, to Karnstein. The tradition,

of course, discolors and distorts a little. He might have been
termed a Moravian nobleman, for he had changed his abode
to that territory, and was, beside, a noble. But he was, in
truth, a native of Upper Styria. It is enough to say that in
very early youth he had been a passionate and favored lover
of the beautiful Mircalla, Countess Karnstein. Her early death
plunged him into inconsolable grief. It is the nature of vampires to increase and multiply, but according to an ascertained
and ghostly law.

"Assume, at starting, a territory perfectly free from that
pest. How does it begin, and how does it multiply itself? I
will tell you. A person, more or less wicked, puts an end to
himself. A suicide, under certain circumstances, becomes a
vampire. That specter visits living people in their slumbers;
they die, and almost invariably, in the grave develop into
vampires. This happened in the case of the beautiful Mircalla,
who was haunted by one of those demons. My ancestor,
Vordenburg, whose title I still bear, soon discovered this, and
in the course of the studies to which he devoted himself,
learned a great deal more.

"Among other things, he concluded that suspicion of vampirism would probably fall, sooner or later, upon the dead
Countess, who in life had been his idol. He conceived a
horror, be she what she might, of her remains being profaned
by the outrage of a posthumous execution. He has left a
curious paper to prove that the vampire, on its expulsion from
its amphibious existence, is projected into a far more horrible
life; and he resolved to save his once beloved Mircalla from
this.

"He adopted the strategem of a journey here, a pretended
removal of her remains, and a real obliteration of her monument. When age had stolen upon him, and from the vale of
years, he looked back on the scenes he was leaving, he
considered, in a different spirit, what he had done, and a
horror took possession of him. He made the tracings and
notes which have guided me to the very spot, and drew up a
confession of the deception that he had practiced. If he had

intended any further action in this matter, death prevented him; and the hand of a remote descendant has, too late for many, directed the pursuit to the lair of the beast.''

We talked a little more, and among other things he said was this:

''One sign of the vampire is the power of the hand. The slender hand of Mircalla closed like a vice of steel on the General's wrist when he raised the hatchet to strike. But its power is not confined to its grasp; it leaves a numbness in the limb it seizes, which is slowly, if ever, recovered from.''

The following Spring my father took me on a tour through Italy. We remained away for more than a year. It was long before the terror of recent events subsided; and to this hour the image of Carmilla returns to memory with ambiguous alterations—sometimes the playful, languid, beautiful girl; sometimes the writhing fiend I saw in the ruined church; and often from a reverie I have started, fancying I heard the light step of Carmilla at the drawing-room door.

DAW
TANITH LEE

"Princess Royal of Heroic Fantasy"—*The Village Voice*

THE BIRTHGRAVE TRILOGY
☐ THE BIRTHGRAVE   (UE2127—$3.95)
☐ VAZKOR, SON OF VAZKOR   (UE1972—$2.95)
☐ QUEST FOR THE WHITE WITCH   (UE2167—$3.50)

THE FLAT EARTH SERIES
☐ NIGHT'S MASTER   (UE2131—$3.50)
☐ DEATH'S MASTER   (UE2132—$3.50)
☐ DELUSION'S MASTER   (UE2197—$2.95)
☐ DELIRIUM'S MISTRESS   (UE2135—$3.95)
☐ NIGHT'S SORCERIES *(April 1987)*   (UE2194—$3.50)

OTHER TITLES
☐ THE STORM LORD   (UE1867—$2.95)
☐ DAYS OF GRASS   (UE2094—$3.50)
☐ DARK CASTLE, WHITE HORSE   (UE2113—$3.50)

ANTHOLOGIES
☐ RED AS BLOOD   (UE1790—$2.50)
☐ THE GORGON   (UE2003—$2.95)
